COMRADE DON CAMILLO

and

DON CAMILLO AND THE DEVIL

*"Bright is the ring of words
    When the right man rings them."*

R. L. STEVENSON

COMRADE DON CAMILLO

and

DON CAMILLO
AND THE DEVIL

*

GIOVANNI GUARESCHI

Illustrated by the Author

THE COMPANION BOOK CLUB
LONDON

This edition is issued by arrangement with
Victor Gollancz Ltd., London

*Made and printed in Great Britain
for The Companion Book Club (Odhams Books Ltd.)
by Odhams (Watford) Limited
Watford, Herts*
S.565.UC.

CONTENTS

*

COMRADE DON CAMILLO

translated from the Italian by
FRANCES FRENAYE

I

GOLD FEVER

THE news exploded like a bomb around Monday noon, upon the arrival of the newspapers. Someone in the village had won ten million liras in the national soccer sweepstakes. The papers gave the name of the winner as Pepito Sbezzeguti, but no one in the town was known under such an exotic name. The bet collector, besieged by a curious mob, threw out his arms hopelessly.

"I sold any number of tickets to fellows from out of town at the market on Saturday," he said. "It must be one of them. Ten million liras! He's bound to show up."

But no one showed up, and the village continued to fret, because they felt sure there was something fishy about the name. Sbezzeguti was plausible, someone of that name might have come to the market. But Pepito was going a little too far. Nobody who dealt in wheat, corn, hay, livestock and Parmesan cheese would be called Pepito.

"It's a phony name, if you ask me," said the proprietor of the Molinetto. "And someone using a false name isn't likely to be a stranger. It must be a villager who doesn't want it known that he played the sweeps. Maybe he doesn't want his debtors to know, or his wife."

The argument was logical enough. The villagers dropped the theory of the winner being an outsider and concentrated upon their fellow townsmen. They concentrated as intently as if they were trying to identify a common thief rather than the winner of a legitimate pool.

Don Camillo followed the affair less passionately but with a certain amount of interest. And because he felt that Christ did not altogether approve of his leanings towards the trade of a detective he offered Him an explanation.

"Lord, it's not a matter of idle curiosity; I'm doing my duty. A man who has received such a favour from Divine Providence has no right to hide it."

"Don Camillo," replied Christ, "Divine Providence may take an interest in the soccer sweepstakes, although personally I doubt it, but surely not in all the publicity about the winnings. The fact of the matter is all that counts and it's quite adequately known. Someone has won a considerable sum of money, but why must you beat out your brains to discover his identity? Your business is to look after those who are less fortunate."

But Don Camillo couldn't rid himself of his curiosity. The mystery of Pepito continued to occupy his mind until finally a great light dawned upon him. It was all he could do not to ring the church bells in exultation, and quite beyond his powers to resist putting on his cloak and going for a walk in the village. In time he arrived at the workshop of Peppone, mayor and blacksmith. Don Camillo stuck his head through the door and greeted his enemy.

"Good morning, Comrade Pepito!"

Peppone stopped hammering and stared at the priest in dismay.

"What do you mean, Father?"

"Nothing at all. Pepito's a diminutive of Peppone, after all, and by some strange chance Sbezzeguti is an imperfect anagram of Giuseppe Bottazzi."

Peppone resumed his hammering.

Don Camillo shook his head.

"What a shame that you're not the Pepito who won the ten millions."

"A shame, yes. In that case I'd be able to offer you two or three millions to go back home."

"Don't worry, Peppone. I do favours for nothing," said Don Camillo, going away.

Two hours later the whole village knew what is meant by an anagram, and in every house Pepito Sbezzeguti was vivisected to find out if Comrade Giuseppe Bottazzi was lurking inside. That same evening the Reds' general staff held a special meeting at the People's Palace.

"Chief," said Smilzo, "the reactionaries have gone back to their old tactics of smearing a good name. The whole village is in an uproar. They say you won the ten millions. There's no time to be lost; you must nail down their slander."

Peppone threw out his arms.

"To say a fellow has won ten millions in the soccer sweep-stake isn't slander. Slander means accusing someone of having done something dishonest, and the sweepstakes are quite on the level."

"Chief, in politics to accuse someone of a good deed is a smear. And an accusation that hurts the Party is definitely slanderous."

"People are laughing behind our backs," put in Brusco. "We've got to shut them up."

"We must print a poster!" Bigio exclaimed. "We must come up with a statement that makes everything clear."

Peppone shrugged his shoulders.

"We'll put our minds to it tomorrow," he said.

Whereupon Smilzo pulled a sheet of paper out of his pocket.

"We've something ready, Chief, in order to save you the trouble. If you approve we'll print it right away and paste up the posters tomorrow morning."

And he proceeded to read aloud:

The undersigned, Giuseppe Bottazzi, declares that he has no connection with the Pepito Sbezzeguti who won ten million liras in the soccer sweepstakes. It is useless for the reactionaries to accuse him of being a millionaire. All it proves is that they are a gang of neo-Fascists.

—Giuseppe Bottazzi.

Peppone shook his head.

"It's all right," he said, "but until I see something in print I'm not going to rush into print myself with an answer."

But Smilzo stuck to his argument.

"Why wait to shoot until someone has shot at you? Good strategy calls for beating the opponent to the draw."

"Good strategy calls for a kick in the pants to anyone who sticks his nose into my private affairs. I can defend myself without help."

Smilzo shrugged his shoulders.

"If you take it like that, there's nothing more to say."

"That's how I do take it!" shouted Peppone, bringing his fist down on the table. "Every man for himself, and the Party for the lot of us!"

The general staff went away grumbling.

"To let himself be accused of having won ten million is a sign of weakness," observed Smilzo. "And besides, there's the complication of the anagram."

"Let's hope for the best," sighed Bigio.

Soon enough the rumour appeared in print. The landowners' paper published an insert that said: *"Scratch a Peppone and you'll find a Pepito"*, and everyone in the village found this exceedingly clever and funny. The general staff held another meeting in the People's Palace and declared unanimously that something had to be done.

"Very good," said Peppone. "Go ahead and print the poster and paste it up."

Smilzo made a bee-line for the printer's. Little more than an hour later the printer, Barchini, brought Don Camillo a copy of the proofs.

"This is bad business for the newspaper," said Don Camillo sadly. "If Peppone really did win the money I don't think he would put out such a statement. That is, unless he's already gone to the city to collect it or sent someone else to collect it for him."

"He hasn't made a move," Barchini assured him. "Everyone in the village is on the alert."

It was late, and Don Camillo went to bed. But at three o'clock in the morning he was awakened by the news of a visit from Peppone. Peppone sneaked in from the garden, and when he was in the hall he peered out anxiously through the half-closed door.

"Here's hoping no one has seen me," he said. "I feel as if I were being followed."

Don Camillo glanced at him anxiously.

"You haven't gone crazy, have you?" he asked.

"No, no fear of that."

Peppone sat down and wiped the perspiration from his brow.

"Am I talking to the parish priest or to the village gossip?"

"That depends on what you came to say."

"I came to see the priest."

"The priest is listening," said Don Camillo gravely.

Peppone twirled his hat between his fingers and then confessed:

"Father, I told a big lie. I *am* Pepito Sbezzeguti."

For a moment Don Camillo was speechless.

"So you did win the millions, did you?" he said when he had recovered his aplomb. "Why didn't you say so?"

"I'm not saying so. I was speaking to you as a priest, and you should have no concern with anything but the fact that I told a lie."

But Don Camillo was concerned with the ten millions. He shot a withering look at Peppone and moved to the attack.

"Shame on you! A proletarian, a Party member winning ten million liras in a soccer sweepstake! Leave such shenanigans to the bourgeoisie! Communists earn their living by the sweat of their brow."

"I'm in no mood for joking," gasped Peppone. "Is it a crime to place a bet in the soccer sweepstake?"

"It's no joke," said Don Camillo. "I didn't say it was a crime. I said that a good Communist wouldn't do it."

"Nonsense! Everyone does."

"That's very bad. And all the worse for you because you're a leader of the class struggle. The soccer sweepstake is a diabolical capitalist weapon turned against the People. Very effective, and it costs the capitalists nothing. In fact, they stand to make money. No good Communist can fail to combat it."

Peppone shrugged his shoulders in annoyance.

"Don't get excited, Comrade! It's all part of a vast conspiracy to persuade the proletariat to seek riches by other means than revolution. Of course that's pure fraud, and by abetting it you're betraying the cause of the People!"

Peppone waved his arms wildly.

"Father, let's leave politics out of it!"

"What's that, Comrade? Are you forgetful of the Revolution?"

Peppone stamped his feet, and Don Camillo smiled indulgently.

"I understand, Comrade," he said, "and I don't blame you. Better ten million liras today than the Revolution tomorrow!"

He went to poke up the fire and then turned around to look at Peppone.

"Did you come here just to tell me you'd won the money?"

Peppone was in a cold sweat.

"How can I get the cash without anyone's knowing?" he asked.

"Go for it, that's all."

"I can't. They're watching me like hawks. And besides my denial is coming out tomorrow."

"Then send a trusted comrade."

"There's no one I can trust."

"I don't know what to say," said Don Camillo, shaking his head.

Peppone held out an envelope.

"You go for me, Father."

He got up and went away, leaving Don Camillo to stare at the envelope.

The next morning Don Camillo set out for the city. Three days later he made his return. He arrived late in the evening, and before going to the rectory went to talk to the Christ over the altar. Opening up his suitcase he said sternly:

"Jesus, here are ten bundles, each one of them containing a hundred ten-thousand-lira notes. In other words, the ten million liras that belong to Peppone. All I have to say is this: he doesn't deserve them."

"Tell that to the sweepstake operators," Christ replied.

Don Camillo took the suitcase away. When he reached the second floor of the rectory he switched the light on and off three times in succession as a signal to Peppone. Peppone replied by means of the light in his bedroom. Two hours later he arrived at the rectory, with his coat collar turned up to hide his face. He came in from the garden, through the door with the heavy padlock hanging from it.

"Well, then?" he said to Don Camillo, who was waiting in the pantry.

Don Camillo pointed at the suitcase, which was lying on the table, and Peppone approached it with trembling hands. When he saw the bundles of banknotes he broke into perspiration.

"Ten million?" he whispered questioningly.

"Ten million cold. Count them for yourself."

"Oh no," demurred Peppone, staring fascinatedly at the money.

"A pretty pile," commented Don Camillo, "at least for today. Who knows what it may be worth tomorrow? A single piece of bad news is enough to bring on inflation and turn it into worthless paper."

"I ought to invest it right away," said Peppone. "With ten millions I could buy a farm, and land always has value."

"It's the peasants that have a right to the land," said Don Camillo. "At least that's what the Communists say. They don't mention blacksmiths. They'll take it away from you, you'll see. Communism is the wave of the future, Comrade. . . ."

Peppone was still staring at the banknotes.

"I have it!" he exclaimed. "Gold! I'll buy gold and hide it away."

"What good will it do you? If the Communists take over, everything will come under the control of the State and your gold will lose its purchasing power."

"I could always deposit it abroad."

"Tut, tut! Like a regular capitalist! You'd deposit it in America, I suppose, because Europe is going Communist for sure. But when America is left out on a limb it will have to surrender to the Soviet Union."

"America's got real power," said Peppone. "The Soviet will never take it over."

"I wouldn't be so sure, Comrade."

Peppone took a deep breath and sat down.

"My head's whirling, Father. Ten million liras."

"Please oblige me by taking them home. But don't forget to send back my suitcase. That's my private property."

"No, Father," said Peppone. "Keep the money for me, will you? I'd rather talk about it when I can think straight, perhaps tomorrow."

After Peppone had gone away Don Camillo carried the suitcase up to his bedroom and went to bed. He was dead tired, but his sleep was interrupted at two o'clock in the morning by the reappearance of Peppone, together with his wife, both of them swathed in heavy coats.

"Forgive me, Father," said Peppone. "My wife just had to take a squint at the money."

Don Camillo brought down the suitcase and deposited it on the pantry table. At the sight of the banknotes Peppone's wife turned deathly pale. Don Camillo waited patiently, then he closed the suitcase and escorted the two of them to the door.

"Try to get some sleep," he said as they went away.

He tried to do the same thing himself, but an hour later he was once more awakened by Peppone.

"What's this?" he protested. "Isn't the pilgrimage over?"

"I came to take the suitcase," explained Peppone.

"Nothing doing! I've stowed it away in the attic and I have no intention of bringing it down. You can come back tomorrow. I'm cold and tired and entitled to my rest. Don't you trust me?"

"It's not a question of trust. What if something were to happen to you during the night? How could I prove that the money is mine?"

"Don't worry about that. The suitcase is locked and there's a tag with your name on it. I've thought of every contingency."

"I appreciate that, Father. But the money's safer in my house."

Don Camillo didn't like his tone of voice. And he changed his own to match it.

"What money are you talking about?"

"My own! The money you went to get for me in Rome."

"You must be crazy, Peppone. I never got any of your money."

"The ticket's in my name," shouted Peppone. "I'm Pepito Sbezzeguti."

"It's plastered all over the walls that you're *not* Pepito Sbezzeguti. You signed the statement yourself."

"I am, though! Pepito Sbezzeguti is an anagram of Giuseppe Bottazzi."

"No it isn't. It's an anagram of Giuseppe Bottezzi. I have an uncle of that name and it's for him that I cashed in the ticket."

With a trembling hand Peppone wrote *Pepito Sbezzeguti* on the margin of the newspaper lying on the table, and after it his real name.

"Damnation!" he exclaimed. "I put an *e* for an *a*. But the money's mine."

Don Camillo started up the stairs to his bedroom, with Peppone following after.

"Don't take it so hard, Comrade," he called out as he climbed into bed. "I won't steal your money. I'll use it for your own cause, for the cause of the downtrodden people."

"Devil take the people!" Peppone shouted.

"You benighted reactionary!" said Don Camillo, pulling the sheet up over his head. "Go away and let me sleep!"

"Give me my money, or I'll kill you like a dog!"

"Take the filthy stuff and go away!"

The suitcase was on the chest of drawers. Peppone seized it, hid it under his coat and ran down the stairs.

When Don Camillo heard the front door slam he gave a deep sigh.

"Lord," he said sternly, "why did you let him ruin his life by winning that money? He doesn't deserve such punishment."

"First you scold me because he didn't deserve such a prize and now you call it a punishment! I can't seem to please you, Don Camillo!"

"I wasn't talking to you, Lord; I was talking to the sweepstake operators," Don Camillo murmured as he finally fell asleep.

2

DON CAMILLO'S REVENGE

"Lord," said Don Camillo, "he's gone a bit too far, and I shall destroy him!"

"Don Camillo," said the crucified Christ over the altar, "they went a bit too far when they hung me up on this Cross, but I managed to forgive them."

"But they didn't know what they were doing! Peppone had his eyes wide open and deserves no pity."

"Look here, Don Camillo," Christ retorted; "ever since Peppone became a senator haven't you been particularly hard on him?"

These words hit home, and Don Camillo resented them.

"You wouldn't say that, Lord," he protested, "if you knew me a little better."

"Oh, I know you well enough," Christ sighed in reply.

Don Camillo knew when to stop. He hastily bent one knee, crossed himself and glided away. But outside the church his resentment was reawakened. Just beside the rectory door some unfortunate fellow had just pasted up a copy of the poster which had aroused his original anger. It was a story that dated back to two years before.

One gloomy winter evening, when Don Camillo was just about to go to bed, someone had knocked at the rectory door. Don

Camillo saw that of course it was Peppone. He motioned him to a chair and handed him a glass of wine, which Peppone drained with a single gulp. It took two more glasses to loosen his tongue, and then he came out with:

"I can't stand it!"

From under his heavy black cape he pulled out a bundle.

"Ever since I've had this in the house I haven't been able to sleep."

It was the famous ten million liras, of course, and Don Camillo replied:

"Then put it in the bank."

Peppone gave a wry laugh.

"That's a very poor joke! How can a Communist mayor deposit ten million liras in the bank without saying where he got them?"

"Convert them into gold and bury it in the ground!"

"That way I wouldn't get any interest on my capital."

Don Camillo was sleepy, but his patience was not yet exhausted.

"Come along, Comrade," he said pacifically; "let's get to the point."

"Well then, Father, you know that businessman who takes such good care of other people's money. . . ."

"No, I don't know him."

"Surely you do. He belongs to your camp. A fellow that gets a lot of business from Church people and then eases his conscience with big donations to religious charities. . . ."

"Oh yes, I have an idea whom you mean. But I've never had any dealings with him."

"But you can get in touch with him very easily. The priest at Torricella is one of his agents."

Don Camillo wearily shook his head.

"Comrade," he said, "just because God gave you an inch, do you have to take a mile?"

"God has nothing to do with it, Father. I had a stroke of good luck and now I want to take advantage of it."

"Then it's perfectly simple. Go to the priest at Torricella and ask him for an introduction."

"No, I can't do that. People know my face too well. If they were to see me hanging around the rectory at Torricella or the businessman's office, I'd lose my reputation. Imagine a Communist getting mixed up with the Church and high finance! If I can keep my name out of it, then it's strictly a matter of money. I can't let it become a political football."

Don Camillo had always taken a dim view of the businessman who earned sky-high interest rates for his clients and then contributed to the building of new churches. But the Torricella priest was a thoroughly decent fellow and, if he had acquired a sports field, a swimming pool, a moving-picture projector and other attractions to compete with those offered by the Reds, it was all thanks to the generosity of this wealthy parishioner. And so Don Camillo suspended his judgment.

"I don't want to get myself involved in any more complications," he said. "Tomorrow evening at this time, I'll arrange to have the priest come over from Torricella. I'll go to bed and leave you to talk with him."

Twenty-four hours later Peppone and the other priest met in Don Camillo's study. They seemed to have reached some agreement, for Don Camillo heard no more of the affair. A year later Peppone was elected to the Senate, and from then on Don Camillo was besieged by some devil.

"Peppone is an ingrate," the devil whispered in his ear. "You were a good friend to him when you went to collect the sweepstakes money, and what has he done for you in return? No sooner was he elected than he made an inflammatory speech in the public square."

Portions of the inflammatory speech had been brought to Don Camillo's attention. In boasting of his electoral triumph Peppone had made scathing references to "*a certain priest who used all sorts of pious platitudes to prevent a victory of the People, a priest who would better be employed as a bellringer if only he knew how to ring a bell.*" Quite obviously Don Camillo was tempted to retaliate by telling the story of Peppone's clandestine sweepstakes winnings.

For two whole years the priest staved off this temptation. He had just about banished it from his mind when he saw the new Communist poster. Just at that time the famous businessman had got his name into the headlines as the central figure of a financial scandal. When the scandal was at its height, Peppone launched this attack against him, in which he included "*certain conniving priests who, for love of money, did not hesitate to join hands with a notorious swindler in order to rob the faithful of their hard-earned savings."*

This shameless accusation was more than Don Camillo could take, and he made up his mind to explode a little bomb of his own.

Peppone came back quite often to the village. He was now a very different man, carrying a brief-case full of state papers and wearing a self-important and preoccupied air, as if the affairs of the whole world weighed upon his shoulders. He greeted the local people distractedly and inspired fear even among his Party comrades. Whenever anyone brought him a problem he said solemnly: "I'll take it up in Rome." He went in for dark, double-breasted suits and conventional felt hats and never appeared without a tie. The poster contained glaring grammatical errors, but since his personality was quite strong enough to overshadow his style, no one dared make fun of them. Don Camillo laid his plans and accosted him at eleven o'clock one night at the door of his house.

"Excuse me," he said, while Peppone was turning the key in the lock, "but do you happen to be one of the poor innocents fleeced by conniving priests who joined hands with a notorious swindler?"

Peppone had succeeded in opening the door and now he had no choice but to let Don Camillo in. At once Don Camillo drove his point home.

"Comrade Senator," he went on, "the next trick is mine. When I tell the whole truth, you'll be the laughing-stock of the whole country. Just wait until your electors find out that you cheated both the tax collector and the Communist Party of your sweepstakes winnings! And how you cheated them again by turning over your ten million liras to a criminal speculator, one of those whom you define as the Enemies of the People!"

Peppone threw out his chest defiantly.

"I'll sue you for libel," he retorted. "You can't prove a thing."

"I'll prove the whole story. Your name is in that man's files. He sent your interest payments by cheque, and I have the cheque numbers."

Peppone wiped a sudden access of perspiration from his brow.

"You'd never play me a dirty trick like that!"

Don Camillo sat down and lighted his cigar butt.

"It's no dirty trick," he said. "It's just a reply to your poster."

Peppone let himself go. He tore off his jacket and threw it on to a sofa and loosened his tie. Then he sat down directly across from Don Camillo.

"You don't need to take revenge," he groaned. "I lost every penny."

"But you'd been getting such exorbitant interest for the past two years that you pretty nearly came out even."

Peppone felt trapped, and in desperation he blurted out:

"Father, will you settle for three million?"

"Comrade, you have no right to insult me with such an offer. That will cost you something extra."

He pulled out a newspaper, unfolded it and pointed out an article on one of the back pages.

"You see, Senator, we know what's going on. We see that you have been given the important job of picking ten deserving comrades whom you're to escort on a free tour of Soviet Russia. We shan't interfere with this project. But as soon as you've left the country we'll let the cat out of the bag. The embarrassment of your Party leaders will add to the fun."

Peppone was speechless. Knowing Don Camillo as he did, he realized that there was no chance of stopping him. His crumpled air moved the priest to compassion.

"Comrade," he said, "you can consider yourself liquidated. That is, unless . . ."

"Unless what?" groaned Peppone, raising his head.

Quite calmly Don Camillo set forth the only means of escaping disgrace. Peppone listened with his jaw sagging.

"Father, you're joking," he said when the priest had finished.

"It's no joke. It's do or die."

"You're mad, Father," said Peppone, leaping to his feet. "Stark, raving mad!"

"Exactly, Comrade. That's why you'd better think twice before you say no. Madmen can be dangerous. I give you until tomorrow night."

Two days later Don Camillo went to the old Bishop, who heard him out patiently to the end of his story.

"Is that all?" he inquired. "I think that with a rest cure in the mountains you may get over it."

Don Camillo shook his head.

"I meant every word," he insisted. "It's the opportunity of a lifetime. Two whole weeks of direct contact with a group of our most ardent Communists and also with the Russians! . . ."

The Bishop looked at him with dismay.

"My son, who put this idea into your head?"

"Nobody. It just came upon me. Who knows? Perhaps it was inspired by the Lord."

"I can't believe it," muttered the Bishop. "Anyhow, you're dead set upon it, and you expect me to let you go without breathing a word to a soul. What if they discover who you are?"

"They won't discover that, I promise you. I'll take pains to disguise myself. I don't mean so much by the clothes I wear as by my frame of mind. That's what really counts. A normal mind has to take on Communist processes of thought, if facial expression and tone of voice are to fit in with the Communist pattern."

The Bishop tapped his cane against the stool where he was resting his feet.

"It's sheer madness, my son," he concluded.

"Yes, Your Grace," agreed Don Camillo.

"But you may go," the Bishop added.

Don Camillo knelt down, and the Bishop laid a wasted hand on his bowed head.

"God be with you, Comrade Don Camillo," he said, raising his eyes to heaven.

He spoke in such a low voice that Don Camillo barely heard what he was saying. But God had no difficulty hearing.

3

DON CAMILLO IN DISGUISE

"GOOD morning, Senator," said the sharp-tongued cleaning woman who was scrubbing the boarding-house floor.

"Good morning, Comrade," cautiously murmured the milkman, who was just making his morning delivery.

"Good morning, you poor fool," said a stout-bodied man who was standing square in the middle of the pavement, waiting for him to come by.

Peppone did not deign to answer; he pushed him aside and went on his way. The scene was Rome, at nine o'clock in the morning. The vast machinery of the capital was slowly getting under way and a remnant of sleepiness still dulled the crisp freshness of the autumn air.

"Good morning, you poor fool," repeated the stout-bodied man, this time in a cordial, almost affectionate manner. "Up in the country this is the beginning of a wonderful day. Mist is rolling off the ploughed fields, the clover is shiny with dew and the vines are heavy with clusters of ripe, honey-sweet grapes, half-hidden by russet leaves. . . ."

Peppone grunted in reply. Did his enemy have to lie in ambush every morning in front of the boarding-house and then buzz about him with the latest village news? To quiet his nerves he lit a cigarette.

"Of course," the other jeered. "A cigar would never do. City people don't like strong smells, and if your landlady were to see you with a cigar butt hanging out of one corner of your mouth, senators would go down in her esteem. A very nice old lady she is, by the way, and you did well to tell her you were an 'independent'. It would be quite a shock to her to find out that you're a Communist."

Peppone threw away his cigarette and loosened his tie.

"Yes, I know that you used to feel more comfortable with your shirt open and a handkerchief knotted around your neck. But a senator can't go around looking like a hayseed. You're a big shot now, with a telephone on your desk and marble tiles on your office floor."

Peppone glanced at his watch.

"Don't worry," said the voice beside him. "You're doing a very good job. You displayed excellent judgment in the choice of candidates for your Russian tour. Only one name is missing from the list."

Peppone took off his hat and wiped the perspiration from his forehead.

"It's all the fault of that speculator! I wish I'd never met him."

"Look here, my boy," said his interlocutor with genuine feeling, "you don't have to let yourself in for any of this. Why go looking for trouble? You can kick off the traces and come on home."

"No, I can't," groaned Peppone.

"Then good-bye until tomorrow, and God help you!"

They had come to the bus stop, and Peppone watched his friendly enemy walk away and lose himself in the crowd. Did the fellow have to haunt him every morning with memories of the past, of days when he had been a simpler but happier man, to tease him with the siren call of "Home, Sweet Home"?

On the bus Peppone sat down across from a man who was reading the Communist daily, *L'Unità del Popolo,* which he held wide open before him, as stiffly as if it were mounted on a wooden frame. Peppone could not see his fellow passenger's face, but this dramatically provocative pose convinced him that he must be a jackass. *"Every Party member should wear a Party emblem in his buttonhole, but to display it ostentatiously is contrary to common sense."* So Peppone himself had decreed in the good old days, when someone had played a miserable, low-down trick on his dog, Thunder. Don Camillo had scolded Peppone for failing to take off his hat when the Blessed Sacrament went by, and Peppone had answered with insulting remarks. Shortly after this, Thunder had come home with all his hair shaved off, except on his rump, where it had been trimmed in the pattern of a hammer and sickle. And every time that Don Camillo met the dog, he tipped his hat in mock respect for the Party emblem.

"Those were the days," Peppone thought to himself, "before people were really bitten by the political bug and a good laugh straightened out their relationship better than any amount of bitter discussion."

The conventionally dressed man across the way lowered his paper and Peppone had to admit that he didn't look like a jackass. His eyes were expressionless, but this was doubtless because the thick lenses of his glasses concealed them from view. He was wearing a commonplace light suit and an even more commonplace grey hat. Somehow or other he was unpleasant, and Peppone was annoyed to see him get off at the same bus stop as himself.

"Sir," the man asked him, "can you show me the way to . . . ?"

Peppone lost all control.

"I can show you the way to go to hell," he shouted.

"Exactly what I wanted to know," said the man calmly.

Peppone strode rapidly away, and the other followed after. Five minutes later he sat down at the same isolated table in a small, empty café. After Peppone had cooled himself off with a heaping dish of ice cream he regained sufficient self-control to speak.

"Your bad joke has gone far enough," he decreed.

"Not a bit of it. This is only the beginning."

"You don't expect me to take you seriously, do you?"

"I not only expect it; I demand it."

"Now, Don Camillo——"

"Call me Comrade Tarocci. . . ." And he took a passport out of his pocket. "There it is, in black and white: 'Camillo Tarocci, linotypist'."

Peppone turned the passport over and over in his hands, looking at it disgustedly.

"A false name, a false passport, false colours."

"No, Comrade, the passport is genuine. It was issued to Camillo Tarocci, linotypist, and I'm practically his spitting image. If you don't believe me, just look at this." And holding out a piece of paper, he explained: "Here you have a membership card of the Communist Party, issued to Camillo Tarocci. Everything's authentic and in good order." And before Peppone could interrupt him he went on: "There's nothing to be surprised about. Some of the comrades aren't what they seem. But since Tarocci is one of the star members of his cell, you have only to write and ask him for the names of half a dozen fellows particularly deserving to be taken along on your tour and then choose him instead. Then while he takes a fortnight's country vacation I'll tag along with you. I'll have a good look at Russia, and when I come back I'll tell him all about it."

It was all Peppone could do to keep his temper.

"I don't know or care whether there really is a hell," he spluttered. "But if there is one, that's where you're going."

"Then we shall meet again in the next life, Comrade."

At this point Peppone's defences broke down.

"Father," he said wearily, "why are you dead set on destroying me?"

"Nobody's dead set on destroying you, Comrade. My presence on your Russian tour isn't going to affect the state of things in Russia. The good things will be good and the bad things will be bad whether I'm there or not. Why are you so nervous? Are you afraid it isn't the workers' paradise that your newspapers make it out to be?"

Peppone shrugged his shoulders.

"As far as I'm concerned," Don Camillo went on, "I'm hoping it isn't as bad as our papers paint it."

"Very fine feelings!" exclaimed Peppone sarcastically. "How objective and disinterested you are!"

"I'm not disinterested at all," Don Camillo retorted. "It's to my interest that the Russians should be happy. That way they'll stay quietly at home and not go bother other people."

A week later Comrade Camillo Tarocci received the news that he had been chosen to go on the Russian tour. Carrying a cheap suitcase he reported at the Communist Party headquarters, along with the nine other tour members. A young Party official received the little group introduced to him by the Senator and issued terse parting instructions.

"Comrades, you have a definite mission to perform. You are to keep your eyes and ears open, not only on your own behalf but also on behalf of your comrades at home. When you come back you must tell friends and foes alike about the technical accomplishments and peaceful spirit of the glorious Soviet Union."

While Peppone visibly paled with apprehension, Don Camillo asked permission to make a statement.

"Comrade," he said, "it's hardly worthwhile to travel so far merely in order to come back and tell our friends something they already know and our foes something they refuse to admit. My idea is that our mission should be to convey to our Russian hosts the joyous and grateful greetings of the Italian people for their liberation from the threat of war."

"Of course, Comrade," muttered the Party official; "that goes without saying."

He went away, sticking out his chest and looking slightly annoyed, and Peppone turned ferociously on Don Camillo.

"When something goes without saying then it needn't be said. Besides, you must speak in a way that shows some respect for the person to whom you are speaking. Obviously you don't know who that was."

"Oh yes, I do," Don Camillo imperturbably replied. "He's a twenty-five-year-old young man, who was about ten when the war began. He never fought with us up in the mountains against the Germans and so he can't possibly know what a terrible thing war is or how psychologically important is Comrade Khrushchev's trip to America to forward the cause of peace and disarmament."

"Well spoken," said Comrade Nanni Scamoggia, a hulking fellow from the proletarian Trastevere section of Rome, with a tough and devil-may-care air about him. "When there's fighting to be done, you'll never see one of these Party big shots on the scene."

"And when these bureaucrats start setting up a bureaucracy ——" added Comrade Walter Rondella, a working man from Milan. But before he could say any more Peppone interrupted.

"We're not here to hold a meeting. If we don't step fast we'll miss the train."

He walked briskly towards the door, shooting Don Camillo an atomic glance loaded with enough power to topple a skyscraper. But Don Camillo preserved the stony expression of a comrade who, whatever the cost, will not deviate a single inch from the Party line.

On the train Peppone's chief preoccupation was not to let the diabolical Comrade Camillo Tarocci out of his sight. He sat directly in front of him in order to block his way. But Don Camillo did not seem to be in a mood for making trouble. He took out of his pocket a book with a red jacket and a gold hammer and sickle stamped upon it and with an impenetrable expression on his face immersed himself in its perusal. At rare intervals he raised his eyes and looked out at the fields and villages gliding by the train. As he closed the book and started to put it back in his pocket, Peppone remarked:

"Must be good reading."

"The very best," said Don Camillo. "It's a collection of excerpts from Lenin." And he added, handing it over for inspection: "Too bad it's in French. But I can translate any part you'd like to hear."

"No thanks, Comrade," said Peppone, closing the book and returning it to its owner.

He looked cautiously around him and breathed a sigh of relief when he saw that all his other travelling companions were either dozing or turning the pages of illustrated magazines. No one had noticed that in spite of the red jacket and the French title, *Pensées de Lénine,* the book was actually a Latin breviary.

At the first stop several of the men got off the train. Comrade Scamoggia came back with a bottle of wine and Comrade Rondella with an extra of an evening newspaper, over which he was shaking his head disgustedly. On the front page there were pictures of Khrushchev's last day in America and the usual crowd of smiling faces around him.

"I don't know what it is, but to see him smile in the company of those grinning mugs is more than I can stomach."

"Politics is a question of brains, not of feeling," said Don Camillo. "The Soviet Union has been struggling all along to

31

achieve peaceful co-existence. The capitalists who fostered the Cold War are the ones who have very little to smile about. The end of the cold war is a capitalist disaster."

But Rondella had all the obstinacy of the typical organized Milanese worker.

"That's all very well. But I have a perfect right to say that I hate capitalists and I'd rather be seen dead than caught smiling with them."

"You have a perfect right to say what you please. But don't say it to us; say it to Khrushchev. By the time we get to Moscow he'll be there. You can ask to see him and then say to his face: 'Comrade Khrushchev, you're on the wrong track'."

Don Camillo was as sly as the slyest Communist secret agent. Comrade Rondella turned pale.

"Either you can't or you won't understand me," he protested. "If I have to handle manure in order to fertilize a field, then I'll handle it. But no one can force me to say that it has a good smell."

"Comrade," said Don Camillo quietly, "you fought with the Partisans, I know. When you were ordered into danger, what did you do?"

"I went."

"And did you tell your comrades that you couldn't stomach the idea of risking your life?"

"Of course not. But what's the connection?"

"War is war, Comrade, whether it's hot or cold. And the man who's fighting for a just cause can't afford to have opinions of his own."

"Drop it, Comrade Rondella," intervened Peppone. "We're going to a country where you won't run into any capitalists, that's one thing sure."

"And it makes me feel considerably better," admitted Rondella.

"The thing I'm happiest about," said Comrade Scamoggia, "is that for a whole fortnight we shan't run into any priests."

Don Camillo shook his head.

"I wouldn't be too certain about that, Comrade. In the Soviet Union there's freedom of religion."

"Freedom of religion? Ha! ha!" jeered Scamoggia.

"Don't laugh! The Soviet Union takes its freedom seriously."

"You mean there are priests there too? Does that filthy breed really defy extermination?"

"It will die out of its own accord, when poverty and ignorance are gone," put in Peppone. "Poverty and ignorance are meat and drink to those black crows."

But Don Camillo was colder and more severe than ever.

"Comrade Senator, you know better than I that in the Soviet Union poverty and ignorance have been done away with already. If there are still priests, it can only be because they have some power which there is as yet no way to overcome."

"What *have* they got?" Scamoggia shouted. "Aren't they made of flesh and blood, like ourselves?"

"No!" shouted back Peppone. "They're the dregs of the earth! They're a band of cowards, hypocrites, blackmailers, thieves and assassins! Even a poisonous snake will go out of his way to avoid a priest, for fear of being bitten."

"You're going overboard, Comrade Senator," said Don Camillo. "Your violence must be based on something personal. Tell me, did some priest do you dirt?"

"The priest's yet to be born that can do me dirt!" protested Peppone.

"What about the priest that baptized you?"

"I was only one day old!"

"And the priest that married you?" Don Camillo insisted.

"Don't argue with him, Chief," laughed Scamoggia. "This comrade is the dialectical, hair-splitting type; he'll always have the last word."

And he added, turning to Don Camillo:

"Comrade, you're a man after my own heart! You know what you're talking about and you hate the priests just as much as I do."

He poured wine into the paper cups and proposed a toast:

"To the Soviet Union!"

"Down with capitalists!" said Comrade Rondella.

"Death to priests!" roared Peppone, looking Don Camillo straight in the eye.

As Don Camillo raised his cup he gave Peppone an eloquent kick in the shins.

It was midnight when the train reached the frontier. The moon was full, bathing in its light the villages perched among the mountains. Every now and then the travellers caught a glimpse of the plains below, with rivers running like ribbons across them and cities that were clusters of sparkling lights. Don Camillo stood at one of the corridor windows, puffing at his cigar butt and enjoying the sight. Peppone came to stand beside him, and after gazing at length out of the window heaved a deep sigh.

"You can say what you like, but when a man is about to leave his country he suddenly appreciates it."

"Comrade, you're indulging in outworn rhetoric and nationalism. Don't forget that our country is the world."

"Well then, why do so many poor fools want to go to the moon?" Peppone asked without thinking.

"Comrade, something distracted my attention, and I didn't hear your question."

"It's just as well you didn't," mumbled Peppone.

4

OPERATION RONDELLA

THE tri-motor plane on which the little group embarked at an airport in East Germany was so noisy that no one could make his voice heard above the din. Comrade Don Camillo was forced to hold his tongue and Peppone enjoyed relative peace of mind. Nevertheless he remained alert, for Don Camillo was a dangerous character even when he was silent. For the moment he was confining his anti-Communist activities to reading the supposed excerpts from the works of Lenin, and Peppone had no cause for worry until the priest closed the book and smote his forehead with one hand, as if he had just had a bright idea. But he quickly neutralized the effect of this alarming gesture by stroking his hair and then dusting off the lapels of his jacket.

"Amen," muttered Peppone with a deep sigh, which cleared his sputtering carburettor. The plane was gradually losing altitude and soon put down its wheels on Soviet soil.

"Lord, my little church seems very far away!" Don Camillo thought as he went down the waiting steps.

"But Heaven is very near," the Lord reassured him.

Don Camillo pulled himself together and resumed the role of Comrade Tarocci.

"Comrade," he said gravely to Peppone, "don't you feel an urge to pick up a clod of this sacred earth and kiss it?"

"Yes, and after that to ram it down your throat," Peppone muttered between clenched teeth.

Notice had been received of the visitors' arrival, and a girl stepped forward to meet them, followed by a man in a flapping, faded raincoat.

"Greetings, Comrades!" she said brightly. "I am Nadia Petrovna, your interpreter, and this is Yenka Oregov from the Government tourist bureau."

She spoke excellent Italian, and if it hadn't been for her fixed stare and the severity of her tailored suit, she might have been a girl from our own part of the world.

Peppone introduced himself and his companions, and after an orgy of handshaking the tourist-bureau official made a little speech welcoming them in the name of their Soviet brothers, co-fighters for the cause of freedom, social justice and peace. He was a stocky fellow, some forty years old, with a shaven head, a square jaw, thin lips, darting eyes and a bull neck. Standing there in the raincoat that came almost down to his ankles, he had the unmistakable air of a policeman. He spoke without moving the muscles of his face and with such wooden gestures that if his speech had not been translated to them they might have taken it for a prosecutor's harangue rather than a welcome. Comrade Nadia Petrovna affected the same official stiffness, but there was something definitely softer about her.

Comrade Nanni Scamoggia was struck dumb, although she was by no means the first pretty girl he had seen in the course of his heartbreaker's career. He was twenty-eight years old and every inch a Roman, with shiny, black, wavy hair, eyes that had a slightly perverse expression and long lashes, an ironical twist to his lips, broad shoulders, narrow hips and feet as small as a ballet dancer's. He wore tight-fitting trousers, a red shirt and a black leather jacket, and a cigarette drooped out of one corner of his mouth. He was half tough, half dandy, quick to use his fists and accustomed to having his way with women.

As the little group crossed the airfield, with Peppone, Comrade Oregov and Comrade Nadia Petrovna leading the way, Scamoggia regained his power of speech.

"Comrade," he said to Don Camillo, "how's *she* for an atom bomb? Do you find her as easy on the eyes as I do?"

"I do," answered Don Camillo, mentally asking the Lord's indulgence. "They don't make girls any prettier than that one."

He spoke loudly, for the benefit of Comrade Rondella, who promptly rose to the bait.

"She's pretty enough," he admitted, "but we've got just as pretty girls at home."

"At home they know how to dress," said Don Camillo. "But put one of them into the clothes Comrade Petrovna is wearing and she'd cut a very poor figure. This girl has real classical beauty; she's not just one of those dolls you see in our cities. Especially in Milan, where they're born knowing all the answers."

"Nonsense, Comrade!" protested Rondella. "There are girls in Milan as pretty as you could hope to see."

"Cool off, Comrade," intervened Scamoggia. "We've got pretty girls, all right, but this one has something special. I can't put my finger on it, but it's there."

"It depends on the environment in which she was brought up. It's environment that shapes the man, and also the woman. This is an elementary truth, but plenty of people don't seem to understand it."

Comrade Rondella had another two cents' worth to put in, but a sudden halt interrupted him.

"Customs inspection," announced Peppone, threading his way back among them. And he added, in Don Camillo's ear: "I hope you aren't carrying anything that will get us into hot water."

"Comrade," said Don Camillo reassuringly, "I know the ways of the world."

The inspection was quickly over, because Peppone had made efficient preparations for it. Every member of the group had the same type of cheap suitcase and all the contents had identical weight. The only thing that gave any trouble was a bottle in the possession of Scamoggia. The customs inspector unscrewed the top, sniffed at the liquid inside and then handed it over to be sniffed by Comrade Petrovna.

"He wants to know why you're carrying a woman's perfume," she explained.

"It isn't a woman's perfume," Scamoggia told her. "It's eau-de-Cologne for after shaving. What sort of lotion do they have around here? Gasoline?"

She started to reply, but she could see that a fellow as tough-looking as this one wasn't to be put in his place so easily. And so she contented herself with translating only the first part of his statement. The inspector muttered something unintelligible and put the bottle back in the suitcase.

"Here they have pure alcohol," she informed Scamoggia. "He says you can keep it for your own personal use, but you're not to sell it."

After they had left the field Scamoggia stopped and reopened his suitcase.

"Wait a minute," he said. "If it's the custom here for men to use pure alcohol, then I'll follow their example. Since this is considered a woman's perfume, then a woman should have it."

He started to give her the bottle, but she drew her hand away.

"Aren't you a woman?" asked Scamoggia.

"Of course," she stammered.

"Then take it. I'm not putting it up for sale; it's a present."

She seemed perplexed, but finally she took the bottle and stowed it away in the bag swinging from her shoulder.

"Thank you, Comrade," she managed to say.

"You're welcome, good-looking!"

Comrade Petrovna tried to give him a haughty bureaucratic stare but succeeded only in blushing like a little capitalist. She ran to catch up with the rest of the party, while Scamoggia closed his suitcase, lit a cigarette and let it dangle from one corner of his mouth, with an air of obvious satisfaction.

A bus was waiting for them, and they climbed in. As Peppone was hoisting his suitcase on to a shelf above the seats Don Camillo tapped him on the shoulder.

"Chief," he said, "there must be some sort of mix-up. I seem to have your suitcase."

Peppone examined the tag and saw that it was indeed his. He took the other one down from the shelf and sure enough it was tagged with the name of Camillo Tarocci.

"Nothing serious," said Don Camillo. "Just as I said, it's a mix-up."

Peppone sat down, across from Don Camillo. After the bus had started a second thought crossed his mind.

"So when we went through the customs I was carrying your suitcase," he said.

"Accidentally, you were."

"And accidentally did your suitcase have something contraband in it?"

"Oh, nothing much. A few holy cards, a picture of the Pope and some communion wafers."

Peppone shuddered all over.

The bus was travelling through an endless expanse of flat country, where scrawny cows were grazing on the meagre autumnal grass. Comrade Petrovna announced that they were going to visit a tractor factory, after which they would be taken to a hotel for dinner and a night's rest.

The factory was on the outskirts of the city of R. It was an agglomeration of dismal grey cement buildings rising abruptly out of the plains to the north.

"This ugliness is the product of what's called an 'industrial civilization', and it's the same the world over," Don Camillo thought mournfully to himself, feeling acutely homesick for his faraway village, where every brick had been put in place by a man's hand and men and things were bound by invisible ties together.

The workers wore the indifferent, bored air common to their kind. Some parts of the factory were staffed exclusively by women, stocky little creatures who did not in the least resemble Comrade Petrovna. At a certain point Comrade Rondella could not help edging up to Don Camillo and saying:

"Comrade, these women don't look as if they'd grown up in the same favourable environment as our charming interpreter!"

Don Camillo made a shattering reply.

"Comrade, you can't look at women factory workers as if they were contestants in a beauty parade! Every self-respecting Communist knows that."

It was no time for an argument, especially as Peppone was shooting dagger looks in their direction.

The visit was prolonged beyond all measure, because a zealous young manager explained in detail even things that required no explanation, with volleys of statistics that Comrade Petrovna had to translate without omitting a single one. Finally they came to the end of the assembly line. Don Camillo seemed to be thunderstruck with admiration at the sight of a finished tractor and said, turning to Peppone:

"Comrade Senator, this tractor is just like the one which the

Soviet government presented to your agricultural co-operative at home!"

Peppone would gladly have committed mayhem. The tractor in question had stubbornly refused to work, and the whole province had laughed about it. Now he was forced to smile and say what a boon it was to his peasant constituents. But when he had finished his little speech the mechanic in him won the upper hand. He took aside one of the engineers and pointed out a certain part of the fuel injection pump, which he explained did not function for such and such a reason. The engineer listened attentively and then shrugged his shoulders since he could make no better reply. Fortunately Comrade Petrovna came over and offered to interpret for him.

"He gets the point," she said to Peppone. "They're waiting for authorization to make the necessary changes."

The engineer laughed and said something more, causing the girl to knit her brow and hesitate for a moment. Finally, without looking Peppone in the face, she added:

"He says the authorization may arrive from one year to the next." She started to rejoin the group, but Scamoggia came to meet her.

"Comrade," he said, displaying a set of teeth as white as those of a Hollywood moving-picture idol, "I didn't hear those last figures about the replacement parts. Could you get the manager to repeat them?"

The manager obliged with a fresh volley of statistics, enough of them to choke an adding-machine. Scamoggia nodded approvingly and shook the manager's hand.

"Thank you," he said to Comrade Petrovna. "You don't know what pleasure you've given me."

"Are you particularly interested in agricultural machinery?" she inquired ingenuously.

"No, but I like to hear you talk."

This was a sacrilegious offence to a temple of labour and Comrade Petrovna paled and stiffened in proper bureaucratic style.

"Comrade . . ." she started to say in a harsh, metallic voice.

She had never been in the Trastevere section of Rome or looked into a pair of eyes like those of Scamoggia. They swallowed her up, and all her rigidity melted away.

R. was a typical Russian city of about a hundred and fifty thousand people, with few automobiles and little traffic of any kind on the streets. The hotel was small and ill kept and Don Camillo found himself in a thoroughly uncomfortable room. He wondered with whom he was to share it, but his doubts were soon put to an end by the arrival of Peppone.

"Look here, Father—I mean Comrade—," said Peppone, "you've got to stop pulling Rondella's leg. Let him alone, even if you don't like him."

"But I do like him," replied Don Camillo. "Where the Party's interests are at stake, I hew to the line. The fellow is sadly muddled; there are remnants of bourgeois ideology in his mind and it's up to us to clear them away."

Peppone threw his hat against the wall. "One of these days I'm going to strangle you," he hissed into the priest's ear.

The group gathered in the dingy dining-room. Comrade Oregov sat at the head of the table, with Peppone on his right and Comrade Nadia at his left. Don Camillo manoeuvred himself into a place opposite Rondella, thus causing Peppone's temperature to boil over. It boiled over again when he saw Don Camillo raise his hand to his forehead to make the sign of the cross as he sat down.

"Comrades," he exploded, "what wouldn't I give if some of those stupid reactionaries who are always talking down the Soviet Union could be with us? If only they could see it with their own eyes!"

"It wouldn't be any use, Comrade," Don Camillo said dismally. What with pretending to smooth his hair and brush the lapels of his jacket, he had successfully made his sign of the cross. "Their own eyes wouldn't convince them. They go around with blinkers."

Comrade Petrovna translated these words, and the tourist-bureau official nodded his shaven head in approval as he murmured a reply.

"Comrade Oregov says that you have hit the nail on the head," she said to Don Camillo, who acknowledged the compliment with a slight bow.

Scamoggia, who was always ready to second what Comrade Tarocci said, added an observation of his own.

"Our country is a century behind. Our stinking industrialists think they know it all, just because they produce a few miserable machines. But if they were to see a factory like the one we visited today, they'd have heart failure. And it isn't one of your biggest and best, is it, Comrade Petrovna?"

"Oh no, it's just a second-rate plant," she responded. "It's the last word in modern technology, but the production is relatively small."

Don Camillo shook his head sadly.

"We Italians ought to feel humiliated to see that a second-rate Soviet factory is so far ahead of the Fiat Company, which is our greatest producer of cars."

Comrade Peratto, from Turin, who so far had had very little to say, was wounded in his local pride.

"That may go for the tractor department, but when it comes to cars, the Fiat's not to be sneezed at. We have no right to belittle the Italian workers who made it what it is today."

"Truth above everything!" exclaimed Don Camillo. "Truth is more important than the pride of the Fiat Company. As long as national pride leads us to condone the backwardness of our social and economic system we shall never learn the lesson of efficiency which the Soviet Union can teach us. A man whose fiancée had only one leg insisted that two-legged women were inferior to her. That's exactly the attitude we have towards our half-baked accomplishments. Here in Russia industry has two strong legs to stand on."

"And what legs!" echoed Scamoggia, looking boldly at Comrade Petrovna.

"I don't see what you're driving at," Comrade Rondella said to Don Camillo.

"A Communist must face up to the truth, even when it is painful," Don Camillo explained. "We've come here to search for the truth, not to indulge in sentimentality."

The tourist-bureau official had followed the conversation carefully, asking Comrade Petrovna to translate every word. Peppone was sitting nervously on the edge of his chair, but fortunately just at this moment the food was brought to the table and the hungry group fell eagerly upon it.

The cabbage soup was not to their liking, but its taste was eclipsed by a savoury roast of mutton. Their hosts had even thought to provide them with wine, which relaxed the tension and loosened their tongues. The subject of the tractor factory was brought up again and Comrade Peratto, in order to wipe out the bad impression he had made by boasting of Fiat cars, called Don Camillo's attention to the ingenuity of a certain device in the Russian tractor factory's assembly line.

"Of course," said Don Camillo; "the Russian people are ingenious and inventive above all others. They have demonstrated their talent not only in the invention of the radio and the sputnik but also in the perfection of all sorts of lesser gadgets. Take the washbasins in our bedrooms, for instance. Instead of having one tap for hot water and another for cold, they join them together in a single outlet which allows you to run water of whatever temperature you choose. This may seem like a small thing, but where else are you to find it?"

Rondella happened to be a plumber and he could not let this go by.

"Comrade, don't be silly. My grandfather knew how to put two taps together. Where do you come from?"

"From the part of Italy that has more Communists than any other; in other words, from the most progressive part of the country. Besides, if I'm silly, I'm in good company. In Churchill's memoirs you can find the very same thing, and nobody can say that Churchill's a Communist."

Rondella's ideas were not muddled; they were crystal clear and he insisted upon expressing them.

"I don't give a damn about Churchill! I say that by exaggerating these things you play right into the enemy's hands. If truth comes above everything, then we must show it some respect."

Don Camillo took off his misted glasses, wiped them and put them back on his nose. Then he broke the silence with these solemn words:

"Truth? Truth is whatever coincides with the interests of the working class. Comrade, you trust your eyes rather than your reason. And your reason is weak, because there are too many capitalistic cobwebs in your brain."

"And you have a brain like a sieve," Rondella retorted angrily. "Besides that, you've gone out of your way to step on my toes ever since we met. When we get back home, I'll take care of you!"

"I'm not as patient as you are," said Don Camillo, "and I'll take care of you here and now!"

It all happened in a flash. Rondella stood up and punched Don Camillo in the jaw and Don Camillo shot him a return blow which toppled him back into his seat. The tourist-bureau official conferred with the interpreter and she passed on what he had to say to Peppone. Peppone got up, took Rondella by the scruff of his neck and hustled him outside.

"Comrade," he said when Rondella had recovered some degree of composure, "the commissar noticed that you were out of sorts. Apparently this climate doesn't agree with you. An hour from now an aeroplane leaves for Berlin, and he can arrange for your finding a place on it. From there you can go straight home."

"With pleasure!" shouted Rondella. "You can't imagine how glad I'll be to see the last of the whole bunch of you."

"Don't take it so hard. We'll see you when we return."

Rondella opened his wallet, took out his Party membership card and tore it to pieces.

"We may meet," he said, "but I'll be on the other side of the street."

Peppone had to give him a kick in the pants, but he did so with sincere regret. When he came back into the dining-room he put on a brave smile.

"It's all settled. He's most grateful for Comrade Oregov's thoughtfulness."

Then he raised his glass and proposed a toast to the victorous Soviet Union, to which Comrade Oregov responded with a toast to peace and the forthcoming liberation of the Italian working-class from capitalist tyranny.

"How about drinking to Nadia?" Scamoggia whispered in Don Camillo's ear.

"Take it easy, Comrade!" was Don Camillo's reply.

The dinner ended on a gay note. An hour later, while Comrade Rondella was flying towards Berlin, with a befuddled head and an aching behind, Peppone and Don Camillo retired to their room.

"Put out the light, Comrade," said Don Camillo. "You can put it on again as soon as we're in bed."

"Ridiculous!" exclaimed Peppone.

"Ridiculous, my eye! A priest can't be seen in his underwear by a Communist senator!"

When the light went back on Don Camillo took a notebook and wrote in it: *"Return to the fold of Comrade Walter Rondella."* Out loud he said:

"Another redskin bites the dust!"

"Only a priest could play so filthy a trick! But you're not putting over anything else on me!"

Don Camillo sighed.

"You'll have to consult the inhabitant of my pen about that."

Peppone stared at it with fascination, while Don Camillo unscrewed the top and extracted a slender object which turned out to be a crucifix.

"Lord," said Don Camillo, raising his eyes to heaven, "forgive me for putting hinges on Your arms and on those of the Cross. But there was no other way I could bring You with me."

"Amen!" roared Peppone, burying his head under the sheet.

5

A FORCED REST

"In illo tempore: Missus est Angelus Gabriel a Deo in civitatem Galilaeae cui nomen Nazareth, ad Virginem desponsatam viro, cui nomen erat Joseph, de domo David, et nomen Virginis Maria. Et ingressus Angelus ad eam dixit: Ave gratia plena; Dominus tecum. . . ."

The aeroplane on which he was travelling together with the druggist, swooped so abruptly that Peppone was left gasping. He wondered confusedly what the Latin was doing way up there in the air and how that hatefully reactionary druggist had come to be with him on the trip to Russia. Before he could settle these questions in his mind the droning Latin broke in on his consciousness again.

"Quae cum audisset, turbata est in sermone eius, et cogitabat qualis esset ista salutatio. At ait Angelus ei: Ne timeas Maria, invenisti enim gratiam apud Deum. . . ."

With enormous difficulty Peppone raised an eyelid which seemed to weigh half a ton. Gradually his eye fell upon a faded tapestry hanging on the wall with Russian characters on it.

". . . et vocabis nomen eius Jesum. Hic erit magnus, et Filius Altissimi vocabitur. . . ."

Peppone opened his other eye and turned completely over.

46

He was aghast to see that at the table which the Soviet hotel administration had allotted to this room Comrade Camillo Tarocci was celebrating Mass. Out of the red-jacketed volume of excerpts from Lenin he was reading the Gospel according to St. Luke.

Peppone leaped out of bed and ran to hold his eye to the keyhole of the door. His heart was pounding and for a moment he thought the only thing to do was to throw a sheet over Don Camillo's head. He thought better of this and began to shuffle around the room, making as much noise as possible in order to cover up the Latin sounds. He would have continued this indefinitely, had not the tinkle of a damned little bell rung in his buzzing ears. He didn't want to listen, but he was forced to acknowledge its reality, and when Don Camillo raised the tin cup which was serving as a chalice, he came to a halt and bowed his head. Steps rang out in the corridor, but Peppone did not budge.

"God help us!" he muttered to himself.

The steps stopped in front of the door; someone knocked and said in almost unrecognizable Italian:

"Time to get up, Comrade!"

Peppone grunted an answer, and the steps moved on to the next door.

"*Ite, Missa est. . . .*" said Don Camillo at last.

"It's about time," gasped Peppone. "You can keep the blessing for yourself."

"Lord, forgive him," whispered Don Camillo, bowing before the tiny crucifix which he had set up on the upturned bottom of an empty water carafe. "He's so jittery he can't think straight."

"I'd like to know if you weren't jittery when they knocked at the door," roared Peppone.

"Did somebody knock? I didn't hear."

Peppone didn't press the point because he knew that Don Camillo was telling the truth. Besides, he was dead tired and only wished he could go back to bed, even if it meant resuming his dream trip with the reactionary druggist.

"You're all ready, and the least you can do is get your trappings out of the way so that I can have room to dress." he said roughly.

"Comrade, you seem to be upset," said Don Camillo with a

47

deadpan face. "Perhaps the climate of the Soviet Union doesn't agree with you."

"You're what upsets me!" shouted Peppone, shoving him through the door.

Then he saw something that upset him still more. The door wasn't locked, and whoever had come to call them could have simply turned the handle and walked in.

Comrade Nadia Petrovna was waiting at the breakfast table. As soon as they were all gathered together she said:

"We may as well start. Comrade Oregov won't be down for some time."

She was wearing her most forbidding bureaucratic manner and she spoke in a cold, impersonal voice, without looking any-one in the eye. Without a single unnecessary movement she lowered herself into a chair. She breakfasted on just a cup of tea, which she sipped distractedly, as if it were an unpleasant duty. It seemed as if she were enveloped in a sheath of ice, but, fortunately or unfortunately, there were cracks in the sheath and from them there issued an agreeable fragrance, which spoiled the effect of frigidity. Forgetful of the fact that she was a servant of the State, Nadia Petrovna had sprayed herself with the eau-de-Cologne given to her by Comrade Nanni Scamoggia. Comrade Scamoggia was sitting at some distance from her, but he had a keen sense of smell and was quite aware of the transformation.

Comrade Yenka Oregov arrived just as breakfast was over. He had a preoccupied air, and after a hasty good morning he took Comrade Petrovna aside. They held a long discussion, making frequent reference to a piece of officially stamped paper which Comrade Oregov had taken out of his brief case. After they had apparently established a course of procedure, Comrade Petrovna addressed herself to Peppone.

"Comrade Yenka Oregov has received from the tourist bureau a definite programme for the whole period of your stay. At nine o'clock this morning you are to visit the Red Star tractor factory."

Peppone stared at her in amazement.

"Comrade, if I'm not mistaken, that is the factory we visited yesterday afternoon."

Comrade Petrovna went back to confer with Comrade Oregov.

"The programme which we have just received states un-equivocally that after resting from your trip yesterday afternoon, you are to visit the factory today. The original programme has been cancelled and therefore yesterday's visit must be considered as not having taken place."

Peppone threw out his arms in bewilderment and she conferred again with her superior.

"The programme is not subject to change, and this afternoon you are scheduled to take a sight-seeing trip around the city. Comrade Oregov does not insist that you pay another visit to the factory and so he suggests that you dedicate this morning to further rest, here in the hotel."

The travellers had not yet fully recovered from the weariness of their journey and so they jumped eagerly at this solution.

"Comrade Oregov is going to the factory to change the record of the date of your visit," said Comrade Petrovna. "I shall be at your service in the lobby."

And she went to sit on a broken-down sofa in the room through which it was necessary to pass going either in or out of the hotel. Her bearing was stiff and proud, but she left a train of fragrant eau-de-Cologne behind her.

Don Camillo went back up to his room, took off his shoes and threw himself down on his bed. But just as he was about to doze off, Peppone began to mutter to himself and pace the floor. After making his ablutions on the plane he had left his safety razor behind him.

"Take my razor and stop making such a racket," said Don Camillo.

"I never use any razor but my own," said Peppone. "And besides, I'm not used to that old-fashioned straight kind."

"Then go downstairs, change some of the liras you've taken from the taxpayers into roubles and buy yourself a new one. The General Store is nearby. Only be careful of the traffic and don't get yourself run over."

From the window there was not a car to be seen except for the bus which had brought them to the hotel, and Peppone was needled.

"The traffic will come in due time," he snorted. "We're not in a hurry. We are satisfied for the moment with the traffic with which we've peopled outer space."

"Buy me some wool socks," Don Camillo shouted after him.

"In the forty years since the Revolution they must have made at least one pair."

Peppone slammed the door in reply.

Comrade Petrovna treated him with the utmost consideration and got the hotel manager to exchange his bank note for a package of roubles. Then she wrote in Russian on a slip of paper: *"One safety razor and a dozen blades; one pair of men's wool socks, medium size."*

The General Store was just across the street and the transaction was speedily effected. As soon as the salesgirl had read the request she handed the items to Peppone and wrote down the price. But when Peppone returned to his hotel room he did not look as happy as might have been expected. He tossed the socks to Don Camillo, who caught them in mid-air and looked at them with evident satisfaction.

"Beauties!" he exclaimed. "We couldn't make anything half so good. The idea of having one longer than another is particularly clever. No man's feet are exactly the same. How much did they cost?"

"Ten roubles," said Peppone, who was unwrapping his razor.

"And what was the exchange?"

"I don't know. All I can tell you is that for a ten-thousand-lira bill they gave me seventy roubles."

"Then they gave you a hundred and fifty liras to a rouble. It's just about the same as the Swiss franc. What did you pay for the razor?"

"Nine roubles."

Don Camillo made some mental calculations.

"The razor was one thousand three hundred liras and the socks one thousand four hundred and fifty."

Peppone was busily lathering his face and did not reply.

"How much would you pay for a razor like this at home?" Don Camillo insisted.

"Two hundred liras for an American brand," admitted Peppone. "I can't believe there's such a difference. It must be a mistake."

"I don't think so, Comrade. You probably got your old razor at a sale and you can't expect them to have such things here. Under the Communist régime both factories and retail shops belong to the State and they don't have to meet any competition.

Besides your razor was American and this one is Russian; obviously there's no comparison between them. Then although the rouble's worth only forty liras on the free market, the tourist rate is a hundred and fifty. Communism hasn't been fighting its way for forty years just to give favourable exchange to visitors from abroad. Your razor would cost a Russian only three hundred and fifty liras."

Peppone had begun to shave. Suddenly he stopped, lathered his face again, changed the blade and started all over. Don Camillo stared at him quite pitilessly, but Peppone went grimly ahead. Then all of a sudden he swore and threw the razor at the wall.

"Comrade, where's your faith?" said Don Camillo gravely. Peppone, his face still covered with lather, shot him a bitter glance. Don Camillo relented; he searched his own suitcase and found an object which he handed over to Peppone.

"Is this that disgusting American razor of yours?" he asked. "I found it on the floor."

Peppone snatched it from him.

"Every day I live I'm more sure that to murder a priest is no crime!"

Meanwhile, as Comrade Petrovna kept watch at the front door, Comrade Scamoggia appeared before her. Before he could open his mouth she said brusquely:

"Comrade Oregov asked you to dedicate this morning to resting up in the hotel. It's not right for you to try to go out."

"I'm not trying to go out," said Scamoggia. "I want to rest up here beside you."

Comrade Petrovna gave him a puzzled stare.

"With so much room in the hotel I can't understand why you choose to rest in this particular spot."

"Must you treat your comrades so very formally?"

"No, only capitalists go in for formality."

"But I'm not a capitalist!" Scamoggia protested.

"You have certain capitalist ways."

"I may have made a mistake, Comrade. If you're willing to help me I'll conduct a self-examination."

Comrade Petrovna was softened by the earnestness of these words.

"Sit down, Comrade," she said, without altogether abandoning her severity. "Tell me about yourself."

"My name is Nanni Scamoggia. I'm twenty-eight years old and I've been a member of the Communist Party ever since I attained the age of reason. I sell and repair scooters."

"What are scooters?"

He pulled out of his pocket a photograph of himself, a muscular figure in white overalls astride a Vespa.

"There you are," he said. "Practically everybody has one."

"Very interesting. And do the other members of your family belong to the Party?"

"My father's a member of the Leghorn section. My mother's dead. My sister is a cell leader in the Dressmakers' Union."

"And your wife?"

"Comrade, do I look like a married man?"

She stared at him severely.

"At your age you need a woman."

"But why should I tie myself down to one woman, when there are so many available?"

Instinctively she drew away.

"There's another instance of bourgeois mentality. Only capitalists exploit women by treating them like playthings. In a socialist society a woman has the same station and dignity as a man."

"Comrade, I didn't express myself correctly. I was speaking of that category of women who hate work and have no political or social principles. They have no dignity and therefore no rights. . . ."

"I understand," she interrupted. "But when a comrade reaches a certain age, he ought to have a family and raise up new members of the Party."

"Comrade, I agree. But we live in a world very different from yours, full of selfishness and hypocrisy. In our country priests have the upper hand and a large number of women are obedient to them. Many of them are secret agents of the clergy, and a man has to watch his step."

"Don't you know any good Communist girls?"

"Yes, quite a few," he said with a weary gesture. "Perhaps it's all my fault, but I don't really care for any one of them."

"I can't believe it, Comrade. Not a single one?"

"Oh, one or two, perhaps. But they're already married."

Comrade Petrovna thought for a moment and then said:

"It's a serious situation, Comrade, I can see. But you're not facing up to it the way you should."

"Comrade," said Scamoggia, letting down his defences, "the years go by, I know, but with our blue sky and bright sun, all the flowers growing around us, the music in the air and the good wine we have to drink, a man has the illusion of being for ever young. Our country has been blessed by God. . . ."

"*Comrade!*" she interrupted. "That's heresy! No country is either blessed or cursed by God. God doesn't exist!"

"I know. Perhaps it's on account of those miserable priests, and all the churches and shrines . . . but somehow we have the illusion that He is really there."

"You're mentally confused, Comrade!"

"Perhaps you're right. But can't you look me in the eye when you tell me so?"

"I mustn't fall into the same error as Stalin," she thought to herself. "You can't expect Russians and Italians to speak the same language. Every country has its own climate and customs. A single key won't open every lock."

But Comrade Scamoggia broke in on her reflections.

"Let's talk about you," he suggested.

"I'm a Soviet woman," she answered proudly. "A Party member and an employee of the Government tourist office. I'm twenty-six years old and I live in Moscow."

"Do you live alone?"

"No, unfortunately I don't," she answered, lowering her head. "I share my room with two other girls. But I have no reason to complain."

"I'm not complaining either!" exclaimed Scamoggia.

Comrade Petrovna raised her eyes and looked at him with surprise.

"What do you mean?"

"I thought you might live with a masculine comrade. Naturally I'm glad to hear you live with two other girls."

She continued to stare at him.

"I don't follow your reasoning," she said.

But this was a shameless lie. It was quite clear from the fact that she turned his photograph over and over in her hands and

53

instead of giving it back to him slipped it into her bag. Even a dyed-in-the-wool Communist bureaucrat is subject to human frailty.

6

THE SPACE CELL

EXCEPT for Don Camillo, every member of the carefully chosen group was a Party militant of long standing—even the ill-fated Rondella, whom Don Camillo had perfidiously broken down and eliminated. Of the eight remaining stalwarts, Comrade Bacciga was perhaps the most solidly grounded in Communist doctrine, which he quoted at length on all appropriate occasions.

But Bacciga came from Genoa, and he was Genoese to the bone. Which means that he was above all a practical man, with a highly developed sense of business. Once Don Camillo had picked him for his next target this very sense of business was his undoing.

It happened on the afternoon of the first officially scheduled day, when the visitors were escorted on a sight-seeing tour of the city. The government-managed General Store, which Peppone had visited in the morning, was the first stop. Comrade Yenka Oregov instructed Comrade Nadia Petrovna to inform the visitors that by 1965 the Soviet Union would be producing eight billion yards of woollen materials a year and five hundred and fifteen million pairs of socks. Then, having assured them that everyone was free to buy what he chose, he stationed himself at the door to assure order.

Comrade Scamoggia wanted to know every detail of the store's operations and managed to draw Comrade Petrovna aside, into the housewares department. Peppone attached himself like a watchdog to Don Camillo and the others scattered in different directions.

The store was full of women, many of whom wore a worker's smock or the uniform of a mail-carrier or a trolley conductor. After making some purchases of food or household goods they went, for the most part, to admire the displays of women's dresses, shoes, underwear and beauty products.

"Your true Communist woman," Don Camillo said to Peppone, *"is remarkable for her lack of vanity and her scorn for everything superfluous.* On this premise there are only two possible explanations of the sight we have before us. Either these women are not good Communists, or else, thanks to the high living standards attained by the Soviet Union, the things they are gaping at with such obvious envy are not to be considered superfluous."

"I don't see what you're driving at," muttered Peppone suspiciously.

"I mean that consumer goods are now so abundant that a woman may allow herself to feel like exchanging her trousers for a pretty dress."

And when Peppone did not rise to this bait, he continued:

"After all the roubles you got for your ten thousand liras, why don't you buy a petticoat for your wife? Of course, a State petticoat, made out of State material by State dressmakers, can't be expected to have the trimmings and fine points of a privately manufactured product."

At this point Peppone could no longer withhold a withering reply.

"It's better for a woman to wear a plain petticoat and to be free, than to shop at Christian Dior's and be a slave."

"Well spoken, Comrade," said Don Camillo, who meanwhile had caught sight of the member of the group he was looking for.

Comrade Bacciga had managed to get away from the others and to engage in conversation with the clerk in the fur department. Their conversation was in sign language and in quotations of bid and asked, which they jotted down in turn on slips of paper. After they had come to an agreement Comrade Bacciga pulled some shiny cellophane envelopes out of his pocket which she nimbly stowed under the counter. Then she wrapped up a mink stole for him to take away and the transaction was completed. Peppone had not noticed what was going on, but Don Camillo had followed every stage of the proceedings and now he was in a hurry to return to the hotel.

But they did not return until evening, for after the General Store they visited a hospital and a ball-bearing factory. Don Camillo went straight to his room, and Peppone, worried by his disappearance, hastened to rejoin him. He found Don Camillo sitting on the floor, studying some pamphlets and papers he had taken out of his suitcase.

"Couldn't you be satisfied with the excerpts from Lenin?" roared Peppone. "What other rubbish did you bring with you?"

Don Camillo did not so much as raise his head, but continued his scrutiny.

"Take this," he said, handing him a loose page, "and learn by heart the passages underlined with a blue pencil."

Peppone took one look at the page and started.

"This is something from the *Militant's Manual*!" he exclaimed.

"Well, what of it? Did you expect me to bring clippings from the *Osservatore Romano*?"

Peppone turned as violently red as the October Revolution.

"I say that this has been taken out of my own personal copy which belongs on the shelves of the local Party library!" he protested. "There's the library mark in it, right there. I'd like to know how . . ."

"Don't be excited, Comrade. You don't suppose I could have acquired my Communist culture in the library of the Archbishop's Palace, do you?"

Peppone leaned over to examine the material on the floor.

"Every bit of it's mine!" he exclaimed in horror. "You've ruined the whole collection! I'll . . ."

"Come now, Comrade!" interrupted Don Camillo. "It's disgraceful to rake up our petty personal differences here in a foreign land. Hurry up and memorize the passages underlined in blue. Those underlined in red are for me."

Peppone stared at him suspiciously.

"You're cooking up some mischief, for sure."

"Nothing of the sort. If you don't want to play the fool, go ahead and learn what I told you. You've got only half an hour."

"Very well. I'll have more to say to you later."

He sat down at the table, fixed his attention on the text and proceeded to learn his lesson. There were only two passages of a few lines each, but he was so indignant that he could have memorized a whole page.

"Now, let's hear you," said Don Camillo, putting the other papers back in the suitcase.

"Comrades!" said Peppone, "Lenin has said: *'Extremes are never advisable. But if we have to choose, we prefer absolute clarity, even if it is narrow and intolerant, to elusive and intangible haziness. . . .'* "

"Good! When I pretend that I can't remember a certain quotation from Lenin, then you are to come out with that. As for the other passage, your cue is when I ask you for the official opinion of the Party."

"For God's sake, what Party do you mean?"

"The one and only Communist Party, of course," said Don Camillo. "Which, as it says in the *Manual, 'demands of all its members that they . . .'* "

" *'That they should, in their personal conduct . . .'* " broke in Peppone. And angrily he recited the whole piece, without omitting a single word or even a comma. Don Camillo listened with a somewhat sanctimonious air and said at the end:

"Good work, Comrade! I'm proud to be your pastor!"

Dinner was abundant and also educational, because Comrade Oregov illustrated with numerous statistics the progress which the Soviet Union would achieve in 1965. At the end, after the customary toasts to peace, the easing of international tension and the inevitable victory of Communism, Don Camillo rose from his chair.

"Comrades," he said. "Party membership obliges every one of us to follow certain principles, to exercise self-examination and constructive criticism of our fellows. . . ."

He talked very slowly, emphasizing every word and looking proudly at Comrade Oregov, to whom Comrade Petrovna conscientiously interpreted him.

"Before his Party conscience, a Communist must scrutinize his every action and question himself as to whether he could have performed it better. He must not hesitate to speak the truth, no matter how disagreeable it may be. Comrade, I can't remember the exact words of Lenin on this subject. Lenin said . . ."

He fumbled agonizingly for the words and Peppone put in:

"Don't fret, Comrade. Lenin said: *'Extremes are never advisable. But if we have to choose, we prefer absolute clarity, even if it is narrow and intolerant, to elusive and intangible haziness.'* "

Comrade Yenka Oregov nodded his head and smiled complacently.

"Thank you, Comrade," said Don Camillo, keeping his eyes on Comrade Oregov. "On this basis I feel myself authorized to speak clearly. The little unpleasantness of yesterday, concerning Comrade Rondella, recalled to me the fifth paragraph of the Party Constitution, which says: *'In case of an infraction of Party discipline every member has a right to be judged by a regular Party organization and to appeal to the assembly of his fellow members and also to higher authorities.'* Now I have this to say: If one member of the group led by Comrade Senator Bottazzi is guilty of an infraction of Party discipline, what Party organization is to judge him? Of course, the Comrade Senator represents the Party and can call his case to the attention of the federation, the regional section or the cell to which he belongs. But if the infraction is committed on Soviet soil and involves a local situation, who is to judge it? I maintain that it is to be judged here and now. Since we are not presently connected with any Party organization, such as those described in paragraph ten of the Party Constitution, I believe we can and should organize our own cell."

When Comrade Petrovna had translated these words, Comrade Oregov voiced no reaction and waited imperturbably for Don Camillo to go on.

"Comrades," he continued, "you look at me as if you were wondering what kind of cell I mean. Not a labour-union cell, since we are not engaged in labour; not a regional section, since this is not where we live. Of course it's true that we didn't come to the Soviet Union to amuse ourselves, but rather to learn and teach, and this is work of a very important kind. And even if we do not live here, the Soviet Union is our spiritual home. Let me tell you, then, what I have in mind."

Don Camillo was obviously sincere, and the others listened to him attentively.

"Comrades, we are a group of travellers who have removed themselves from an outworn, decrepit civilization and journeyed to a civilization which is in the pride of its youth. We are the crew of a flying machine which has left behind it the decaying world of capitalism and is making a voyage of exploration over the fascinating world of socialism. Our little crew is composed not of isolated individuals but of a group of men united by a single faith and a single will: to spread Communism throughout the globe. No, we are not a labour-union cell, or a regional cell, we are an interplanetary cell, a space cell. For the world from which we come is more distant from the socialist world than this planet of ours from the moon. And so I propose that our group organize itself into a cell named after the one man who embodies the Soviet people's desire for peace and progress: Nikita Khrushchev!"

Comrade Oregov was so overcome with emotion that he stood up, amid ringing applause, and pumped Don Camillo's hand for at least ten minutes. Don Camillo conferred with him through the interpreter, and then said:

"In the name of the Italian Communist Party and in agreement with the representative of the Communist Party of Russia, I announce the constitution of the 'Nikita Khrushchev Cell!'"

The nine cell members held an immediate meeting, a very simple matter since they were all seated around the table, and pursuant to paragraph twenty-eight of the Constitution they voted for officers to represent them. Comrade Camillo Tarocci was elected leader; Comrade Nanni Scamoggia secretary and Comrade Vittorio Peratto treasurer. Peppone did not vote and it was not until he was raising his glass in a toast to the officers that he realized that the leader was to be Don Camillo. It was all he could do to choke down his glass of wine.

"Comrades," Don Camillo announced gravely, "I want first of all to thank you for this expression of confidence and to promise that I shall do everything I can to deserve it. I propose we start functioning without delay. Is there a suggestion of any business to be brought before the meeting?"

When no one spoke up, he jumped into the breach himself, to the accompaniment of an anguished glance from Peppone.

"Then, Comrades, I have something to suggest. No real Communist is afraid of the truth. The Party teaches us to be intolerant of failings, dissatisfied with anything that falls short of perfection. A Party member who is incapable of criticism, who does not demand a maximum of effort both of himself and his comrades cannot hope to be a leader or to win outsiders to the cause. Among the obligations listed in paragraph nine of the Constitution is that of 'leading a private life of exemplary integrity'. Comrade Bacciga, do you admit that this aftenoon, in the course of our visit to the General Store, you bought a mink stole?"

"I do," replied Comrade Bacciga, turning deathly pale. "Comrade Oregov authorized us to buy anything we wanted."

"Correct. Do you further admit that you paid for the stole not with money but with nylon stockings which you brought from Italy? If you don't admit it, then you're a liar. And if you do, then you're admitting at the same time that you are party to one of those black-market transactions which are notoriously damaging to the Soviet economy, in short, that you're a saboteur. In either case your private life is not an example of integrity. With this I rest my accusation. Now the comrades will listen to your defence."

While Comrade Bacciga struggled to collect his thoughts Comrade Petrovna translated Don Camillo's words for the benefit of Comrade Oregov. When Comrade Bacciga did stammer a few lame excuses, they were unanimously judged to be insufficient. First, he had defrauded the Soviet customs; second, he had sabotaged the Soviet economy; third, he had betrayed the trust of his Soviet comrades. Comrade Oregov looked like a Robespierre come to judgment, and Comrade Bacciga had to conduct his self-examination before him.

"The frank admission of your fault is in your favour," Don Camillo concluded. "But that is not enough. On this matter I shall ask the opinion of Comrade Senator Bottazzi."

Striking up as authoritative a pose as the circumstances would allow him, Peppone replied:

"The Party does indeed demand that every comrade's personal conduct should be an example to others. It cannot be indifferent towards behaviour which lowers it in the public esteem. According to Marxist-Leninist philosophy, a Communist's private and Party life are one. The Party organization exercises a disciplinary function; it corrects such members as subordinate social responsibility to personal well-being and thereby tar themselves with the capitalist brush."

He delivered this harangue with such conviction that for the second time Comrade Oregov favoured him with an approving smile.

"But self-examination and condemnation do not atone for a crime," Don Camillo added. "Even priests, who are the embodiment of hypocrisy and dishonour, tell a penitent that he must make amends for his sin, and in the case of theft he must return the stolen goods to their rightful owner."

"Comrade, you don't know priests!" Peppone interjected angrily. "They're much more likely to connive with the thief than to condemn him."

"I was speaking of what they *should* do rather than of their actual practice," Don Camillo explained. "Certainly Comrade Bacciga's barter must be considered a theft."

After some further talk Comrade Scamoggia entered a resolution:

"I move that the stolen object be restored to the Soviet Union. Let Comrade Bacciga give it to Comrade Nadia Petrovna."

There was a chorus of murmurs, interrupted by Comrade Petrovna in person.

"I am grateful for your kind thought," she said, "although it is to some extent 'tarred by the capitalist brush', as the Comrade Senator was saying. But I have already told Comrade Oregov that you would like to give the stole to his wife, Comrade Sonia Oregovna."

This ingenious solution won a round of applause. Comrade Bacciga had to hand over the stolen stole to Peppone, who then presented it to Comrade Oregov, on behalf of the newly formed "Nikita Khrushchev Space Cell". As for the nylon stockings, they were entirely forgotten, that is except by Comrade Bacciga. When Don Camillo closed the meeting by sentencing Comrade Bacciga to six months of suspension from all Party activity, the latter shot him a look of fierce resentment. As they were going upstairs he caught up with his persecutor and hissed:

"Comrade, the Communist Party isn't big enough to hold the two of us!"

"Then surely the dishonest member should be the one to drop out," said Don Camillo.

Before putting out the light Don Camillo opened his famous notebook and wrote down: "*No. 2—Comrade Bacciga, morally liquidated.*"

Peppone stretched his arm out of bed, snatched the notebook and read the annotation. Then tossing it back to Don Camillo he said:

"Your next entry will be: '*No. 3—Liquidated: the undersigned, by Comrade Peppone.*'"

Don Camillo looked down his nose.

"Comrade," he replied, "you forget that you're talking to a leader. And a Communist leader isn't so easily liquidated."

"You don't know your Communist Party!" retorted Peppone.

7

POLITICS ON THE ROAD

"COMRADE, have you the Party files of the members of our group with you?"

Peppone, who was busy shaving, wheeled angrily around. "That's strictly my affair."

"Our affair, you mean. Now that I'm a cell leader I'm entitled to know my men."

"You're entitled to go straight to hell, and take your cell with you."

Don Camillo raised his eyes to heaven.

"Lord, did You hear him? Of all the Communist cells in the world this is the only one to have an accredited chaplain, and he says it can go to hell!"

Everything has its limits, and when a safety razor is used like a hoe it can be a very dangerous weapon. Peppone was hacking away at his chin, and his chin began to bleed. But how can a Communist senator have any peace of mind when he has brought with him to Russia a priest disguised as a Party militant of long standing and this diabolical Vatican emissary has set himself up as the leader of a cell? While Peppone was swabbing his nicked chin Don Camillo managed to replace in his room-mate's suitcase the files which he had deftly taken out of it for study.

"Comrade, if those files are so very private," he said, "let's

64

forget them. But don't be surprised if I make some embarrassing errors."

Just then Scamoggia came to tell them that the bus was waiting in front of the hotel.

It was a grey autumn morning. Women in men's overalls were washing and sweeping the streets, running the trolley cars, tarring a paved square and doing construction work on a new building. In front of a *Gastronom* a long line of women, in simple but more feminine clothes, was patiently waiting. Don Camillo leaned towards Peppone and whispered in his ear:

"These women not only have men's rights; they have women's rights as well!"

Peppone did not even look up. He and Don Camillo were sitting on the back seats of the bus. Comrade Oregov and Comrade Petrovna sat in front, directly behind the driver, and the eight other comrades occupied the seats between. Whenever Comrade Petrovna stood up to translate some remark of Comrade Oregov she faced the entire group. This seating arrangement also allowed Don Camillo to talk in a low voice either to Peppone, who was sitting just across the aisle, or to Comrades Tavan and Scamoggia, who were sitting in the two seats directly ahead. Now that Don Camillo had liquidated Comrade Rondella of Milan and shaken the faith of Comrade Bacciga of Genoa, he was gunning for Comrade Tavan.

"*Tavan, Antonio, forty-two years old, a native of Pranovo in the province of Veneto. Party member since 1943. Tenant farmer. Active, loyal, trustworthy. To be used only in peasant circles, on account of his limited acquaintance with social and economic problems. Socialist father. His family has worked the same land for 120 years. A skilful and hard-working farmer.*"

This was the description which Don Camillo had pilfered from Peppone's files, and now the peasant Tavan was a marked man.

They had left the city behind them and were travelling across the desolate countryside.

"We are now going through the 'Red Flag' *sovkos*," Comrade Petrovna was explaining, "one of the first of its kind to be established after the Revolution. It has a total area of 30,000 acres, of which 10,000 are under cultivation, and is equipped with fifty-four tractors, fifteen reaping machines and fifteen trucks. There are three hundred and eighty agricultural workers. At the present time there are six thousand *sovkos* in the Soviet Union, with a total of four million head of cattle, six million hogs and twelve million sheep. . . ."

Rising up out of the wide, flat land they suddenly saw signs of human habitation, small houses clustered around large buildings with corrugated iron roofs, silos, barns and warehouses. As the bus bumped over a narrow dirt road, they noticed dozens of huge tractors abandoned hither and yon over the ploughed fields and covered with rust and mud. In the inhabited area other tractors, trucks and agricultural instruments stood about on the ground, exposed to the weather, in front of the farm buildings.

"Four million head of cattle!" exclaimed Don Camillo with a deep sigh.

"That's quite a number!" agreed Peppone.

"When you add those to the twenty-seven million of the *kolkhos*, they come to thirty-one million."

"Colossal!"

"By the end of 1960 there are supposed to be forty million," Don Camillo went on. "But for the time being there are still two million two hundred head less than there were in 1928, before collectivization."

Peppone could not see what Don Camillo was after.

"Comrade," Don Camillo explained, "the Soviet Union is the only country in the world where everything is out in the open, where there is a public statement of whether or not things are going well. These are official statistics and from them we must conclude that whereas there has been enormous progress in science and industry, agriculture is still lagging. Volunteers have had to be sent from Moscow, Kiev and other cities to break ground in Siberia."

He threw out his arms in mock sympathy, then aiming his words at the ears of the peasant Tavan he added, ostensibly to Peppone:

"Comrade, you've seen the condition of those tractors and you can judge for yourself the validity of my conclusions. I tell you that the trouble is this: peasants are peasants the world over. Just look at the way things are at home. Who are our most backward people? Peasants! Yes, I know that the day labourers are struggling to improve their situation, but they are workers. Just

66

try to change the ways of a peasant or a tenant farmer! See if you can make him class-conscious or involve him in the proletarian movement!"

Comrade Tavan had pricked up his ears and was not losing a single word of the conversation going on behind him.

"And now consider the state of things here in Russia," continued Don Camillo. "What people are holding the country back? The hard-headed *kolkhos* holders, who don't give a hang for the collectivized land and insist upon cultivating the few acres which the government has generously given them for their own private use. There are eighty thousand *kolkhos* and six thousand *sovkos*, but the *kolkhos* peasants have seventeen million head of privately owned cattle as compared to fourteen million collectively owned between *kolkhos* and *sovkos* together. Those peasants don't deserve to own any land at all. And, mark my words, it will be taken away from them."

Comrade Tavan's ears had turned bright red.

"Look again at our own country," said Don Camillo. "Who promoted the black market during the war? The peasants! And who promotes it here? The peasants of the *kolkhos*! With us, where is it that the priests still have most power? Among the peasants! And in the Soviet Union how do the surviving priests continue to retard the general progress? Thanks to the roubles they collect from the *kolkhos*!"

Comrade Tavan's ears were no redder than the cheeks of Peppone.

"Comrade," said Don Camillo, by way of winding up his peroration, "here we have a country that has beaten world records in every domain and won first place in the race to the moon. But among the *kolkhos* you still find selfish obstruction to progress. Beware of peasants! They're an ugly lot, I tell you!"

"Well spoken, Comrade!" said Scamoggia, from his seat in front of Peppone. "People make me laugh when they talk about giving the peasants land. Give it to them, and see what they'll do! They'll starve us! The land should be publicly owned, cultivated by the State. And peasants should be treated like workers. Just because the peasants work the land, are they to have its produce? Then why shouldn't a worker in an automobile factory be given a car? Who gave us our Fascist régime? The peasants! Wasn't a black shirt their everyday working garment

67

in Emilia and Romagna, where you and the Comrade Senator come from . . . ? Just look at the way that stupid fool out there is assassinating that tractor . . . !"

The careening tractor in the immediate vicinity of the bus seemed dangerously out of control. As a matter of fact the driver was not a peasant; he was a Government farm-bureau agent. But although his ineptitude was not forwarding the sixth Five-Year Plan it fitted in most opportunely with the purposes of Don Camillo.

"Lout!" called out Scamoggia as the tractor passed alarmingly close by.

But the lout took this interpellation for a friendly greeting and raised a clenched fist in reply. Comrade Tavan's ears had grown deadly pale. Peppone scribbled something on a scrap of paper and handed it to Don Camillo. For the benefit of their companions he said:

"Make a note on what we are seeing for the report we are to take back home."

But on the paper he had written:

"Keep your mouth shut, or I'll fracture your shin!"

Don Camillo nodded gravely. Meanwhile Scamoggia was distracted from his diatribe against the peasants by an explanatory harangue from Comrade Nadia Petrovna.

"We are not stopping at the 'Red Flag' *sovkos*, because it is concerned only with the cultivation of grain. The grain has already been harvested and there is nothing for us to see. We are proceeding now to the *kolkhos* at Grevinec, a co-operative enterprise covering four thousand acres of land which goes in for truck gardening and for raising cattle and hogs as well. It is completely autonomous and receives no Government aid, although the Government farm-bureau supplied its mechanical equipment. . . . Just now, Comrades, we have crossed the *kolkhos* boundary line. . . ."

This last bit of information was quite superfluous, because, although the terrain was the same as before, the general picture was entirely different. Here everything was the way it should be; the fields were tidily ploughed and the grazing livestock well fed. The village houses were the usual wooden shacks, but each one had its own neatly trimmed orchard and vegetable garden, a chicken yard, a hog run and a stall for the cow. Two solidly constructed buildings housed the administrative offices and the community school. Comrade Petrovna explained that ninety-seven per cent of the *kolkhos* were electrified, but unfortunately this one belonged to the more primitive minority.

In order to reach the heart of the village the bus had to go over a typically rutted road, and so while it was still half a mile away the "Space Cell" group requested permission to get out, stretch their legs and cover the remaining distance on foot. The mud had dried and hardened, and by taking care not to stumble into the ruts the visitors were able to walk without too much difficulty. Along the way they were overtaken by a horse and cart. In the cart sat a chubby man wearing high boots, an oilskin raincoat with a fur collar and a fur cap. Don Camillo scrutinized him attentively and hastened to catch up with Comrade Petrovna.

"Who is that fine gentleman, Comrade?" he asked her.

Comrade Petrovna laughed. She passed the question on to Comrade Oregov, who seemed to share her amusement.

"Comrade, you have eagle eyes," she said to Don Camillo. "That 'fine gentleman' is a priest."

"What? A priest?" exclaimed Comrade Scamoggia, who was of course walking at Comrade Petrovna's side. "What business has he here?"

She looked at him severely.

"Comrade, do you remember Paragraph 128 of the Constitution: *'In order to assure freedom of conscience, the Church is separate from the State and the Schools from the Church. Every citizen has a right to observe religious practices or to conduct antireligious propaganda, as he chooses.'* "

"But that fellow's not a citizen, he's a priest!" said Scamoggia indignantly.

Comrade Petrovna laughed again and when she had explained the reason for her hilarity to Comrade Oregov he once more chimed in.

"Comrade," she said, "in the Soviet Union priests have the same rights as anyone else. As long as they do not go in for obnoxious proselytizing, no one disturbs them. If someone wants a priest, he is free to pay for his services."

Scamoggia turned to Don Camillo.

"Comrade, you were right. And to think that one of my

reasons for wanting to come here was to get the priests out of my hair!"

"Priests are the lowest order of creatures on earth!" roared Peppone. "When Noah got into the ark, he didn't want to take any snakes along, but God Almighty shouted to him: 'Noah, without priests how am I to survive?'"

When Comrade Oregov was informed of this witticism he laughed louder than ever and took it down in his notebook. Don Camillo laughed too, unenthusiastically, and fell back to the end of the line, where Peppone was walking.

"Comrade, that's cheating!" he protested. "I didn't tell you the story that way. Noah didn't want to take *donkeys*, and God said: 'Without Communist senators I wouldn't have any fun!'"

"My version is better," retorted Peppone. "Only I owe an apology to the snakes."

"You fraud!" hissed Don Camillo. "You're taking advantage of the fact that I'm a cell leader!"

They walked along in silence for a moment and then Peppone returned to the attack.

"I saw that fellow myself," he muttered; "all of us saw him. But you were the only one to detect the smell of a priest. The call of the blood, no doubt! But don't fool yourself. When we come to power you won't go about in a cart, or a car or even on your own two feet. Dead men don't stir."

"That's all right with me," said Don Camillo, calmly lighting the butt of his cigar. "Under a Communist régime anyone who stirs is dead, and one dead man's as good as another."

As they entered the village Scamoggia turned around and shouted back to Don Camillo:

"Comrade, you were right again when you said priests live off the ignorance of the peasants. Just look at that fellow now!"

In one of the vegetable gardens the priest was busily talking to an old couple. Don Camillo saw him plainly and so did Comrade Tavan. Once more the latter's flapping ears turned crimson. Comrade Petrovna shook her head.

"Don't get excited, Comrade," she said to Scamoggia. "He's in contact only with a few old people. That's the way it is all over. When they die off, then God will die, too. Even now He lives only in the minds of those who were brought up in an era of superstition. And when God is dead, the priests will follow. The Soviet Union has plenty of time ahead of it; we can afford to wait."

She spoke in a loud voice and even Don Camillo, at the end of the line, heard her.

"God can afford to wait too," he mumbled in the direction of the silent Peppone.

Comrade Salvatore Capece, a thirty-year-old Neapolitan, with an expressive face and flashing eyes, was standing nearby, and Don Camillo said to him provocatively:

"Comrade Petrovna has really got something, don't you agree?"

"She's got plenty," Capece eagerly responded. "I don't mind telling you that she's right up my alley."

Don Camillo smiled.

"From the way she keeps looking at you I think you've taken her fancy," he remarked.

Comrade Petrovna hadn't intentionally looked at him at all, but Capece was more than ready to swallow Don Camillo's flattery.

"Comrade, you know what's what," he agreed. "A woman can't be anything else but a woman."

And he quickened his step in order to rejoin her.

"You'll go to any lengths to stir up trouble, won't you?" said Peppone.

"Comrade, I've got to get busy while God is still alive. Tomorrow may be too late," said Don Camillo.

8

CHRIST'S SECRET AGENT

GREVINEC was prepared for the Italian visitors' arrival; the propaganda and publicity director was waiting for them at the entrance to the village and led them to the administrative headquarters of the local soviet, where the district Party leader and the head of the *kolkhos* gave welcoming speeches, translated by Comrade Nadia Petrovna. Peppone made a carefully rehearsed speech in reply and followed the local custom of joining in the applause.

Besides the bigwigs there were several minor dignitaries whom Comrade Petrovna introduced as the directors of the various departments: cattle and hog breeding, fruit, vegetable and grain production, machinery repairs and so on. The room in which the reception was held was barnlike in structure, furnished with a rough wooden table, rows of chairs and a portrait of Lenin on the wall. The reception committee had adorned the gilt-framed portrait with green branches, but this decoration attracted less attention from the guests than did the presence of numerous bottles of vodka on the table.

A glass of vodka, downed as rapidly as if it were red wine, is stimulating to both heart and body, and Peppone responded promptly and intensely to it. After Comrade Petrovna had explained that this particular *kolkhos* was a recognized champion in the production of pork, milk and cereals, he asked for the floor. Standing squarely in front of Comrade Oregov, he began to speak, quite extemporaneously, pausing after every sentence to give Comrade Petrovna time to translate it.

"Comrade," he said, "I come from the province of Emilia, where, exactly fifty years ago, some of the first and most successful people's co-operatives were established. In this region agriculture is highly mechanized, and the pork, dairy and cereal products are tops in quantity and quality alike. In my village my comrades and I have founded a co-operative of farm workers which was honoured, not long ago, by a magnificent gift from the Soviet Union!"

Here Peppone pulled out of his brief case a sheaf of photographs, which he handed over to Comrade Oregov. The photographs showed the triumphant arrival in the village of "Nikita", the gift tractor, and its operation on the co-operative's land. They were passed around to all those present and received unanimous approval.

"In our country the undermining of capitalism is under way," Peppone continued. "It is not yet in the final stage, but it is making progress, as Comrade Tarocci, who comes from the same region, can testify. Inevitably the privileges of the landowners and clergy will be wiped out, and a new era of liberty will begin. Soon agricultural co-operatives modelled on the *kolkhos* and government projects modelled on the *sovkos* will replace the slave-labour conditions which form such a shameful hangover from the past. You can understand how deeply interested I am in the Russian *kolkhos*. I should like to ask Comrade Oregov and your leaders to show me every detail of the Grevinec operation."

Comrade Oregov replied that he did indeed understand the importance of the Italian comrade's request and would do everything in his power to satisfy it. He parleyed with the *kolkhos* leaders, and Comrade Petrovna transmitted the gist of their deliberations to Peppone.

"Comrade, everyone appreciates your interest in the technical and organizational aspects of our undertaking. But if I were to act as an intermediary between you and the *kolkhos* leaders for the whole time of your visit, your comrades would not be able to make the complete tour of the area which the programme

73

provides for them. Fortunately, among the technicians here present there is one who can give you complete information in your own language."

She paused to beckon to one of the Russian group, and a thin, dark man between thirty-five and forty years old, in mechanic's garb, stepped forward.

"Here we have a man whose job is concerned with farm-machinery supplies and repairs, Stephan Bordonny, an Italian . . ."

"Stephan Bordonny, citizen of the Soviet Union," the thin man interrupted, holding out his hand to Peppone, but looking reproachfully at Comrade Petrovna. "Yes, I am a Soviet citizen, and so are my children."

Comrade Petrovna smiled to cover up her embarrassment.

"I stand corrected, Citizen," she said. "I should have specified that you are of Italian origin. While the rest of us make a general tour, you will be a private guide to Comrade Senator Bottazzi."

She went to join the group and Don Camillo started to go after her, but Peppone blocked the way.

"You are to stay with me, Comrade Tarocci," he said firmly, "and to take notes on everything we see."

"At your orders, Comrade," said Don Camillo wryly.

"Are you a Party member, Comrade?" Peppone asked their guide.

"No, I haven't yet been accorded the honour," the other replied with an impersonal and detached air.

Citizen Bordonny gave definite answers, which Don Camillo transcribed in his notebook, to every question asked by Peppone, but it was plain that he did so in the least possible number of words. He knew every detail of the *kolkhos'* operation and cited exact dates and figures, but without any comment of his own. He courteously refused the cigar and the cigarette which Peppone and Don Camillo in turn offered him. Because they were smoking he finally took out of his pocket a piece of news-paper and a pinch of *makorta* and deftly rolled a cigarette. They visited the wheat silos and then the warehouse used to store fertilizers, sprays and small agricultural tools. Everything was listed and in perfect order.

In one corner of the warehouse was an odd-shaped, brand-new machine and Peppone asked what it was used for.

"It's for carding cotton," Bordonny replied.

"Cotton?" exclaimed Don Camillo. "Do you mean to tell me that in this climate you can grow cotton?"

"No," said Bordonny laconically.

"Then what are you doing with this machine?"

"It came here by mistake. We had asked for a threshing machine for our wheat."

Peppone shot Don Camillo an atomic glance, but Don Camillo had caught on to a good thing and had no intention of letting it go.

"So are you going to adapt it to threshing?" asked Don Camillo.

"No," their guide said icily. "We've put together a machine of our own."

"And how do you suppose the other fellows who ordered the carding machine are managing to handle their cotton?"

"That's not our affair."

"Mix-ups of this kind shouldn't be allowed," said Don Camillo with a curtness which equalled Bordonny's.

"The area of your country is a hundred and fifty thousand square miles, and ours is eleven million," answered the other.

At this point Peppone intervened, at the same time stepping with an utter lack of delicacy on Don Camillo's foot.

"Citizen Bordonny, are you in personal charge of this operation?" he inquired.

"No. I have only a limited share of the responsibility."

"I'd like to see some of the larger machines," said Peppone.

The warehouse for the larger machines was not much to look at. It was a big, wooden barn with a rusty corrugated-iron roof. But inside it was truly impressive. The beaten-earth floor was immaculately clean and the machines were polished and lined up as if for exhibit at a fair. Citizen Bordonny knew the date of purchase, the oil and gasoline consumption and the horsepower of every one.

At the far end of the building there was a workshop with brick walls. It contained a strict minimum of tools but it was kept in such perfect order that Peppone was very nearly moved to tears. A tractor was currently under repair and the various parts of its motor were lined up on a workbench. Peppone picked up one of the parts for closer examination.

"Who's been working on this?" he asked.

"I have," said Citizen Bordonny indifferently.

"With this lathe?" asked Peppone, pointing in surprise to an instrument that had something vaguely lathe-like about it.

"No, with a file," the guide answered.

Hanging from a big hook on the wall there was a connecting rod, tied together with heavy string. Bordonny took a screwdriver and struck the rod, causing it to ring like a bell.

"It's out of balance," he said. "I can tell from the sound. All it takes is a practised ear."

Peppone took off his hat and wiped the perspiration from his forehead.

"What do you know about that?" he exclaimed. "I thought there was only one man in the world who used that system. And here in the middle of Mother Russia I find another!"

"Who's that?" asked Don Camillo.

"The mechanic at Torricella," said Peppone. "A perfect wizard, who specialized in tuning racing-cars. A fellow that didn't look as if he had a penny to his name, but racers used to send him their cars from all over Europe. During the second year of the war his machine shop was hit by a bomb aimed at the bridge over the Stivone. He and his wife and two children were killed on the spot."

"Only one of his sons," said Bordonny. "The other was lucky enough to be in the army." There was a new tone in his voice as he added: "I'm happy to know someone who remembers my father."

They left the building in silence. Outside, the sky was black with an impending storm.

"I live in that house over there," said Bordonny. "We'd better take shelter there before it starts to pour. While we're waiting I can answer any further questions."

They reached the house just as the first drops of rain were beginning to fall. It was a simple dwelling, but cosy and warm,

76

with smoke-blackened beams on the kitchen ceiling. Peppone had not yet recovered from his surprise when they sat down at the long table.

"The last time I went to your father's machine shop was in 1939," he said, as dreamily as if he were talking to himself. "Something was wrong with my little second-hand car and I couldn't get at the trouble."

"It was a connecting rod," said Bordonny. "And I was the one who fixed it. My father used me as a helper. Tell me, how did the car run?"

"It's still running. . . . So that slight boy with a lock of dark hair dangling over his forehead . . ."

"I was just nineteen," said Bordonny. "And at that time you didn't have a moustache, as I remember."

"No," said Don Camillo. "He grew that when he was thrown in jail for drunkenness and disorderly conduct. Of course his real crime was anti-Fascist agitation, and eventually it did him a good turn. After the war he won the status of political prisoner and martyr to the cause. That's how he became first mayor and then senator."

Peppone brought down his fist on the table.

"That's not the whole story!" he protested.

Bordonny was staring at Don Camillo.

"Your face isn't unfamiliar either," he said. "Do you come from the same place?"

"No, no," Peppone hastily interpolated. "He's been living around there, but he comes from another town. You couldn't possibly have known him. Tell me, how did you get here?"

Bordonny shrugged his shoulders.

"What's the use of going back over things which the Russians have generously forgotten?" he said in a voice which had once more turned cold. "If you want more explanations about the *kolkhos*, I'm ready to give them to you."

But Don Camillo did not leave it at that.

"My friend, don't let the fact that he's a Communist senator stand in your way. We don't have to consider politics. You can talk as man to man."

Bordonny looked in the eyes of first the one and then the other.

"I have nothing to hide," he asserted. "Everybody here at

Grevinec knows my story. But since they don't talk about it, I'd rather not talk about it either."

Don Camillo held out his pack of Italian cigarettes.

Outside there was a raging storm, and rain beat against the windowpanes.

"For seventeen years I've been craving one of those cigarettes," said Bordonny, lighting one up. "I've never got used to *makorta* rolled in newsprint. It makes my stomach turn over."

Greedily he inhaled a few puffs and then let the smoke trickle slowly out of his mouth.

"It's a simple story," he said. "I was on the Russian front, at a truck repair centre, and one day the Russians walked in and took us over. It was at the end of 1942, and the wind and snow were murderously cold. They drove us ahead of them like a flock of sheep. Every now and then one of us fell to the ground and they left him with a bullet in his head on the muddy snow. I fell, too, but I knew enough Russian to make myself understood and when a Russian soldier gave me a kick and said 'Get up!' I was able to answer. '*Tovarisch*,' I said, 'I can't go on. Let me die in peace.' I was one of the last prisoners in the column and the others were already a hundred feet away, almost lost from sight in the snow. He aimed above my head and muttered: 'Hurry up and die, then, and don't get me into trouble.' "

Just then somebody bundled up in dripping burlap came into the kitchen. Unwinding this covering she revealed herself to be a handsome woman no more than thirty years old.

"My wife," said Stephan.

The woman smiled, murmured a few incomprehensible words and disappeared up a circular stair.

"God willed that I should live," Bordonny went on. "When I came to I found myself in a warm *isba*. The place where I had fallen was half a mile from here, between the woods and the village, and a seventeen-year-old girl who had gone to collect kindling had heard moans coming out of a pile of snow. She had strong arms and she tugged me along by my coat collar, like a sack of potatoes, without even setting down her bundle of wood."

"They're good people, these Russian peasants," said Peppone. "A fellow called Bagò, from Moinetto, was saved in the same way."

78

"Yes a lot of fellows owe them their lives. But this girl wasn't Russian; she was a Pole whose family had been moved here because there was a shortage of agricultural workers. They shared what little food they had with me and kept me hidden for two days. I realized this couldn't go on for ever, and since the girl and I managed to communicate with each other in broken Russian, I told her to go and report that a lost Italian soldier had stumbled in on them only a few hours before. Reluctantly she consented to go. Soon she came back with a man armed with a pistol and two others with guns. I raised my hands and they beckoned to me to follow them. The Polish family's hut was the one farthest from the centre of the village, and I had to walk a good distance with the guns sticking into my back. Finally we came to the open space where you saw the silos. A truck loaded with bags of wheat was standing there and an unfortunate fellow was ruining the motor trying to get it started. I was so outraged that I turned to one of my captors and said: '*Tovarisch*, he's going to run down the battery and then he'll never get it going at all. The injection pump must be choked; tell him to pump out the gasoline.' My guard was amazed to hear me use a few Russian words. 'What do you know about it?' he asked suspiciously. 'That's my trade,' I told him. The battery was rapidly dying, and he pushed me over to the truck and ordered the driver to do what I had said. The face that looked out of the cab window was that of a very young boy in soldier's uniform. He didn't know what pump I was talking about, because he'd never driven a diesel before. I asked for a screwdriver, threw up the hood and cleaned out the fuel injector. 'Now it will start,' I said, and a few minutes later he drove it away.

"They shut me up in a small room of the local soviet but left me a cigarette for company. Ten minutes later they came back, and holding their guns against my back, pushed me over to a shed where there were primitive arrangements to repair tractors and agricultural machinery. They pointed out one of the tractors and told me to find out what was the matter with it. I asked for some boiling water to pour into the radiator and then tried to start it. Then I got down and said: 'It's a cylinder. The whole motor has to be taken apart and the cylinder made over. It will take quite some time.' With the miserable tools they gave me I worked like mad for forty-eight hours. Just as I was putting back the whole block an officer and two men armed with sub-machine-guns came along. They looked on while I put more boiling water in the radiator and tried the motor. God meant me to live, because it started right up and ran like a dream. I ran it around the shed and then brought it back to its original place. I wiped my hands on a rag, jumped down and stood in front of the officer with my arms above my head. They all started laughing. 'He's all yours, Comrade,' said the officer to the district Party leader. 'It's your responsibility; if he runs away, you'll pay for it.' I joined in the laughter, 'Captain,' I said, 'Russia's a big country, and I'm not likely to run any farther than that isolated *isba*, where there's a girl I've taken quite a fancy to, even if she did report me.' The officer looked me up and down. 'You're a good Italian worker,' he said. 'Why did you come to fight against the workers of the Soviet Union?' I told him that I came because I was sent. My only military activity was truck repairs and the only Russians I'd killed were two chickens I had accidentally run over. . . ."

The storm was raging more fiercely than ever. Bordonny got up and talked into an old army field telephone in one corner. Then he came back and said:

"They say you may as well stay here. The rest of your party is stuck over at Barn No. 3, which is at the other end of no-where." And he sat down.

"Well, what happened next?" asked Don Camillo.

"I worked like a dog at repairing their machines and putting the workshop in order. By the time I was able to stop and think, the war was over. The Polish girl's father died, and we got married. As the years went by she and I were both given Soviet citizenship."

"And didn't you ever think of going home?" asked Don Camillo.

"What for? To see the mass of rubble where my father and brother were rotting away? Here they treat me as if I were one of their own, in fact better, because I'm good at my job. At home there's no one to remember me. I'm just one of the prisoners of war who disappeared in Russia. . . ."

Just then there was a loud noise and the door was thrown open. In came a stream of water and a strange wriggling monster that looked like a giant centipede. From somewhere Bordonny's wife appeared on the scene and rushed to close the door. The shiny oilskin covering of the monster fell to the floor and out popped half a dozen children, one handsomer than the next, ranging from six to twelve years of age.

"Your disappearance in Russia has been time well spent, I can see that!" exclaimed Don Camillo.

Bordonny stared at him again.

"I *do* have a feeling I've seen you before," he repeated.

"It's unlikely," said Don Camillo. "But even if you have, forget about it."

They were well-brought-up children and, although for the first few minutes they made quite a racket, a few words from their mother were enough to calm them down. They sat down on a bench near the stove and began talking in a low voice together.

"They're still small," the woman apologized in surprisingly good Italian. "They forgot that their grandmother is sick in bed upstairs."

"May we pay her a visit?" said Don Camillo.

"That would make her very happy. She seldom has a chance to see anybody."

They went up the circular stair to a low-ceilinged attic room. A shrivelled old woman was lying in a bed made up with neatly pressed white sheets. Bordonny's wife said something to her in Polish and she whispered a reply.

"She says may the Lord bless those who visit the sick," the wife explained. "She's very old and she can't help thinking in terms of the past."

At the head of the bed there was a holy picture and Don Camillo bent over to examine it.

"It's the Black Madonna!" he exclaimed.

"Yes," murmured the wife, "the protectress of Poland. Old Poles are Catholics. On account of her age you must forgive her."

She spoke cautiously and there was a vague look of fear in her eyes.

Peppone put in a reassuring word.

"There's nothing to forgive. In Italy young people are

Catholics, too. It's quite all right as long as they're on the level. Our enemies are the priests, because they mix politics with religion."

The old woman whispered something into her daughter's ear and the latter shot an enquiring glance at Bordonny.

"They're not here to do us any harm," he told her.

"Mother wants to hear how is . . . the Pope," his wife stammered.

"He's all too healthy!" answered Peppone.

Don Camillo extracted something from an inside pocket. The old woman stared at it with wide-open eyes and then reached out a bony hand. She whispered excitedly into her daughter's ear.

"She wants to know if that's really he."

"Himself and no other. Pope John XXIII."

Peppone turned pale and looked around him with a worried air.

"Comrade," said Don Camillo, taking him by the arm and impelling him towards the door, "go downstairs with Citizen Bordonny and see if it's still raining."

Peppone started to protest, but Don Camillo cut him short.

"Don't interfere with me, Comrade, if you value your skin."

And he stayed alone with the two women.

"Tell your mother she can talk freely, because I'm as much of a Catholic as she is."

The two women spoke at length together and then the younger one reported:

"She wants to thank you and give you her blessing. Now that she has that picture she feels that she can die in peace. It was very hard for her to see my father die without the last rites of the Church."

"But there are priests of a sort, who are free to visit you, aren't there?" asked Don Camillo.

She shook her head.

"They seem like priests," she explained, "but they are emissaries not of God but of the Party. What good are they to us Poles?"

The rain was still coming down in buckets. Don Camillo took

off his jacket, pulled the hinged crucifix out of the false fountain pen, stuck it into the neck of a bottle and set it up on the bedside table. Then he took out the aluminium cup which served for a chalice.

A quarter of an hour later, Peppone and Bordonny, alarmed by the long silence, came upstairs and looked in the door. Before their startled eyes Don Camillo was celebrating Mass and the old woman, her hands folded and her eyes filled with tears, was following his every motion. After she had received communion it seemed as if new strength were flowing through her veins.

"*Ite, missa est. . . .*"

The old woman whispered breathlessly into her daughter's ear and the latter went to stand beside her husband.

"Father," she said excitedly, "will you marry us before God? Until now we've been married only in the sight of man."

Outside the rain was still coming down as hard as if clouds from all Russia had converged upon Grevinec. There was no wedding ring, but the old woman slipped a worn gold band off her fourth finger.

"Lord," said Don Camillo, "don't take it amiss if I skip a few words or even a few sentences. . . ."

Peppone stood there like a stone until Don Camillo pushed him down the stairs.

"Go and bring them up here, the whole lot of them!" he ordered.

The rain had begun to diminish, but Don Camillo was so wound up that he could not stop. In the twinkling of an eye he baptized all the children. And yet he did not, as he had threatened, skip a single word, much less a sentence. Only God could have given him the wind to get through it.

The whole thing lasted an hour, or perhaps it was a minute. Before he knew it Don Camillo was sitting once more at the kitchen table, with Peppone at his side and Bordonny across from him. The sun had come out and the children's eyes were shining in the dark corner. Don Camillo counted them: twelve for the children, four for their parents and two for the old woman. She was not with them downstairs, but her eyes were indelibly imprinted on his memory, for he had never seen a look such as theirs before.

Just then Comrade Nadia Petrovna appeared at the door.

"Is everything all right?" she inquired.

"Everything's perfect," said Don Camillo.

"We are most grateful to Comrade Oregov for assigning us a guide as competent as Citizen Stephan Bordonny," added Peppone, shaking their host's hand and starting towards the door. Don Camillo was the last to leave the house, and at the threshold he turned around to make the sign of the cross.

"*Pax vobiscum,*" he murmured.

And the old woman's eyes responded:

"*Amen.*"

9

THE RAINS CAME TO STAY

As it was categorically stated on the visitors' programme, they were guests of the Grevinec *kolkhos* for lunch, and this spontaneous generosity aroused the expected enthusiasm among them. Peppone had prudently arranged for Don Camillo to sit beside him, and now Don Camillo whispered in his ear:

"Comrade, I have no use for people who find everything abroad superior to what they have at home, but I can't help saying that this bowl of healthy cabbage soup is infinitely preferable to our bourgeois spaghetti."

"Comrade," muttered Peppone, "after the trick you played this morning, you deserve a soup made of boiled nails and arsenic."

"This one is just about as good," retorted Don Camillo.

But, as usual, the vodka and roast mutton were highly satisfactory and Peppone was inspired to make a little speech, cast in a conventional mould, to which Comrade Oregov made an equally conventional reply. Luckily Don Camillo was in top form, buoyed up by two glasses of liquid fire and the heartwarming experience of the morning. From a ramp built of quotations from Marx, Lenin and Khrushchev he launched an oratorical sputnik which sent even Comrade Nadia Petrovna into a state of perceptible ecstasy as she translated it and caused the eyes of Comrade Yenka Oregov to shine with a reflected glow.

Don Camillo spoke of the *kolkhos* as if it were a living, breathing being, and his hearers got a new and agreeable feeling that they were happy and important people. After he had reached an operatic conclusion, Comrade Oregov leaped up and pumped his hand interminably, talking all the while in a rapid-fire patter.

"Comrade Oregov says that the Party needs men like you for its rural propaganda," Comrade Petrovna told him, "and he wishes that you would stay here. We have accelerated courses for learning Russian."

"Please thank Comrade Oregov on my behalf," answered Don Camillo. "After I have gone home and had time to make arrangements for my wife and children I may take him up on his offer."

"He says that you can have all the time you want," Comrade Petrovna assured him. "You can count on him to facilitate your return."

More vodka was brought to the table, and the visitors did not get away until the middle of the afternoon.

The torrential rain had transformed the road into a river of mud and the bus had some difficulty getting started. After five miles or so they came to the crossing of the road leading back towards the "Red Flag" *sovkos*. The irrigation canal running alongside had overflowed and the road was under a good fifteen inches of water. With Comrade Oregov's authorization the driver took a left turn in the direction of Tifiz and for a couple of hours the truck rolled over a narrow, winding track which was blessed with a solid bottom.

Unfortunately it began to rain again and the driver was faced with further trouble. The bus skidded from one side to the other, threatening to go off the road, and under continuous abuse the differential got out of order. The rain gave no indication of letting up and darkness was beginning to fall. Since the village of Tifiz was only two or three miles away the driver was sent ahead to bring back a tow truck or a tractor. But he came back with disappointing news. The only piece of working machinery in Tifiz was attached to the grain elevator. Since this offered no help out of the present situation and the *kolkhos* at Tifiz belonged to the distressing six per cent without telephones, the group had no choice but to walk the rest of the way. They set out, with a bitter wind blowing into their backs and mud up to their ankles.

By the time they came to the village it was completely dark and, since it was one of the unfortunate eight per cent without electric light, its aspect was anything but welcoming.. The assembly room of the rural soviet was filled with sacks of fodder, but in a voice of unprecedented volume and severity Comrade Oregov gave orders that it should be cleared without delay. A group of men armed with brooms concluded the cleaning operation, leaving the visitors covered with dust at one end of the room, which had only kerosene lamps to light it. Don Camillo found himself standing next to Comrade Tavan, the tenant farmer, and he proceeded at once to undermine his morale.

"Comrade," he said audibly to Peppone, "do you remember what I said to you about the peasants this morning? At the *sovkos* which is run directly by the government, everything functioned efficiently. But here, where the *kolkhos* people manage their own affairs, there is nothing but disaster. Trucks and tractors are not running and the assembly room is used for a storehouse. Isn't it very much the same at home? At Le Pioppette, where many peasant houses have been rebuilt since the war, what do you find? Potatoes in the bathtub; kindling wood and chickens in the garage, while trucks and tractors rust outside. Believe me, Comrade, peasants haven't the stuff in them to live as free men under a socialist régime. All they know how to do is obey orders. How ridiculous to speak of 'giving the peasants land'! The land must belong to the State, every square inch of it. We must set up government-directed *sovkos* until such time as the peasants have acquired some sense of responsibility."

"That's not the half of it, Comrade," chimed in Scamoggia. "It will take centuries for sense of any kind to penetrate their noodles."

The surrounding light was dim, but Tavan's flapping ears had turned red enough to shine even in complete darkness. Don Camillo was getting ready to shoot off some more of his ammunition, but the heel of Peppone's right shoe came down on a corn on his left foot. If a gun barrel had been stuck into his belly, Don Camillo would have had no thought of surrender. But a corn irritated by a long walk in wet weather was strongly conducive to silence.

As the dust subsided, Comrade Oregov was seen standing with his legs wide apart in the middle of the room, issuing imperative orders. Trestles and boards were assembled to make a long table. Someone brought out a roll of burlap, and soon the table had a cloth upon it. Heat began to fan out of the stove, extra kerosene lamps provided more light and the table was set with plates, knives, forks, spoons and glasses. Comrade Oregov glanced at the corner where Peppone and his little band were awkwardly standing and guessed at the growing tension among them. In the twinkling of an eye he summoned three girls to pass around the vodka. After two good drinks the visitors' faith in the ultimate triumph of socialism was fully restored. That is, except in Don Camillo, whom the vodka cast into a deep depression.

Because they were prey to a genuinely Communist hunger they fell like wolves upon the bowls of steaming cabbage-and-potato soup. When he saw that their appetites were satisfied, Comrade Oregov called upon Comrade Petrovna to express his deep regret for the inconveniences of the afternoon. Don Camillo was once more in a diabolical mood and he stood up to respond to the apology.

"Actually we have enjoyed the adventure," he began, "because Comrade Oregov gave us a splendid example of how a Communist leader should behave. In my country there is a proverb which says that the master's pride lends nobility to his horse. In our era of mechanization and social progress, which has swallowed up both horse and master, it might be more apt to say that Comrade Oregov is ennobled by the rightful pride which the Communist Party takes in his achievement."

Comrade Oregov was delighted with this witticism and with the compliment which Don Camillo had paid him.

Peppone, as a senator, a Party official and leader of the mission, carried a brief case bulging with important secret papers. In the course of the dinner he imprudently put the brief case down on the floor, and Don Camillo, who was as usual sitting beside him, had an opportunity to open it and quickly examine the contents. Underneath the papers he found a bottle of brandy and a piece of excellent salami. Peppone became aware of his neighbour's discovery only when he quite unexpectedly heard Comrade Oregov thanking him for his generous gifts and insisting upon dividing them among all those present. The gifts, of course, were the bottle of brandy and the salami.

"Comrade," said Don Camillo, when he came back from making the presentation, "that was a splendid gesture. Just as splendid as the round of vodkas which you offered us with the change from your ten-thousand-lira bill."

Peppone shot him an angry look.

"He who laughs last laughs best," he retorted. "We have a long way to go before we get home."

Comrade Oregov was sitting at one end of the long table. At his right were the director and political secretary of the *kolkhos* and at his left Comrade Nadia Petrovna. Beside Comrade Petrovna was Comrade Salvatore Capece of Naples, who had wedged himself in between her and Comrade Nanni Scamoggia.

The brandy and salami showed typical bourgeois inertia and never got away from this end of the table.

"Comrade," said Capece, turning the full force of his melting eyes upon Comrade Petrovna, "if I had a guitar I could make a far prettier speech than that of Comrade Tarocci."

Comrade Petrovna said something to the director of the *kolkhos*, and he disappeared from the table. Nobody noticed, because the heat of the room, the vodka and the cigarette smoke had reduced the whole company to a state of somnolent euphoria. But when he came back, they were aroused by a loud shriek from the throat of Comrade Capece.

"It's a guitar!"

The *kolkhos* of Tifiz did not have a single working machine, but it did have a guitar, and also an accordion with a boy who knew fairly well how to play it. While Comrade Capece was tuning the guitar, the boy struck up a march on the accordion. At this moment the habitually taciturn tenant farmer, Tavan, had a sudden inspiration. He snatched the accordion from the boy's hands and sounded a chord which reduced the whole company to silence. Then he played 'The Horsefly' and 'The Mazurka of Migliavacca', and played them so well that the size of his ears became almost unnoticeable.

Comrade Salvatore Capece was ready to join in, and to the accompaniment of the accordion he burst into song. He sang '*O sole mio*', and all Naples was in his voice, from the Vomero to Possillipo, from Zi' Teresa to '*Funiculi, funicula*', from Moonlight on the Bay to the Problem of the South. If he hadn't given them an encore they would have torn him to pieces.

He sang half a dozen more songs, and Comrade Nanni Scamoggia began to foam at the mouth, because the singer never took his eyes off Comrade Nadia Petrovna and she was in a state of obvious enchantment.

Then Comrade Tavan broke into a polka. This had a magic effect. In a second, table and tableware were swept away and anyone who wanted to go on drinking had to take refuge in the adjacent *kolkhos* office, which was also the repository of the vodka. Everybody began to dance and the only one actually to take refuge from the horrendous sight was Don Camillo, who found the picture of Lenin on the office wall to keep him company.

Comrade Salvatore Capece finally tossed aside the guitar and began to dance with Comrade Nadia Petrovna. He held on to her so jealously that when Peppone had something urgent to get translated she had almost literally to tear out of his arms.

"Comrade," said Peppone when he had drawn her off into a corner, "after a day's hard work a man is entitled to some good, clean fun. And if a fellow is a spoil-sport, like Comrade Tarocci, and refuses to join in, then he deserves to be punished. Don't you agree?"

"I do," she answered promptly.

"Comrade Tarocci has many of the qualities of leadership, but in his own house his jealous, reactionary wife leads him by the nose. Even now, when he's thousands of miles away from home, he's afraid of letting himself go. He's simply got to join the dance!"

"Leave it to me!" said Comrade Petrovna.

Five minutes later a band of laughing girls burst into the office and pulled Don Camillo out into the main room and on to the dance floor. Peppone thoroughly enjoyed the scene, and while Don Camillo was being whirled about by the prettiest of the girls he signalled to Comrade Vittorio Peratto, the photographer from Turin, who whipped out his flash-camera and snapped a sensational picture. After that every one of the girls wanted to have her picture taken dancing with Don Camillo, and when the roll was finished Peppone said to Comrade Peratto:

"You're responsible to me for the negatives, and don't you forget it!"

There was a short pause while the windows were thrown open to clear the room of smoke, and fresh bottles of vodka were uncorked. But the gaiety did not subside. Comrade Li Friddi, the Sicilian, produced a mouth organ; Comrade Curullu, the Sardinian, gave an imitation of a drunk trying to fit a key in a keyhole in an attempt to sneak back into his house late at night; Comrade Gibetti, the Tuscan, sang an operatic air in a shrill falsetto voice, and Comrade Bacciga, from Genoa, held the whole company spellbound with a bag of magician's tricks.

"Organized recreational groups and television have raised the cultural level of the working class," Don Camillo said pantingly to Peppone.

"No doubt about it," Peppone replied. "And I have an idea that back home a display of picture postcards would be much better propaganda than any number of political manifestos."

"What sort of pictures?" inquired Don Camillo.

"Pictures of our beloved parish priest in false clothing, kicking up his heels at a dance."

"Don't count your chickens before they're hatched," retorted Don Camillo. "As you said yourself, we have a long way to go before we get back home!"

The dancing had resumed, and a little man about forty years old accosted Don Camillo.

"Comrade," he said in Italian, "are you the head of the group?"

"No, this stuffed clown beside me is the head. I'm only the cell leader."

"Well, I have something to tell you both. If your Neapolitan friend over there doesn't let go of that girl, the fellow from Rome is going to break his bones."

Without pausing to find out how the stranger happened to speak Italian, Peppone rushed away to forestall any possible trouble. Don Camillo made some wild gesture, and the stranger laughed and showed that he understood.

"Vodka, that's what you want, isn't it?" he inquired.

"*Da da!*" responded Don Camillo, still unable to believe that the man spoke his language. And he pointed towards the office which was also the vodka cellar.

Once they were in the office they were able to talk freely.

"I am a Rumanian," the stranger informed Don Camillo.

"Then how do you happen to speak Italian with a Neapolitan accent?"

"Because I come from Naples, that's why. In 1939 I was a sailor, and I met a Rumanian girl and followed her to Rumania."

"Did you catch up with her?" asked Don Camillo.

"I caught up with her all right, but not in time."

"What do you mean? Was it too late? Had she already married another man?"

"No, it was too soon, and I had to marry her myself. Fortunately the war came along and the Russians moved into Rumania. They were recruiting agricultural workers and I volunteered to go. . . ."

While the stranger was telling his story, Peppone was waiting for a chance to get hold of Comrade Petrovna. At the end of a mazurka he took her away from Comrade Capece and whirled her into a waltz.

"Look here, Comrade," he said; "I have something to tell you. Comrade Scamoggia is an asset to the Party, but he isn't politically mature. He's subject to capitalistic errors. . . ."

"I've noticed them," said Comrade Petrovna. "But I think he'll outgrow them with time."

"I quite agree. But tonight they have taken the upper hand, and if you don't stop dancing with that guitar player, he may make trouble. I thought I'd tip you off, because I'm sure you wouldn't want the party to wind up in a fight."

They finished the waltz together and then parted company. Peppone went to the office, and Don Camillo brought him up to date on the Neapolitan's story.

"He's never been mixed up in politics," he explained. "He just wants us to help him get out of hot water."

Peppone shrugged his shoulders.

"He went looking for trouble, didn't he? Why didn't he stay in Rumania?"

"Because of my wife," the stranger explained. "I had to get away from her. And it's easier for a Neapolitan to be a Rumanian in Russia than it is in Rumania! I could be perfectly happy here, because I'm a barber and hairdresser, the only one for miles around. I go from one *kolkhos* to another, giving shaves and haircuts. But my real speciality is permanent waves. . . ."

"Permanent waves?"

"Women are women the world over, Chief, and if they have a chance to pretty themselves up they'll starve themselves to death to pay for it. As soon as one girl got a permanent, all the rest of them wanted one, too. My reputation spread like wild-fire. . . ."

"I see," said Peppone. "But that doesn't explain why you're in hot water."

"Chief, can't you imagine what it is to be a young man in the middle of this enormous Russia? It's not true what they say about free love. When I came here from Rumania, I had that idea in mind. But if you start flirting with a Russian's wife or his girl, he'll beat you up just as promptly as the next one. At the first *kolkhos* I went to I was caught red-handed and kicked out in no time flat. At the second I had the same bad luck, and so on, right down the line."

"Well, why worry?" laughed Peppone. "Aren't there eighty thousand *kolkhos* to choose from?"

"Yes, but I'm only one man!" the barber retorted.

Peppone couldn't stop laughing, and Don Camillo decided to take advantage of his good humour.

"The poor fellow's joking," he put in. "The truth is he's crazy to get back to Naples. Can't we give him a hand?"

"What do you mean? We can't take him back in a suitcase, can we?"

"No. But Comrade Rondella was sent home, and you have travelling papers for a group of eleven."

"You're crazy! Under Comrade Oregov's eagle eye?"

"He can't keep tabs on us for ever."

"Don't be a fool," said Peppone. "The fellow can stay here and pursue his barber's trade and let the married women alone."

"I don't call that Communism!" said the barber.

"It's a funny story," admitted Peppone, "but I refuse to get mixed up in it." And he went out of the room.

"Don't desert me," the barber implored Don Camillo. "I'm not asking you to get yourself in trouble. Just tell me where you're going and when. I can get myself kicked from one place to another. Only God Almighty can stop a Neapolitan from going home, and Khrushchev isn't God."

Don Camillo copied out the tour schedule.

"That's all I can do for you," he said. "And forget that we ever met. I've forgotten it already."

The main room was more tumultuous than ever and Peppone was searching desperately for Comrade Petrovna. He was desperate because Comrade Capece and Comrade Scamoggia had disappeared also. Finally he caught sight of the girl and grabbed her by the arm.

"What's happened?" he asked her.

"I got there too late," she admitted. "They went out together and by the time I overtook them it was all over."

"Where is Capece?"

"In the haystack of Barn No. 7."

"And Scamoggia?"

"He's holding a cold compress to Capece's black eye."

"Nobody else knows about it?"

"Only Comrade Capece, who has the black eye for a souvenir, and Comrade Nadia Petrovna, who got slapped in the face!" She clenched her fists angrily. "He had the nerve to hit me!" she added.

This was no laughing matter. Comrade Petrovna was not an ordinary woman; she was high up in the Party and a Government employee.

"I quite understand," said Peppone gravely. "Shall I beat him up or shall I report him to Comrade Oregov?"

"There are times when personal feelings have to be sacrificed for the good of the Party," replied Comrade Petrovna. "Just let the whole thing go. Comrade Scamoggia is still under the influence of vodka. When he comes to himself he'll see the stupidity of his behaviour."

Peppone shook his head.

"Comrade, Lenin has instructed us to tell the truth, no matter how disagreeable it may be. I happen to know that Scamoggia didn't have a single drop of either vodka or brandy. He wasn't drunk; he knew perfectly well what he was doing."

Comrade Petrovna looked more beautiful than ever and her

eyes shone as if with tears. One cheek was slightly redder than the other and she covered it with her hand.

"Comrade," she said humbly, "it's not easy for me to admit, but I'm afraid I too am not politically mature."

Don Camillo suddenly appeared at Peppone's side.

"Anything wrong?" he queried.

"No, everything's in good order," said Peppone sternly.

10

THREE STALKS OF WHEAT

DURING the night a furious wind out of nowhere swept over the plains and froze the soggy ground over. Don Camillo was the first to wake up, roused by the stentorious snoring of Peppone. Long icicles hung at the windows, but an agreeable warmth came out of the big stove. All around, on improvised cots, his eight companions, overcome by the vodka and uproarious gaiety of the night before, lay in a deep sleep. Don Camillo, like all the rest, had slept with his clothes on, and Peppone lay on the cot next to his own.

"If he didn't snore so shamelessly," Don Camillo thought to himself, "I'd be almost sorry to have given him so many headaches."

He looked around and silently called the roll. Yes, except for Comrade Yenka Oregov and Comrade Nadia Petrovna, they were all there, and Comrade Salvatore Capece still had a wet compress over his black eye.

"Lord," said Don Camillo, "have pity on these poor fellows and shed light upon their darkness."

He lowered his legs over the edge of the cot and started to put on his shoes. He got the left one on all right, but the right one seemed stuck to the floor. Apparently the lace was caught in a crack. He gave it a hard jerk, and Peppone suddenly stopped

96

snoring. The reason for this coincidence was the simple fact that Peppone had tied Camillo's shoelace around his ankle.

"Comrade," Don Camillo said to him reproachfully, "I can't see why you mistrust me."

"After all the tricks you've played under my waking eyes, who knows what you might do while I'm asleep!"

They went to wash up at a pump outside. The icy wind slashed their faces and the inhabitants of the thatch-roofed houses all seemed to have shut themselves up inside. But suddenly there were signs of life. A big truck arrived, and Comrade Oregov, with a group of local men, suddenly appeared on the scene to greet it. Peppone and Don Camillo went to join them.

A boy jumped down from the truck and asked for help in unloading a motor-cycle. Then the driver got out and reported to Comrade Oregov. When he turned down his fur coat collar they saw that he was none other than Citizen Stephan Bordonny. The boy had ridden on the motor-cycle to get mechanical assistance from Grevinec, and now the visitors' bus driver, accompanied by Comrade Nadia Petrovna, came to see what was to be done next.

"Don't worry," Comrade Petrovna said to Peppone, after Comrade Oregov and Bordonny had held a brief consultation. "He has brought over the necessary parts and the bus will soon be repaired."

"Won't they have to tow the bus here?" asked Peppone.

"That's impossible," she told him. "The road is frozen over and the truck is too light for its tyres to get a good grip on the ice. They're going to carry out the repairs on the spot."

"I'm a mechanic myself," said Peppone. "If you'll give me a pair of overalls, I'll be glad to lend a hand."

Comrade Oregov was pleased with this offer, and Comrade Petrovna told Peppone that a pair of overalls would be provided.

"Make it two pairs," said Peppone. "Comrade Tarocci here is mechanically minded, and we can use his help."

Comrade Oregov approved of this plan and went off on the motor-cycle to the neighbouring village of Drevinka, whence he intended to notify his superiors by telephone of the forced delay.

"Comrade," Peppone said to Comrade Petrovna, "that leaves you in charge of the rest of the group. If any of them misbehaves, don't hesitate to discipline him. I call Comrade Scamoggia to your particular attention, because he's a troublemaker."

"I thought all night long about the way he insulted me," she replied. "He owes me an explanation."

There was a cold look in her eyes, but it was softened by the brand-new permanent wave which the Neapolitan barber had found time to give her hair.

By now the overalls had been found, and Peppone and Don Camillo drove away in the truck. Peppone confided to Don Camillo that he was alarmed by Comrade Petrovna's formidable air.

"That woman is in a dangerous frame of mind. She's quite capable of taking up lipstick and nail polish, if she can lay her hands on them."

"I don't doubt it," Don Camillo replied. "When it comes to politics, women are always extremists."

During the ride in the truck Citizen Bordonny did not open his mouth and behaved as if he could not understand what his two Italian passengers were saying. The bus driver had climbed in the back, lain down and fallen asleep, but Bordonny was not taking any chances.

Bordonny had brought all the necessary tools, and as soon as they reached the stranded bus he saw what was to be done. The rear end of the bus was easy to jack up, but in order that the jack shouldn't slip on the ice it was necessary to lay a board for it to stand on. The bus driver flatly refused to crawl underneath. His reluctance was natural enough and Peppone was surprised to hear Bordonny argue so violently with him. He tried to put in a word, but Bordonny went on shouting and finally the bus driver turned around and walked away in the direction of the *kolkhos*.

"To hell with him!" Bordonny muttered when the other had gone.

"I don't know that he's to be blamed," said Peppone, shaking his head. "He just didn't want to risk being pinned down under the bus."

"Bawling him out was the only thing I could do to get him out of the way," Bordonny explained.

Soon the truck was jacked up and work begun. While

98

Bordonny was loosening screws and taking off nuts, he talked to his companions.

"This was the site of a fierce battle just before my capture, around Christmas of 1942. The Russians attacked in overwhelming numbers and when we retreated we left many of our dead behind. A group of some thirty artillerymen and *bersaglieri* were surrounded and taken prisoner, many of them wounded or sick. The Russians shut them up in a barn at a *kolkhos* near the one you've just visited at Tifiz, and when we retook the area a day later we found them dead. The Russians had machine-gunned them rather than let them get away. I was there when the bodies were discovered, and it was a terrible sight."

Don Camillo and Peppone went on working, although their fingers were numb with cold.

"We gathered up the dead bodies and buried them," Bordonny continued. "If you will walk for three-quarters of a mile towards the north you'll see a wagon track leading to the right. Just a hundred yards before you actually reach it, there's an irrigation ditch, with an overgrown hedge on one side. If you go a couple of hundred feet along the hedge you'll come to a big oak tree whose trunk is covered with ivy. The burial ground is right there, in the rectangle bounded by the road, the wagon track, the ditch and a line parallel to the road leading from the wagon track to the oak tree."

They worked on for another half hour without speaking.

"I can do the rest alone," said Bordonny. "In case anyone comes I'll sound the horn. If you look under the ivy you'll find something there."

Don Camillo walked resolutely away and Peppone had no choice but to follow him. The sky was dark and the wind continued to blow over the bare plain.

"If the wind lets up there'll be snow," said Don Camillo.

"I hope there's enough to snow you under," retorted Peppone.

They broke into a run and soon they came to the ditch. There was a thick coat of ice on the bottom and Don Camillo clambered down on to it to pursue the rest of the way. When they came to the great oak tree, which raised its bare branches towards the dark sky, they climbed up through an opening in the hedge. Before them lay a wide field, still covered with green stalks of wheat.

For a moment they stood still, gazing at the desolation of the scene. Then Don Camillo forced himself to take a few steps forward and with a trembling hand thrust aside the twining ivy. On the trunk of the tree there was carved a date: *Dec. 27, 1942*, and the single word *Italia*, with a cross above it.

Don Camillo let the ivy fall back, while Peppone slowly took off his cap and looked out over the field, thinking of the wooden crosses that were no longer there, of the scattered bones buried in the cold ground.

"*Requiem aeternam dona eis, Domine, et lux perpetuus luceat eis. . . .*"

Turning around he saw that at the foot of the oak tree, under the rude cross that Bordonny had carved upon it, Don Camillo was saying the Mass for the Dead.

"*Deus, cuius miseratione animae fidelium requiescunt: famulis et famulabus tuis, et omnibus hic et ubique in Christo quiescentibus, da propitius veniam peccatorum; ut a cunctis reatibus absoluti tecum sine fine laetentur. Per eumdem Dominum. . . .*"

The tender stalks of wheat quivered under impact of the wind.

"*My son, where are you?*"

Peppone remembered the despairing outcry of the headline over a newspaper story he had seen in the last years of the war.

"*Where are you, my son?*"

Bordonny was intent upon his work, but he kept one ear cocked for any approaching sound. When he heard someone coming from the direction of the *kolkhos*, he sounded his horn as a warning. It was not, as he had feared, the bus driver, but one of the Italians, the fellow with the big ears. He was walking very slowly and, as soon as he drew near, Bordonny halted him.

"Lend me a hand, Comrade, until the others return."

Tavan took off his coat and fell willingly to work, and meanwhile Peppone and Don Camillo hurriedly retraced their way. When they got to the bus, Peppone said to Tavan:

"Hand that tool over to me."

Comrade Tavan wiped his hands on a rag and put on his overcoat. He hung about Don Camillo, who had lit a cigar butt, and finally got up his courage to say:

"Comrade, if you're not busy, I'd like a word with you."

"The experts have taken over," Don Camillo replied. "There's no reason why we can't talk." And they started walking up the road together.

"Comrade," said Comrade Tavan with a slightly embarrassed air. "You have said a great many true things, with which I have to agree. But I can't go along with you when you condemn the whole peasant class. In the city, workers are thrown together; they are in contact with modern progress and in the centre of the political scene. Whereas peasants live in isolation and can't be expected to have any community feeling. It's hard to get new ideas into their heads; most often they don't understand them. But a few of them have caught on and are trying to improve their lot."

Comrade Tavan's dark-skinned, bony face and his flapping ears were somehow disarming.

"I know that you're a loyal and hard-working Party man," said Don Camillo. "Perhaps I spoke too hastily. In any case, I didn't mean to wound your class pride."

"You were right," the other replied. "The peasant class is just about the way you describe it, but it's in the process of change. It's the old people who are still holding it back, and in the country old people carry a lot of weight. They have all sorts of wrong ideas, but because they've worked like dogs all their life long, it's hard to contradict them. The Party has all the answers, but the old people still hold the reins. It appeals to their reason, but they listen to their hearts. Even when they are capable of thinking clearly their hearts still rule over their heads."

"Comrade, I'm from peasant stock myself and I know exactly what you mean. That's the peasant problem in a nutshell. And that's why we must step up our propaganda."

They walked on without speaking.

"Comrade," Tavan said abruptly, "my wife and children and I live with my father, who is seventy-five years old, and my mother, who is seventy-three. Our family has been settled on the same piece of land for over a century. My father and mother don't go into the village more than once a year and they've only once been to a big city. How am I to straighten out their ideas, especially after what happened to them? . . ."

Don Camillo looked questioningly at him.

"Comrade, if there's anything on your mind, come out with it. You're talking man to man, not to the Party."

Comrade Tavan shook his head.

"I had a brother five years younger than myself," he explained, "and he died in the war. My father managed to accept it, but my mother has never been reconciled. When she heard that I was making this trip she was beside herself, and I had to promise to do what she asked."

"Where was your brother killed?" asked Don Camillo.

"He went where they sent him," said Tavan, "and he was killed just here, in the battle that took place around Christmas of 1942." There was obvious relief in his voice. "My mother made me promise that I'd do everything I could to find the cross that marks his grave and put this in front of it. . . ."

And out of his pocket he pulled a wax votive candle.

"I understand, Comrade," said Don Camillo. "But how can you hope to find the place where he is buried?"

Tavan drew a faded photograph out of his wallet.

"Here it is," he replied. "The regimental chaplain gave this to my mother. There's the cross with my brother's name, and on the back are the name of the nearest village and a local map."

Don Camillo turned the photograph over and then gave it back to him.

"Don't you see, Comrade?" asked Tavan anxiously. "It's just about here, and somehow I must find it. But how can I ask these people to tell me?"

They had walked quite a way up the road and by now they were not far from the irrigation ditch and the oak tree, the very one that was marked on the map.

"Walk faster," said Don Camillo, at the same time quickening his own pace. When they came to the ditch he halted. "This is the road, here's the ditch with the hedge running along it, and there's the tree." And followed by Comrade Tavan he retraced his way along the bottom of the ditch and climbed out of it just below the oak. "There," he said, pointing at the wheat field, "this is the place where your brother lies."

He lifted up the ivy and showed him the cross and the date carved on the bark of the tree. Comrade Tavan looked out over the field, and the hand that was holding the candle trembled.

Don Camillo took a few steps forward, bent down and dug a hole in the earth. Tavan understood and put the candle into the hole and lighted it. Then he stood up and stared straight ahead, holding his cap in his hand. Don Camillo took a knife from his pocket and cut out a clod of earth with three slender stalks of wheat growing in it. He put the clod in the aluminium cup which he always carried with him for use as a chalice. "I'll get hold of another cup somehow," he told himself. And he said to Tavan:

"Take this to your mother."

Then they walked back to the edge of the field.

"Make the sign of the cross, Comrade," said Don Camillo. "I'm going to do the same thing myself."

From where they stood they could see the flickering flame of the votive candle.

Then the sound of the horn caused them to hasten their steps back to the bus. Just before they got there Don Camillo stopped.

"Comrade," he said, "your mother will be happy, but the Party can't possibly approve."

"I don't give a damn about the Party," said Comrade Tavan emphatically.

And he fingered the cup containing the clod of earth and the stalks of wheat as tenderly as if they were alive.

II

THE CELL GOES TO CONFESSION

THERE were few passengers aboard the train for Moscow and soon Don Camillo found himself alone in a compartment. When Peppone saw him pull out the famous book of excerpts from Lenin he went off in disgust to chat with Comrade Nadia Petrovna and Comrade Yenka Oregov, who had set up their headquarters at the front end of the car. Don Camillo put away the disguised breviary and took out his notebook.

"Thursday, 8 A.M. Tifiz *kolkhos*. Stephan Bordonny. War cemetery. Mass for the Dead. Comrade Tavan, 3 P.M. Departure by train."

Thursday? Was it only Thursday? He could hardly believe that he had been in the Soviet Union for no more than seventy-nine hours.

Once more darkness was falling, and not a single tree or house broke the monotony of the wind-swept plain. There were only endless wheat fields, which in his mind's eye he could picture green and alive under the summer sun. But no amount of imagination was sufficient to warm his heart. He thought of the winter landscape of his native Bassa, with its heavy fog, drenched fields and muddy roads. There no wind was too icy to extinguish the natural warmth generated by the touch of man. A peasant trudging through that landscape did not feel cut off from the rest of the world. Invisible life-giving threads bound him to his fellows. Here there were no such bonds. A man was like a brick in a wall, a necessary but interchangeable part of the national structure. At any moment he might be discarded and thrown on the scrap heap, and then he had no reason to go on living. Here, in short, man was desperately isolated and alone. Don Camillo shuddered. Then he was roused by the thought:

"Where the devil is that rascal Peppone?"

The door of the compartment creaked, and he saw the inquiring face of Comrade Tavan.

"Am I disturbing you?" Tavan asked.

"Come on in and sit down," replied Don Camillo.

Tavan sat down on the opposite seat. He took a roll of cardboard out of his pocket, and after a moment's hesitation showed it to his companion.

"Only a few more days and they won't have to suffer any longer," he explained, pointing to the cup containing the three stalks of wheat, which he had concealed inside. "They can get air from the open end of the tube. Do you think I ought to punch holes in the side as well?"

"No, I think they're quite all right the way they are. The important thing is not to let them get overheated."

Tavan stood the tube up against the back of the seat.

"But later on . . ." he began.

"Later on? When do you mean?"

"When I'm back home. . . ."

Don Camillo shrugged his shoulders.

"Comrade, I don't see anything difficult about transplanting three stalks of wheat."

"The difficulty's with my mother," said Tavan. "What am I going to say? 'This is some wheat that . . .'?" He paused and looked out the window. "With eleven million square miles of land why did they have to sow wheat in that particular place?" he muttered.

Don Camillo shook his head.

"Comrade," he said, "if a country has twenty million war dead of its own, it can't make much ado over the fifty or a hundred thousand left on its soil by the enemy."

"That's not something I can tell my mother," objected Tavan.

"I'm not recommending it. Let your mother go on thinking about the wooden cross which the photograph showed over her son's grave. Tell her that you lit the candle in front of it. As for the three stalks of wheat, do whatever your heart prompts you. If you keep them alive and transplant them, then their seed will somehow keep alive the memory of your brother."

Tavan listened with a gloomy air and Don Camillo changed the subject.

"Comrade," he said, "what makes you raise such sentimental and bourgeois questions?"

"I like to discuss them," said Tavan, picking up the roll of cardboard and starting to go away. Before leaving he looked again out of the window.

"Eleven million square miles, and they had to pick on that one acre . . ." he repeated.

Don Camillo did not remain long alone. A few minutes later the door swung open again and Comrade Bacciga from Genoa came in. He sat down across from Don Camillo and because he was a hard-headed, direct sort of fellow he came straight to the point.

"Comrade," he said, "I've been thinking things over, and I see that you're in the right. This is no place to make deals in minks and nylons. And I'm sorry for the stupid things I said after you'd denounced me."

"I owe you an apology, too," said Don Camillo. "I should have talked to you man to man instead of bringing the matter up in front of the whole cell. But the fact is that Comrade Oregov had seen what you were at, and I wanted to clear it up before he did."

Comrade Bacciga mumbled something under his breath and then said:

"He got the stole, didn't he, even if the deal was illegal?"

"At least the story went no farther," said Don Camillo consolingly.

"Yes, but I got the short end of the deal," said Bacciga.

"You paid for your fun, that's all, Comrade," said Don Camillo.

"But what am I going to say to the person who gave me the stockings and told me to bring back the mink stole in return?" He went on grumbling under his breath and then added: "Comrade, let's be frank. Last night I saw the trick the Senator played

106

on you and I heard him saying you have a bossy wife. Well, my wife is ten times as bad, I can tell you. She's the one that got me into it, and if I don't bring back the goods not even Comrade Togliatti himself can save me. I can't haul her up in front of the Party organization, because she's a stinking Fascist as well. Her daughters will take her side, and they're even worse than she is."

"Stinking Fascists, too?" inquired Don Camillo.

"Worse than that! They're Christian Democrats. Storm troopers, I call them!"

"I understand," said Don Camillo. "How can I help you?"

"Comrade, I work on the docks, and so I always manage to have a few American dollars in my pocket. America stinks, too, but dollars always come in handy. Do you get the point?"

"Not exactly, no."

"Comrade, for the sake of keeping peace at home I'm willing to part with my dollars. Is there anything wrong about that?"

"About your spending your dollars? Not a thing. The Soviet Union needs dollar exchange."

"I thought so," said Bacciga with relief. "And while we're about it, can you give me an idea of what they're worth?"

Don Camillo was thoroughly informed.

"The official exchange is four roubles for a dollar, but tourists are entitled to ten. Reactionary papers claim that there's a black market as well, and you can get twenty. But of course that's the usual anti-Communist propaganda."

"Of course," said Bacciga. "So once we get to Moscow I can do what I like with my money, is that it?"

"It's perfectly legitimate, Comrade."

Comrade Bacciga went away satisfied, but Don Camillo had no time to make a note of what had happened because Comrade Salvatore Capece was already at the door. The cold compress had been effective and his left eye was now circled with only a rim of pale blue.

"Comrade," he said, sitting down across from Don Camillo, "I don't know how you do it, but you gulp down that vodka as if it were brandy. But it's still vodka. There's no telling what it may do to you, and after the mischief is done, well it's irrevocable."

Don Camillo nodded assent, and the other went on:

"The Senator told me that he'd settle with me later. Meanwhile I have a black eye and a lump as big as a nut on the back of my neck. What more of a settlement can he want? My wife's active in our local Party cell, and if there's any talk about all this foolishness she's sure to hear about it. She's hot-blooded and jealous. I needn't say any more, because it seems that you have to cope with very much the same thing."

"Don't worry, Comrade," said Don Camillo; "I'll take it up with the Senator myself."

Capece leaped to his feet with a look of obvious relief.

"Salvatore Capece, that's my name!" he exclaimed. "If you ever come to Naples, just ask for Salvatore Capece. Everyone there knows me!"

By now so much had happened that Don Camillo felt he really must jot it down. But fate would not have it that way. Before he could pull out his notebook Comrade Peratto blew in. As a Piedmontese from Turin he lost no time beating around the bush.

"Comrade," he said, "yesterday we had quite a bit of fun. That's always the way when there's drinking. But now the effects of the vodka are gone and I'm cold sober. The Senator can say what he likes, but I'm a professional photographer, not an amateur. And so here's the roll containing all the pictures I snapped last night. Do what you want with them."

Don Camillo accepted the roll.

"I'm grateful, Comrade. It's very decent of you."

"It's a matter of professional ethics," said Comrade Peratto, preparing to take his leave, "and also of masculine solidarity. My own wife is growing more jealous every day. I'll tell the Senator the film was exposed to the light."

After Peratto had gone Don Camillo lifted his eyes to heaven. "Lord," he said, "after all this I'm almost ashamed of not having a jealous wife." Then he took out his notebook and wrote down: "Wives are the opium of the people." Before he could add anything more Comrade Scamoggia appeared at the door. He threw himself down on the seat across from Don Camillo's, lit a cigarette and then let it hang from one corner of his down-turned mouth. He looked unusually serious and it was plain that there was something on his mind. Don Camillo looked at him inquiringly for a moment, and then as the other gave no signs of speaking he decided to complete his notes.

"Comrade!" Scamoggia interrupted, and Don Camillo hurriedly put the notebook away.

"Something wrong?" he asked innocently.

"Comrade, you know what happened last night," Scamoggia began.

"Have no fear about that," Don Camillo reassured him. "Capece was just here, and everything's in good order."

"Capece? What's he got to do with it?" said Scamoggia, very much surprised.

"He got the black eye, didn't he?" exclaimed Don Camillo.

"Oh, perhaps he did," said Scamoggia distractedly. "That's not what I came to talk about."

"Then I'm completely in the dark," said Don Camillo.

Scammogia puffed the cigarette smoke slowly out of his mouth.

"Last night, in a moment of weakness, I hit somebody in the face."

"Yes, I know," said Don Camillo impatiently.

"Oh, I don't mean Comrade Capece. I mean the girl."

Don Camillo was thoroughly taken aback.

"You mean to say you hit Comrade Petrovna? How could you do a thing like that?"

Comrade Scamoggia threw out his arms as if to indicate that he himself could give no explanation.

"Comrade Petrovna is an intelligent woman," said Don Camillo. "She'll understand that it was all on account of the vodka."

"I hadn't been drinking, and she knows it," said Scamoggia. "That's the whole trouble." He threw his cigarette on the floor and stamped it out. Don Camillo had never seen him in such a state of depression.

"Don't be melodramatic, Comrade," he said. "She's a lovely girl."

"Exactly," said Scamoggia. "She's worth her weight in gold, and I can't treat her as if she were just a casual pick-up. I have no right to lead her on."

Don Camillo's country, La Bassa, was hundreds of miles from

Rome and he couldn't fathom the workings of Scamoggia's city-slicker mind.

"Lead her on?" he said. "What do you mean?"

"It's no joke!" shouted the Roman heartbreaker. "When Nanni Scamoggia hits a girl in the face, it's not without some reason. Do I look to you like the kind of man that roughs up a woman just for the fun of it?"

Don Camillo shook his head.

"I see. You're afraid the girl has got the idea that you're seriously interested in her."

"Exactly."

"You don't want to get married, is that it, and you're afraid to tell her."

"That's it."

"Then it's perfectly simple. Just let things coast along, and in three days, when you go home, she'll realize that she has to get over it."

"But *I* won't get over it. That's the point."

Don Camillo saw that the situation was even more complex than he had imagined.

"In that case I can't give you any advice," he admitted.

"Yes, you can. You know how to think straight, and I'm counting on you. We had a long talk last night, after it was all over. I had to explain."

"Quite right."

"In a few months she'll be coming to Rome as interpreter to a guided tour. And then . . ." And after a moment of hesitation he added: "Comrade, can I trust you?"

"Just as if you were talking to your confessor."

"I wouldn't be caught dead in the confessional!"

"Quite right," said Don Camillo. "Nevertheless there are priests who have died rather than reveal the substance of a confession. If I were a priest that's the kind I'd be. So you can speak quite freely."

"When she comes to Rome she'd just as soon stay there, in order to be with me. Is it right for me to encourage her?"

"No," said Don Camillo peremptorily. "That would be dishonourable. A Comrade Scamoggia can't behave that way. There's a much more natural and honourable solution."

"What's that?"

The girl's very good at her job and probably she enjoys the favour of the Party. When we get to Moscow she can doubtless obtain permission for you to stay here. The Soviet Union needs men with strong convictions and technical ability. Once you've settled yourself here the rest will be easy. You can satisfy both your heart and your conscience. Surely that's better than involving an innocent, lovesick girl in an affair in a foreign land."

Scamoggia's face lighted up.

"Comrade, my mind wasn't working and you've set it back on the right track. As you say, it's all quite simple. I'm glad I unburdened myself to you."

And after vigorously shaking Don Camillo's hand he went away.

"Lord," said Don Camillo, "the Comrade shepherd's job is to bring the lost sheep back to the Party fold."

"Not so," said the Lord; "that's the job of Comrade Devil!"

But perhaps this was not the Lord's voice; perhaps it was the voice of the wind howling over the steppes. Don Camillo had to leave the question unanswered because Peppone was standing before him.

"Why haven't you come to talk with us," said Peppone, "instead of sitting here and staring out of the window?"

"Comrade," said Don Camillo gravely. "A cell leader has a lot to do if he's to live up to his Party responsibilities."

Peppone stared at him suspiciously and then shrugged his shoulders. No matter how diabolical his enemy might be, what harm could he do shut up in a compartment of a train travelling through Mother Russia?

12

IN THE JAWS OF HELL

THIS was Peppone's great day! They had visited a tractor factory and a *kolkhos* and travelled by train for twenty consecutive hours through an endless expanse of fertile, cultivated land. These things had given them some idea of the Soviet Union's agricultural resources and industrial efficiency, but they had not made an overwhelming impression. Indeed, a series of regrettable accidents had tipped the balance in favour of the West. But now, Peppone reflected, all doubts and misconceptions would be swept away; the Western point of view was doomed to annihilation. The luxurious, ultra-modern bus in which they were driving down the broad streets of Moscow was quite unlike the rickety vehicle in which they had been transported across the muddy roads of the Ukraine, and around them were not thatch-roofed hovels but towering skyscrapers. Don Camillo, the disguised representative of the Western point of view, was momentarily speechless.

"Don't let it get you down, Comrade," Peppone whispered into his ear. "Even what you can see with your own eyes is a mirage created by propaganda. Meanwhile, if you want some exercise, you can take a little walk around the Kremlin. The circumference only measures three miles."

He was repeating the data furnished by Comrade Nadia Petrovna, but there was as much pride in his voice as if he had built Moscow with his own two hands. As for Comrade Yenka Oregov, the visitors' admiring exclamations made him tremulous with joy. He was no cold and indifferent bureaucrat; in return for his salary of a thousand roubles a month he gave at least ten thousand roubles' worth of zeal and enthusiasm. He was happy in the conviction that he was a humble but essential part of the gigantic structure of the Communist State. "It takes a hundred kopeks to make a rouble and a thousand times a thousand roubles to make a million roubles. But without my kopek the million roubles would not be complete." This was the way he saw it, and his reasoning was not as absurd as it might have seemed, because the investment of a single kopek gave him the feeling that he was a millionaire. The visitors' gaping admiration filled him with pride, but when he saw that they had digested all they could of the wonders of Moscow he instructed Comrade Nadia Petrovna to inform them that the preliminary part of their tour of the city was over.

"Comrade Oregov says that you may want to stretch your legs," she announced, "and he advises you to return by foot to the hotel. It's only a few hundred yards away."

They got out of the bus in the middle of an imposing square. As if he had suddenly remembered an unimportant detail, Comrade Oregov wheeled around and led them into a small building which housed an escalator. The next thing they knew they were carried down into the bowels of the earth.

"Comrades," said Comrade Petrovna, when they got to the bottom, "this is the subway!"

The famous Moscow subway was grandiose in the Babylonian manner. Everywhere there was decoration: bronze and marble statuary, bas-reliefs, paintings and gleaming glass. It seemed almost as if the carpeting must be made of mink. Peppone and his companions were overpowered, and Comrade Oregov glowed with satisfaction. The first to speak was Comrade Scamoggia.

"Comrade," he said in a subdued voice to Comrade Petrovna, "next to you, this is the most gorgeous sight of the Soviet Union!"

She was taken by surprise but recovered herself sufficiently to answer:

"Comrade, this triumph of Soviet art and industry doesn't lend itself to jokes."

"But, Comrade, I'm not joking," Scamoggia insisted.

He spoke so earnestly that for a moment Comrade Petrovna forgot her Party dignity and gave him a capitalistic smile. Meanwhile Peppone nudged Don Camillo.

"Comrade," he said with a grin, "can you imagine what that priest with whom we have both had some dealings would say?"

The subway was beginning to be crowded with people: men and women in the usual ill-fitting clothes, with the usual gloomy expression on their faces.

"I know what he'd say," replied Don Camillo. "He'd say that it's better to eat steak out of an earthenware dish than an onion served on a golden platter."

"Materialism of the lowest degree!" said Peppone. But his imagination lingered over the steak.

These were the days of the famous thaw, and the Soviet government had chosen to lodge the visitors in the very best hotel. It was a structure as magnificent as the subway, with over a thousand rooms, elaborate reception halls and elevators in every corner. After lunch Don Camillo sat in an armchair in the lobby to watch the people go by. They were of every race and colour: black, brown, yellow and all shades of white, apparently coming from every corner of the globe and jabbering in a variety of languages. Soon the watchful Peppone came to sit down beside him.

"It's like the tower of Babel," remarked Don Camillo.

"So it seems," Peppone agreed. "But although they speak so many different tongues, they manage to understand one another. They all think the same way; that's the power of Communism. Did you notice the crowd we saw this morning standing in line to visit the tomb of Lenin? Because he brought light into darkness, men come from everywhere to pay him their respects."

Don Camillo gazed earnestly at Peppone.

"Comrade, when you were mayor you didn't know any of these things."

"Yes, I did. I knew them just as well as I do now, only I wasn't aware of it. Later I thought them over and crystallized my ideas. It's just what happened when Jesus Christ was in fashion. Only in the case of Christ it was superstition that bound men together, whereas now it's reason. The truth was always there, but it took Lenin to light a torch by which all men could see it. That's why every visitor to Moscow wants more than anything to visit his tomb."

"But isn't there somebody else in there with him?" asked Don Camillo.

"There is and there isn't," said Peppone. "Anyhow, Lenin is the one people come to see. You'll have a chance to look at him yourself."

"No, I won't," said Don Camillo, shaking his head.

"We're going there shortly, all of us," said Peppone. "I've just been talking over plans with Comrade Oregov."

"I have no debt of gratitude to discharge," said Don Camillo. "I don't follow the vagaries of fashion, and for me Christ is still the only true Light."

"But you have duties, as a cell leader."

"My duty as a priest comes first," said Don Camillo. Pulling a postcard out of his pocket, he set it down on a nearby table and began to write.

"I hope you're not up to some more of your tricks," grumbled Peppone.

"Isn't it legitimate for a fellow to have a friend whose address happens to be the Bishopric Square?"

"Except for the fact that nobody besides the Bishop has that address!"

Don Camillo held out the card for inspection.

"That's why I'm able to address it to plain Mr. So-and-so, which happens to be the bishop's name!"

Peppone glared at the card and gave it back to him.

"I'm not sticking my nose into your personal affairs."

"Nevertheless, if I were you, I'd add my signature," Don Camillo advised him.

"Are you crazy?"

"What if Christ were to come back into fashion?" insinuated Don Camillo.

Peppone took the card and scribbled his name at the bottom.

"Don't get me wrong," he said sternly. "It's only because your bishop happens to be a very lovable man."

Don Camillo got up and slipped the card into a mailbox attached to a column in the hall. When he came back he found the whole group gathered together.

"According to your wishes," said Comrade Nadia Petrovna, "we're going to visit the tomb of Lenin."

Don Camillo started to go along with the others, but at the door he stumbled and turned his ankle. If Peppone had not braced him with one arm he would have fallen flat on the floor.

"We'll send for the hotel doctor," said Comrade Petrovna. "I trust it's nothing serious, but you'd better stay here and rest."

Don Camillo seemed so very disappointed that Comrade Oregov felt the need to console him.

"You'll be able to visit the tomb another time," he said cheeringly.

And so Don Camillo hobbled back to his chair. He rubbed his ankle and of course it was immediately restored to normal. With a sigh of relief he pulled out of his pocket the famous book of excerpts from Lenin.

A half-hour went by, and Don Camillo was so completely absorbed in his thoughts that he forgot that he was Comrade Tarocci. Just at this point a voice said:

"Father!"

Don Camillo looked up and then kicked himself for his stupidity. But it was too late to cover it up. In the adjacent chair, which had been vacated by Peppone, sat a thin, dark-haired man about forty-five years old. Don Camillo recognized him at once and spontaneously called him by name.

"Comassi!" he exclaimed.

The newcomer held an open copy of *Pravda* before him and leaned over towards Don Camillo as if he were translating an article on the front page for his benefit.

"I knew you the minute I saw you," he explained, "even if you weren't wearing your cassock."

"I wanted to see Moscow," said Don Camillo, "but I had to wear suitable clothes."

"You mean you're still a priest?" the newcomer muttered.

"What else could I be?" said Don Camillo.

"So many people have switched their allegiance. . . ." said the other.

"My allegiance is of a kind that can't be switched. . . . But tell me, what are you doing here?"

"I came with a group of comrades from Prague. That's where I'm living. We go back tomorrow."

"And I suppose you'll report that I'm a Vatican spy."

"Don Camillo, you know me better than that!"

The Comassis were a good churchgoing family from Castelletto; only young Athos had fallen away. His story was the same as that of many of his contemporaries. On September 8, 1943, when Badoglio signed an armistice with the Allies, he cast off his soldier's uniform and made for home. Then when he was called up to the army of Mussolini's short-lived Fascist republic, he took to the hills. He was not seen again until April of 1945, when the Partisans came out of hiding and with them many last-minute recruits who had foresightedly grown long beards in order to appear veterans of the Partisan struggle. Young Comassi wore a red kerchief around his neck and held a position of command. He assumed charge of local operations, which consisted largely of obtaining forced contributions of money from the landowners, each one in proportion to the area of his land. Fists flew and many a landowner was lucky to escape with his life.

Seventy-five-year-old Count Mossoni, together with his seventy-year-old wife, a servant girl and a dog, lived quietly in an isolated manor house in the centre of the plain. One morning when their tenant farmer came to deliver a can of milk nobody answered the bell. He walked into the house and found it empty. Only the dog stood in one corner and could not be persuaded to leave it. The farmer called in some neighbours and they found that the dog was standing guard over the rim of an old, indoor well. At the bottom of the well lay the bodies of the count, the countess and the servant girl. Apparently thieves had broken in during the previous night, jimmied open a safe hidden behind a portrait hanging on the second-floor drawing room wall and killed all three human occupants of the house.

A dozen people had seen young Comassi leave the village by car that evening with a group of young toughs and a strange man who was apparently their leader. Other witnesses had noticed the car going up the Mossoni driveway. The three young toughs had kept watch outside while Comassi and the stranger went in. Twenty minutes later they all drove away together.

These were dangerous times and no one dared come forward and testify against them. For three years the affair was forgotten. But during the elections of 1948 posters were stuck up in the village telling the whole story of the murder and pointing out what kind of men the Reds were trying to put in power. The three young toughs were able to prove that they hadn't gone into the house and claimed they had never known the identity of the stranger. As for Comassi, he had once more disappeared. That is, until this moment, when Don Camillo discovered him at his side.

"What are you doing in Prague?" he asked him.

"They say I have a good voice, and I make news broadcasts in Italian."

"That's a dirty job," said Don Camillo. "Does your family know?"

"No, they don't. But I'd like them to hear my voice and know that I'm alive."

"That wouldn't make them very happy. They're better off thinking that you're dead."

"But I want them to know," Comassi insisted. "That's my whole purpose in speaking to you. God must have meant to give me this chance."

"God! This is a fine time to remember Him! He wasn't in your thoughts when you murdered those poor old people!"

Comassi made an abrupt motion as if there were something he felt impelled to say. Then, apparently, he thought better of it.

"I understand," he murmured. "I can't expect you to believe me. But since you're a priest, you can't refuse to hear my confession."

The hotel lobby was thronged with people of every race and tongue. Black, brown and yellow faces mingled together and a discordant clamour filled the room. Don Camillo felt as if he were in the jaws of hell, and yet God was there, perhaps more vividly than anywhere else in the world. Christ's words rang in Don Camillo's ear: "Knock and it shall be opened unto you. . . ." He made the sign of the cross and Comassi followed his example, cautiously and deliberately, because there were hundreds of watchful eyes around him, beyond the paper curtain of the *Pravda*.

"O God of infinite mercy, here at Your feet is the sinner who has offended you . . . humbly seeking Your pardon. . . . Lord, do not turn me away . . . do not despise a humble and contrite heart. . . . *Cor contritum et humiliatum non despicies.* . . ."

In an almost inaudible voice Comassi repeated the prayer which Don Camillo recalled to him. Then he said what he had to say, and the words came from his heart, although he seemed to be reading them from the newspaper.

". . . we went in and threatened them with a gun. At first they wouldn't reveal the hiding place, but finally they did. . . . The leader told me to go up to the drawing-room on the second floor and take the money while he kept an eye on them. When I came back he was all alone. He took the money saying that it would all go to the Cause. . . . Then, just before the election, when the posters told the story, they helped me to get away. . . ."

"Why didn't you protest your innocence?"

"I couldn't. He was a higher-up of the Party. . . ."

"Then why don't you come forward now?"

"I can't. It would be even worse now than then. The Party would be involved in a scandal."

"You mean to say that you still respect the Party?"

"No, but I'm afraid. If I said anything they'd liquidate me."

"But what is the leader's name?"

The name was one so much in the news that Don Camillo could hardly believe it.

"Nobody must find out what I have told you, but I want my father and mother to know that I'm not a murderer. That much you can tell them. And I want them to listen to my radio broadcasts, not on account of what I say but simply in order to hear my voice. That way I can feel that I'm still alive, and not just a dead man crying in the wilderness. . . ."

He pulled a sealed envelope out of his pocket and surreptitiously transferred it to the pocket of Don Camillo.

"Here's the whole story, with my signature. You mustn't open the envelope, but you can tell that man that it is in your possession and that I want to go home. . . ."

Comassi was very pale and his voice trembled.

"*Ego te absolvo* . . ." said Don Camillo.

Comassi seemed to have recovered his peace of mind. He folded the newspaper and handed it to Don Camillo.

"You can keep it as a souvenir," he said. "You've never heard a confession in a stranger place than this. . . . Forget what I said to you about the letter; I should never have said it. There's nothing to be done, really. . . . I've passed the point of no return."

"Don't be so sure, Comrade," said Don Camillo. "God still has an outpost in Prague: He's better organized than you may think. Meanwhile I'll see to it that your father and mother listen to your broadcasts, not on account of what you say, but simply in order to hear your voice."

Comassi got up.

"God!" he said. "Who could have imagined that someone would speak to me of God in a place like this?"

"God has outposts everywhere, Comrade," said Don Camillo, "even in Moscow. God's organization is very old, but it's still working."

13

COMRADE NADIA'S COFFEE

"Comrade, I'm in trouble," said Scamoggia.

"Everyone has to stew in his own juice," replied Don Camillo.

"It's not my own trouble," Scamoggia explained; "it's some-body else's. Only it's been passed on to me and my duty is to pass it on to my immediate superior. Then you'll report it to the chief and he'll report it to the echelon above him. Isn't that the correct official procedure?"

Don Camillo, wearied by the Babylonian tumult of the lobby, had gone upstairs and thrown himself down on his bed.

"If it's an official matter, yes," he said, pulling himself into an upright position. "Sit down and tell me more about it."

Scamoggia shrugged his shoulders.

"I'll give you the story," he said, "and you can decide for yourself how official it is. Do you know Comrade Gibetti?"

"Of course," said Don Camillo.

Actually he knew only what he had read in Peppone's files. Gibetti was a Tuscan, forty years old, an electrical engineer, an active Partisan, well grounded in Party ideology. He had had no occasion to size the fellow up at first hand, because, like the Sicilian Li Friddi and the Sardinian Curullu, Gibetti was close-mouthed and never revealed what he was thinking.

"I like him," said Scamoggia. "He's tough, like myself. And as a Partisan he risked his life without flinching."

"I know that," said Don Camillo.

"Did you know that during the war he fought here in Russia, somewhere near Stalino?"

"In view of his subsequent Partisan record, that's not to be counted against him."

"I agree, Comrade; it shouldn't matter, but in his case it does."

"Why so?"

"During the war he was only twenty-three years old. In spite of instructions he had an urge to fraternize with the enemy. And when the enemy happens to be a stunning seventeen-year-old girl, you can see that the fraternizing might go too far. It did, but then came the retreat, and it was all over."

Don Camillo threw out his arms.

"It's not a pretty story," he said, "but in war such things are bound to happen. In every country there are girls who got themselves into trouble with foreign soldiers."

"Yes," admitted Scamoggia, "but it's unusual to find a soldier who goes on thinking of an enemy girl for seventeen years after the war is over. And that's Gibetti's story." He puffed at his cigarette and then went on: "He told me all about it. Originally he wanted to take the girl home. He dressed her up in an army uniform and with the help of his comrades started to carry out this plan. Then his unit was encircled by the Russians and because he was afraid she might be shot he sent her away. He gave her all the tins of rations that he could get out of his friends and told her to hide out in an abandoned *isba*, where he promised to pick her up again if they escaped from the Russians' clutches. 'But if we're killed or captured,' he said, 'wait until it's all over and then go home. You can say that the Italians carried you away.'

"The battle lasted three days, and at the end the Russians had to beat a retreat for fear of being encircled in their turn. Gibetti returned to the *isba*, but she was no longer there. He went back to Italy with the thought of her still haunting his mind. After the armistice he took to the mountains as a Partisan, but he still hadn't forgotten her. At the end of the war he joined the Party, but even that was no help to him in retracing the girl. All he could do was send letters to her by any Party comrade who went to Russia. Either the letters never got mailed or else they didn't reach their destination; in any case he had no reply. Finally, seventeen years later, he found a chance to come to Russia himself, and at this particularly favourable time when the tension between the two countries is relaxed.

"On our original programme we were to visit Stalino, and the girl supposedly lives close by. But there has been a change of plans and he doesn't know what to do. That's why he told me the story. 'You're on good terms with Comrade Nadia Petrovna,' he said. 'See if you can't do something for me. I'm willing to stay here, if necessary; I'd do anything to find that girl.'

"I told him to leave it to me and trust my discretion. Then I went to Comrade Nadia. She's a woman with a head on her shoulders and the first thing she said was that she must look into the girl's present situation. I gave her the name and address and she wrote to a friend of hers who holds down an important post in Stalino."

Scamoggia paused and took a typewritten sheet from his pocket.

"Here's the reply," he said.

Don Camillo turned the paper over in his hands.

"This doesn't mean anything to me," he said. "I don't know Russian."

"Here's Comrade Nadia's Italian translation," said Scamoggia, handing him another sheet of paper.

The letter was brief. It said that a Soviet mechanized unit had found the girl, clad in an Italian army coat, at an *isba* near the enemy lines. She claimed that the Italians had brought her there after they had withdrawn from the village of K., against her will, but that she had finally escaped them. She was taken back to K., handed over to the village authorities, accused of collaboration with the enemy and executed on the spot.

"But I can't tell this to Gibetti," Scamoggia concluded. "If you think he ought to be told, go ahead and tell him. If you don't, remember that he's dead set on staying here because he thinks he can find her. It's too much for me, and I'm washing my hands of it."

And he strode out of the room leaving Don Camillo alone. The Soviet Union has more than its share of devils and one of them began tugging at Don Camillo's cassock, the cassock which he still wore in spirit beneath his disguise. The devil

123

whispered: "Go ahead, Don Camillo! Here's your chance to sink Gibetti!" But Don Camillo booted him away. A moment later Peppone came through the door and Don Camillo grabbed his arm.

"After all, you do outrank me," he said, shoving the papers into his hand. "I'm putting this little affair right in your lap."

Then since the papers alone were not sufficient to make his point he proceeded to furnish a full explanation. Peppone turned around to lock the door and then gave vent to his feelings.

"The élite!" he shouted. "Ten hand-picked men! And what do we see? Rondella made trouble from the start and had to be sent home. Scamoggia came with bottles of perfume in his pocket and the idea of playing Don Juan, and Capece went and set himself up as his rival. Bacciga's purpose was to deal on the black market, Tavan's to light a candle on his brother's grave, Peratto said he was going to take pictures for the Party paper and on the side he's selling others to the capitalist press—he thinks he's put it over on me but I know perfectly well what he's up to. And now Gibetti, who seemed to be beyond reproach, is contributing to the confusion! Is it possible that not a single man came to see the Soviet Union? Has every one of them got some personal motive up his sleeve?"

"You're too hard on them, Comrade," said Don Camillo consolingly. "Curullu and Li Friddi are as pure as driven snow."

"A pair of dummies, that's what they are! They don't say a word for fear of compromising themselves."

"And then you've forgotten Comrade Tarocci!"

"Tarocci?" mumbled Peppone. "Who's that?" Then he came to himself and stood with his legs wide apart, wagging his thumb in Don Camillo's face.

"You!" he shouted. "You'll send me home with a heart attack if you don't watch out!" And he threw himself on his bed in exhaustion. His usual aggressiveness had crumpled and he could hardly speak. "You're nothing but a blackmailer! You've got me into such a mess that if it became known I'd be a laughing-stock the world over. Ever since I ran into you in Rome my life has been hell. Every time you open your mouth my heart skips a beat and my stomach turns over. I have nightmares all night long and when I get up I feel as if all my bones were broken." He paused to wipe the perspiration from his brow. "If you wanted to get me down, you can be happy. I'm down and out."

Don Camillo had never seen Peppone in such a low state of mind or imagined that he could be at such a total loss as to what to do. He felt strangely sorry for him.

"God is witness that I never meant you any harm," he expostulated.

"Then why did you get me into this play-acting? There's no iron curtain any more. You've seen that there are people from every country in the world travelling around. You could have come here in plain clothes on your own. I'd have paid your fare. This way you may not have cost me money, but you've made me suffer the pains of the damned, and my pains aren't yet over. Perhaps it gives you some pleasure to travel at the expense of the Soviet Union. . . ."

Don Camillo shook his head.

"I didn't want to see the Soviet Union as a tourist. I wanted to see it through your eyes. It's one thing to see a show from the audience and another to be behind the scenes with the extras. Unless the Party has completely addled your brain you must know that I was on the level."

Peppone got up and went over to the stand where his suitcase was lying. He started to open it but stopped halfway.

"You've even taken my brandy!" he exclaimed. "What were you after when you insisted on giving it to Comrade Oregov, I'd like to know?"

"Nothing," said Don Camillo. "It was my loss as well as yours, because now I have to give you some of mine."

He produced his own bottle, and after swallowing a glassful Peppone was once more able to cope with the situation.

"Now then," said Don Camillo, once more showing him the two sheets of paper, "what do you propose to do?"

"Take care of it yourself," said Peppone. "I don't want to hear anything about it."

Don Camillo went straight to Gibetti's room. There he tackled the thorny matter without delay.

"Comrade Scamoggia has bad news, but he couldn't bear to tell it to you himself, so I'm here to tell you."

Gibetti leaped up from the bed where he was lying.

"You may as well forget about that girl," said Don Camillo. "She's married and has five children."

"It can't be true!" said Gibetti.

"Comrade, you know Russian, don't you?" said Don Camillo.

"No."

"Then how did you manage to fraternize with her so closely?"

"We understood each other without words."

"And how did you manage to write to her?"

"I knew how to write her name and the name of her village, and I got someone to teach me how to say: 'I'm still thinking of you. I'll be back. Write me a letter.' And she had my address."

Don Camillo pulled the typewritten Russian sheet out of his pocket.

"Here's the report from her native place. You can get someone to translate it for you and you'll find in it everything I've been saying."

Gibetti looked searchingly at the letter.

"Her name and the name of the village are there, all right," he admitted.

"And so is the rest of what I told you," said Don Camillo. "In case you don't believe me, you can easily enough check on it when you get home."

Gibetti folded the paper and tucked it into his pocket.

"I shan't do anything of the sort," he replied. "I trust you completely. Next time I lose my head over a woman I'll just look at this paper and find a quick cure." He smiled sadly and went on: "Comrade, you know my Party record, don't you? Well, I did what I did, and many things I shouldn't have done as well, chiefly for the purpose of getting myself to Russia and looking for the girl. How am I to behave from now on?"

"Go right on fighting for the Cause."

"But my cause was Sonia and now someone else has taken it over."

Don Camillo shrugged his shoulders.

"Think it through, Comrade, that's all I can say. I've talked to you not as a Party comrade but as a friend. In my Party capacity, I know nothing of the whole affair."

"I do, though, to my sorrow," mumbled Gibetti as he threw himself back on to the bed.

The group met over the dinner table, all except for Gibetti, who was feeling sick. Comrade Oregov was in good spirits, because the afternoon programme had gone off well. Comrade Bacciga was sitting beside Don Camillo, and managed to whisper in his ear:

"Comrade, I've made my deal. I exchanged my money and bought another mink stole."

"But how are you going to get it through the customs back home?" asked Don Camillo. "You can't very well pass off a mink stole as part of your personal linen."

"I'll sew it on to my overcoat collar. Plenty of men's overcoats are trimmed with fur. By the way, our reactionary press was, as usual, in error."

"I don't doubt it," said Don Camillo. "But what's the connection?"

"You told me that, according to the rate of exchange quoted by the reactionary papers, I'd get twenty roubles for every dollar. But I got twenty-six."

The vodka was going around and the conversation grew more and more gay.

"Comrade Tarocci," said Scamoggia, "it's a shame you couldn't come with us. A visit to the tomb of Lenin is something never to be forgotten."

"Quite right," said Comrade Curullu, who was sitting nearby. "To see the last resting-place of Stalin makes a tremendous impression."

The mention of Stalin was not exactly tactful, and Don Camillo hastened to fill in the awkward silence that followed.

"Of course," he said diplomatically. "I remember how impressed I was by the tomb of Napoleon in Paris. And Napoleon is a pigmy alongside Lenin."

But Comrade Curullu, fortified by vodka, would not stand for a change of subject.

"Stalin, that's the great man," he said gloomily.

"Well spoken, Comrade," chimed in Comrade Li Friddi. "Stalin is the outstanding hero of Soviet Russia. Stalin won the war."

Comrade Curullu downed another glass of vodka.

"Today, in the line of workers waiting to visit the tomb, there were some American tourists. The girls were dressed as if they were going to a preview of a Marilyn Monroe picture. Little idiots, I call them!"

"Quite right, Comrade," Li Friddi assented. "I was just as disgusted as you. Moscow isn't Capri or Monte Carlo."

"If Stalin were still alive, those little idiots wouldn't have been allowed to enter the country. Stalin had the capitalists scared to death."

Peppone, with the aid of Comrade Nadia Petrovna, was doing his best to distract Comrade Oregov's attention. But at a certain point Comrade Oregov pricked up his ears and demanded a translation of what was being said at the other end of the table. Peppone sent a mute S O S signal to Don Camillo.

"Comrades," Don Camillo said gravely to the two recalcitrants, "nobody denies the merits of Stalin. But this is neither the time nor the place to speak of them."

"Truth knows neither time nor place!" Comrade Curullu insisted. "Even if today the Soviet Union has conquered the moon, the truth is that the Party has lost the revolutionary inspiration for which two hundred and fifty thousand men laid down their lives."

"Policies have to be adapted to the circumstances of the moment," Don Camillo timidly objected. "The end is what counts, not the means."

"The fact is that Stalin got everything he wanted without bothering to set foot outside the Soviet Union," insisted Curullu.

Don Camillo relapsed into silence and let the vodka take over. Little by little, all the comrades, except for Peppone, were overcome by nostalgia for Stalin. Peppone sat with clenched jaws, waiting for the inevitable explosion. Comrade Oregov confabulated excitedly with Comrade Nadia Petrovna and then leaped to his feet, pounding with his fist on the table. His eyes were feverishly bright and he was pale as a ghost. There was an icy silence until he shouted in strangely accented but comprehensible Italian:

"Long Live Stalin!"

He raised his glass, and the others leaped to their feet and followed suit.

"Hurrah!" they all shouted together.

Comrade Oregov drained his glass and the rest of them did the same. Then he dashed it to the floor and they did likewise. Comrade Nadia Petrovna abruptly announced:

"Comrade Oregov wishes his Italian comrades a very good night."

The party broke up in silence. Don Camillo and Peppone were the last to leave the private dining-room, and Comrade Nadia Petrovna blocked their way.

"Comrades," she said, "may I offer you a cup of coffee?"

They stared at her, perplexed.

"It will be brewed in Italian style," she explained smiling. "My house is only a short distance away."

Behind the ancient palaces and the American-style skyscrapers lay a proletarian section of the city. Comrade Petrovna lived on the fourth floor of a shabby house whose stairways reeked of cabbage and cooking oil. Her apartment consisted of a single room, furnished with two couches, a table, four chairs, a wardrobe and a stand for the radio. The curtains at the windows, some tasselled lampshades and the rug on the floor were obviously meant to be decorative, but did little to alleviate the bleakness of the surroundings.

"This is the comrade with whom I live," she said, introducing the girl who had opened the door. Although the girl was older, stockier and more rustic in appearance than Comrade Petrovna she was obviously cut from the same cloth. "She's an interpreter of French, but she speaks a fair amount of Italian as well," Comrade Petrovna added.

The coffee was already brewing over an alcohol burner in the middle of the table.

"We make it here," Comrade Petrovna explained, "because we share a kitchen with the next apartment, and it's across the hall." The flavour was unexpectedly delicious, and the two girls were gratified by their guests' appreciation. "I hope you're enjoying your trip to our great country," said Comrade Petrovna when the compliments were over.

Peppone, who was in a jovial mood, launched into an enthusiastic recapitulation of the wonders of the journey. But Comrade Petrovna's friend cut him short.

"We know all these things," she said. "Talk to us about Italy."

"Comrades," said Peppone, throwing out his arms in mock despair, "Italy is a small country, which might be a wonderful place to live in if it weren't infested with capitalists and clergy."

"But there's a good bit of freedom, isn't there?" put in Comrade Petrovna.

"On the surface the country is free," answered Peppone. "But the priests are secretly in control and they have spies everywhere. By the time we get home they will know every detail of our travels."

"Really?" said the other girl.

"You can tell her better than I," said Peppone, turning to Don Camillo.

"It's the truth," admitted Don Camillo. "I can swear to it."

"How terrible!" exclaimed Comrade Petrovna. "And how does the average worker get along? Comrade Scamoggia, for instance?"

"Scamoggia isn't an average unskilled worker," Peppone explained. "He's an expert mechanic with a busy workshop of his own."

"Approximately how much money does he make?" she asked with an apparently casual air.

"If you figure thirty liras to the rouble, then he makes about seven hundred roubles a month," said Peppone after a quick mental calculation.

The two girls exchanged a few words in Russian together and then Comrade Petrovna went on:

"It all depends on the purchasing power of the lira. How much does it cost, in roubles, to buy a man's suit or a pair of shoes?"

"That varies, according to the quality," put in Don Camillo. "A suit may cost anywhere between seven and fourteen hundred roubles; a pair of shoes anywhere from seventy to three hundred and fifty."

"What about the suit you are wearing?" asked Comrade Petrovna's room-mate of Peppone, fingering its luxurious senatorial fabric.

"Forty thousand liras," he replied.

"That's about one thousand three hundred and fifty roubles," interpolated Don Camillo.

"But to return to Scamoggia," said Peppone, "I repeat that he's a special case. Scamoggia . . ."

"Scamoggia, Scamoggia!" exclaimed the room-mate. "I'm always hearing that name. Is he the individual who behaved so dreadfully at the Tifiz *kolkhos*? I don't see how such a fellow can keep on belonging to the Party."

"He's not a bad fellow at all," said Peppone. "You mustn't judge him from appearances. He's a sharp-witted and loyal Party man."

"Perhaps his parents were unenlightened and didn't bring him up the right way."

"No, there's nothing wrong with his family. You have to know Rome to understand him. When Roman men are away from home, they put on a devil-may-care air. But within their own four walls they don't dare open their mouths for fear of their wives."

"Is Scamoggia afraid of his wife?" the room-mate inquired.

"Not yet. He hasn't got one," said Peppone, laughing. "But once he's married he'll be like all the rest."

Comrade Nadia Petrovna came back into the conversation with a question about Italian citrus-fruit production, which Peppone answered with a volley of statistics. She listened attentively and insisted on serving a second cup of coffee. Then she offered to guide the two men back to the hotel, but they insisted that they could find it alone. On the way, Peppone remarked that few Italian women had achieved such political maturity as that of Comrade Nadia Petrovna and her friend.

"Can you imagine one of our girls interested in heavy industry and fruit production in the Soviet Union?"

"No, I can't," said Don Camillo with a dead-pan expression. "An Italian girl is interested only in the young man who's courting her. She wants to make sure he isn't married, to find out about his family background, salary and reputation."

Peppone came to a sudden halt, as if some suspicion were crossing his mind.

"Are you insinuating that . . ."

"I'm insinuating nothing," retorted Don Camillo. "No Communist senator would come to Moscow as a marriage broker. He has more important things to do than to look out for pretty girls for his Party comrades."

"Quite right!" roared Peppone, oblivious of his companion's irony. "Pretty girls are far from my thoughts, and so are married women, in spite of the fact that my wife wants me to bring back some furs just like her neighbour's."

This was obviously a sore point, and when he had got it off his chest he felt better. It was ten o'clock in the evening and an icy wind swept through the deserted streets. Moscow seemed like the capital of Soviet melancholy.

14

THE NEXT-TO-LAST WAVE

THEY left Moscow for the airport by bus early in the morning, when there was no one to be seen except street cleaners. Young girls and middle-aged women were spraying the streets with water, running mechanical sweepers and brushing up what these left behind with brooms. Don Camillo pointed out to Peppone how their every gesture seemed to indicate pride in the privilege of doing a man's work.

"It's a comforting sight," he concluded, "and one you can't see anywhere except in the Soviet Union."

"I shall be still more comforted on the day when in our own country we conscript priests for this job," mumbled Peppone.

An icy wind which seemed to come straight from the tundras of Siberia blew, unimpeded, through the empty streets. Only in the vast Red Square did it find human targets. What looked like bundles of rags, waiting for the street cleaners to come and carry them away, revealed themselves on second glance to be pilgrims lined up for the ritual visit to the mausoleum. Peasants from Uzbekistan, Georgia, Irkutsk and other remote parts of Russia had been ousted from their trains in the middle of the night and now sat, huddled together like sheep, on their suitcases, until such time as the approach to the tomb should be opened.

"Comrade," said Don Camillo, "how different this is from the days when poor mujiks travelled in wagons to St. Petersburg and camped out for days in the park until they had a chance to see the Tsar and his German bride."

"It's one thing to be a slave performing an act of submission to a tyrant and another to be a free citizen paying tribute to his liberator," Peppone retorted.

"Besides the fact that many of them come to make sure of the fact that Lenin and Stalin are really dead."

Peppone smiled blandly.

"When I think that by midnight tomorrow I shall be unloading the lot of you at the Milan railway station, I have to pinch myself to be sure it isn't a dream. Enjoy your fun while you can. The time is running out. . . ."

The adventure was nearly over. At nine o'clock the plane would disembark them at S., where they were to visit a shipyard, then they were to travel for three hours by boat to the city of O. and board another plane for Berlin. The boat trip was Comrade Oregov's idea. Planes, trains, buses, trolleys and subways had all contributed to a demonstration of Soviet efficiency in the field of transportation, but a voyage by sea was necessary to complete it. Comrade Oregov had submitted his final project to the higher-ups and was visibly proud that it had been accepted.

Punctually at nine o'clock the plane landed at S. The airfield was small, commensurate with the size of the town which had no importance except for its shipyard. In the broad, well-defended harbour, equipped for all possible repairs, there were ships of every description. Comrade Bacciga of Genoa felt immediately at home and was more loquacious than he had ever shown himself before. Among the various craft there was a gleaming new tanker and he described its tonnage and fittings with such familiarity and technical skill that Comrade Oregov felt his guidance was quite unnecessary. He left the little group of Italians in Comrade Nadia Petrovna's charge and went off to the shipyard to arrange the details of the visit.

Comrade Bacciga was in top form. He had a ready answer to every question and exclaimed at intervals:

"Shipbuilding is a Genoese speciality, but these fellows are experts and I take off my hat to them."

Don Camillo was on the alert, and after Bacciga had several times announced this opinion he said:

134

"They're experts, all right, and from away back. Just look at that old schooner! Isn't it a beauty?"

The others followed Don Camillo along the quay until they came to a place where the schooner was in full view. It seemed to be straight out of a nineteenth-century engraving, and yet a fresh coat of paint and varnish made it look at the same time brand-new.

"It's wonderful what respect the Russians have for everything that harks back to their glorious past!" Don Camillo exclaimed. "Comrades, this ship bears witness to a long and noble tradition." Then, after a few minutes of silent admiration, he turned to Bacciga. "Comrade longshoreman, for centuries we have been masters of the art of shipbuilding, but to see a schooner like this we had to come all the way to the Soviet Union."

Comrade Nadia Petrovna had gleaned further information from one of the workers.

"*Tovarisch* is the ship's name," she informed them. "It's used for cadet training."

"Three thousand tons," put in Comrade Bacciga, turning suddenly upon her. "It was originally called the *Cristoforo Colombo* and was a training ship of the Italian Navy."

Comrade Petrovna blushed.

"Forgive me, Comrade," she muttered. Then because she had caught sight of Comrade Oregov, walking towards them in the company of a shipyard official, she went to receive instructions. Peppone tugged at Don Camillo's sleeve and drew him apart from the others.

"Can't you keep that big mouth of yours shut?" he whispered. "Now you've made a real blunder."

"It wasn't a blunder at all," said Don Camillo. "I knew all along that it was the *Cristoforo Colombo*. I'll never forget how badly I felt the day when they took it and the *Giulio Cesare* away."

Comrade Bacciga was standing nearby and Peppone turned to vent his ire on him.

"Couldn't *you* have shut up about it?"

"How could I, Chief?" said Bacciga. "I recognized it from the start."

"A loyal Party member wouldn't have allowed himself any such recognition."

"I may be a loyal Party member, but don't forget that I'm also a professional longshoreman," Bacciga retorted.

"What do you mean by that?"

"Water's water everywhere," said Bacciga, "but there's a big difference between the sea and the Po River. I can't look at the *Cristoforo Colombo* with as little emotion as if it were a river barge."

"The sailors of the famous cruiser *Potemkin* weren't of the same stamp as you," said Peppone sarcastically.

"But then they weren't Genoese," said Bacciga.

At eleven o'clock, with their heads crammed full of statistics, the Italians finished their tour of the shipyard. Their ship was not due to leave for another hour, and while Comrade Nadia Petrovna took the main body of the group to look at the town, Comrade Oregov, Peppone and Don Camillo went to have a drink in a workers' canteen. Comrade Oregov worked on a report of the day's activities, while the other two fortified their spirits for the coming sea voyage. A bitter wind and a mass of clouds in the sky seemed to foretell a storm.

The canteen was ill-lit and dirty, but it served excellent vodka. After the second round Peppone confided to Don Camillo:

"I'm afraid of being seasick. How about you?"

"Not in the least. Priests have been storm-tossed for nearly two thousand years, and they've always managed to come out alive."

"We'll see if you can still crack jokes when we're on the high seas," said Peppone.

Soon the cold wind drove the rest of the group indoors. They didn't look as if they had had much fun, and the dourest of them all was Comrade Curullu. After they had all sat down and a glass of vodka had loosened their tongues, Comrade Curullu proceeded to let off steam.

"Do you know where we have been, Comrade?" he asked Don Camillo.

Don Camillo put away his book of excerpts from Lenin.

"In a church!" Curullu continued. "And do you know what was going on?"

Don Camillo shrugged his shoulders.

"A wedding!" said Curullu excitedly. "Complete with priest

136

and all the usual rubbish!" And he added, turning to Comrade Scamoggia: "And to think that you came here in the hope that there'd be no priests cluttering up the landscape! You should have seen this one! He was sleek and well fed and rigged out in even fancier vestments than ours. And the bride and groom! There they were, all dressed up, with their hands folded in prayer and a sickly, angelic smile on their faces! It was enough to make your stomach turn over."

"A disgusting sight to see in the Soviet Union!" chimed in Comrade Li Friddi. "You'd have thought we were in a backward village in Sicily."

They all looked expectantly at Don Camillo, and he had a ready reply.

"Comrades, the Soviet constitution allows every citizen to practice his own personal religion. And as long as the priests don't corrupt young people under eighteen years of age with their teachings, they are free to exercise their trade. This is nothing so very startling. The whole story of religious persecution is Vatican propaganda."

Comrade Oregov had pricked up his ears and with the aid of Comrade Nadia Petrovna was following the conversation. Don Camillo looked to him for a sign and he hastened to respond.

"He says that Comrade Tarocci is quite right," said Comrade Petrovna. "Paragraph 124 of the Constitution is observed to the letter. The Council for the Orthodox Church and the Council for Religious Bodies see to it that there is complete freedom of conscience; in fact they help the churches solve practical problems."

"That makes it perfectly clear," said Don Camillo. "The priests don't do whatever they please, as they do at home; they do only what the Constitution allows. It's quite a different situation."

"But it adds up to the same thing," protested Comrade Li Friddi. "Priests are priests, wherever you find them."

Don Camillo laughed.

"Comrade, in this enormous country there are only twenty-six thousand churches and thirty-five thousand clergy."

"That's too many of both," muttered Comrade Curullu.

"Remember that in 1917 there were forty-six thousand

churches and fifty thousand priests, and in 1945 there were only four thousand churches and five thousand priests," said Don Camillo.

"Is that true?" Comrade Curullu asked incredulously, turning to Comrade Oregov.

After the usual translation Comrade Nadia Petrovna replied on his behalf:

"Those figures are substantially correct. Today priests and their churches receive no money except from their parishioners. During the war the Orthodox Church gave full patriotic support to the war effort. And the Party uses non-violent, dissuasive means to combat superstition."

But vodka caused Comrade Curullu to give further vent to his disillusionment.

"Comrade," he said to Comrade Petrovna, "if in the last fourteen years the number of priests has grown from five thousand to thirty-five thousand, how can you say that there has been a combat against superstition?"

Comrade Petrovna hesitated a moment before relaying this question to Comrade Oregov, and he listened to her with a bowed head, as if he were personally responsible for this betrayal Finally he looked up and threw out his arms in despair. There was no need for Comrade Nadia Petrovna to translate for him. This was the end of the discussion. Comrade Oregov returned to working over his report and the visitors spoke of other things. The canteen was filled with smoke, and Don Camillo felt a need of fresh air. He went out on to the street, and Peppone followed after. The wind had died down and they were able to stroll quietly up and down, side by side. Finally Peppone exclaimed:

"Thirty-five thousand priests. After a bloody revolution and thirty-two years of sacrifice on behalf of the people!"

"Don't get excited, Comrade," said Don Camillo soothingly. "Numbers shouldn't alarm you. These Russian priests are only government employees. They call the Pope an enemy of peace, and their old Patriarch Alexis once referred to Stalin as having been 'sent by God'. But although Communism has won over the priests it has lost the war against religion. And it has lost two other wars: the war against the peasants and the war against the *bourgeoisie*. After four decades of struggle the Soviet Union has gained atomic supremacy and conquered the moon; it has installed science in the place of superstition and subjugated both its own people and the peoples of the satellite nations; it has killed off ten million peasants in the process of agricultural reform and eliminated the old middle class. Yet today, in their search for God, the Russians are spending their hard-earned roubles to build churches. Agricultural production is below the pre-Revolutionary level and the Government has been forced to allow the peasants to have a portion of privately owned land and to sell its produce on the free market. At the same time there is a new and increasingly powerful *bourgeoisie*. Don't take offence, Comrade, but you yourself, with your well-tailored, double-breasted dark blue suit, the two salaries which you receive as a senator and a Party leader, your bank account and your intention of buying a high-powered car, are a budding bourgeois. Can you deny it?"

"What do you mean, a 'high-powered car'?" I'm going to buy a second-hand standard model."

Don Camillo shook his head.

"It isn't the horsepower that counts; it's the principle of the thing."

Peppone took a leather case out of his pocket and extracted a big Tuscan-type cigar. Don Camillo, who for the past two days had been longing for the familiar aroma, heaved a formidable sigh and said bitterly:

"There you are! The *bourgeoisie* feast while the people are famished!"

Angrily Peppone broke the cigar in two and offered half of it to Don Camillo.

"Thirty-five thousand priests weren't enough," he muttered; "you had to come and join them!"

At this moment they heard the ship whistle.

The *Partisan* was a light but powerful and up-to-date craft, which ploughed steadily and speedily through the water. The first hour of the voyage left nothing to be desired. Unfortunately the devil intervened; the sky darkened again and the wind began to blow. In order that the giant waves should not throw the ship on to the rocky shore, the captain steered farther out to sea in search of calmer weather. But the storm only increased in intensity and soon the ship was dangerously drifting. A sailor came down into the saloon and hurled a pile of canvas objects on the floor.

"The captain says to put on the life jackets and go up on deck," said Comrade Nadia Petrovna.

On deck all hell seemed to have broken loose. Rain poured down from the sky and waves beat mercilessly against the sides of the ship. The sky was pitch black and the wind was howling. The wheel rotated wildly and two lifeboats were swept away. All eyes were turned on the captain, who stood clinging to the rail of the bridge. He knew that all those present were looking to him for safety, but he avoided their gaze and stared helplessly out over the water. How long would the ship hold together? A giant wave lifted the stern and it seemed as if the bow would sink into the sea. After the wave had broken over the deck and the ship had regained its balance, the passengers looked around and counted their numbers. They were all there: Peppone and his group, Comrade Oregov and Comrade Petrovna, the captain and the six members of the crew. Huddled together, holding on to whatever object came to hand, they had miraculously survived the first inundation. But how would they manage to survive another? The ship slid along the side of the next wave and down into the hollow. Then it came to the surface again, but one of the portholes was shattered and the hold began to fill with water. Hopelessly Peppone turned to Don Camillo:

"For the love of God, do something!" he shouted.

Don Camillo summoned all his self-control.

"Lord," he said, "I am happy to die in Your service."

Forgetful of where he was and of the fact that none of his companions except Peppone knew him except under the name of Comrade Tarocci, he bared his head and reached into his pocket for the crucifix concealed in a fountain pen. He held it up over their heads and they fell on to their knees before him, even Comrade Petrovna, the captain and the crew. Only Comrade Oregov kept his cap pulled down over his eyes and clung to the stairway which led to the bridge, looking at the sight with amazement.

"Lord," Don Camillo prayed, "have mercy on Your unfortunate children. . . ."

As he spoke a wave dashed against the side of the ship and another threatened to break over the deck.

"Ego vos absolvo a peccatis vestris, in nomine Patris et Filii et Spiritus Sancti. . . ."

He traced a sign of the cross in the stormy air, and his hearers crossed themselves and crept forward to kiss the crucifix. A mountain of water broke over the deck, but God had other designs for them and did not allow it to sweep them away. They rose to their feet, suddenly confident that the worst was over. All of them had noticed that Comrade Oregov had neither taken off his cap nor fallen to his knees, but only now did they mentally question the consequences. He was standing stock-still, with clenched jaws and blazing eyes. Comrade Nadia Petrovna, the captain and the members of the crew were alarmed by his menacing stare, but the Italians were so happy to be alive they paid no attention.

The ship was still shaken by the storm, but the sailors were able to man the pumps while the passengers went to wring out their drenched clothes. Comrade Oregov's attitude was quickly forgotten. As the storm gradually subsided shipboard life returned to normal. Two hours later men were talking among themselves just as they did every day. After all, nothing so very extraordinary had happened. A heavy sea, decks awash with water, a shattered porthole, two lifeboats swept away—the everyday occurrences of a sea voyage. No one thought of Comrade Oregov until the ship reached port and Comrade Nadia Petrovna mentioned his name. The gangplank was in place and Peppone and his group were about to walk down it when Comrade Nadia Petrovna planted herself in their way.

"We must wait for Comrade Oregov," she said with a tremor in her voice.

Just then the captain came along and led her away below deck. He brought her back a few minutes later and smilingly shook Don Camillo's hand.

"Kak trevòga, tak do Bògo," he said.

"We can disembark," Comrade Petrovna explained. "Unfortunately one of the last waves carried Comrade Oregov away. The Party has lost an able and devoted servant. A valiant soldier is dead."

When they set foot on land, Don Camillo looked anxiously out to sea, half-expecting to see the ghost of Comrade Oregov between the lowering clouds and the storm-tossed water.

"May God forgive you your sins!" he said to himself, trying to convince himself of the truth of the captain's story. If the captain had written in his log that two lifeboats and Comrade Oregov had been lost at sea, what reason was there to doubt him?

The departure of the Berlin plane was delayed by the storm. In the bus which carried them to the airfield Don Camillo found himself sitting across from Comrade Scamoggia.

"Well, Comrade," he said, "the time has come to say good-bye. You'll be staying on after we have gone away."

"No, I'm going with you," Scamoggia replied.

"Wasn't Comrade Petrovna able to persuade you to stay?"

"I never even mentioned the possibility. I feel I'm still needed by the Italian Communist Party."

"Very good, Comrade! A Party stalwart must subordinate love to duty."

Comrade Scamoggia sighed and looked out of the window. The bus came to a stop at the airfield gate and they all got out. Comrade Nadia Petrovna and Peppone went into the office with the group's travelling papers. The police official glanced over them and passed on the list of names to his interpreter, who proceeded to call them out one by one.

"Pierto Bacciga. . . ."

Bacciga came in, and both Peppone and Comrade Petrovna confirmed his identity. When his name had been checked, Comrades Capece, Gibetti, Li Friddi and Peratto followed.

"Walter Rondella. . . ."

Peppone forgot that Comrade Rondella had been ignominiously shipped back home. He looked up and saw the Neapolitan barber whom they had met at the Tifiz *kolkhos* standing brazenly before him. Already he had approved the fellow's name as that of Rondella and Comrade Petrovna had assented. When Comrade Tarocci was called in Peppone was tempted to disavow him. But this vengeful impulse had no time to take root in his mind.

"Ten entries, ten exits," said the interpreter, as he handed the papers back to Peppone.

As they walked towards the plane Don Camillo asked Comrade

Petrovna to tell him the exact meaning of the Russian words which the ship captain had pronounced at the moment of disembarkment.

"He was summing up what happened during the storm," she replied. "In dire extremity man remembers his God.' "

"An outdated Russian proverb," muttered Don Camillo.

As the travellers climbed into the plane Comrade Petrovna shook hands with them, one by one. When it came to the Neapolitan barber, who was also a refugee from Rumania, it was all she could do to contain her laughter. But the sight of Comrade Scamoggia froze the smile on her lips. Don Camillo was the last to climb aboard.

"Good-bye," he said.

"Pray for me, Comrade," Comrade Petrovna whispered, and there were tears rolling down her cheeks.

For a long time after the plane had left the ground Don Camillo could not stop thinking of the sorrowful expression in her eyes. Then he looked down at the endless expanse of mist-covered fields and remembered a Russian phrase which he had jotted down in his notebook: *"Spasitjel mira, spasi Rossiu!*—Saviour of the world, save Russia!"

15

THE STORY THAT HAS NO END

"LORD," said Don Camillo to the crucified Christ above the altar, "for two whole weeks I've been back in my own familiar surroundings, and I still can't get over the feeling of distress from which I suffered during my travels. Mind You, Lord, it was distress, not fear; I had no reason to be afraid. I was deeply ashamed, like an old soldier used to fighting out in the open when he finds himself under false colours, charged with penetrating the enemy ranks in order to plot their destruction. The crucifix concealed in a fountain pen, the breviary masked as a volume of excerpts from Lenin, the clandestine Masses celebrated before a bedside table! . . ."

"Don't torment yourself, Don Camillo," Christ answered gently. "You weren't a coward, trying to knife his neighbour in the back; you were trying to help him. Would you refuse a dying man a drink of water if it were necessary to lower yourself to practise deceit in order to bring it to him? The heroism of a soldier of Christ is humility; his only enemy is pride. Blessed are the meek . . ."

"Lord, you are speaking from a Cross that has all the glory of a throne, a throne which you won in open battle, without the humiliation of disguise. You never appeared to men in the likeness of the Devil. . . ."

"Don Camillo, didn't the Son of God humble himself when

he consented to live like a man and die like a common criminal? Just look at your God, at His wounded side and the ignominious crown of thorns on His head!"

"Lord, I am looking at You," insisted Don Camillo, "but I see only the divine light of Your supreme sacrifice. No light at all, not even the wavering flare of a match, illuminates the wretched figure of 'Comrade Don Camillo'."

Christ smiled.

"What about the light you kindled in the eyes of the old peasant woman of Grevinec? And the candle you lit on the unmarked grave of a soldier whose family did not even have the satisfaction of knowing where he lay? Then think back to the storm at sea and the terror of your miserable companions at the thought that their last hour had come. When you held up your crucifix and asked God to forgive them their sins, did they ridicule the transformation of Comrade Tarocci into a priest of the Church? No, they fell down on their knees and tried to kiss that tiny figure with the collapsible arms. Haven't you ever wondered what got into them?"

"But, Lord, any other priest would have behaved the same way," murmured Don Camillo.

"Remember that only Peppone knew who you were. For all the others you were simply Comrade Tarocci. How do you explain their change of heart?"

Don Camillo threw out his arms. Only now did he realize what an incredible episode it had been.

"You see," said Christ, "that some light must have been shed by 'Comrade Don Camillo'."

For most of the two weeks since his return Don Camillo had been trying to put his travel notes in order for the Bishop's perusal. It was no easy job for, although the Bishop was old and forgetful, he had very exacting notions of grammar.

Ever since they had said good-bye at the Milan railway station, Don Camillo had had no news of Peppone. The Neapolitan barber had dropped out of the group in West Berlin; Comrade Tavan, with his three stalks of wheat, had left the train at Verona, and Don Camillo had got off, along with Comrade Bacciga and Comrade Peratto, at Milan.

"Shouldn't you travel with us as far as Parma or Reggio

Emilia?" Scamoggia had asked him. But Don Camillo claimed to have urgent business in Milan. This was quite true because there he had left his cassock and he was in a hurry to recover it. Peppone had counted his little troop and just as Don Camillo was leaving the train he heard him shout gaily at Scamoggia:

"There are only six of us from now on. Take this money and buy six bottles of wine. I want to treat you."

Peppone's laughter continued to ring in his ears and he racked his brain to know what had caused it. On the evening of the fourteenth day after his homecoming Peppone himself turned up to give him an explanation. For a moment Don Camillo failed to recognize his old friend. He had left him wearing a double-breasted dark-blue suit, a white shirt and a grey silk tie, and now here he was in his outfit of times long gone by: a corduroy jacket, wrinkled trousers, a cap pulled down over the back of his head, a handkerchief knotted around his neck and a peasant's black wool cape over his shoulders. Don Camillo stared at him for some minutes and then shook his head.

"How silly of me to forget," he exclaimed, "that the representative of the working class has to carry his load in a senatorial suit in Rome and in the rig of a mayor in his native village. It must be hard lines for you to travel only at night. Won't you sit down?"

"I can say what I have to say standing up," grumbled Peppone. "I've come to pay my debt." He pulled a candle out of his pocket and put it down on Don Camillo's desk. "This is to thank the Lord for having saved me from shipwreck."

" 'In dire extremity man remembers his God', as the Russian sea captain said," answered Don Camillo. "Usually when the extremity is past he proceeds to forget Him. I congratulate you on your good memory."

"And this is to thank the Lord for saving me from a certain priest whom the Devil sent to torment me," added Peppone lugubriously, drawing forth another candle, a giant one, four feet long and eight inches in diameter.

Don Camillo's jaw dropped.

"I had it made to order," Peppone explained. "It's big, if you like, but if it were really to represent the danger of that priest it would have to be four times bigger."

"You flatter me," said Don Camillo. "A country priest doesn't really deserve such consideration."

"There are country priests more dangerous than the Pope in person," said Peppone. He threw a parcel and three letters on to the desk and added: "These were sent to me with the request that I should turn them over to Comrade Tarocci. I don't like it, not a bit. I warn you that if I receive any more I shall burn them."

Don Camillo opened the parcel, which was full of photographs, and looked hastily at one of the letters, which was addressed in the same writing.

"They are . . ." he began.

"I'm not sticking my nose into your business, Father," said Peppone.

"But they pertain to Comrade Tarocci, who as cell-leader is obliged to inform his superior. They are pictures sent by Comrade Peratto, and he says I am to do what I please with them. Look at this group, where we are in the front row together. Doesn't it interest you?"

Peppone snatched the picture, examined it, and said between clenched teeth:

"I hope you're not going to get me into any more trouble!"

"Don't worry, Senator. Comrade Peratto has sent another set, of a strictly unofficial nature, which he asks me to place without mentioning his name. The Party doesn't pay him very well and he wants to make a bit of money."

"Would you play a dirty trick like that?"

"It's up to you. What if we fail to give him satisfaction and he sends a picture that has me in it to a Party paper?"

Peppone lowered himself into a chair and wiped the perspiration from his forehead. While he looked through the pictures Don Camillo read the second letter and informed him of its contents.

"This one is from Comrade Tavan. He thanks me for my good advice and says it has done wonders for his mother. He has planted the three stalks of wheat and goes to look at them every day. 'If they were to whither,' he says, 'I'd feel that my brother was even more dead than before.' And he sends his best wishes to the Comrade Senator."

Peppone only grunted in reply.

The third letter was a very short one, enclosing some money.

"It's from Comrade Gibetti," said Don Camillo. "When he got home he began to wonder about the contents of the Russian letter which told the story of the girl with whom he was in love. Finally he got it translated and found that she was dead. He has sent me a thousand liras to say a Mass for her soul. I'm going to send back the money and tell him I'll say a Mass for her every month."

Peppone brought his fist down on the desk.

"Who the devil told these fellows that you were a priest?" he thundered. "That's what I'd like to know!"

"Nobody told them. They simply got the idea."

"But how did they get it?"

"It was a question of seeing the light," said Don Camillo. "Since I'm no electrician, I can't explain."

Peppone shook his head.

"Perhaps the fault is mine. Perhaps there on the ship my tongue slipped and I called you 'Father'."

"I don't remember your doing any such thing."

Peppone showed him a picture in which Comrade Oregov occupied a prominent place.

"When I saw him for the last time," he said with bowed head, "the fury of the storm was over. How did it happen that a wave washed him into the sea? What happened up on the deck after we had gone below?"

"Only God can say," said Don Camillo. "And He alone knows how often the poor fellow is in my thoughts."

Peppone gave a deep sigh and got up.

"Here are the pictures I'd choose," he said.

"Agreed," said Don Camillo. "And what am I to do with the candles?"

Peppone shrugged his shoulders.

"The big one can be for the escape from shipwreck," he muttered.

"That's what you said for the smaller," Don Camillo reminded him.

"The smaller can be for the escape from the priest," shouted Peppone, and he went away without saying good-bye.

Don Camillo went over to the church. There was no candlestick large enough to contain the giant candle, but he managed to fit it into a big bronze vase. When he had put both candles on the altar and lit them Don Camillo said:

"Lord, Peppone is mindful of you."

"And of you, too, if I'm not mistaken," Christ replied.

When the Bishop had read Don Camillo's report, he sent for him. "Now give me the whole story," he said.

Don Camillo talked for several hours uninterruptedly and when he had finished the Bishop exclaimed:

"It's incredible! Conversion of Comrade Tavan and Comrade Gibetti, liberation of a Neapolitan barber, communion given to the old Polish woman, the marriage of her daughter to an Italian veteran and the baptism of their six children, the veteran's confession and rehabilitation, a Mass for the Dead celebrated in a forgotten cemetery and the absolution given to eighteen persons in imminent danger of death! And besides this you became a cell leader. All in the space of six days in the territory of the anti-Christ! I can hardly believe it!"

"Your Grace, besides my word there are the photographs and the letters. And I have a senator for a witness."

"A senator!" groaned the old man. "Then the damage is irreparable."

Don Camillo looked bewildered.

"My son, can't you see that under these conditions I'll simply have to raise you to the rank of *monsignore*."

"*Domine, non sum dignus*," he murmured, raising his eyes to heaven.

The Bishop shook his head.

"Just what I said myself, many years ago, but no one paid any attention. God be with you!"

In the month that followed, the Russian adventure ceased to occupy Don Camillo's mind. But one morning as he was coming out of the church he caught Smilzo pasting a poster on the rectory wall. He did not make his presence known but when Smilzo came down from the ladder and almost knocked him over, he asked:

"Comrade, what if someone were to tear down your poster while the paste is still fresh and ram it down your throat?"

"Father, no man alive would do a thing like that!" Smilzo replied.

"Just suppose such a man *is* alive and standing here before you!"

He had taken hold of the lapels of Smilzo's ragged jacket and seemed to have no intention of letting them go.

"All right. . . . That would be a very different situation." Don Camillo went on in a different tone:

"Look here; do I ever stick up posters on your 'People's Palace'? Why do you have to inflict your political idiocies on me?"

"This isn't politics," said Smilzo. "It's the announcement of a cultural event."

Without releasing his grip on Smilzo's jacket Don Camillo looked up and read a notice to the effect that Senator Giuseppe Bottazzi was to talk the following evening about his recent trip to the Soviet Union. A period of questions and answers would follow.

"You're right," he said, letting go of Smilzo's jacket. "It's a strictly cultural proposition. Where can I get a ticket?"

"Everybody's welcome and entrance is free," said Smilzo, straightening out his lapels. "And there are no holds barred on the questions."

"Even questions from me?"

"Even from the Bishop," said Smilzo, beating a cautious retreat. "We particularly want to educate the clergy."

He had retreated too far for Don Camillo to lay hands on him again, and besides the priest had other matters on his mind. He went into the rectory and picked up his pen. Half an hour later a boy delivered a letter to Peppone, which read as follows:

"*Dear Comrade Senator: I can hardly wait to come to to-morrow night's meeting. Just let me submit one advance question: Why are you looking for trouble? Best regards from—Comrade Tarocci.*"

In the late afternoon Peppone was unexpectedly called to Rome and the next morning Smilzo had to add a postscript to the poster: *Because of the unavoidable absence of the speaker the meeting is postponed to an indefinite date.*

Once more, when he climbed down from the ladder, Smilzo found himself face to face with Don Camillo.

"Too bad!" said the priest. "Who knows how long the clergy will have to remain wrapped in the ignorance of the Dark Ages?"

Smilzo quickly picked up his ladder and retreated to a position of safety.

"Don't you worry, Father. We'll open their eyes!"

No later date was ever announced, and after rain had washed the poster away it received no further mention. Six months went by, and because Don Camillo had no opportunity of talking about his Russian trip he began to wonder whether it was all a dream. But one morning, when he was putting his papers in order, the sexton came to tell him that a stranger was at the door. To his utter amazement Don Camillo saw, over the sexton's shoulder, the face of Comrade Nanni Scamoggia.

"How did you get here?" he asked.

"There are such things as trains," said Scamoggia. "And I persuaded Comrade Bottazzi to give me your address."

"I see," said Don Camillo, although he didn't see at all. "What's the reason for your visit?"

Scamoggia was still the same devil-may-care fellow as before. This was quite plain from the way he lit his cigarette and threw himself into a chair. But his nonchalance did not deceive Don Camillo, who remembered the tears in Comrade Nadia Petrovna's eyes.

"I have a problem, Comrade . . . I mean Father. It's that girl. . . ."

"Yes. What happened to her?"

"She came to Rome two months ago with a Russian women's delegation. When they left she cut loose and stayed behind."

"So what did you do?"

"In my Party position I couldn't have dealings with a traitor to the Soviet Union. . . ."

"So what next?"

"In order to marry her I had to leave the Party," said Scamoggia, tossing his cigarette butt into the fire.

"Is that the problem?"

"No, it's this. We've been married for a month now, and every day she says the civil ceremony isn't enough. She wants a church wedding."

"I don't see much to worry about," Don Camillo observed calmly.

"You wouldn't," said Scamoggia. "But don't forget that the very sight of a priest turns my stomach."

"I understand, Comrade. You have a right to your own opinions. But if that's the case, why have you come to me?"

"Because if a priest does have to be dragged into it, I'd rather he were a regular fellow. And you're a sort of ex-comrade, like myself. In fact, you're my former cell leader."

"Not a bad idea," said Don Camillo.

Scamoggia went to open the door and shouted:

"Nadia!"

A second later Comrade Petrovna entered the room. As soon as she saw Don Camillo, she rushed to kiss his hand.

"How revolting!" muttered Scamoggia. "So short a time in this country and she knows all the rules!"

All their papers were in good order and the marriage ceremony was a rapid affair. Peppone had to accept the job of giving the bride away. But he did it with a smile. Before the couple went away Don Camillo took the girl aside and asked her to tell him the true story of Comrade Oregov.

"It was an ugly affair," she explained. "When the rest of us went below deck, Comrade Oregov ordered the captain to lock us all up and put handcuffs on you and Comrade Bottazzi. He raved about betrayal, and Vatican spies and commissions of inquiry. Finally he appeared to be quite mad. He and the captain came to blows and the captain knocked him against the rail. Just then a wave swept him away. This is the whole truth, but only the captain, you and I know it. It's all very sad. . . ."

After the bride and groom had left, Don Camillo and Peppone sat warming their hands at the fire in the study. For some time they were silent, and then Don Camillo exclaimed:

"I must jot that down before I forget it."

He pulled the famous notebook out of his pocket and said aloud as he was writing:

"Two more conversions and another marriage . . ."

"Put down whatever you like," roared Peppone. "It will all go on your bill on the day of the Great Uprising!"

"Won't you give me a small discount?" asked Don Camillo. "I'm an ex-comrade, after all."

"We'll let you choose the place where you are to be hanged," jeered Peppone.

"I can tell you that right now," retorted Don Camillo. "Right beside you!"

It was a cold winter day and the mist rising from the river clouded over the end of this newly finished story, which already was older than time.

A Note from the Author

THIS book—the latest of the series of *The Little World of Don Camillo*—was published in instalments in the last fourteen issues (1959) of *Candido*, the Milanese weekly which I founded in 1945 and which played a propaganda role of recognized value in the important general election of 1948 when it contributed to the defeat of the Communist ticket.

Candido is no longer in existence. It suspended publication in 1962, chiefly because the Italians of the "economic miracle" and the "opening to the Left" have lost all interest in the anti-Communist struggle. The present generation of Italians is made up of "purists", that is, of conscientious objectors, anti-nationalists, and do-gooders. It grew up in the school of political corruption, of neo-realist films and of the sexual-sociological literature of Left-wing writers. It is not a generation at all, but a degeneration.

What a wonderful place was the poverty-stricken Italy of 1945! We came back from the starvation of the Nazi prison camps to find our country a heap of rubble. But through the ruins in which so many innocent victims had died a fresh breeze of hope was blowing. What a difference there is between the material poverty of 1945 and the spiritual poverty of the newly rich of 1963! The wind that blows among the skyscrapers of the "economic miracle" stinks of sex and sewerage and death. In the prosperous *dolce-vita* Italy all hope of a better world is dead.

There is only an unholy mixture of hell and holy water, as we face a new generation of priests who are no brothers of Don Camillo.

In the newly rich Red Italy *Candido* could not survive, and indeed it died. And the story which came out in instalments in 1959, although it lives on because of the vitality of its characters, is out-of-date. Its essentially light-hearted quarrel with Communism is understandable only in the light of the time at which it was written.

The reader may at this point object: "If the attitude towards Communism has changed and your story is out-of-date, then why didn't you bury it in the tomb of *Candido*?" To which I reply: "Because some few people have not changed their attitude and I have an obligation of loyalty towards them."

I dedicate my story to the American soldiers who died in Korea, the last brave defenders of the besieged West, to them and to their dear ones, who have some reason to hold to their opinions.

Likewise I dedicate it to the Italian soldiers who died in Russia and to the sixty-three thousand of them who were shut up in Soviet prison-camps and of whose fate nothing is known. To them in particular I dedicate the chapter entitled *Three Stalks of Wheat*.

I dedicate it further to the three hundred priests who were assassinated by the Communists in the province of Emilia during the bloody days of Italy's "liberation", and to the late Pope Pius XII, who blasted Communists and their accomplices. And to the Primate of Hungary, the indomitable Cardinal Mindzenty and to the heroically martyred Church of his country. To all of these I dedicate the chapter entitled *Christ's Secret Agent*.

The last chapter, *A Story That Has No End*, I dedicate to the late Pope John XXIII. This is not only for obvious reasons but also (if the reader will forgive me) for a motive of a very personal nature. After Pope John died in June 1963, the statements issued by public figures the world over included one from Vincent Auriol, the socialist president of France when Pope John was Apostolic Nunico to Paris. In this statement Auriol said (and I quote him verbatim): "On New Year's Day of 1952, mindful of my disputes with the mayor and the parish priest of my town, he sent me as a present a book by Guareschi, *The*

Little World of Don Camillo, with these words on the flyleaf: 'To Monsieur Vincent Auriol, president of the French Republic, for his amusement and for his spiritual profit, from J. Roncalli, Apostolic Nuncio.' "

The Don Camillo of 1959 is the same as the Don Camillo of 1952, and I have written this story—even if it is out-of-date —for the "amusement" and (forgive my heavy-handedness) for the "spiritual profit" of the few friends I have left in the disjointed world of today.

Giovanni Guareschi

Roncole-Verdi, 16 August, 1963

DON CAMILLO AND THE DEVIL

First published August 1957

OPERATION SAINT BABILA

SAINT BABILA was perpetually in Don Camillo's way, but Don Camillo didn't know how in the world to get rid of him. On that far-away day when he first came to take over the parish he found Saint Babila in the sacristy, and there he left him. Every now and then he moved him from one corner to another, but Saint Babila continued to be cumbersome, because he was in the form of a life-size terracotta statue, six feet tall and heavy as lead.

In the beginning the statue must have been properly robed and vested, with artistically painted face and hands, but the passage of time had caused all the ornamentation to fall to pieces, leaving the terracotta crude and bare. If it hadn't been for the worn inscription "Saint Babila, B——" (for Bishop) on the base, no one would have thought there was anything holy about it. Several generations of acolytes had chosen to use it as a coat-rack, and as a result the head and shoulders looked as if they had been thoroughly sandpapered. From the waist down it might have been modelled with a shovel, and from the waist up brushed with a chicken feather.

For years, then, Saint Babila had been a nuisance to Don Camillo. Any number of times he had thought of getting rid of him, but even though it is made of identical material, a saint's statue is not the same thing as a chipped kitchen pot. You can't take a hammer and smash it, or simply toss it into the dustbin. And even if banished to the cellar or woodshed it remains just as cumbersome as before. Don Camillo had in mind at one point to haul it all the way to the barn, but he was afraid that the loft floor would collapse under its weight. If only it had been made out of bronze, he could have melted it down and recast it as a bell. But how can a sacred image, sculptured in terracotta, be destroyed without profanity? One day, however, Don Camillo did find the answer, and he hurried at once to the sacristy to talk it over with Saint Babila.

The saint stood in one corner, his worn head and shoulders emerging from a crude vestment whose folds, moulded by some rustic potter, made it look as if it were a piece of corrugated sheet-iron.

"I have it!" said Don Camillo. "And it's for your good as well as mine." Then, removing the incense-pot censer which an irreverent acolyte had hung round the saint's neck, he continued:

"This is no place for you. Here there's no telling who may lay dirty hands upon you and fail to show the respect that is your due. I'm going to take you to a refuge where no one can touch you and you can abide in safety for ever and for ever. No, I'm not going to bury you underground, either. Underground means death, and running water is life-giving. . . ."

Don Camillo fancied he detected a grimace on the saint's worn face, and he protested impatiently:

"What about the 'Christ of the Deep Sea' near Portofino? Wasn't his statue purposely lowered into the ocean bottom? You've no reason to make trouble! . . ."

Saint Babila made no trouble, and that very night Don Camillo proceeded to carry out his plan. It required an immense physical effort, because the statue weighed over three hundred pounds. Finally, however, without being seen by a single soul, he succeeded in removing it from the sacristy and loading it on to a wagon. A few minutes later, with his overcoat pulled up to his hat-brim, he got into the driver's seat and drove towards the river. The night seemed particularly propitious to an Operation Saint Babila. It was freezing cold and the countryside was deserted.

When they reached the river, Don Camillo persuaded the horse to go all the way down to the water's edge, where with the help of two long boards he pushed the statue on to a rowing-boat. Then, having loosened the rope by which the boat was tied up, he took the oar and rowed towards midstream. He had a very clear idea of where he was going. The river, at this point, was so wide that it seemed like the sea and had a particularly deep bottom. This was to be the resting-place of Saint Babila.

At the last minute the saint abandoned his docile behaviour and made so much trouble that Don Camillo nearly fell overboard. But eventually the statue resigned itself to making the plunge and disappeared into the river.

When he got back home Don Camillo put the horse in the stable and before going to bed went to pay his respects to the Christ over the main altar.

"Lord," he said, "thank you for not letting Saint Babila drag me into the water. I have reason to be happy tonight, because Saint Babila is settled *per omnia saecula saeculorum,* and that means for ever and ever."

"*Amen,*" murmured Christ with a smile. "But remember, Don Camillo, that in human events there are no absolutes."

Operation Saint Babila had taken place between eleven-thirty and one-forty-five of a freezing November night, without a single soul to see. Don Camillo had conducted it with extreme prudence and had no cause for worry. But since in human events there are no absolutes, it happened that at one-forty-seven of the same night Comrade Peppone, the Communist mayor of the village, was awakened by a pole knocking against the shutters of his bedroom window. He got up and cautiously opened the shutters, to find that one of his Party henchmen, Smilzo, was standing below, at the far end of the pole, trembling with cold and excitement.

"Chief," he shouted, "something very serious has happened."

Peppone went downstairs to open the door. As soon as Smilzo was in the house he exclaimed:

"A sacrilege!"

"A sacrilege?" echoed Peppone. "Who's guilty of a sacrilege?"

"The priest!" shouted Smilzo.

Peppone took hold of Smilzo's ragged jacket and shook him violently.

"Smilzo, you must have been drinking."

"Not I, chief. The priest has committed a sacrilege, I tell you. I saw him with my own eyes and followed him the whole way. Do you remember the dusty statue of Saint Babila that stood in one corner of the sacristy?"

Peppone did remember. "Saint Babila, B——" (for Blessed Virgin, he imagined), he must have read those words a thousand times on the base of the statue, which had most often been seen serving as a rack for coats and vestments.

"Well, I saw that statue, I tell you. He put it on a wagon and took it down to the river, then he transferred it to a boat and threw it into the water. I didn't see him actually throw it but I heard the splash, and when the boat came back there was no more no statue. That's a sacrilege, Chief!"

This was quite obviously true. Otherwise Don Camillo would not have feared the light of day. If he had done it all alone, in the dead of night, then there must have been something reprehensible about it.

This was the period of "peaceful co-existence", when the Reds changed their line and passed themselves off as quiet folk, with a genuine respect for other people and especially for other people's religion. Peppone wasted no time. He got dressed and went with Smilzo to check up on what had taken place. Peeping through the sacristy window he saw that the statue had disappeared. Then he found the imprint of the horseshoes and the track left by the wagon-wheels, all leading down to the river. On the shore there was a still more important piece of evidence. While Don Camillo was transferring the statue to the boat, a fragment had been chipped off and now lay there, bearing witness to the truth of Smilzo's story. With all these elements in hand, Peppone sent Smilzo to gather his henchmen together. At eleven o'clock the next morning the village was plastered with posters carrying the following message:

"Citizens:

"Under cover of darkness a sacrilegious hand profaned the Lord's House and stole the sacred image of the Virgin Saint Babila. In order to abolish its veneration and to uproot even its memory from the hearts of the faithful, this same sacred image was then, most nefariously, thrown into the river.

"Before this ignoble deed the local section of the Communist Party cannot but lay aside its political enmity towards the clerical intriguers. Along with all good Christians we deplore this loss and intend to organize a searching party, whose mission is to

restore Saint Babila to the place of honour which she held before.
—GIUSEPPE BOTTAZZI."

Everyone that read these words hastened to the church, and since the whole village read them the church was soon over-crowded and Don Camillo was in serious trouble. People wanted to know how, when and why, and he couldn't very well answer: "There was no theft and no sacrilege. I am the one that threw the statue into the river." Suddenly now that the statue was gone, all the villagers, including those who were completely unaware of its existence, declared that it was the church's most treasured possession. Words could not express the resentment they harboured against the thief.

When Don Camillo could stand no more, he threw out his arms in a gesture of despair and fled to the rectory, where he took to his bed with a raging fever.

"Poor Don Camillo!" said his parishioners. "He's overcome by sorrow."

Meanwhile the proponents of the "peaceful co-existence" line had gone into action, and the next morning they were hot on the trail, down by the river. From a motor-boat, where he cut the figure of an admiral, Peppone directed dredging operations. In the area pointed out by Smilzo not a single inch of the river bottom was left untouched. And when the workers came back to the shore for lunch, Peppone announced:

"If we're unsuccessful we'll call upon the union of deep-sea divers. Saint Babila shall be found; we have sworn it before God and the people!"

This fine phrase made the round of the entire village. Meanwhile, after lunch, the dredging was resumed, and soon the search centred about the deepest part of the river. All of a sudden a cry passed from mouth to mouth on the shore:

"They're getting hot!"

And half an hour later there was a loud explosion of joy:

"Saint Babila is found!"

Don Camillo was still nursing his fever and trying to keep his mind off his troubles when they were quite forcibly called to his attention. A crowd of excited men and women burst into his room shouting:

"Father, they've fished up the statue!"

"Father, they're forming a procession on the bank of the river!"

"Father, the procession is on its way, bringing the statue home!"

"The whole village is marching, and a lot more people from the country around!"

"Father, you'll simply have to get up and receive them!"

The procession was indeed drawing near. When Don Camillo sat up in bed and looked out of the window he could see a multitude of people winding their way along and singing: "Look down on the people, Thou Blessed One", to the music of the local brass band. There was nothing to do but get dressed and go downstairs. He threw open the church door and stood there, waiting for Saint Babila.

They had put the statue on a litter, borne on the shoulders of the eight liveliest devils of Peppone's gang, with Peppone himself and his closest cronies preceding it. Behind the litter came the brass band, followed by some two or three thousand people. Those of the villagers who had stayed at home scattered flowers from their windows.

When the head of the procession reached the church square and the litter-bearers were in front of the door, Peppone signalled to them to lay their burden gently down. The winding line broke up and rushed forward. When the crowd had gathered round him Peppone turned to Don Camillo and said in a thundering voice:

"Father, the people's callous but honest hands have brought you back the venerable image of their protectress, Saint Babila, stolen by some sacrilegious criminal but washed and purified in the waters of our country's mightiest river!"

Don Camillo wished for his eyes to be transformed into loaded machine-guns, but all he could do was bow his head as if to say: "Thank you, Mr. Mayor. May the heavens open and strike you dead!"

After this a group of true believers took the place of Peppone's henchmen and Saint Babila was carried triumphantly into the church. Naturally the statue could not be banished to the sacristy. The image of Saint Lucius, patron of dairy-farmers, was moved out of one of the chapels in order to give it an honoured place.

An hour later, when peace and quiet were restored, the wife of Bigio came to the church to have her latest offspring baptized. The baby was a girl, and if she hadn't been the offspring of a rascally infidel, she might have been called pretty.

"What do you want to call her?" asked Don Camillo between clenched teeth.

"Babila," the mother answered defiantly.

"That won't do," said Don Camillo.

"And why not?" said the mother with a sarcastic laugh. "Just because our Party fished the saint out of the river?"

"No," said Don Camillo glumly. "Because Babila is a man's name."

The woman shook her head and turned to look at the saint. On the base was printed: "Saint Babila, B——."

"Saint Babila, Blessed, I suppose," she said, laughing again.

"No," said Don Camillo, "that *B* is for 'Bishop'."

The mother, the godparents and their friends looked at one another disappointedly.

"A bishop!" the mother muttered ill-humouredly. "We might as well have left him at the bottom of the river!"

"Very well, then," said Don Camillo, grinding his teeth; "what's to be the name?"

The little group wore a puzzled air.

"Palmira, like our leader, Palmiro Togliatti," one suggested.

"Marilyn," said the godmother, who was a passionate reader of film magazines.

And Marilyn it was.

2

PEPPONE'S PILGRIMAGE

SELDOM had there been such a miserable autumn; when it didn't rain cats and dogs, it drizzled. If, by virtue of some miracle, the sun peeped out in the morning, by afternoon there was a fog thick enough to be cut with a knife and even wetter than water. The ground was damp and rotted, and the peasants were at their wit's end because they saw no prospect of sowing the wheat. Mules and oxen sank up to their bellies in the lush grass, and tractor wheels could only spin idly, becoming more and more heavily weighed down with mud. No one but a madman would have ventured out if he didn't have to, that is, no one but a madman or a hunter, because a hunter is only a madman who hasn't been shut up in an institution.

On this mid-November afternoon a hunter was walking, or rather ploughing his way, along the Canal. He wore high rubber boots, and every now and then he had to stop and wipe them, because the mud stuck to them and pulled him down. He hadn't yet fired a single shot and it seemed unlikely that he would fire one, but he continued to trudge along, accompanied by a totally unenthusiastic dog. At a certain point the dog was so disgusted that he turned round and started for home.

"Thunder!"

The dog stopped, looked round at his master and trotted farther away.

"Thunder! Come here!"

The hunter's voice was charged with anger, and the dog finally went to him, growling.

"As long as I'm here, you've got to stick by me," he said, as the dog came near.

And if the dog could have spoken he would doubtless have said:

"Just because you're a jackass, Reverend, doesn't mean that I have to be one too!"

Don Camillo continued to mutter under his breath for a while, and then, when the fog began to close in around him, he decided that Thunder's idea wasn't such a bad one, after all. After a decent silence, he said:

"If you want to go home, run along. I'm tired of having you underfoot."

He shot the last round from his shotgun and hung it, with the barrel pointing down, under his heavy coat, from the right shoulder. Just then Thunder pricked up his ears, moved a few feet forward and stiffened all over.

"Why did it have to be just now?" grumbled Don Camillo, reaching under his coat for the gun.

But hardly had he extricated it than he realized that Thunder was pointing to no ordinary game, for he was barking, in deep, gloomy tones, in the direction of a clump of acacias. Don Camillo attempted to quiet him and then took up his stand behind a mulberry tree. He saw the acacia branches move, and a moment later there appeared a shadowy, tall human figure, without a head, advancing slowly upon him. All of a sudden Thunder leaped forward, barking joyfully now, as if in recognition. Don Camillo saw that this was no headless ghost, but a big man, holding a coat over his head. Actually, the coat was over the head of the child he was carrying on his shoulders.

"For a minute I thought you were a man without a head," said Don Camillo, when the giant stopped in front of him. "And considering the little use that head of yours is to you, I wasn't so very far wrong."

The man stuck his head out from the folds of the coat.

"Father," he said, "if it weren't for the respect I bear your dog, I'd give you the answer you deserve."

"Take it easy, Peppone," Don Camillo said with a laugh. "I didn't mean to insult you."

"I shall insult you, though, Father, if you don't remove yourself and let an honest man go his way."

"Strictly speaking, you're not going your way; you're poaching on someone else's property. But, be that as it may, no one is stopping you."

"Then, Father, don't block the whole path; I don't want to wet my feet in the grass. Instead of wasting your dog's time, you'd do better to go and pray to your Boss to send us a bit of sun!"

"My Boss needs no advice from me," said Don Camillo, stepping aside. "He knows when to make the sun shine or the rain fall."

"It doesn't seem that way to me," said Peppone, starting to walk along. "Your Boss goes in for politics instead of attending to business."

Don Camillo did not bother to reply, but slung his gun over his shoulder and walked along, behind Peppone. Once they had left the Canal, Peppone said, without turning round:

"How much longer are you going to trail me?"

"I'm going my own way," Don Camillo replied. "A hunter's way is through the open fields. But, if I may ask, where are *you* going?"

"Where I please," shouted back Peppone. "Hasn't anyone a right to find the fields open but you?"

"Yes," said Don Camillo. "But I have a right to find it very odd indeed that a man should go walking in the mud with a five-year-old child on his shoulders who would be much better off at home."

"My son is my own concern," roared Peppone. "Kindly keep your mind on your own affairs!"

"That's just the point. I baptized him and entered him in my books. That's why I have a right to say that your head must be full of cotton-wool if you carry him around on a day like this."

Peppone did not answer, because just then he slipped in the mud and would have fallen to the ground had not Don Camillo bolstered him up from behind.

"Do you see what I mean?" the priest asked him. "You might have knocked his brains out."

"It's all your fault!" shouted Peppone, stamping his feet in order to shake off some of the mud that had stuck to them. "You needle me until I can't see where I'm going."

Don Camillo opened his coat, took off his shotgun and set it up against another mulberry tree.

"Give the child to me, while you wipe your big horseshoes," he said, lifting the burden from Peppone's shoulders.

Peppone cursed to himself as he plucked a branch and angrily scraped the mud off his boots. It was a tedious job, and the little boy whispered restlessly into Don Camillo's ear:

"Piggy-back, please!"

"Be quiet!" said Don Camillo gruffly.

The little boy pouted and made as if to cry. In order to avoid a scene, Don Camillo lifted him up to his shoulders. As he raised his arms his coat started to slip off, and he stopped it only by leaning against a tree.

"Catch it, will you?" he shouted to Peppone.

"Catch what?" asked Peppone aggressively.

"My coat. It's about to fall into the mud."

Peppone stopped scraping and went to pick up the coat. From the priest's shoulders the little boy signalled to his father, pointing repeatedly at his own head.

"No," said Peppone. "Wait till I take you back. He wouldn't like it."

"What wouldn't I like?" roared Don Camillo.

"For him to put your coat over his head."

"Go on, throw it over his head, and hurry up with what you're doing," said Don Camillo, holding fast to the little legs that swung down over his chest.

Peppone threw the coat over the child's head, and for a minute the priest's eyes were covered. When he had parted the folds and looked out he saw Peppone balancing unsteadily on one foot and then falling backwards into a puddle.

"Neat work!" the priest exclaimed. "If the 'cells' of your Party are as solid as the cornerstone, then the revolution will be here soon!"

"If your hind quarters were as wet as mine," Peppone grumbled, "you'd display a little more Christian charity!"

He struggled to his feet and came over to take back his son, but Don Camillo stepped away.

"Leave him with me," he said; "with my rubber boots I'm

not so likely to stumble. Take my gun, and when we reach the road I'll turn over this little monkey to you."

"I'm not going to the road," said Peppone glumly.

"Then where are you going?"

"I'm going where I see fit. Give me back my boy and let me alone."

Don Camillo peered out from among the folds of his coat at Peppone.

"Look here, wild man, this child has a raging fever. If you don't take him straight home . . ."

"Taking him home wouldn't help," muttered Peppone. "For two months now it's come on him every evening, and the doctor can't find a cure. Give him back and stop bothering me!"

"*Quo vadis*, Peppone?" asked Don Camillo, shaking his head.

"*Quo vadis* wherever I please, and *quo venisti*, too, in spite of all the cursed clergy in the world put together! I'm going where I have to go."

"Can't you go by the road?"

"No, I tell you! I have to cross the fields. I don't mind humbling myself before Almighty God, but I won't be a laughing-stock of priests and priest's pets."

Don Camillo looked hard at Peppone's agonized face.

"Very well, I won't say another word. Let's get going."

"I'll carry the child."

"No; he's safer on my shoulders. And no use carrying the shotgun. We may as well leave it here and Thunder will keep watch over it."

The fog had closed in on them and it was wetter and wetter underfoot, but they kept on walking. For part of the way they moved in a direction parallel to that of the road, but neither of them mentioned it. The distance of seven miles seemed interminable. Finally, just before the fog made everything invisible they arrived at their destination. It was a big brick building, darkened by age, which rose at one side of a little-travelled road, with barren fields, where once upon a time rice had grown, all round it. Three hundred years earlier it had been a mere chapel, but later it had become the sanctuary of the Madonna of the Fields. Peppone, with a rough gesture, took his son into his arms.

"You stay outside," he said brusquely to Don Camillo. "I don't want you spying on me."

Don Camillo waited at the door, while Peppone hoisted the little boy on to his shoulders and went in. The church was cold and half-dark, and not a soul was there. The Madonna of the Fields was the only living thing, with her eyes gleaming from above the altar. Don Camillo kept watch at the door. For several minutes he knelt down on a stone and told the Madonna all the things that Peppone probably didn't know how to tell her. When he heard the door creak he got up.

"If you have anything to say, you can go in now," said Peppone.

"I've had my say already," said Don Camillo.

And they started back across the fields, with the child under the coat, on Don Camillo's shoulders. The fog was so thick that towards the end they nearly lost their way. Don Camillo whistled, and Thunder came to guide them. It was dark when they reached the rectory, and Peppone said:

"I'll take back my load."

He slipped off Don Camillo's coat and saw that the child's head was reclining on his.

"The little fellow's asleep," he murmured.

"Not as fast asleep as you might think," said Don Camillo.

"What do you mean?"

"If your neck were as wet as mine, you wouldn't have to ask," said Don Camillo, handing the child over.

Peppone stood for a moment as if he had something important to say, but could not find the words.

"I hope you won't go around telling how we tough Reds go back in an emergency to . . . our childhood," said Peppone hopefully.

"I'm no tell-tale," said Don Camillo. "But if only you weren't such a silly fellow . . ."

"Don't ask the impossible," said Peppone firmly.

Don Camillo ran to kneel down in front of the main altar.

"Forgive me, Lord," he said, "if I wasn't here for vespers."

"Absence excused!" Christ said with a smile.

3

THE NEW LOOK

WHEN the official news came through, along with the first directives, Peppone was staggered. In the good old days he had fought like a lion to have one of the village streets called after Joseph Stalin and had even given his name to the Consumer's Co-operative. As if this were not enough, the great hall of his emporium and meeting-place was decorated with a bigger-than-life-size portrait of the great man.

Such was Peppone's discomfiture that when he had called his henchmen together he found himself for the first time with nothing to say. All he did was toss the sheet of paper containing the directives on to the table and throw out his arms in a helpless and disconsolate manner. The others read the paper through and looked at one another. Then Smilzo summed up the situation.

"What fault have we, Chief, if we believed what the higher-ups told us? Anyhow, it's all perfectly simple. We take down the street sign, change the Co-operative's name and splash a bucket of white-wash over that wall. Stalinism has gone down the drain."

They had met in the Co-operative, and on the wall in front of them was the gigantic portrait of the moustachioed post-humously purged Leader, Peppone looked at it very sadly. He suffered not only from the blow to his faith, but from a vivid memory of the amount of money the portrait had cost. He himself had insisted that it be a fresco, because, as he had declared at the unveiling, "it must endure as long as the glory of the father of all peoples, that is, forever and ever".

In the great hall were gathered only Peppone and his general staff; the hoi polloi were playing cards and listening to the radio in two other rooms. Thus they were spared the sight of the discredited leader, while Peppone and his intimates could discuss the situation more freely. Naturally enough, when Don Camillo's voice suddenly boomed forth in their midst they started as if a cannon had sounded.

"Good evening," he said heartily, and went to sit down at a small table.

"This hall is reserved for private deliberations," Smilzo told him.

Don Camillo settled back in his chair, stuck a cigar butt between his lips and calmly lit it.

"Is there some celebration?" he asked, after he had blown a smoke-ring up at the ceiling.

"When a visitor sees that he's not wanted," put in Peppone, "the least he can do is go away without stopping to argue."

"Certainly," said Don Camillo. "But when a visitor is taking advantage of his last chance to admire a masterpiece of art which is about to be destroyed, then, wanted or not wanted, it's his duty to remain."

He scrutinized the painting on the wall with a connoisseur's eye and then ended:

"Because it's a fresco, you'll have to scrape and replaster the wall. Twelve square yards of plastering are no joke."

There was no reply. Peppone clenched his fists but held his tongue.

"Oh well, politics is politics. I don't run the same risk, thank heaven. My Leader's held his own for nearly two thousand years."

Peppone jumped to his feet.

"Father," he said, "if you want to pick a fight, you've come to the right place."

Don Camillo shook his head.

"Never again, Mr. Mayor, never again! We've fought quite often enough over that fellow with the bushy moustache. I came simply to indulge in the legitimate satisfaction of seeing you destroy the image of your former god."

173

Peppone brought his fist down on the table and shouted:
"You shan't have that satisfaction!"

Again Don Camillo shook his head.

"Mr. Mayor, you've misunderstood me. I don't say that you must take a hammer and start to knock off the plaster in my sight. I just want to know that you've given orders for the demolition. Farewell, Face! . . ."

Peppone brought down his other fist on the table.

"I'm giving no such orders. As long as I live, that face won't be touched."

"Then you're disobeying the higher-ups. You're running foul of Party discipline."

"No, I'm not," shouted Peppone. "The Party doesn't order me to give satisfaction to a rascally priest or other such garbage."

When Don Camillo had left home it wasn't with the intention of getting Peppone into so much trouble, but now that things had taken this turn he let him stew in his own juice.

"Well, do as you see fit," he retorted blandly. "But at least I'll have the satisfaction of seeing Stalin's name obliterated from the façade of the Co-operative and the street sign."

"You shan't see anything at all!" shouted Peppone.

Peppone got into really hot water because the reactionary papers took up the story and carried pieces about "deviations", "Stalinist factions" and "possible splits". Very soon a bright young man was sent from national headquarters. He called a meeting of Peppone's chief henchmen and addressed them as follows:

"The reactionary papers are printing the usual absurd stories, but there's no use contradicting them. The only answer is to go ahead and get rid of the painting and the street sign and the name on the façade of the building, as originally intended."

The man from headquarters was a stickler for discipline, the sort of young Party worker that wears spectacles and a double-breasted suit. But he made no impression on Peppone.

"My personal prestige is at stake," Peppone told him. "We're not getting rid of anything. I won't hear of giving that miserable priest such satisfaction."

The man from headquarters tried to explain that where the dignity of the Party is involved, that of the individual must take second place. He brought in the dangers of the "personality cult" and its terrible consequences. Then, when he saw that Peppone was still looking askance at him, he thought up a compromise solution.

"Comrade, I know how to reconcile our points of view. We'll send you off on a mission, and while you're away, your men will obey our orders to wipe everything out."

Bigio was a man of few words, and those he did speak tumbled out of his mouth like bricks falling from the top of a scaffolding.

"It will have to be *your* men that carry out *your* orders. We're not wiping out a thing. You got us into all this trouble. Why couldn't you tell us before he died just how things stood?"

The man from headquarters looked round and then explained that he was only a link in the chain of command.

"Very well, then," he concluded. "I'll make a report on your objections."

He did exactly this, and as a result Peppone received an ultimatum; either to knuckle under or else to be expelled from the Party for indiscipline and other damaging reasons.

It was a peremptory letter, and having read it several times Peppone went to the rectory and threw it down in front of Don Camillo. Don Camillo read it over and over in his turn and then came out with the single word:

"Garibaldi."

"Garibaldi?" mutter Peppone suspiciously. "Where does he come in?"

"Because he has the same first name as Stalin, and you can leave the first half of the inscription on the façade of the Co-operative the way it is. As for the painting, you don't need to deface it. You can just pierce a hole and put in a glass door connecting the great hall with the pergola and the bowling-alley. As for the street sign, never mind about that. One day it will fall, all by itself."

Peppone pounded his fists on the table and thrust his chin out in the direction of Don Camillo.

"I said I wasn't going to give you any satisfaction!"

"I don't want any. You've won, and this is my surrender. You're the stronger of the two."

"Father, I can't trust you. There's something here that doesn't meet the eye."

"Only a little common sense," said Don Camillo, shaking his

head. "I'd rather have a live Peppone than a dead Stalin. It's better to thumb a nose at Stalin than at you. Just think it over and see if you don't agree."

Peppone thought for a moment, and then said:

"From my point of view, you're quite right."

"From mine too. . . . Lambrusco wine or Fontanella?"

"Lambrusco," said Peppone without hesitation.

It was an unusually fine bottle and so were the two that followed. At a certain point Peppone raised his glass and shouted:

"Hurrah for Garibaldi!"

"Hurrah!" said Don Camillo, clinking his glass against the other.

Then they had to drink a toast to the conscripts born in 1899, iron men, one and all.

"We ninety-niners! . . ." exclaimed Peppone.

And he said these three words in such a way that they were as meaningful as a long oration.

4

THE CASE OF THE DISAPPEARING DOG

DON CAMILLO'S dog, Thunder, had fallen from grace, and was punished by being tied up, for several weeks, on a chain. Just when it seemed as if he had mended his ways he made for the garden gate, returned to the gay life and for several days on end failed to put in an appearance.

"The fact that the hunting season is over doesn't dispense you from the everyday duties of a well-bred dog," said Don Camillo. "You're not a mutt or a stray, you have a pedigree. *Noblesse oblige*, and although you're quite free to go out by yourself, you must come home at night."

Thunder cocked his head and listened with a penitent air, but these high-sounding words went in one ear and out the other. Don Camillo was genuinely fearful of losing his beloved pet. Even the loss of his indispensable motor-cycle would have been less difficult to bear. But fate willed, perversely, that Don Camillo should lose his dog. Thunder disappeared on Saturday morning while Don Camillo was saying his first Mass. For a couple of days the priest hoped for his return, then he betrayed his worry by making inquiries of his neighbours. No one in the village had seen him, and gradually Don Camillo extended his search to the outlying farms.

Actually, his first thought had been to question Peppone, for Peppone was the only other person for whom Thunder felt affection. One day Peppone had even gone so far as to say: "Politics may divide us, but Thunder makes us one. Nevertheless, come the revolution, Thunder won't save you from the fate you so richly deserve!" Now Peppone was just the man to whom Don Camillo wanted to turn, but the political situation was unusually tense, and if he had made any contact with the Red leader, an earthquake might have ensued. In the long run, however, after he had exhausted all other possibilities, Don Camillo did have to knock at Peppone's door, that is he wrote him a letter.

"*Dear Mr. Giuseppe Bottazzi:*

My dog, Thunder, has been missing for two weeks past. If you can give me any news of him, I shall be most grateful. Yours very truly . . ."

The answer came by return of post:

Dear Mr. Priest:

If your dog has run away, it means that he, too, has got wise to you. Very truly yours . . ."

Don Camillo did not abandon his quest, and after a month had gone by he asked Barchini to print fifty notices, which he proceeded to post in the surrounding district: "*Lost: Hunting dog. Reward to anyone bringing information which leads to his return.*"

After three days Don Camillo received a missive with crudely printed letters and no signature at the bottom:

"*Reverend: If you want to find your dog, without having to give any reward, go to the acacia grove at Pragrande and look in the vicinity of the sewer.*"

Without losing a single minute, Don Camillo set out across the fields in the direction of Pragrande. He didn't have to look far, because near the sewer entrance there was a pole sticking out of the ground, with a dog-collar wired to it, and a crudely printed sign saying: "*Here lies one of the two dogs of the rectory. He was run over by a truck: too bad, because the other one is more of a dog than he.*"

With his stick Don Camillo dug up the loose earth round the pole. After he had gone down a couple of feet he replaced the dirt and went away. Back in the rectory he shut himself up in his bedroom in order to quiet the sorrow and indignation that welled up in his breast. Turning the collar over and over in his hands he repeated to himself: "They killed him . . . they killed him. . . ." There was no doubt in his mind: out of sheer spite, someone had murdered the dog. But who could it be? In spite of his resentment, Don Camillo could not bear to think that the murderer was someone he knew. No one in the village could have been so vile. There were people who might have killed a man, but never a dog, just in order to hurt the master. All day long he was in the dumps, and when evening came he was as exhausted as if he had unloaded a transatlantic steamer. He had no wish to talk, and when he went to close the church and found the old Desolina Fiorini waiting to see him he started to dismiss her roughly.

"Father," she said mysteriously, "I have a secret to tell you."

"What is it?" asked Don Camillo curtly.

"I read the notice about the dog. . . ."

"Well . . ." said Don Camillo, taken by surprise.

"It's no use your offering a reward. Someone knows where the dog is, but he's not talking."

"Well, you can talk, can't you?" panted Don Camillo. "Don't you trust me?"

"I trust you, Father, but I don't want to get in trouble with those people. . . ."

"What people?"

"The usual people, Father. Didn't the dog disappear on the twenty-fourth of last month?"

"Yes."

"Well, I saw him with one of them on that day."

Don Camillo could contain himself no longer. The old woman's caution was driving him crazy. Still, it would have been unwise to put too much pressure upon her.

"Speak up, Desolina," he said. "After all, you know me."

"I know them, too. . . . This wasn't the first time your dog had gone out with them, either. First he took up with the ring-leader; he was always underfoot in the workshop. After that he shifted his attentions to the ringleader's right-hand man. I must admit I was shocked to see the company your dog was keeping."

"They made the overtures," protested Don Camillo. "And what does he know of politics?"

"Nothing, of course, Father. But I know that it could only come to a bad end. Anyone that takes up with the Reds . . ."

179

"Desolina," said Don Camillo prudently, "when you speak of 'the ringleader's right-hand man', do you mean Smilzo?"

"Yes," she said unwillingly, after a fearful look around her. "That was his special friend. I saw them go off more than once together, on Peppone's truck. . . . On the twenty-fourth of last month, which was a Saturday, that's exactly what happened. Only that time Smilzo came back alone."

Don Camillo had heard all too much. After reassuring the old woman, he went back to the rectory and brooded over his wrong in bed. He slept very little, rose at dawn and as soon as he had said Mass made straight for the workshop of Peppone. It looked suspiciously like a coincidence that Smilzo should be on the scene as well. But Peppone was obviously unprepared to see Don Camillo turn up at this early hour and with such an angry look on his face.

"Did you have a bad night, Father?" he asked.

"I did. But I slept better than someone with a dungheap where a conscience should be."

"For instance? . . ." asked Peppone threateningly.

"For instance the fellow who murdered my dog simply in order to spite me."

Peppone shook his head.

"The loss of the dog has affected his mind," he muttered. "There's nothing to do but let him have his say. He's dreamed that somebody killed the dog and come to tell us about it instead of going to a soothsayer who might have interpreted the dream in terms of a winning lottery number."

"I didn't dream it at all," said Don Camillo, pulling Thunder's collar out of his pocket, along with the letter and sign. "I found him dead over at Pragrande, and with this sign for a tombstone."

Peppone read both documents.

"Too bad," he said. "But you're barking up the wrong tree. Here there are people that would have been glad to kill you in order to please the dog, but none that would have killed the dog just to spite you."

"This isn't the wrong tree at all," Don Camillo insisted. "I'm looking for a fellow who on the twenty-fourth of last month rode off on the truck belonging to a certain Giuseppe Bottazzi, who rode off with my dog and rode back without him."

Peppone took a step forward.

"You're barking up the wrong tree, Father, I tell you!"

"The police sergeant won't bark up the wrong tree, though, after I've told him my story and given him the names of witnesses."

"I'm not afraid of you or the police, either. If somebody killed your dog, we can't do anything about it. The sins of priests who have sold their souls to America are visited upon innocent dogs!"

"We'll see who has the last laugh!" shouted Don Camillo, moving towards the door. "Ten minutes from now there's going to be an H-bomb explosion, and then the fun will begin."

Smilzo had turned as pale as the lady of the camelias. He grasped Peppone's arm and pleaded.

"Chief, don't let him go!"

But Peppone stared at him in amazement and shook him off.

"What's the matter, you fool?" he asked.

Don Camillo had stopped to look round.

"I'll expose you and your whole miserable gang," he shouted towards Smilzo. "No use your putting on an act like that with me."

"Father, I didn't kill your dog, I swear it!" Smilzo exclaimed.

"Good for you! Then swear that you didn't write this sign and this letter. And while you're at it, swear that you didn't take Thunder away with you on Peppone's truck on the twenty-fourth of last month?"

"I'm not swearing indiscriminately," Smilzo objected. "I simply swore that I didn't kill your dog."

"And what dog is buried at Pragrande, then?"

"I can't tell you," said Smilzo. "I found him dead on the road a week ago and buried him there. He looked a lot like Thunder, that's all. Afterwards I wrote you an anonymous letter in order to make you stop whining about your lost dog."

Peppone took Smilzo by the lapels of his jacket and shook him as if he meant to make a single hash out of brains and belly.

"Come out with the whole story," he shouted, "or I'll kill you like a dog."

After Smilzo had caught his breath, he told everything he knew.

"Thunder and I were great friends. He's a good dog; you'd never suspect he belonged to a priest."

Don Camillo picked up a hammer.

"Be calm, Father," said Peppone. "There's no use scaring an innocent witness like me. . . . Go ahead, Smilzo."

"We were friends, as I say. Every Saturday, when I went round to the markets with Peppone's truck, he came along. Once we stopped in a tavern at Peschetto and a fellow asked me if I'd sell the dog. I said that he wasn't mine, that I'd found him on the road. He said he had to have the dog to go hunting and put a thousand-lira note into my hand. I had had a good bit to drink, so I took it and went away. A mile farther on, I realized what a fool I'd been and started to go back for Thunder. While I was turning round Thunder himself ran up and made a flying leap on to the truck. We stopped at the next tavern along the way and drank up the thousand liras."

"You lout!" said Don Camillo disgustedly. "Did you teach him to drink, as well?"

"That was just a manner of speaking. I drank red wine and he ate a dish of red meat, such as I wager he never enjoyed when he was with the clergy."

"Never mind about the clergy," said Peppone. "Tell what you have to tell."

"There isn't much more," said Smilzo. "The following Saturday I thought over what had happened. Before stopping to eat lunch in Fornella I took off the dog's collar, smeared him with mud and took him in with me on the end of a piece of rope. Of course the rope was tied around his neck in clerical style, so that it could be slipped off, and I had showed him how to get free. I went to a tavern frequented by hunters and there I found a man who wanted to buy him for two thousand liras. And so on, and so on."

"What do you mean, 'and so on'?"

"I mean that I drove a mile or so down the road, stopped and waited for Thunder to catch up with me. When he came we had another bout of eating and drinking, just as before. In short, I'd found a first-class racket. I sold him, he ran away, and then we split the profits."

"And did he enjoy this game?"

"Of course he enjoyed it. He hasn't sold his soul to America, like you. He understands the economic situation and the necessity of sharing the wealth."

Once more Don Camillo picked up the hammer.

"And where is Thunder now?" he demanded.

"Last time I saw him was at Castelmonti, where I sold him for three thousand liras, but he never came back. I suppose he never managed to get away. That's the whole story. I didn't kill him; I only pretended he was dead in order to stop your whining about him."

"Good enough," said Don Camillo, waving the card in the air. "Theft, embezzlement, libel . . ."

Peppone felt he had to step in.

"To say that you're more of a dog than Thunder isn't libel; it's no more than the simple truth."

"We'll see what the court has to say," said Don Camillo. "I for one shan't let you off so easily."

"For once it's not a matter of politics," said Peppone. "Smilzo may have done wrong, but he did it entirely on his own, and with the complicity of your dog, who didn't hesitate to second him. Your legal action is directed at a private individual. If you want to send him to jail, go right ahead."

Don Camillo brought the hammer down on the anvil.

"I don't want to send anyone to jail. I want my dog! Between a thief who sells another man's dog for three thousand liras and a brute who cheats him by paying only a twentieth of the real value, there's not much to choose. But the dog is mine, and I want him back."

Peppone took his jacket off the hook and slipped it on.

"Shut your holy mouth," he said. "You shall have your dog." And followed by Smilzo he went out and climbed into his truck.

"I'm coming along," said Don Camillo.

"To Castelmonti," said Peppone, as Smilzo took the wheel. "We'll inquire in the tavern who bought the dog and then ransom him, by fair means or foul."

The truck speeded over the dusty roads of the lower Po valley in the direction of the distant hills. But after seven or eight miles Smilzo abruptly threw on the brakes.

"What's the matter?" Peppone asked impatiently.

Smilzo opened the door and a dog leaped into the cab. The dog was Thunder. Nobody said a word, and Smilzo turned round and made for home. After a mile the silence was broken by an angry growl and again Smilzo came to a sudden stop.

"What's the matter now?" asked Don Camillo.

"Our understanding is that at the first tavern we stop and divide the spoils," Smilzo explained. "I still owe him his share from the last time."

With Thunder at his heels he got out and went into the tavern in front of which he had stopped the truck. Peppone followed suit, leaving Don Camillo alone. It was as hot as summer, and under the metal top of the cab Don Camillo soon began to perspire. Finally he got out, went into the tavern and asked for a glass of water.

"Come in, Father," said the host, going by with a huge bowl of spaghetti in his arms. "Your friends are waiting for you in the next room."

The room was shady and quiet, and the spaghetti emanated an ambrosial odour. Don Camillo sat in front of a heaping plateful, and only then did Thunder abandon his reserved air and show his adoration. But Don Camillo was not to be corrupted.

"I'm paying for what I eat," he said stoutly. "No dishonestly gained bread for me!"

"Nor for me," said Peppone. "Every man must pay for himself, and the devil take the hindmost. But Smilzo's paying for both himself and Thunder."

"Then I'll pay for you, Peppone," said Don Camillo. "That way Smilzo and I shall both have dog guests!"

And he proceeded to enjoy his meal, because having the last word made it worthwhile to pay for an entire regiment.

5

VICTIMS OF WAR

MILCO didn't know how to begin, but finally he managed to say:

"It's about that German woman. Today is the twenty-sixth, and she'll be here the day after tomorrow."

He seemed to be intensely worried, and Don Camillo couldn't see why.

"Every twenty-eighth of March since 1946 she's descended upon you. She may just as well come this year, too."

Milco shook his head.

"You don't know the whole story, Father," muttered Milco; "that's why you can't understand."

True enough, Don Camillo knew no more than did the rest of the village. The story went back to the end of September 1943, when a small detachment of Germans had occupied the village. Among them was Sergeant Fritz, who functioned as quartermaster. He himself was lodged in Milco's house at La Torretta, not very far from the village, between the highway and the Stivone River.

At this time Milco was thirty years old, but he had stayed at home because of a lame leg and also because, in spite of this disability, he was the only man able to run the farm. Milco's wife was not strong, and his extremely healthy son was only eleven years old. There were no other members of the family, and in time of war, when agriculture is just as important as heavy industry, there can be no question of leaving the land deserted and unproductive.

Sergeant Fritz was a good-natured fellow, the same age as Milco, who went about making war as another man might have gone about store-keeping or accounting. Good German that he was, he had a weakness for Italian wine, and when he had drunk a bit more than necessary he would pull out of his wallet the photograph of a handsome, blonde young woman and a ten-month-old blond baby boy, which invariably moved him to tears.

Sergeant Fritz was happy in Milco's house, and both Milco and his wife treated him like one of the family. He had a happy-go-lucky temperament, and since he was in charge of the commissary department he never came back to the farm empty-handed. The sergeant stayed in Milco's house until 28 March, 1945. On the evening of that day he did not come back, and the next day he was fished out of the Stivone River, near Brugello. But it was plain that he had not drowned, for three bullets from a P-38 had gone clean through his head. In those days the Partisans were very active, and Sergeant Fritz had run into one of their bands.

The twenty-eighth of March after the war was over, a blonde young German woman and her blond baby came to La Torretta. The woman knew about four words of Italian and Milco knew about four words of German, so that they were able to understand one another.

"I am the widow of Sergeant Fritz," she told him, "and I have come to lay flowers on his tomb."

Milco took her to the cemetery, and she laid her flowers at the foot of the crude wooden cross on which was written the Sergeant's life story:

Fritz Hauser
2 March 1925–28 March 1945

Milco and his wife asked the woman and her child to stay with them for a whole week. The woman talked about the dreadful conditions in Germany and the difficulties she had encountered on her trip. But above all she talked about Fritz. She said that Fritz had written her a very moving account of Milco and his family, and that she had come not only to visit his tomb but also to pay a tribute of gratitude to them, in short, to thank them for all they had done for her husband.

"I had to sell every last bit of gold I possessed in order to make the journey," she told them. "Now I have nothing. But I hope to find a job, so that next year I shall have another money to come see you again."

She kept her word, and turned up promptly the next year and the one that followed. Punctually, on every twenty-eighth of March, she came with her child to stay for a week at La Torretta. By now everyone in the village knew her and her story. Whenever they met her in the street, they greeted her profusely because, among other things, she was "a fine figure of a girl". She had the generously proportioned sort of beauty which is especially appreciated in the fertile Po valley.

Don Camillo was still perplexed.

"I don't see what it is that requires such special understanding," he muttered. "No one can criticize you for letting her stay in your house, even if you're a widower. After all, you don't live there alone; you have your son and his policewoman of a wife with you. And your wife—God rest her soul!—was already dead when this German woman came last year. What has happened since then to change the situation?"

Milco hesitated for a moment and then said abruptly: "I simply don't want to see her again!"

Don Camillo shrugged his shoulders.

"Well, then, why have you come to me? That's none of my business. If you don't like her face, just write her a letter and tell her to stay away."

But Milco had something more on his mind, as was plain to see from the way he twisted his hat in his hands.

"As long as my wife was alive, I could talk things out with her. But now, who is there for me to talk to?"

By now the channel of communication was opened, and Don Camillo had only to let Milco have his say.

"Father, you remember how it was. I was tied up with the Resistance movement, and they had put me in charge of transmitting their radio messages. I had the radio hidden under a barrel in my barn. On that evening of 28 March 1945 Fritz caught me red-handed. . . ."

"Fritz caught you?" stammered Don Camillo.

"Yes. As usual, after we'd finished supper, I said: 'I'm going to have a game of cards with Ronchini.' And as usual, he said: 'Good luck to you!' I went out and started to walk across the fields, but when I reached the beech-tree I stayed there for a quarter of an hour and then retraced my steps. There was a little door at the rear of the barn which I was the only one ever to use. I slipped through it and took out the transmitting apparatus, just as I had done a hundred times before. But this time the worst possible thing happened: Fritz burst in and caught me at it. . . ."

He paused and wiped the perspiration off his forehead.

"A light went on, and there was Fritz standing before me, quite beside himself with rage. 'Traitor!' he shouted, with his hand on the butt of his pistol. I had my own finger on the trigger of a loaded P-38, which was always in my pocket, and I beat him to the draw. . . . Cursed war! . . ."

And he stopped again to wipe his forehead.

"If he hadn't called me 'Traitor', perhaps I wouldn't have shot him, but the word sounded like a death sentence. . . . It was dark and rainy outside. I loaded his body on to my shoulders, carried it down to the river and threw it in. The Stivone was running high and the body was swept a couple of miles downstream, to the place where it was later found. No one had the slightest suspicion. My wife was the only one ever to know, and now she's dead."

Don Camillo pondered for several minutes over this story. Finally he muttered:

"What can I say? Am I to call you a patriot or an assassin? Your own conscience must be your guide."

"That's why I'm here," Milco exclaimed. "I can't look at it from the patriotic angle. Even if I were to get a medal, I'd still consider myself guilty of murdering Fritz. I can't sleep at night. . . . The first time that German woman came and started to thank me for all I'd done for her dead husband, I thought I'd go through the floor with shame. . . . I killed him and she thanks me! And the fatherless child calls me uncle! No, I can't stand it any longer. I can't live through fifty-one weeks of the year dreading the fifty-second. I don't want ever to see her again; I don't want my stomach to turn over. Father, you can't imagine what I've gone through in the last ten years."

"Yes, I can imagine," said Don Camillo. "And I'm glad

that you suffered. It shows that your conscience is working."

"Yes, it is," said Milco excitedly. "That's why I came here. I'm not looking for comfort. You can say what you please, but the fact remains that I murdered Fritz. You'll have to help me shake off that woman. I haven't the heart to do it, but surely you can tell her the whole story."

"I?" exclaimed Don Camillo, with wide-open eyes.

"Yes. She's arriving the day after tomorrow. You must talk to her. . . . It isn't right that she should thank me for my kindness and treat me like a friend. I'm taking something that isn't due. She must be told that I killed her husband, and then she must tell her son. That way she'll never come back, and my sufferings will be at an end."

Don Camillo shook his head.

"No, Milco, if you really have a conscience, then you mustn't seek to evade further suffering. It's not enough to repent; you must make amends as well. If the sight of this woman makes you suffer, then you must thank God for letting you see her. And why should you wish to hurt her still more? Aren't you satisfied with having killed her husband?"

Milco waved his arms wildly.

"Of course I don't want to hurt her!"

"Well, that's just what you're going to do. She trusts you and thinks of you as one of the family, and you'd rob her of this last illusion. If her presence gives you pain, so much the better. I'll say a prayer for you."

After Milco had gone away, Don Camillo went into the church to pray for him. But it was a very strange prayer.

"Lord," Don Camillo said to the Christ on the altar, "in this filthy land, there are tens of thousands of persons who killed tens of thousands of others. And they're not sorry; in fact, they brag about it. They want medals and positions; they want to be deputies to parliament, senators and publishers; they want their pictures in the school-books of the nation! . . . Now here's a poor devil who has suffered ten years just because he killed a man, and we are powerless to help him. We can't say: 'Look here, Milco. . . . When Fritz caught you with the radio, he called you a traitor, didn't he? Well, you could have called him the same thing! While you were in the barn working for the

Resistance Movement, your wife, abetted by Sergeant Fritz, was working for Germany . . . without thought of resistance!' . . . No, Lord, we can't tell this to Milco, because his wife revealed it on her death-bed, and a priest can't violate the secret of the confessional. Lord, You know best, but is it right, I ask you?"

"Yes, it is, Don Camillo," Christ answered. "The sin of the wife doesn't cancel the sin of the husband. Each one has to pay. . . ."

March 28 rolled round, and with it came the Germans. As soon as Don Camillo heard of their arrival he hurried out to La Torretta, where Milco greeted him like a long-lost friend. It was a fine, sunny day and while the little boy played in the yard with the dog, his mother, Milco and Don Camillo went to look at the fields, which were just stirring from their long hibernation.

"You haven't much colour in your cheeks," said Don Camillo to the German woman.

"I work at a factory in a big city, where there's lots of smoke," she explained.

"That's no good," said Don Camillo gravely. "And don't you have to pinch and scrape all year in order to make this visit?"

"I don't mind pinching and scraping," she answered with a smile.

"Why don't you come and live here, near Fritz?" said Don Camillo. "That would make Fritz happy, I'm sure."

She stared at him in amazement.

"Don't you like it here?" Don Camillo asked her.

"Oh, very much! Italy is the most wonderful place! But I have a home and a job. . . ."

Don Camillo waved in the direction of Milco's house.

"Why not have a home and a job here?"

Don Camillo had no gift for parlour games, and so he came straight to the point:

"You marry him . . . he marries you . . . I perform the ceremony . . . that way everyone will be happy!"

The woman was thirty-seven years old, but she still knew how to blush and proceeded to do so. Milco was forty-two and too old for blushing, but he turned pale. Don Camillo was no matchmaker, and now embarrassment overcame him.

"Very well," he said. "Think it over. When you're ready you'll find me in my office. *Guten Abend*."

And with that he went away.

Apparently they did think it over, for three days later Milco came to see him.

"Well, Father, you shall have your way, and we'll get married."

"Exactly. It's your way, too, I trust."

Milco heaved a sigh.

"Here's hoping that to have her around all the time won't give me more pain than ever. If my conscience still hurts me . . ."

"Let's get this straight, Milco," said Don Camillo. "Where Fritz is concerned, things are just the same. You took away his life, and you can't restore it. That will have to stay on your conscience. But when it comes to the woman and child, it's a different matter. You deprived her of her husband, but you're giving her another . . . and there'll no longer be a fatherless boy. Don't mix your accounts!"

"God help me, that's all I can say!" exclaimed Milco.

"He's helped you already!" retorted Don Camillo.

6

STRANDED IN THE STRATOSPHERE

WHEN the carnival came for the mid-May holiday that year, the
tents had to be pitched on the grounds that usually served as
a livestock market. The whole region was in a political ferment
and the Left-wingers planned to hold a series of meetings in the
village square.

The carnival's improvised pitch was out of the way, on the
outskirts of the village, along the road to Molinetto. But there
were two startling new attractions: a big autodrome and a
stratospheric merry-go-round. The stratospheric merry-go-
round was a cornucopia of steel rods resembling the skeleton of
an inverted umbrella. At the top end of every rod, there was a
miniature aeroplane, and when the merry-go-round revolved,
every rider could raise or lower his vehicle by simply pressing
a lever.

The rectory was no more than three or four hundred yards
away, and every evening, when Don Camillo retired to his room,
on the second floor, he looked for half an hour or so out of the
window at the revolving merry-go-round before drawing the
curtain and going to bed. There is nothing in the least sinful
about riding on a merry-go-round, either on the ground or in the
air, but it is an amusement in which a priest cannot indulge.
People have eyes to see and not much grey matter for thinking,
and the sight of a priest on a merry-go-round would surely

rouse them to derision. All this Don Camillo ruefully understood.

The autodrome and the stratospheric merry-go-round were the carnival's two great money-makers, and late in the evening, when the other attractions had closed down, they continued to draw the crowd. And the merry-go-round stayed open longest of all. Don Camillo did not fail to notice this fact, and one fine evening, after the autodrome had stopped running, he went downstairs and out of the house and walked, in a studiedly indifferent manner, across the alfalfa field behind the rectory. When he had reached the hedge bordering the Molinetto road he stood behind it and bided his time. Across the way, the carnival booths lay in darkness, with only the merry-go-round, in the centre of a small island of light, still turning.

Don Camillo's plan was eminently simple. As soon as the last load of riders had dismounted and started home to bed, he would come out from behind the hedge and ask the proprietor to let him enjoy a ride. He did not have long to wait before the merry-go-round came to a halt and a group of young fellows got down, leaped on to their motor-scooters and rode noisily away into the night. Don Camillo stepped across the ditch and walked straight towards his goal. The proprietor of the merry-go-round, who had stepped into the cabin to count his receipts, jumped when the great dark mass appeared before him.

"First priest you've ever seen?" asked Don Camillo.

"No, Father, but the first one I've ever seen out at this late hour. What can I do for you?"

"I sleep over there," said Don Camillo, pointing to the rectory, "and you've no idea of how your cursed music disturbs me."

"I'm truly sorry," said the man, throwing out his arms to signify that there was nothing he could do about it. "But a merry-go-round without music would be a funereal affair. Late in the evening, I turn the volume very low, but after dark the slightest sound seems to be booming."

"I quite agree," said Don Camillo. "But after you've upset so many of my evenings you ought to be ready to do me a favour."

"Certainly, Father; anything you say."

"Then give me a ride on your machine. And I mean right away."

The proprietor assumed a sincerely regretful air.

"Father, I'll have to ask you to be patient. I'm waiting for a group that arranged to have a couple of rides all together. There they are now."

Don Camillo wheeled round with the intention of making his escape, but it was too late. The group was directly behind him, and at its head stood Peppone.

"Our beloved parish priest!" he exclaimed. "Were you expounding the view that it's a mortal sin to ride on the merry-go-round?"

"No, I was simply saying that the music keeps honest folks from sleeping."

"Oh, is that it? I thought for a minute that *you* were the one that couldn't sleep."

Smilzo, Bigio, Brusco, Lungo and Fulmine, in short all the rest of the gang, had paid no attention to the encounter but were gaily clambering into their seats in the planes.

"And what has brought you here, Mr. Mayor?" asked Don Camillo in his turn. "Did you come to give your bad boys some wholesome recreation?"

"Come on, Chief!" called out Smilzo from the merry-go-round.

"Go along, Mr. Mayor," said the smiling Don Camillo. "The bad boys are calling. What fun to see such a great hulk of a mayor flying a miniature plane!"

"Not half as much fun as to see a great hulk of a priest like yourself at the same occupation!" Peppone retorted.

"The fact is, however, that I shall see a flying mayor, but you're not going to see a flying priest."

"Well, enjoy the sight while you can," roared Peppone, striding towards the merry-go-round. "And don't fail to write a sensational article about it in the scandal sheet with which you plaster the village walls."

Peppone hoisted himself into a plane while the proprietor prepared to start up the motor, which was inside the cabin.

"Have fun, Father!" repeated Peppone. "Tell all your good little boys and girls that the Communist administration is spending the taxpayers' money on nocturnal orgies!"

The motor began to run, and out of a loudspeaker came the muted notes of a sprightly march.

"Give her gas, boss!" shouted Peppone, as his plane swung in front of the cabin. "That way the good Father will have a lullaby to put him to sleep."

"Shut your big trap!" sounded a voice directly behind him, and when Peppone turned round he saw that Don Camillo was in the plane following his.

By now the merry-go-round was turning at full speed and everyone was having a good time. But soon the damp night air got the better of Don Camillo.

"Tell that fellow down there to go a little more slowly," he shouted to Peppone.

Peppone pressed the lever and his plane dipped down. As it swung past the cabin he started to call out, but the words stuck in his throat.

"What about it?" shouted Don Camillo.

Peppone muttered something unintelligible and pointed to the cabin. Then Don Camillo went down in his turn and caught sight of what had startled Peppone. What he caught sight of was this: three men with handkerchiefs over their faces, all the way up to the eyes, and revolvers in their hands. The proprietor stood facing the wall and the three men were pushing the barrels of their revolvers into his back, while a fourth one of them dipped into the cash-register drawer and transferred handfuls of paper money to a brief-case. Meanwhile the merry-go-round was whirling at full speed, to the customary musical accompaniment.

The robbers were not satisfied with what they had taken, and two of them went with the proprietor to the trailer where he had his sleeping quarters in order to dig out something more. When they came out they were more dissatisfied than ever and began to manhandle their victim.

"It's no use insisting," he protested. "I took the rest of the money to the bank this morning. Look in my wallet and you'll find a receipt for it."

They found it and tore it angrily into a thousand pieces. And the merry-go-round kept on turning.

"Stop this thing, blast you!" shouted Smilzo as he passed by.

One of the bandits aimed a revolver threateningly in his direction and all the members of Peppone's flying squad pressed their levers simultaneously until the little planes were every one high flying. At this point the merry-go-round really looked like an umbrella turned inside out by the wind. The bandits were furious that their haul was so meagre, but their leader had an abundance of bright ideas.

"We'll separate those fools up there from their money," he suggested, and raised his face to shout in their direction:

"Empty your pockets, or else we'll shoot the brains out of you."

"Go to hell!" answered Peppone.

The leader gave an order to his second-in-command, who went into the cabin and turned a handle which caused the planes to whirl faster. Peppone's men cried out, but the bandits' third-in-command turned up the music until it drowned their cries. After half a dozen rounds, the leader jerked his head and the second-in-command brought the velocity to a little less than it had been before.

"Put your money in your handkerchiefs, knot them and then, when you pass in front of the cabin, throw them in. I'm giving you exactly half a minute to do what I say."

When the half-minute was up, he went on:

"Beginning with that fellow all in black, start throwing them in!"

Don Camillo, who was obviously the one answering this description, took what little money he had in his pocket and threw his knotted handkerchief into the cabin, and the others followed his example. The bandit leader picked them up and counted the money.

"Too little!" he shouted. "Throw your wallets with all the rest in them, or else I'll step up the speed. . . . I give you exactly five seconds. Beginning with that fellow all in black, start throwing them in!" Don Camillo, knowing he had practically nothing in his wallet and feeling that this was certainly one time that the poverty of the clergy paid off, threw his wallet. The others followed somewhat more reluctantly but soon seven wallets landed at the leader's feet; they were duly emptied and tossed into a corner. Then the leader turned to the proprietor.

"Don't stop that merry-go-round until a quarter of an hour after we've gone. And you'd better not try to double-cross us, because we'll know how to find you again. We'll set your whole outfit on fire and roast you alive."

Then the four of them ran for the car they had left on the road and drove away at top speed.

"Stop us, damn you!" shouted the high flyers to the proprietor below. But he was shaking with fear and let the merry-go-round run for the full quarter of an hour which had been enjoined upon him. Then the motor came slowly to a stop and the umbrella gradually closed. The seven took twenty minutes to collect sufficient strength to get out of their planes. Finally they joined the proprietor in the cabin and picked up the empty wallets from the floor. So far, no one had said a word, and now Peppone was the first to speak, grasping the lapels of the proprietor as he did so.

"If you breathe a word of what went on here tonight, I'll not only smash your head, but I'll see to it that you can't hold your carnival in any of the villages in our control."

"And those in *our* control won't have you either," added Don Camillo.

Then all seven of them trudged across the field together. Behind the rectory they said goodbye.

"When all is said and done, we had a very pleasant if somewhat expensive evening, did we not, Mr. Mayor?" said Don Camillo.

Peppone answered him with a roar which shattered the velvety stillness of the night and roused echoes miles and miles away.

Don Camillo slept well that night, dreaming of a heavenly merry-go-round which transformed even the most black-hearted customers into little children roaring with delight.

7

THE RAINS CAME

THE weather continued to be wretchedly unseasonable. After a few sunny days, just enough for the ground to begin to dry, there came another downpour. It had started raining early in July of the preceding year, just when the wheat most needed sun. Then, when the wheat crop was practically ruined the implacable rain went on to kill off the grapes. There was no opportunity to do the regular autumnal sowing, and immediately after Christmas, when the rain finally stopped, it was followed by an unprecedented fall of snow. And as soon as this melted there came more rain. The peasants were beside themselves, because the sprouting wheat was yellow instead of green, and many of them had to give back the seeds distributed by the beet-sugar manufacturers. Both oxen and tractors risked bogging down if they were taken out, for the irrigation canals were filled to overflowing and the fields were one vast sea of mud.

That Tuesday was a market-day, and the arcades around the square were crowded with peasants and tenant farmers, condemned to idleness by the bad weather. Their talk was all of the farm chores which the rain had prevented them from accomplishing, and some of them went so far as to involve the Deity in their tribulations.

"I don't see why Almighty God has it in for us poor farmers!"

As Peppone and Smilzo came out of a café together they

caught this exclamation on the wing, and Peppone was quick to turn it to his advantage.

"Almighty God has nothing to do with it, my friends. He's attending to His own business, and there's no use in dragging Him in. The fault lies with those people who are exploding the universe."

Peppone was a natural rabble-rouser. He knew just when to put in a word and had an infallible eye for spotting the one man in the crowd that would make a perfect foil. This time it was Girola, one of the oldest peasants for miles around, who was standing in the front row of the little assembly.

"You there, Girola," said Peppone, "in all the ninety-seven years of your life, have you ever seen anything like this crazy weather?"

"No," said Girola, slowly shaking his head. "I've seen a bit of everything, storms and floods, and hurricanes that lasted for days or even weeks at a time. But an upset like this, going from one year over to another, is something I've never seen."

"And what do you say is the cause?" asked Peppone.

"Who knows?" muttered Girola, shrugging his shoulders.

"Don't say that, Girola," Peppone shouted, warming up to his subject. "You know, and you've been heard more than once to voice your opinion. There's no reason for you to keep mum about it now. No one's going to claim that it's a fairy-tale, that the rain comes only when God wills it."

So saying Peppone pulled a newspaper out of his pocket.

"Girola's not the only one to have seen clearly; now scientists have reached the same conclusion."

And Peppone held up the headlines for all to see. No one could say that this was a Party publication; it was an independent newspaper with a Rightist slant.

"Here is the voice of world science," Peppone continued, "and it says that we are quite right to be disturbed in our minds over the explosion of the Americans' hydrogen bomb. Their atomic energy has got out of control, and there's no telling what may happen. If you want to read about the damage caused in a three-hundred-mile radius by this last explosion, you can buy the paper. Just to bolster up Girola's opinion, I can tell you this much: a group of Swiss scientists has studied the matter thoroughly and concluded that the earth's balance is threatened by the atomic bomb. Here it is:

> "'Atomic explosions have created powerful currents in the upper atmosphere, moving in the direction of the North Pole. When the resulting centres of condensation reach the Pole, they are precipitated in the form of snow and ice. Such artificial precipitations may affect the balance of our planet: already the North Pole is eighteen per cent heavier than the South.'"

Peppone lifted his head from the paper and looked triumphantly about him. But his satisfaction was marred by the sight of a newcomer to the group, whose presence was anything but welcome. Nevertheless he asked a rhetorical question:

"What is the meaning, then, of this lack of balance between the poles? I never went further than the fifth grade and don't know a word of Latin, so I turn the problem over to an eminent Dutch scientist.

> "'Dr. Schneider, director of the Legerkusen Laboratories in Holland, says that the radio-active particles launched into the atmosphere by atomic explosions act as nuclei of condensation and determine the precipitation of rain and snow.'

"So why hold it against Almighty God if we have three feet of snow or a whole year of rain? The Americans are to blame."

Don Camillo had made his way up to the front row of Peppone's interlocutors, and when Peppone once more lifted his head from the paper, he immediately encountered the priest's eyes. They angered him to the point where he became aggressive.

"Yes," he repeated. "Don't hold it against God, hold it against the Americans. Unless the Reverend Father, here present, has such regard for America that he'd rather you took it out on God!"

"No indeed!" exclaimed Don Camillo. "God has nothing to do with human folly. And He meant men to use their brains to think clearly. We've no business to hold anything against God; let us rather examine ourselves."

"Father, let's stick to the point," said Peppone. "The criminal stupidity of which we are talking is not ours, it's the Americans'. We're speaking of the hydrogen bomb, you know."

Don Camillo nodded assent.

"Right, Mr. Mayor. These things are too serious to be mixed with political propaganda. We must truthfully say that all the disasters, present and future, inherent in experimenting with the atomic bomb are to be laid at the Americans' door. Because, as the mayor has just told us, only the Americans have the bomb."

Without stopping to think, Peppone retorted:

"Nonsense! The Russians have the bomb too, and in a form a hundred times more powerful. It's no use your trying to twist the facts."

Don Camillo shook his head mournfully.

"Things are even worse than I thought, Mr. Mayor. If it goes on raining, these people will have to be told that the Russians, as well as the Americans, are to blame."

The little crowd laughed, and Peppone gritted his teeth.

"The Russians are not in the least at fault," he protested. "The Americans had the bomb first, and the Russians were forced to develop it for the sake of self-protection."

Don Camillo threw out his arms in mock despair.

"Mr. Mayor, if I were to shoot off my gun, whom would you blame? Me?—or the inventor of gunpowder?"

"And if I were to shoot off a gun at you," shouted Peppone, "whose fault would that be? Mine—or that of the bell-ringer at Torricella?"

"Neither one," said Don Camillo calmly. "I'd say it was the fault of those who taught you to deny God and shoot at the defenceless clergy."

"No one has taught me to deny God or shoot at the clergy!" shouted Peppone.

"Then your masters' teaching programme isn't up-to-date. But they'll catch up in time. That's what they've taught everywhere else."

At this point Smilzo stepped forward.

"Chief, there's one thing we have been taught, and that's not to let an adversary who's in patent bad faith bait us. Don't waste time arguing with him."

But Peppone was like a dog with a bone, and wouldn't let go. "We're not to be trapped by professional baiters," he said, "but this is an amateur. He deserves a lesson, and we shall see that he gets it."

Peppone had recovered his aplomb and now he turned to Don Camillo with a smile.

"Father, you say that atomic disasters are due to Americans and Russians alike, because both of them have the bomb. But can you tell me this? Why has public opinion been aroused only now, after the explosion of the American hydrogen bomb? Why is it that committees of scientists and statesmen have chosen to protest at this particular time? Because we've had ten months of rain and can't sow our beets? Is that it?"

"That I can't say, Mr. Mayor."

"Then I'll tell you. Public opinion and world science have been mobilized for a very good reason. The explosion of the last bomb has proved that atomic energy has escaped the American's control. When they set off bombs, nowadays, they don't know what may happen. That's the scientists' opinion, not mine. And who, may I ask, has been clamouring for years for mutual control of atomic energy? Russia or the United States? Russia, Father! America is to blame for having lost control of the atom, while Russia has kept it."

Don Camillo looked as if he were hard hit by the logic of Peppone. After a pause he said:

"Mr. Mayor, I can't say you're altogether wrong. You admit, then, that the American bomb is more powerful than the Russian?"

"I admit nothing of the sort!" shouted Peppone. "The Russians have the most powerful bomb by far. Only they haven't lost control of it, like the Americans. An effect obtained by calculation and one due to mere chance are two different things altogether."

Don Camillo nodded his head.

"Mr. Mayor, what do you say to continuing the argument with your hands?"

"Hands, feet, machine-guns, cannons, anything you say. . . ."

"Don't misunderstand me; I don't want to get you into a boxing-match. The rain has let up, and we can play a game that may prove to be amusing."

In the middle of the square there were still some remnants of the carnival: a shooting-gallery, a merry-go-round and an instrument for measuring a fellow's strength by means of a hammer. The test was to swing a hammer and bring it down on an iron base to which there was attached a measuring-rod and a mobile block which rose, under the blow, to a point numbered between zero and one thousand. If the block went all the way to the top it rang a bell and won a prize. When the two men stood in front of the instrument Don Camillo said:

"I'm the United States, and you're Russia; does that suit you, Mr. Mayor?"

The crowd ringed them round and listened in silence.

"The iron block is atomic energy. Is that clear?"

"Yes."

"I'm America, and since I've lost control of atomic energy I strike at random, not knowing how far I'll go. You're Russia and in full control; you strike a calculated blow."

Don Camillo took an enormous handkerchief out of his pocket and put it over his eyes.

"I'll just take one last peek in order to see where I'm to place the blow."

Then Peppone and he each took a hammer.

"Ready?" said Don Camillo.

"Ready," said Peppone.

Don Camillo spread his legs apart, raised the hammer and brought it down. The block went up to six hundred.

Peppone struck the next blow and sent it up to seven hundred.

With his second blow Don Camillo sent it up to eight hundred and ten.

Peppone nine hundred.

Don Camillo nine hundred.

Peppone struck wildly and went back to eight hundred and fifty.

"Russia's weakening," jeered a reactionary at Peppone's shoulder.

And Don Camillo proceeded to score nine hundred and ten. Peppone summoned all his strength, clenched his teeth and struck a blow that would have shattered an anvil. The iron block went up like a V-2; it passed the thousand mark and hit the electric bell. When he heard the bell ring Don Camillo laid down his hammer and took the handkerchief away from his eyes.

"It happened to you," he said, "but it might just as easily have happened to me. Anyhow, now that we've hit the ceiling and made the world go up in flames we may as well go and have a glass of wine together."

Peppone was perplexed for a moment and then exclaimed:

"No, Father, the comparison doesn't hold water. The fault is yours. If we were to make an agreement to control atomic energy, neither of us would hit the ceiling."

"Exactly," said Don Camillo, "if we knew what the ceiling was. What if it were seven hundred and fifteen or six hundred and three? Do either American or Russian scientists know the limit of Divine Patience?"

It was raining again, and after witnessing the contest, the little crowd had once more taken refuge under the arcades. Don Camillo and Peppone were left alone beside the atomic machine.

"Devil take all bombs!" muttered Don Camillo.

"It's Almighty God's fault for having created Americans and Russians," said Peppone ill-humouredly.

"Don't be blasphemous, Comrade," said Don Camillo severely. "The human race has a big bill to pay, and the present generation has to make up for the deficiencies of the one that preceded it. We're late in coming upon the scene."

"Then the late-comers are fools," observed Peppone.

"No, Comrade; the only fools are those that haven't won a good place for themselves in the eternal life to come."

Peppone pulled the lapels of his coat together and said wryly:

"And while we're waiting for the life to come, it just goes on raining."

8

MADE IN USSR

"Don Camillo," said the old Bishop, "your letter grieved me, not so much for what it said as for what I read between the lines. What is the meaning of your discouragement? Have you lost the faith that has been your bulwark for so long?"

"My faith is unaltered, Your Grace," said Don Camillo sadly; "it's a question of technique, of mechanics."

And when the Bishop looked at him in astonishment he went on to say:

"The young people are getting away from me. It's as if they were racing off on motor-cycles and I were panting after them on foot. It's not faith that's lacking, but a motor-cycle."

"That's not good reasoning, Don Camillo; it's a play on words."

"Nevertheless, Your Grace, it reflects the true situation. I don't want to compete with the devil on his own ground; just because young people would rather dance than listen to my sermons, I shan't hold wild parties in the rectory. But because they are so dead set on the films, I want to show some that are a cut above the average. That's the point of what I'm trying to say."

"How can that be the point, Don Camillo?" said the Bishop, throwing out his arms in bewilderment. "Haven't you been putting on educational pictures for the last five or six years? What's so new about that?"

"The practice isn't new, Your Grace. And neither is the

projector. It's an obsolete model, practically falling to pieces, and . . ."

"That's quite enough, Don Camillo," the Bishop interrupted. "If the Good Lord lets obsolete models—such as myself—endure so long, it must be because they're still useful in one way or another. No, Don Camillo, you're trying to trick me. It's not true that you *need* a motor-cycle, you just wish you had one!"

But Don Camillo wasn't really trying to trick him. His 16-mm. projector was no longer a machine, it was the ghost of a machine that might have been. And a motor-cycle without a front wheel and saddle is a far less serviceable vehicle than shank's pony. Even the best film, when it came out of Don Camillo's projector, was a cinematographic omelette, and the sound track was a cacophonic zigzag.

"The only thing I can suggest doing," said the big-city repairman to whom Don Camillo had taken it, "is adding it to the rubbish, that is, if the Department of Sanitation will consent to take it!"

When he went back to the village Don Camillo was strongly tempted to throw the thing in the river, but he could not give himself this satisfaction until he was sure of obtaining a replacement, or at least of obtaining the money with which to buy one.

In spite of his remonstrances, the old Bishop did not send Don Camillo away empty-handed. He gave him all the money he could, and although it wasn't very much, Don Camillo went home feeling happy. The first step was taken. There were thousands more steps to go before he reached his goal, but they did not weigh upon him. No landslide ever starts until the first pebble has fallen from the top of the mountain.

And so, after due time, came the promised day, and the arrival of the projector, a brand-new model with a sound-track as smooth as velvet. Don Camillo whitewashed the walls of the room and varnished the chairs. He rented a superlative film and posted announcements at every street corner. The afternoon before the great event he ran up and down the streets so often that inevitably he ran into Peppone.

"Is the mayor going to honour us with his presence tonight?" he asked. "It's such a big occasion that our first citizen should really be on deck."

"What big occasion do you mean?" asked Peppone in astonishment.

"The opening of the new picture palace."

"I've never heard of any picture palace, old or new," answered Peppone. "All I know is that for some years past you've shown magic-lantern slides for the benefit of choir-boys."

Don Camillo let this sarcasm go by.

"Let the dead bury their dead," he suggested. "We have a real hall and a fabulous new projector."

"Fabulous as it may be, you're probably coming in on the last guard's van, as usual."

"After you've been to one of our new shows, you'll see that this guard's van is up at the head of the train and moving faster than even a diesel engine."

"Fast or slow, the film is a superannuated medium," said Peppone. "It's dead as a doornail, and there's no place for it outside a church hall."

"What medium is in step with the times, then?" asked Don Camillo. "The evening class in everyday revolution?"

"Leave politics out of it," said Peppone. "Progress has left the film behind. The coming thing is television."

Just then Smilzo arrived upon the scene and threw out the question:

"Chief, what do you say? The expert is here and wants to know where to put the aerial."

"Wherever he thinks best. I deal in combustion-engines, and television's not up my street."

Smilzo hurried away, and after swallowing a lump in his throat, Don Camillo asked:

"Is our mayor a pioneer television owner?"

"Not myself personally, but the workers' Party who place it in the vanguard of progress. The TV set is for the People's Palace, and tonight is the first showing. But we shan't offer you any competition, Father. The set is a product of the State Radio Plant of Moscow, and only Party members are invited. I can't ask you to come, Father, much as I regret it, that is, unless you take out a membership card."

"I admit that I'd like to see what this thing called television is all about," said Don Camillo between clenched teeth, "but I can wait a little bit longer."

"*Fate vobis*," said Peppone, throwing out his arms.

Don Camillo went home with a queasy feeling in his stomach and took his troubles to the Christ on the main altar.

"Lord," he panted, "Peppone and his gang have a TV set!"

"They're not the only ones in the world, are they?" Christ answered. "And it's not a death-dealing machine, is it?"

"They're not the only ones in the world, but they're the only ones in the village."

"But why do you worry? Are you afraid that the appeal of something so new may lure some of your followers into the bear's lair?"

"No, only Party members can enjoy it. But I had hoped that my film hall would attract some of Peppone's hangers-on, and I could save them from the bear's embraces."

Christ sighed.

"Are these your weapons, Don Camillo?" he asked. "I didn't have any machines with which to seize men from the devil's grasp and put them on the path of righteousness."

"Lord, forgive me," said Don Camillo, humbly bowing his head. "But the devil didn't have any machines then, either. If the devil rides a motor-cycle, why should I pursue him on foot?"

"Don Camillo, I can't follow your cycling metaphor. But the vehicles that carry men to heaven or hell are just the same now as they were then."

The television set poisoned Don Camillo's entire evening, and in spite of the success of the film show, he was unable to sleep. Something about the affair was not clear in his mind, and the thought of this elusive, shadowy zone would not let him rest. The next morning, when he looked out of the window that gave on to the church square and saw the television aerial rising above the People's Palace, he was suddenly enlightened. That afternoon he managed to run into Peppone again and said to him brusquely:

"In this television business, are you following a directive from the higher echelons, or did you think it up yourself?"

"What do directives have to do with television?" asked Peppone. "I do what I please."

"Then you're a jackass, Peppone. Only a jackass could imagine that anyone in this village would take out membership in the Communist Party for the sake of seeing the idiocies projected by your teletrap, 'made in USSR'. Who believes that they have television sets in Russia?"

"Oh, I forgot that in Russia they don't have either watches or bicycles!" said Peppone, throwing out his arms. "According to you, this set of ours, which has 'made in USSR' on every single part, is really a 'product of USA', is that it? As you like! Those that have television can enjoy it, and the have-nots will just have to swallow their bile!"

Don Camillo's anger was plain to see, and he did well to go away without answering this last sally. When he reached the rectory he had to hear some first-hand reports on the village reaction to the new TV.

"It seems to be positively wonderful."

"And it was really made in Russia, so they say."

"The Reds who went to the first showing are wild with joy. They say the Americans had better go and bury their heads in the sand."

That night Don Camillo turned over and over in his bed, and his long quest for sleep was thwarted by the chatter of several noise-makers who wagged their tongues immediately under his window, on the church square.

"Too bad, though, that when they have colour TV we'll need a new set."

"A new set? Not a bit of it! They haven't got colour at all in America, but in Russia they've had it for the last two years. And the sets made for export are geared to both black-and-white and colour. Did you see that red lever on the right side? You just pull it down, and there's the whole rainbow."

"If I were Peppone, I'd put it on display at the Party's retail store, so that everybody could see. That way they'd stop saying that we keep it to ourselves because it's either home-grown or made in America."

"Not on your life! They can say what they like, but if they want to see, they'll have to join the Party!"

Don Camillo was a captive audience. And when they stopped talking so loudly and began to laugh and whisper, he jumped out of bed and glued his ear to the aperture of the shutters.

". . . a hall just as dismal as the other . . ."

". . . films more idiotic than ever . . ."

". . . and they say the sound is ear-splitting . . ."

". . . but what should he know about machines? They saw him coming . . ."

". . . you know what it is, when a man has a wad of money, whether it's a few liras more or less . . ."

In order not to burst with rage, Don Camillo dived back into bed, where he didn't shut an eye before morning. But by the time morning came he had swallowed his anger and his brain was functioning in a normal manner. "A canny player plays his cards close to the chest, and no one can guess what he has up his sleeve. If you're not showing your Soviet TV set, it's because the whole thing's a big story. You'll puncture your own balloon, if I give you time, Comrade Peppone!"

And so Don Camillo inaugurated a policy of complete indifference. When anyone spoke of the famous Russian TV set, he answered with a smile:

"If the Russians have the atomic bomb, why shouldn't they have TV sets and send them to their friends abroad?"

"What about the colour TV?"

"They've always been colourful! Why shouldn't they apply this quality to television?"

And so one, two, three months went by. Every evening there was a change of the guard at the People's Palace, and a different group went to see the show, gathering afterwards below Don Camillo's window, on the church square, for an exchange of extravagantly laudatory impressions. Don Camillo was rudely awakened, and had to listen in grim silence. He held out for some time, but on perhaps the ninetieth occurrence it was too much for him to endure. "Enough is enough!" he muttered to himself. "I've taken all I can, God forgive me!"

This was ten days after the snowstorm which had caused the collapse of the roof of the People's Palace and the attic below. The roof and the attic ceiling had been promptly repaired, but the night watchman's quarters were still uninhabitable, because the walls had been soaked with water and the cement was not yet dry enough to permit removal of the scaffolding. The watchman, Lungo, and his wife and child were temporarily quartered elsewhere, and from midnight to four o'clock in the morning the People's Palace was empty.

One foggy evening a man went through the open door leading to the courtyard and climbed resolutely to the attic, where he lay for several hours in ambush. At midnight Lungo let down the iron curtain at the front of the retail store, gathered up the day's receipts and accounts, inspected the premises, locked the doors and went to his mother-in-law's house. The intruder had such self-control that he waited two hours more before going into action. Slowly he made his way to the ground floor and the assembly hall. All the shutters were closed, and he was assured of complete privacy. With the aid of a torch he surveyed the scene. What he was looking for seemed to be veiled by a piece of cloth at the opposite end of the room. He walked over, removed the cloth and gazed upon a shiny, new TV set, surmounted by a metal plate bearing the inscription "Made in USSR". It wouldn't have been very hard to nail a plate of this kind on to a case containing an American or British or Italian machine, and so the investigator detached the back cover. At this point his eviction was so great that he dropped the torch on to the floor.

"Lord," panted Don Camillo, throwing himself on to his knees before the altar, "something utterly astounding has happened. A fellow who accidentally got into the People's Palace last night took a look at the famous Russian TV set. And what do you think was inside the case? Nothing! Did you hear me? N-o-t-h-i-n-g! The case was empty!" And after wiping the perspiration from his brow he went on: "Yes, Lord, empty! For ninety consecutive evenings those poor fools have taken turns going in groups to the People's Palace and then coming out to tell of the miraculous things they've seen. What colossal nerve, Lord! For three months no one has let the cat out of the bag. Just imagine the fun there'll be tomorrow, when the secret is known! The Russian TV! And yet I'll wager that if the discoverer doesn't tell his story they're quite capable of keeping up the farce indefinitely. Isn't it utterly ridiculous? Are they stark mad, to play a part like this, without ever giving themselves away? Self-discipline, they call it, but I have another name . . . Lord, you aren't even listening. . . ."

"I was thinking of the sorrows of the world, Don Camillo, not of the tall tales you've been telling. What is it, then, that the visitor to the People's Palace saw?"

"Lord, a fellow accidentally got in there last night and saw the famous TV set," said Don Camillo, hanging his head. "It's authentically 'made in USSR'."

Don Camillo didn't breathe a word to a soul, but a week later when he ran into Peppone he couldn't resist remarking:

"Comrade, when will your faithful give up the game of the empty box?"

"When the time is ripe, Rev.!"

"Isn't it all very silly?"

"Just try getting up something equally silly among your highly respectable people!"

To this Don Camillo found no reply.

The next morning the village was startled by an amazing piece of news. A short circuit had caused the famous TV set to go up in flames.

"*But the enemies of the People have no cause to rejoice,*" said the poster which Peppone put up on the façade of the People's Palace. "*The working class, no matter how ground down it may be, will have another TV!*"

They took up a collection, and ten days later the People's Palace no longer had an empty box; it had a box full of TV.

"It's not nearly as good as the Russian set we had before," proclaimed Peppone's henchmen, "but it's better than nothing."

And from their point of view, they weren't so very wrong.

9

INFLATION IN THE PO VALLEY

THE question of television continued to be a sore point with Don Camillo, and smart salesmen have a way of sensing such things. The young man with the handsome tan briefcase was all smiles when he came to the rectory, insisting that all he wanted was to make the acquaintance of the most famous priest of the lower Po valley. Don Camillo still had some hundred jars of "Atomic Floor Wax" in the basement, and he wasn't going to fall for sales talk, no matter how many blandishments went with it.

"Thanks for your kind words, but I really don't need a thing."

"Father, you misunderstand me," the young man protested. "I'm no salesman, I work for Guardian . . ."

"I see, it's life insurance . . ."

"No, Father, you must be thinking of some other organization. 'Guardian Purchases' is an entirely different matter, as you can see for yourself."

These last words meant that he had managed to open his briefcase and put a dazzlingly illustrated catalogue into Don Camillo's hands.

"Motor-cycles, bicycles, cameras, typewriters, refrigerators, radio and television sets . . . 'Guardian' buys all these things direct from the makers at such a discount that it can make house-to-house sales on the instalment plan, with no increase over the list prices."

Don Camillo tried to give back the catalogue, but the young man would have none of it.

"Don't worry, Father, I'm not here to sell. I only mean to give you an idea of all the lines we carry. If ever you want to buy any of these things, I'm sure you'll come to us. For instance, some day you'll surely get a television set, and it'll be worth your while to look over our large assortment. . . ."

The smiling salesman must have been Satan in disguise, or else how could he have known that Don Camillo was crazy to have a television set? But so far nothing serious had happened. Just to look at photographs of television sets didn't mean promising to buy one. The young man made this very clear.

"You have here an enormous range of models, from the cheapest to the most luxurious, all of them well-known makes. You can see for yourself that we charge the normal retail price, and the payments are extraordinarily easy. We call ourselves 'Guardian Purchases' because our system actually guards and protects you. The debt you contract with us practically pays itself."

Don Camillo was so taken with the television sets that he forgot about the store of useless wax in the basement. But he did not forget that his personal finances were disastrously low. And so, after feasting his eyes on the catalogue, he insisted on returning it.

"I'll keep what you told me in mind," he said by way of farewell.

"Thank you," said the salesman, tucking it away in his brief-case. "Just let me repeat that you needn't worry about the money. The day you decide to make your purchase just let me know and I'll come to write out the contract and pick up the initial pay-ment. Of course, if here and now you happen to have as little as five thousand liras, it would be even simpler. . . ."

He must indeed have been Satan in disguise, or else how could he have known that, besides the burning desire for a television set, Don Camillo had exactly five thousand liras in his wallet? In any case, when he walked out of the rectory he had them in his pocket, together with a signed contract and a sheaf of signed promissory notes. Of course, he said that these notes were a mere formality and Don Camillo mustn't worry about meeting them. Don Camillo didn't worry. For some time he had warm feelings about the smiling young man, because the television set was a beauty and worked very well. But one day he found himself in trouble.

At the end of the fourth month Don Camillo couldn't meet the payment. The television set was his own personal luxury and he had to pay for it out of his own personal funds, which at this point were not merely low but virtually non-existent. Eighteen thousand liras aren't so very much, but if a poor country priest hasn't got them, what is he to do? He can't work overtime or give private instruction in the catechism. There was no excuse for appealing to his wealthier parishioners, for no object or institution of charity was involved. And no matter how poor he was, Don Camillo had his dignity. He couldn't borrow money to meet the payment due for a television set; after all, it was an extravagance and he ought never to have taken it if he didn't have extra means.

Finally he wrote to "Guardian Purchases", but they wrote back that although they appreciated the unusual circumstances in which he found himself and were truly sorry, there was nothing they could do. The note had been sent to the bank and he must either pay up or submit to the bank's demand for payment. Complications increased, because Don Camillo was unable to pay the next instalment either. This time he did not have the nerve to write; he simply said a prayer and waited for pandemonium to break loose. The situation was particularly delicate for this reason. Although with time Don Camillo would doubtless have been able to restore his affairs to good order, a local election was at hand, and this was not the moment to have the bank publish his name. Don Camillo was not a candidate for office; he was not even enrolled in any political party. But the Christian Democrats' opponents were sure to seize any pretext for attacking a priest. Furthermore, to tell the truth, Don Camillo had been active in the last national election and the Christian Democrats had discussed their tactics with him. He broke out into cold perspiration at the thought of what Peppone and his gang would do if they had the bank's list of bad accounts in their hands.

After a number of sleepless nights and tormented days, the time for the bank bulletin's publication came round, and Don Camillo went all the way to the city to get a copy. Sure enough, the first thing he saw was his own name. He went back to the village in a state of great dismay and shut himself up in the rectory where nobody could see him. For he imagined that everyone must be in the know. That evening he ate no supper and could not even make up his mind to go to bed, but paced up and down the hall, with black thoughts crowding his mind. Peppone and his gang had acquired a formidable weapon against him, and he could just hear the accusations they would make in political meetings. His horror was all the more intense because he seemed to hear the crowd laughing. He must do something —anything—about it. And so, abruptly, he did.

Peppone was still hammering away in his workshop, and the sight of Don Camillo caused him to start.

"You must have something on your conscience," said Don Camillo.

"A priest flitting about by night is bound to startle even an honest man," said Peppone dryly. "What do you want?"

There was no use making a short story long.

"I want to talk with you, man to man."

"What about?"

"The promissory notes."

Peppone threw his hammer into one corner.

"I have something to say, man to man, too," he said. "And I'd like to point out that, in spite of our enmity, I've never made political capital out of your personal misfortunes."

"I can say the same thing," said Don Camillo.

"I'm not so sure about that," Peppone grumbled. "But there's one thing that *is* sure: if you dare to be funny about my overdue note, I'll wring your neck."

Don Camillo thought he must have misunderstood.

"What's your note got to do with me?" he asked.

Out of his pocket Peppone pulled a crumpled paper, which he thrust roughly at the priest.

"If you haven't seen or heard about it, you'll be sure to see or hear tomorrow. On the list of notes that have not been honoured there's one signed by your humble servant, Giuseppe Bottazzi."

And there, under the letter *B*, was listed a note for twenty thousand liras in Peppone's name. Don Camillo had never noticed it simply because he was so intent upon looking for his own.

"Is that the only thing of interest you found?" he asked shaking the bulletin in front of Peppone's nose.

"I confine myself to my own business," said Peppone. "I wanted to know if I was there, and there I was."

Don Camillo put the bulletin into his hand, pointing to a certain line. Peppone read and re-read it, and then stared hard at Don Camillo.

"No!"

"Yes!" Don Camillo exclaimed. "Devil take 'Guardian Purchases'!"

Peppone started.

" 'Guardian Purchases'? A most agreeable young fellow with a big tan briefcase?"

"Exactly."

"And did you get a refrigerator, too?"

"No, a television set."

Peppone launched into a tirade against instalment buying, an institution worse than the atomic bomb. Just a spot of cash and a trifle to pay every month, a debt that pays itself. . . . Then when you're unable to pay, you see that you were the trifler, and two hundred thousands liras of debt are . . . two hundred thousand liras. Finally he calmed down.

"Well, since my refrigerator is working perfectly well, and you're in the same boat, there'll be no political consequences. Why worry? Don't you agree?"

"That's what I say," said Don Camillo. Then a sudden thought caused him to turn pale.

"What about the third ticket?" he shouted.

The third ticket was a group of candidates put up by the Rightists, who were opposing both Peppone's Reds and the Christian Democrats' Shield and Cross. These candidates would have a cogent argument against both their adversaries, and the village would enjoy no end of laughter. Pietro Follini, the Rightist leader, was a fast thinker and an eloquent speaker. Peppone too turned pale.

"The idea that because of these filthy notes they may bracket me with the wearer of a clerical collar makes me see red!" he shouted.

"And the idea of being dragged down to the level of a godless fool makes me see black!" retorted Don Camillo.

They mulled it over for a quarter of an hour, and then Peppone pulled on his jacket and said:

"I'll go through the fields, and you go along the river. We'll have a showdown with that miserable Pietro Follini. First, you try to make him see reason. If he doesn't respond, I'll make him see stars."

Follini had gone to bed, but he came downstairs when he heard Don Camillo calling. Great was his amazement when he saw Peppone beside him.

"Have you set up a common front?" he asked. "I'm not surprised. Reds and clericals have the same end in view: dictatorship!"

"Follini, keep your wit for political meetings," said Peppone. "See if you can grasp what Don Camillo is going to tell you."

They went to sit down in the parlour, and Don Camillo at once showed Follini the bank bulletin.

"Have you seen that?" he asked.

"Yes, I've seen it. I went to the city this morning for the express purpose of buying it. When I saw my name, I took it hard. But when I saw the names of the priest and the mayor, I felt better."

Don Camillo took back the bulletin and thumbed nervously through it. Under the *F*'s there was Pietro Follini, listed as owing forty thousand liras. The three men looked at one another in silence, until Don Camillo said:

"I owe 'Guardian Purchases' twenty thousand liras for a television set; he owes them the same for a refrigerator. How about you?"

"I owe them forty thousand for a television set *and* a refrigerator. Both of them are working very well."

"Same here!" said Peppone.

"Same here!" echoed Don Camillo.

Follini opened a bottle of wine. They drank together and before Don Camillo went back along the river he muttered:

"I'm glad there's not a fourth ticket!"

And before Peppone went back through the fields he mumbled:

"We're neatly matched. Television against television, refrigerator against refrigerator, and promissory note against promissory note! It's democracy in action!"

10

THE DEVIL SWISHES HIS TAIL

MICHAELMAS was close at hand, and festive preparations were under way, when the bombshell burst. It burst in the form of a notice posted by Don Camillo.

> "*For too many years the coming holiday has been celebrated with indecent public dancing in the square. It is time for all good Christians to join in outlawing this immoral spectacle. If foolish folk of both sexes and all ages must cavort like monkeys to the accompaniment of jungle cacophony, let them find a place more appropriate to their carnival than the square in front of God's house.*
>
> "*It is prohibited by law to organize public dancing or other offensive activities in the neighbourhood of a church, and I call upon the duly constituted authorities to enforce this prohibition.*"

Of course, the notice sent Peppone into a paroxysm of anger, for he and his gang were the sponsors of the "indecent public dancing" in question. The "Public Welfare Committee" was called into immediate session at the People's Palace, and proceeded to discuss counter-measures to this act of clerical aggression. When Brusco was called upon to speak, he declared:

"We have all the time in the world to counter-attack. Just now we must concentrate on obtaining a permit for the dancing. After that is cleared, the priest can protest till he's blue in the face."

The majority seconded him, and Peppone went by bicycle to police headquarters.

"I was just about to bring you the permit," the sergeant told him.

"So we can go ahead with our dancing, just as in previous years?" asked Peppone with relief.

"Yes, you have the all-clear of the provincial police. Only you mustn't dance in the square. The carnival ground isn't the legal distance from the church."

"But, Sergeant," Peppone exclaimed, turning purple with rage, "the distance was legal enough for the past seven years! What's the matter with it now?"

"The distance was never legal, Mr. Mayor. But as long as the priest didn't kick, the police winked at it. Now that there's been a protest, we've had to open our eyes. It's a matter of only a few yards, and it's up to the priest's discretion."

"But if we can't dance in the square, where *can* we dance?" asked Peppone in dismay.

"Anywhere you like, just as long as the carnival is set up at a legal distance from the church. The permit is issued under that condition."

Peppone called the committee together again and explained the situation.

"This cursed village seems to be laid out in a way designed to benefit the clergy and poison honest working people! If you take away the square, there's no space large enough to hold a carnival. It's either the square, or the outskirts; there's no other alternative. And if you stage it in the outskirts, what happens? First, you miss the crowd from the cafés and taverns on the square; second, you have to pay rent for the use of the land; and third, you are humiliated by having to operate in the middle of a sea of mud, littered with fallen apples."

Brusco had a word to put in.

"Chief," he said, "since the sergeant told you it was up to the priest's discretion, why don't we go and talk reason to Don Camillo?"

Peppone pounded the table with his fist.

"I'll never lower myself to the level of a priest! Never!"

"I didn't say you should be the one to go parley with him. There are twelve of us, all able to speak up and hold our own.

Let's write our names on slips of paper and then draw one out of a hat. Tell the barman's son to bring us something to write on."

And so, after each one had written on and folded his sheet of paper and thrown it into Brusco's hat, the barman's son proceeded to the drawing.

"Peppone!" he announced.

"Did it have to be me?" Peppone groaned.

Bruscho threw out his arms.

"Never mind; I'll go," muttered Peppone. "Brusco, you stay here, and the rest of you can go on home."

When Brusco and he were alone together, Peppone picked up the hat and took out the eleven remaining ballots. He unfolded them, one by one, and spread them out in a row on the table.

"Look at those, Brusco, and then tell me whether or not you're a bunch of rascals!"

Brusco examined the ballots and saw that every one bore the name of Peppone.

"Brusco," Peppone shouted again, seizing his companion by the shoulder; "is this the way the comrades rat on their leader?"

"No, Chief, it only goes to show what confidence they have in him!"

"Father," said Peppone, sitting down on the chair which Don Camillo pointed out to him, "have we come to the point where we have to argue over a matter of inches?"

"I'm not arguing over inches," Don Camillo replied. "I'm raising a moral question, which defies all measurement."

"But in past years you didn't raise any moral question. There wasn't anything wrong then, so what can there be now?"

"There was always a moral question involved, Mr. Mayor. But I was hoping you would see it for yourself."

"It's much simpler than that," jeered Peppone. "The fact is that you were more afraid of us in past years."

"I was never afraid of a living soul, and you know it," said Don Camillo, shaking his head. "If I didn't step in before, it's just because I knew people were incapable of seeing the light. It's no use arguing with madmen. Now the atmosphere is calmer, and the question can be raised. When people have lost all sense of proportion there's no point in talking about inches. Everything has its proper time."

"I see, Father," assented Peppone. "According to you, the Communists have lost strength and so you can speak your mind. You may think as you please, but I consider you're making a mistake. One day you'll find out that the Communists still count."

"I don't doubt it, Comrade; otherwise I should have ceased to combat them. Wolves stay wolves, and sheep can't be anything but sheep. When the wolves are prowling around the sheepfold, the sheep daren't stick out their noses, but when the wolves go back to the woods, the sheep may come out and nibble a few blades of grass."

"So I'm a wolf, am I?" muttered Peppone.

"Yes."

"And you're an innocent lamb, is that it?"

"Exactly."

"A fine lamb you are!" shouted Peppone, leaping to his feet. "You're a Bengal tiger!"

As he went towards the door, Don Camillo called out: "See you soon, baboon!"

Peppone, still fuming, informed the committee of the upshot of this conversation.

"Curse that priest! Devil take him and his legal distance! We'll dance in the outskirts, but with two orchestras playing so loudly that they'll be heard on the square. It's only a matter of finding the right location."

While Peppone was holding a meeting in the People's Palace, Don Camillo addressed a group of landowners whose property lay in the outskirts of the village.

"I called you together," he said, "because you are good Christians and hence lovers of law and order. Once more the day sacred to Saint Michael is going to be defiled by the Reds' public ball. I have managed to prevent its being held, quite shamelessly, on the square. But the Reds won't give up so easily; they'll simply transfer it to the outskirts. Even there, they'll be checkmated, because you'll refuse them the use of your land. I trust you are all in agreement."

His eight hearers were all ferociously anti-Red, but Don

Camillo's words were not greeted with the enthusiasm which he had expected. They said nothing, and stared at the mat on the oval table before them.

"Well, then?" said Don Camillo in amazement. "If you don't see things in the same light, just say so."

They stared at one another, until finally Cerelli said what was on all their minds.

"Father, you're quite right. But to tell the truth, I don't see the necessity for a clash with the Communists on this particular occasion. If they ask me for the use of a piece of land and are willing to pay for it, why should I say no?"

The other seven admitted that they felt the same way. Don Camillo crossed his arms over his capacious chest.

"Very well. Your priest calls for your help and you refuse to give it."

"No," said Cerelli. "We'd do anything for you, Father. But you mustn't ask us to do more than we feel like doing."

"And what if I were to ask you to do something involving no risk and giving you a chance to make some money?" asked Don Camillo, bringing his fist down on the table. "How would you feel about that?"

"It sounds good, Father."

"Splendid! How much do you think Peppone may offer you for your land?"

They said somewhere between fifteen and twenty thousand liras.

"Excellent," said Don Camillo. "Then the eight of you must agree that anyone who wants your land must put down a sixty-thousand lira deposit. Just think, some one of you may actually pocket that much money!"

This idea won his listeners' favour.

"Good," said Don Camillo. "But we'll have to be sure that no one puts anything over on his neighbours by accepting less. Are you willing to give me your word of honour that nothing less than a deposit of sixty thousand liras will induce you to do business?"

They all swore, and shook hands on it. It's not that way in the city, but in the Po valley, when a man gives his word it is considered binding. And so Don Camillo went to bed with his mind at rest. To spend sixty thousand liras for a couple of days would be utter folly, and Peppone's plans were doomed from the start. It wasn't really the season for a carnival, anyhow; the bulk of the dancers would come from other villages near by. Without the usual contributions from the storekeepers on the square and faced with the prospect of digging up sixty thousand liras in cash, Peppone would have to surrender.

Peppone knew nothing of the trouble which Don Camillo was brewing for him, and the next day he sent Smilzo out on a reconnoitring mission.

"Go and see about renting some land. Remember that you are fortunate enough to be dealing with eight separate owners. If any one of them asks too much money, you can afford to pass him by in favour of one of the seven others. Don't worry about their doing you in. Rich people don't know how to organize such a thing as joint action. Their only wish is to rub up against one another. So remember that I don't want to spend more than twelve thousand liras, to be paid when the carnival is over."

Smilzo went bravely off, and when the first landowner he approached asked for sixty thousand liras cash, he laughed in his face. He laughed again when the second made the same demand. But the third aroused no more than a faint smile, and the fourth wiped that off his face. When he had finished making the rounds, Smilzo came gloomily back to where he had started.

"Chief," he began, "two hours ago you said that rich people were too stupid to organize a joint action."

"Well, what of it?" asked Peppone.

"You're dead wrong, Chief. This time they've all banded together and none of them will rent his land for less than sixty thousand liras, paid in advance."

Peppone began to describe in a loud voice that sink of iniquity which was the soul of Don Camillo. He concluded his tirade by saying:

"Comrades, there are two alternatives before us: either to concede the clericals' victory, or to squeeze out sixty thousand liras. Choose! But think first which course is the more expensive in the long run."

"Chief, we haven't really an idea of the market prices," Brusco observed.

"But you have an Ideal, for which you are willing to die, haven't you?" Peppone shouted.

Brusco wanted to answer that pledging one's life to an Ideal and promising to pay sixty thousand liras are two quite different things. Especially when the liras have to be put down on the spot, for a man who pledges his life to an Ideal isn't compelled to die in advance for it. But he did not say any of these things, and so it was decided that a clerical victory would cost more grief than the outlay of sixty thousand liras. Because none of the Committee had brought any money, Peppone was the one to fork out.

Don Camillo took it hard when he learned that Peppone had put down sixty thousand liras in cash for the rent of a field to the left of the Molinetto road, just outside the village. He hadn't anticipated any such blow. And when he read posted announcements of the carnival, he took it even harder. The posters made extravagant promises: prizes for the best single dancers, the best-matched and most ill-assorted couples and the presence of two orchestras, together with well-known popular singers.

"They're getting up something tremendous," his informants told Don Camillo. "It's advertised in the villages for miles around, with a special appeal to their Party groups. Yes, it's become a political football, an act of resistance to clerical interference."

Don Camillo lost his head. Wasn't the whole fault his? Hadn't he asked for trouble? If he hadn't intervened, the carnival tents would have been pitched on the square; Peppone and his gang would have organized the usual uninspired celebration.

Yes, Don Camillo lost his head. Whenever this happened the consequences were disastrous, for the devil's tail began to swish with anticipation. After having foamed impotently at the mouth with anger, one whole day long, Don Camillo called his most reliable follower, Gigi Lollini.

"Gigi," Don Camillo said to the young man, "have you seen what those damned souls are up to now?"

"Yes, Father, I have."

"Gigi, we've got to make it fail. You must form a committee and set up another carnival, just across the way. If the Reds have two orchestras, then hire three; if they have three contests,

226

stage half a dozen. You have a head start, because while Peppone's had to advance sixty thousand liras, you'll get the land for next to nothing. Go to Cerelli, whose place is just opposite the one rented by Peppone. Only don't let on that I'm in any way concerned. A parish priest can't sponsor a forty-eight-hour dance marathon."

Lollini was a violent anti-Red and undertook the assignment with enthusiasm. He scuttled away and went first to rent some of Cerelli's land. Soon he came back to the rectory.

"Father, that old skinflint wants sixty thousand liras. I asked the other six, and they told me that they had all promised to accept no less. After imposing these terms on Peppone, they feel they must stick to their guns. The main thing is that they don't want trouble. . . . I found some fellows to go into partnership with me, but they refuse to spend more than fifteen thousand liras, and I haven't any cash to advance myself."

Yes, the devil's tail was swishing ominously. Don Camillo paced up and down the rectory hall and then said:

"I can get my motor-cycle later on. Here are the sixty-five thousand liras I've been saving up; I'll give you but five of them."

"Don't worry, Father, you'll get them all back. We have a programme that will put the Reds to shame, and we'll give it plenty of publicity. . . ."

The next day the village was filled with posters announcing "the carnival of the century", put on by the "Good Fun Company". Afternoon and evening dancing were to appropriately honour the feast of Saint Michael.

The morning of the last day before the celebration Smilzo and Lollini came to blows over trifles. Soon after noon a truck arrived with material for the Red's carnival, and two hours later, while it was still being erected, came the material for Don Camillo's, just across the way. At two-thirty, the rival gangs met in the middle of the road and beat each other up enthusiastically. By evening, both carnivals were nearly ready, but it looked as if the next day were going to be the saddest Michaelmas the village had ever known.

"Lord," said Don Camillo to the crucified Christ on the main altar, "if You don't step in, tomorrow is going to be ugly for all of us. Everything in this crazy village revolves round politics, even an immoral but non-political ball. Because of the rivalry between the two groups which have organized the dances, it's likely that the celebration will end in a free-for-all fight. Unfortunately, a minister of your church is mixed up in it, because he ill-advisedly supported one group against the other. He had good intentions, Lord. . . ."

"Don Camillo!" the Lord interrupted, "you know what's paved with good intentions! And since when does the end justify the means?"

"Lord," whispered Don Camillo, "unless it's a lie circulated by God's enemies, You Yourself once drove the money-changers from the temple. Of course, I don't say that beating people up is a sin, but after all . . ."

"Don Camillo, how do you dare criticize your own God?"

"I'm not sacrilegious, Lord, but I do say that when one of God's creatures has an ailing tooth, then even if the dentist hurts him by pulling it out . . ."

"Don Camillo," Christ said gravely: "why do you walk in the tortuous path of sophistry?"

"Because I've got off the right track, Lord, and I wish someone would put me straight, with a swift kick, if need be."

Slowly Don Camillo raised his head to look at Christ's face, but his eyes remained on the feet, nailed to the Cross.

It was a terrible night for Don Camillo. He woke up at four o'clock and ran to the window. It was raining, raining buckets and torrents. And as the hours went by, it continued to rain. It rained all day, and by midnight the floor boards of the two carnivals were floating in mud. It rained all of three days more, and amid the downpour both carnivals were dismantled and shipped away. Then, when God willed it, out came the sun, and Don Camillo ran into Peppone.

"Father," Peppone said bitterly, "your manoeuvres cost me sixty thousand liras out of my own pocket."

"They cost me the same," sighed Don Camillo.

"That makes me feel better," said Peppone.

"Then we're even," put in the priest.

"But on Michaelmas of next year . . ." Peppone began, threateningly.

"You mean, if it isn't raining . . ."

"I forgot that you clericals are in on God's little secrets," Peppone shouted angrily. "But it won't go on like this forever. There'll be a day of reckoning!"

"That is, if it doesn't rain, Mr. Mayor!"

"We'll fight with umbrellas," Peppone said solemnly, as if he were speaking for history.

And in order not to spoil the effect, Don Camillo said nothing more.

II

RING OUT THE OLD, RING IN THE NEW

DON CAMILLO was called to the Bishopric, but since the old Bishop was ill Monsignor Contini received him.

"Tell me all about the 'Bridge' church."

This was the last question Don Camillo had expected and for a moment he was so taken aback that he could not open his mouth.

"The 'Bridge' church? Forgive me, Monsignore, but I don't know what you mean."

"It's not so hard to grasp. There's a building within the boundaries of your parish known as the 'Bridge' church, isn't there?"

"Yes, Monsignore."

"Well then, tell me all about it."

Don Camillo gathered his thoughts together and then told the brief story.

"The so-called 'Bridge' church was until fifty years ago in an independent parish in the Pioppetta section. Then, as the village grew, the Pioppetta parish was integrated with ours. But the 'Bridge' church remained officially open, by virtue of a yearly Mass celebrated on St. Michael's day."

Monsignor Contini shook his head.

"According to what I'm told, there's something more to say. The faithful who live out that way would be happy if Mass were said there every Sunday. Isn't it so?"

"Undoubtedly, Monsignore. The Pioppetta section is quite

far out, and the road leading to the centre of the village is in miserable condition. To come in every Sunday is a real hardship, especially for the old people."

"Then everything we have been told is true. We are distressed only that you shouldn't have been the one to inform us."

"But, Monsignore, no one from the Pioppetta section has ever said anything to me."

"Very well. But when you've noticed a number of people from there failing to turn up at Sunday Mass, especially during the winter, you might have thought to report the situation. In any case, now that it has been reported, we shall see that something is done about it. Every Sunday and holy day of obligation Mass shall be said at the 'Bridge' church."

Don Camillo bowed his head.

"With God's help, I shall carry out the Bishop's orders."

"With God's help and the help of the young priest we are going to send to assist you. We aren't asking you to make an unreasonable effort.

Don Camillo's mouth fell open.

"But, I really don't need . . ." he stammered.

"Don Camillo," Monsignor Contini interrupted him, "we know your good will. But for all of us the years are going by. You're getting to be, well, shall we say, a mature man. . . ."

"I?" exclaimed Don Camillo, throwing out his chest. "I can still carry a three-hundred sack of wheat up to a second story!"

"I don't doubt it! But your job is not weight-lifting, and muscles are not the prime requisites."

"Monsignore, I've always carried out my priestly mission. . . ."

"I'm sure of that, Don Camillo. But we can't expect you to go beyond the call of duty. We shall send you a bright, enthusiastic young fellow, who'll relieve you of some of the drudgery of parish work. The rectory is big enough to lodge him, and the generosity of Divine Providence is unfailing, so that you'll have no trouble in putting him up."

"I shall obey orders, as faithfully as ever."

"As *almost* ever," his superior corrected him. "We know Don Camillo and esteem him at his just worth, but in all truth we can't say that he is an example of perfect discipline. Don Camillo

231

is an honest, diligent priest, but he has a bit of temperament . . . or am I mistaken?"

"No, Monsignore. I admit to my weaknesses."

"Let's forget about them," said Monsignor Contini, "When you go back to the village, put the 'Bridge' church in order, so that it can be turned to full-time use as soon as possible."

"Monsignore," said Don Camillo, throwing out his arms. "When it was a matter of saying only one Mass a year, I brought the necessary supplies with me. But what are we to do now? The church is an empty shell."

"There are people in your village who are not only well off, but who have means far beyond their needs. You must make the rounds of all those who are in a position to give. Tell them that by contributing to this little church they will warm their ailing Bishop's heart."

These words particularly caught Don Camillo's attention.

"Is he so very ill, Monsignore?"

"Yes, but there's no reason to be alarmed or to spread the alarm. It's nothing you can put your finger on, but simply the effect of old age. What His Grace needs above all is complete rest and peace of mind. We must not allow him to worry."

"He needn't worry about the little church under my jurisdiction!" exclaimed Don Camillo. "All that he wishes shall be done. Even if I have to use brute force . . ."

"Come, come, Don Camillo! . . ."

"That's just a manner of speaking."

The "Bridge" church was in a sorry state. The walls were sturdy enough, but the ceiling looked like a sieve; the plaster was in tatters, the floor uneven and the pews cracked or cracking. Even a minimum amount of repairs called for a considerable sum of money, and the collection of such a sum called, in turn, for what seemed like an infinity of patient endeavour. When Don Camillo had drawn up an estimate of the costs, he drew a deep breath as well. "I'll do everything I can, and Divine Providence will look after the rest," he concluded.

His campaign got off to a lame start, when he knocked first at the door of Filotti, the richest land-owner in the vicinity. Don Camillo spoke of the old Bishop and of the pleasure it would give him to hear that the little "Bridge" church was back in use. But Filotti shook his head.

"Father, when you've asked for money for the poor or for the Orphan Asylum, I've always been happy to contribute. But this time I don't feel like giving. The village church is quite sufficient. And, frankly, I don't see why, at this point, I should help to finance propaganda directed against my own class."

"Come now!" exclaimed Don Camillo. "Have I ever supported propaganda against landowners?"

"Father, I'm not speaking of you personally. I refer simply to what I read in your newspapers and the speeches made by your senators and deputies to parliament."

"The Church has neither senators nor deputies!" Don Camillo protested.

"That isn't the way you sounded around election time," said Filotti calmly.

Don Camillo's second stop was at the house of Valerti, who listened quietly to all he had to say and then likewise shook his head.

"Why should I give you money?" he asked. "It would mean that those of us whom you call 'neo-Fascists' would be blasted from two pulpits instead of one."

Without seeking to defend himself, Don Camillo continued his rounds, but his third visit was no more fortunate than the other two, for Signora Meghini hardly waited for him to end his plea before she started violently shaking her head.

"Father, if you're looking for money with which to open a second church, go to the Republicans. Don't forget that you refused Absolution to all of us who voted for the Monarchist Party."

Don Camillo went next to Moretti, a landowner of pronounced clerical tendencies. Moretti listened piously to all he had to say, and answered with a sigh:

"Since you speak of the Bishop, I can't say no. But mind you, it's only for his sake."

"Very good," said Don Camillo, "but why must you tell me that only the good Bishop inspires you? Have I failed to please you in some way."

"Not you personally," said Moretti, shaking his head. "But

233

generally speaking, I can't approve of combating Communism by attacking the upper class."

Don Camillo pocketed Moretti's contribution and went to knock at still another door. Perini opened it in person and gave him ill-humoured attention.

"There's not much I can do, Father," he said. "My family just manages to get along, from day to day. Here's my mite, but let's hope that the new priest is up-to-date."

"Up-to-date?" exclaimed Don Camillo. "What *do* you mean?"

"It's time people got it into their heads that the world is turning definitely to the Left. We militant Catholics insist upon a social programme, and until the clergy catches up with us, Communism will continue to gain ground. And Communism's no joke, Don Camillo. Don't go imagining that all Communists are like Peppone!"

Don Camillo said that he imagined nothing of the sort, and went to knock at the next door. He made a hundred or more visits, and everywhere he received a reply like one of those quoted above. After several days of going from place to place he unburdened himself to the crucified Christ on the main altar.

"Lord," he said, "the rich reproach me for championing the poor, the poor accuse me of conniving with the rich; the whites call me black, the blacks call me white; to the reactionaries I'm a subversive, and to the radicals I'm an obstacle to progress; and as for the Reds, they won't listen to me at all. Am I truly the most ineffective of God's ministers?"

Christ sighed and then answered:

"Don Camillo, you're a skilled hunter and fisherman, aren't you?"

"Yes, Lord."

"You hunt with a gun and fish with a hook and line, don't you?"

"Yes, Lord."

"Then if one day you were to see fish flying through the sky and birds slithering under water, would you still fish with a hook and line and hunt with a gun?"

"No, Lord, I'd fish with a gun and hunt with a hook and line."

"That's where you're wrong, Don Camillo! Because you'd fail completely in both endeavours."

"Lord, I don't understand."

"Many do not understand, Don Camillo, because they look at mere words instead of realities."

Don Camillo collected only enough money to repair the roof of the abandoned church, and it was with a heavy heart that he reported to the Bishopric.

"Never mind, Don Camillo," said Monsignor Contini. "Divine Providence will take care of the rest."

And indeed, after Don Camillo had finished patching the roof, money came from the city for the rest of the repairs. As soon as the work was all done he went to give the good news to Monsignor Contini.

"Then next Sunday you can celebrate the first regular Mass at the renovated church," the Monsignor told him.

Don Camillo's face lit up with joy.

"Monsignore, does that mean you're going to leave me in charge?"

"No, Don Camillo, that would make too heavy a load for you to handle. The new curate is to join you tomorrow. But for a while you'll officiate at the 'Bridge' church, while he takes your place in the village. After that, you'll take turns for a while, before settling upon a definite division of labour."

"I don't see the reason for so many changes, Monsignore."

"That's not hard to understand. I know the mentality of your village people. They have a mistrustful and hostile attitude towards anything new. The faithful from the outskirts would be quite capable of making the arduous trip to the centre of the village rather than go to a Mass celebrated by a *new* priest. But if you are there for the first few Sundays, they'll surely come. Then, when they've fallen into the habit of going to the renovated church, they'll continue to do so after your assistant has taken it over. The Bishop wants you to follow this procedure."

"May I speak to His Grace?" asked Don Camillo, humbly bowing his head.

"His Grace is very ill. He must have complete rest."

"I'd only like to wish him well."

"He can't talk to anyone. Even listening tires him. The doctor's orders are that he is not to talk or listen or read. Yes, the good man is seriously ill."

Don Camillo sighed.

"Where is the Bishop's room?" asked Don Camillo. "As I go out, I'd like to look up at his window."

"It's on the third floor, but the window gives on to the courtyard, so that no noise can disturb him. I'll try to find a propitious moment for conveying your good wishes to him."

"Thank you, Monsignore," said Don Camillo, bowing his head.

"When the new curate arrives, I trust you'll give him a hearty welcome and tell him about the local political situation. He's an extremely capable young man, and up-to-the-minute on social problems."

"Yes, Monsignore."

Don Camillo went slowly down the majestic stairs. When he reached the empty front hall he paused for a moment to look into the courtyard, surrounded by arcades, like those of a convent or monastery. The entrance to the courtyard was just across from the front door, and Don Camillo pushed it open and went in. The courtyard garden was untidy, filled with snow and surrounded by high walls. Don Camillo raised his eyes to look at the long row of windows on the third floor. Which one, he wondered, belonged to the old Bishop? Behind the blackened trunk of a withered tree, he waited for some sign of life from the third floor. But nothing moved, and after lingering for some time, he went away, with his feet soaked from the snow and a chill in his heart.

12

THE NEW CURATE

At nine o'clock the sky abandoned its ambiguous and threatening air; the clouds were brushed away and the sun's honest face started beaming. After the unseasonably stormy weather which had prevailed all through the Spring, Don Camillo at last found cause to rejoice as he hoed his garden. But his joy was short-lived, for the bell-ringer's mother came to disturb him.

"Father, the young curate has come," she announced.

Don Camillo was prepared for the shock and took it with apparent nonchalance.

"Bring him along, then," he said, still intent upon his hoeing.

The old woman looked perplexed.

"I just showed him into the hall," she muttered.

"Well, since I'm not in the hall, but out in the garden, show him out here."

The old woman went away and a few minutes later the young priest was standing at Don Camillo's side.

"Good-day, Father," he said.

Don Camillo straightened up, and the young priest added: "I'm Don Gildo."

"Very happy to see you, I'm sure," said Don Camillo, giving him a handshake powerful enough to strangle a boa constrictor.

The young priest paled, but he had been instructed in sports and sportsmanship, and so he managed to smile.

"I have a letter from the Bishop's secretary," he said, holding out a large envelope.

"If you don't mind, I'll look at it right away," said Don

237

Camillo, taking the letter out of the envelope. After he had finished reading it, he added: "I told the Bishop's secretary that I was still able to carry on. But since it is the Bishop's will to relieve me of part of my burden, then there's nothing I can do but bid you a hearty welcome."

Don Gildo bowed politely.

"Thank you, Don Camillo. I am at your service."

"Those are kind words; I have something for you to do at once."

He went over to the cherry-tree, took down a hoe that was hanging from one of the branches and put it into the young priest's hands.

"Two of us can finish the job more than twice as quickly as one," he observed.

The young priest stared first at the hoe and then at Don Camillo.

"To tell the truth," he stammered, "I've no experience of instruments of this kind."

"That doesn't matter. Stand beside me and do exactly what I do."

The young priest flushed with annoyance. He was sensitive, and besides, he had his dignity.

"Father," he said, "I have come to look after souls, not gardens."

"Of course," said Don Camillo calmly. "But if we are to have fresh fruit and vegetables on our humble table, then the garden must receive some looking after."

He went on hoeing, while the young man continued to stand helplessly beside him.

"Well," said Don Camillo at last, "you mean you really won't help this poor, feeble old man?"

"It's not that I don't want to help you," the other protested. "But the fact is that I came here as a priest."

"The first requisite of the priesthood is humility," said Don Camillo.

The young priest clenched his teeth and started, somewhat ferociously, to lay about him with the hoe.

"Don Gildo," observed Don Camillo mildly, "if I have offended you, take out your resentment on me rather than on this innocent ground."

The young man made an effort to wield the hoe more gently. It took two hours to finish the work. When the two priests, splattered with mud up to their knees, came back to the rectory, it was eleven o'clock.

"We've just time to do another little job," said Don Camillo, leading the way to the shed, where there were some elm logs to be sawed.

Not before noon did Don Camillo call a halt. The young man had stored up so much bile in the last three hours that he had no inclination to touch his food. After a single spoonful of soup, he pushed the bowl away.

"Don't worry if you seem to have lost your appetite," Don Camillo told him. "It's the change of air."

Don Camillo had a tremendous appetite himself, and after he had cleaned up two big bowls of vegetable soup with salt pork, he resumed the conversation.

"How do you like the place?" he asked.

"I've hardly had a glimpse of it," the young man replied.

"It's a village just like any other," Don Camillo told him, "with good people and bad. The only difficulty is in telling which is which. As far as politics goes, the Reds are very strong. And the trouble is they seem to be getting stronger. I've tried everything possible, but things continue to worsen."

"It's all a question of method," the young man assured him.

"Have you a new method better than the old?" Don Camillo asked curiously.

"I don't mean to make any comparison, and I don't pretend to have found a sure cure. But I do say that we must approach the question from a fresh point of view, or at least without the blinkers which have prevented us from seeing social realities. Why are the Communists so successful among the lower classes? Because they say to them: 'Come with us if you want to be better off; we take away from the rich and give to the poor. The priests promise you pie in the sky, but we invite you to cut yourselves a slice here on earth'."

Don Camillo threw out his arms.

"Quite so, Don Gildo, but we can't embrace the materialistic point of view."

"That isn't necessary. We must cease creating the impression that we defend the *status quo*. We must speak of rights as well

239

as duties. Of course, if everyone did his duty, he would automatically respect his neighbour's rights. But we have to assert the rights of the poor in order to compel the rich to do their duty. That way, Communism will cease to have any meaning."

Don Camillo nodded gravely.

"Very true. In other words, we should compete with the Communists on their own ground, even to the point of breaking the law of the land."

"Exactly. When the law of the land upholds privilege and permits poverty, then it is contrary to justice and hence to divine law."

Don Camillo threw open his arms.

"My dear Don Gildo, I can follow your train of thought, but I'm too old to adapt myself to it. I haven't the mental agility any longer. You'll have to forgive me."

Because the curate's mental agility was youthfully intact he poured out a stream of big words, expressive of concepts that were startlingly new. He was aware, moreover, of having a definite mission.

"Father, we know where we're going, and we shall surely attain our goal. You've done a remarkable job, under truly difficult circumstances, and it's high time you had someone to help you. And I don't mean only to help you hoe your garden or saw wood."

"Forgive me," said Don Camillo humbly. "I had no idea how widely read and excellently trained you were."

The curate had scored a conspicuous triumph. That very afternoon he began making his own contacts in the village and laying plans for future action.

Three days later Don Camillo said to his new assistant:

"You came at just the right moment. I need a complete rest. If it isn't too much for you, I wish you'd take my place entirely for a while. The weather has got me down. I need warmth and dry air, and for months it's done nothing but rain."

This suited the curate perfectly. He answered enthusiastically that Don Camillo should have no worry at all, for he would shoulder everything, gladly. And so Don Camillo went into retirement. He went no further than the second floor of the rectory, whose two large rooms looked out, one over the garden and the other over the sports field. The bell-ringer's old mother brought him his food, and he stayed there, in complete seclusion. In one room he had his bed and in the other a small field altar where he said Mass every day, all alone, but very close to God. He had brought up a box of books and spent a great part of the time reading. After two weeks had gone by the old woman broke her habitual silence and said:

"Don Camillo, as soon as you feel up to it, come back downstairs. The new curate is making plenty of trouble."

"Trouble? He seems like a very quiet young man."

"Quiet? He's not a priest, he's a permanent political rally. Lots of people are staying away from church."

"Don't let yourself be disturbed. New days, new ways. They'll get used to him in the long run."

But the new ways really weren't going over, and a few days later the bell-ringer's mother made a new report, which epitomized the whole situation.

"Father, do you know what Peppone said yesterday? He said that as soon as Don Gildo succeeded in emptying the church completely, he'd take him on as group chaplain."

After another interval of a few days, she informed Don Camillo of the answer Filotti had given to somebody who asked why he hadn't been seen at Mass lately. "I'd rather go and listen to the harangues Peppone gives in the People's Palace. He's not nearly so insulting."

Don Camillo held his counsel as long as he could. But after forty days he knelt down impatiently in front of the crucifix on the camp altar and said:

"Lord, I bowed humbly to the Bishop's will. I withdrew in order to give Don Gildo complete freedom. You know, Lord, how much I've suffered all this time. Forgive me if I go downstairs, take Don Gildo by the scruff of his neck and dispatch him back to the city."

It was eight o'clock in the morning, and because Don Camillo wanted to look his best when he finally put in an appearance, he decided to shave. Throwing open the shutters, he discovered that it was a radiantly beautiful day. He paused to take in the peace of the sunlit scene. But a minute later he heard a loud noise. He drew back, but continued to look out at the boys of the "Invincible" soccer team as they ran nimbly on to the field and started at once on a practice game. Forgetting his beard, he watched them play, but to his sorrow they were far below standard and continually fumbled the ball.

"If they play that way against Peppone's team, they'll take a terrible beating," he reflected.

Just then Don Gildo ran out on to the field and stopped the game in order to confabulate with the players.

"So he's going to ruin my team as well as everything else," roared Don Camillo. "If he doesn't decamp, I'll smash him into small pieces!"

But the curate seemed to have no intention of vacating the centre of the field. At a certain point he took over the captain's place and with the ball between his feet, embarked upon a breathtaking display. Don Camillo cast prudence to the winds and flew, rather than walked, down the stairs. When he reached the field he took Don Gildo by the collar and hauled him into the rectory.

"Take off your cassock, put on a jersey and a pair of heavy shoes and go on with your coaching!"

"How can I?" the curate stammered.

"Wear long trousers, a mask and a fake moustache, if you insist, but go ahead and play! You've got to lick that team into shape."

"But my mission, Father . . ."

"Your mission is to secure a victory of our team over the Reds. That will be a knock-out blow."

The "Invincibles" shattered the Red "Dynamos" and made mincemeat out of them. They celebrated madly, while Peppone and his team were in the dumps. That evening Don Camillo gave a banquet in honour of the curate. After it was over he said:

"From now on, forget about your social programme and concentrate on the soccer team. I'll look after the Communist menace!"

13

THE CHAMPION

RENZO was the sort of fellow that for twenty-five years had
jumped on to his racing cycle every morning and ridden all the
way to the city to buy the daily *Sport Gazzette*. Of course, he
could have bought it on the village square a little later in the
day, but that wouldn't have given him the same joy. To pedal
fifteen miles to the city and back was his only regular occupation.
The rest of the time he was ready to accept any odd job he
could get, as long as it allowed him time to buy his paper and
read the section concerned with cycling.

Renzo wasn't touched in the head and he wasn't a loafer or
a drinker. Cycling was his only interest, and he knew everything
there was to know about it. Because he devoured not only the
cycling section of the *Sport Gazzette*, but every single piece of
printed matter on the subject of bicycles and bicycle races that
he could lay his hands on. Renzo was forty years old, and during
all the twenty-five years that he had been under the sway of this
ruling passion people considered him of no account whatsoever.

Then, all of a sudden, thanks to the Marshall Plan for aid to
western intellectuals, the television quiz game was imported
from the U.S.A. and Renzo's life took a new turn. When he
heard that one of the programmes was to feature a cycling
expert, he hurried to glue his eyes on the screen at the Molinetto
tavern. And when the master of ceremonies opened the sealed

envelope and began to read out the cycling questions, Renzo came up with everyone of the answers. The first evening, the tavern habitués took a mild interest in what he was saying; the second week, when he continued to say the right thing, their interest grew. Then, the third week, when the questions got really tough and the expert was shut into a cabin, Renzo's quick thinking caused quite a sensation. The final week, the expert fell down badly on the three decisive questions, but Renzo knew better than he, and the tavern habitués were visibly impressed.

"Why, he could be in the big money!" they exclaimed.

This wasn't the end of the story. Another amateur expert was called on to the programme and walked away with the maximum prize. And the Communist mayor of Reggello, where he came from, organized a big reception, with a brass band and speeches, and hailed him as a man who had brought honour and distinction to his native town.

At this point Peppone called his henchmen together.

"Any political party that manages to enroll Renzo will have a big attraction for the masses. Local elections are just round the corner and we need all the votes he can bring in. Renzo has got to join up, cost what it may!"

They discussed the problem far into the night and the next morning, when Renzo was mounting his bicycle to ride to the city, he found Brusco, Bigio and Smilzo in his way.

"Renzo," they said, "why don't you join the Communist Party? We can get you a road-worker's job and give you a new suit into the bargain."

"I don't want to be mixed up with political parties," said Renzo, and pedalled away.

The comrades saw that there was no point in pressing him too hard, and so Renzo was able to go and buy the *Gazzette* as usual. But at the Pioppaccia intersection a group of Christian Democrats was lying in wait.

"Renzo," they said; "you're a God-fearing man, and you owe it to yourself to join God's party. If you sign up, we'll get you a job at a garage and a new suit of clothes."

But Renzo shook his head.

"I joined God's Party when I was baptized," he retorted.

The stakes were high, and there were hard-headed men on

both sides. When the Reds made their second attack they had more to offer: the post of road-work inspector, a suit, an overcoat and a dozen handkerchiefs.

The Christian Democrats were not slow to match them, holding not only the job at a garage and the suit of clothes, but an overcoat, a raincoat, a dozen handkerchiefs and six pairs of stockings as well. This moved Peppone to come forward with a desperate last-minute bid: a brand-new racing cycle. After which, their rivals could propose no less than a motor-scooter.

"Choose any make you like," they said to Renzo, "and we'll foot the bill."

"No," was Renzo's reply.

At this point they lost patience and their leader said shrilly: "What the devil *do* you want, then? A car?"

"I don't want anything," explained Renzo. "I don't give a hang about political parties. I get round very well on my bicycle and I don't need either an overcoat or a raincoat."

By this time the espionage and counter-espionage departments had had ample time to function. The Reds were acquainted with the Christian Democrats' tactics, and vice-versa. Since Renzo showed no signs of giving in, and all the while television quizzes were becoming more and more popular, Peppone disregarded his position in the Party and fell back on that of mayor. He called representatives of all the democratic parties to a meeting in the town-hall and addressed them as follows:

"My fellow-citizens! When the spiritual and material interests of the community are at stake, partisan politics must take a back seat. We have gathered together out of concern for the general welfare, and I am speaking as one of you. The achievements of the champion from Reggello and the praise given him by his mayor point to the necessity of forming a non-partisan committee to present our candidate for television honours and win for ourselves the same glory."

These stirring words met with loud applause, and the committee turned out to have five Communist and five Christian Democrat members. They went to work at once and closed their first session with a highly satisfactory order of the day. The next morning they went in a body to Renzo's house and set forth the situation.

"Renzo, this is no question of politics or political parties. It involves the interests of the whole village, not to mention your own. You must get on the next television quiz. We'll start the ball rolling, somehow or other, and put you over. Because the good name of the village is at stake, we'll get you a whole outfit of new clothes, send you to Milan by car and give you some cash besides. That way you can win the prize money and our village will be in the headlines. Besides, the *Sport Gazzette* is published in Milan and you'll be able to get it hot off the press."

But Renzo only shook his head.

"The *Gazzette* I buy in the nearest city is quite good enough for me. I don't have to go all the way to Milan."

"And what about the money? You're not too high-and-mighty for that, are you?"

"I said I didn't want to get mixed up in politics, didn't I?" said Renzo.

"But this isn't a matter of politics. No one's asking you to join any party."

Renzo continued to shake his head.

"Five of you offered me a road-work job, and the other five a job in a garage. I simply don't trust you."

The next step was logical enough. Peppone with his five Reds and Piletti with his five Blacks converged upon the rectory. Don Camillo greeted them with considerable perplexity.

"Father," said Peppone, "I am speaking as first citizen of the village and representative of all the rest. You're the only man who can convince Renzo that it's not politics but a matter concerning the village reputation. He has a good chance of winning the jackpot of the television quiz programme and so he simply *must* compete for it."

Don Camillo stared at him with amazement.

"Do you mean to say that you want to put the village idiot on the air?"

"Who else is there?" said Peppone. "You, Father? Do you know when and in what race Girardengo had cramps in his right leg?"

"No, I don't," admitted Don Camillo.

"Well, we need a fellow that knows just this kind of thing. And that means Renzo. He may very well win the big prize."

"What? Renzo win five million liras?"

At this point Piletti, the leader of the Christian Democrats, intervened:

"Father," he said with some annoyance, "I'm afraid I'll have to remind you of something you surely know, since it isn't among the rules of the quiz contest: 'Blessed are the poor in spirit, for theirs is the kingdom of heaven.'"

"Come, come," Don Camillo retorted; "I have a distinction to make there. The Gospel doesn't tell us that the 'poor in spirit' are village idiots."

"This is no time to bicker about trifles," put in Peppone. "You know perfectly well how things stand, and it's your job to tell Renzo that politics don't enter into them."

Don Camillo threw out his arms and exclaimed:

"May the people's will be done!"

"Renzo," the priest said. "If I guarantee that politics has no part in this affair of the television quiz, will you believe me?"

"Yes, Father."

"And if I give you my word of honour that they want to help you only in order that you may win the big money and put our village in the public eye, will you believe me?"

"Yes, Father."

"Then accept their offer, and sign up for the quiz."

"No, Father."

Don Camillo was frankly puzzled.

"Renzo, you simply don't want to be quizzed. Tell me why."

"Because I have my dignity, Father."

Don Camillo did not insist. He paced up and down the room and then came to stand with outspread legs right in front of his interlocutor.

"Renzo, if you're giving up all that money, you deserve some recompense. I'll hire you as bellringer."

Renzo was taken with this idea. What more suitable occupation could he hope to find? He thought it over for five whole minutes and then shook his head.

"I can't do it, Father. The bells have to be rung in the morning, and that's when I go to the city to buy the *Sport Gazzette*."

"But exactly the same paper is sold here!" shouted Don Camillo.

Renzo laughed.

"No, Father; the city paper is an entirely different thing. . . ."

In matters of stubbornness Don Camillo was something of an expert but in this case all he could do was mutter some semi-biblical phrases about the stiff-necked race of sport fans.

14

THE CARBURETTOR

THE newspapers were still full of the story of the child whose life had been saved by the miracle drugs sent by plane from America. Even after the child had recovered they continued to feature the story. According to the Hammer-and-Sickle crowd, it was nothing but a propaganda stunt cooked up by the United States ambassadress.

It all happened in a village on the big river, some twenty miles from the parish of Don Camillo, and so when the dispute was at its hottest Peppone felt he must step in, in order, as he said, "to protect the good reputation of the lower Po valley". His version of the tale was embroidered with so much fancy that Don Camillo found it necessary to run into him—by sheer chance, of course—under the arcade in front of the café, just as he was holding forth on the whys and wherefores of the miraculous cure. As soon as Peppone saw the priest's bulky form looming on the horizon he raised his voice to announce:

"Of course, where political propaganda is concerned, anything goes. But there is a limit to everything, and when it comes to exploiting a helpless child, I draw the line. Any family man will understand what I mean, but naturally one that wears a long black skirt and has no hope of having any children can't be expected to realize . . ."

The bystanders turned to look at Don Camillo, and feeling their eyes upon him, he nonchalantly shrugged his shoulders.

"Mr. Mayor," he said blandly, "if the patient was a child there was no way of saving an adult, was there?"

"What do you mean by 'save'?" retorted Peppone. "There was never any real danger."

"Well, if you're a medical authority, I've nothing more to say."

"I never claimed to be a medical authority," said Peppone. "But specialists stated that there was no need to bring the medicine from overseas when it was available in Holland."

"I'm quite willing to bow to the specialists' opinion. But there's one detail which you and the rest of the comrades seem to have overlooked. The baby didn't need the milk of a contented Dutch cow or the air flailed by a Dutch windmill. He had to have a certain gamma globule which is the exclusive property of the state of Michigan, so why shouldn't the United States ambassadress send there for it?"

Peppone shook his head and laughed loudly.

"*Latinorum latinorum!* When they're at their wit's end they come out with their *latinorum*, their *alpha* and *gamma* and *omega* and all the rest, and if you're not a Latin scholar, you can't reply."

"Mr. Mayor, *gamma* is a Greek letter and not a Latin one. And anyhow, scientists rather than priests gave this hæmoglobin its name."

"Very well," said Peppone, pulling another Soviet propaganda card out of his sleeve, "but what about the Madonna that appeared to the child in a dream? Didn't the priests think up that one?"

"Mr. Mayor," said Don Camillo, with an expression of astonishment on his face, "the clergy does not interfere with children's dreams, or with those of adults, either. They dream when and what they please."

"Listen to this, though," shouted Peppone. "While the plane commandeered by that platinum fox of an ambassadress was flying over the Atlantic, the sick child did dream. And what did he dream about? The Madonna! In his dream the Madonna carried him to Paradise and introduced Jesus Christ, who said that thanks to the United States and Clare Booth Luce, the story would be crowned by a happy ending."

"What was the child to dream, Mr. Mayor?" asked Don Camillo, throwing out his arms in resignation. "Was Lenin to carry him off to the Kremlin and Stalin to explain the Five-year Plan?"

Someone in the group laughed and Peppone grew angrier than ever.

"Let's keep politics out of it!" he exclaimed. "We'd never saddle a child with a dream of this kind. First, because we don't make propaganda out of children, and second, because we don't have to resort to fairy stories. . . ."

" . . . And third, because no one would believe them if you did," Don Camillo concluded.

"And who believes *your* fairy stories, may I ask?"

"There are people, quite a few of them, who not only believe in Paradise, but are willing to behave in such a way as to go there, people that live good, quiet lives and trust in Divine Providence."

Peppone pushed his hat back on his head and placed his hands of his hips.

"Divine Providence, eh? When the medicine came from the U.S.A.! If it had come from Russia, the Reverend here would have said it was a work of the devil!"

"No, Mr. Mayor. The Reverend, as you call him, uses his God-given faculty of reason. He'd never say anything quite so stupid, because he knows that Divine Providence knows neither nation nor party."

"Amen," muttered Smilzo.

"In any case," Don Camillo continued, "this time Divine Providence came from the West rather than the East."

"Then hurrah for America, and down with Russia!" shouted Peppone.

"Hurrah for America, if you insist. But why down with Russia? Russia did no harm in this affair; Russia didn't prevent the child from getting well. I am quite capable of cool detachment, Mr. Mayor, and I'm not afraid to say that this is one instance—perhaps the only one—in which Russia did no damage whatsoever. But, Mr. Mayor, instead of yelling Hurrah for America, why not yell Hurrah for Divine Providence, since Divine Providence cured the child?"

Peppone was as red in the face as the October Revolution.

"Why didn't Divine Providence stop the child from getting sick, in the first place?" he asked.

"Divine Providence didn't bring about the sickness," Don Camillo explained. "Sickness is a product of Nature, and Nature is governed, fortunately, by very rigid laws. If we fail to observe them, then trouble is bound to ensue. As a skilled mechanic, you know, Mr. Mayor, that a motor runs smoothly just as long as its single parts are in good order. If a carburettor is out of order, is it the fault of Divine Providence or of the dirt that got into it? Everything connected with Matter is in the providence of Nature. There is sickness even in Russia, which was created not by God but by Lenin."

Peppone had gradually relaxed and at the end of Don Camillo's little harangue he turned to Smilzo and said with a smile, pronouncing every word slowly:

"Smilzo, apropos of the carburettor, would you ask the Reverend whether when this mechanic gets the dirt out of the carburettor he represents Divine Providence?"

Smilzo looked over at Don Camillo, and asked:

"Has the defendant heard the plaintiff's demand?"

"Yes," Don Camillo replied. "The plaintiff's complaint is a weakness of the brain, but at any rate the defendant has heard it. The mechanic doesn't represent Divine Providence; all he represents is a screwdriver, with a man attached to the handle. All this lies in the realm of the very lowliest kind of matter. Everything happens in accord with natural rather than divine law."

This reply seemed to give Peppone further satisfaction.

"Let's put it differently, Father," he said. "Let's say that the carburettor isn't working for lack of a screw. Unfortunately, it's an American carburettor, and we haven't the right screw to replace it. What are we to do? Scrap the car? Fortunately the United States ambassadress sends a plane to Washington to get it; the screw is put in and the car moves. We're still in the realm of matter, because a humble carburettor is the protagonist of our story. But since the new screw comes from the U.S.A. we must shout Hurrah for Divine Providence. If the carburettor comes from the East you reason one way, and if it comes from the West another."

Peppone's gang hooted their approval, and Don Camillo let them hoot to their hearts' content. Then he said:

"My reason works the same way in both directions."

"Bunk!" shouted Peppone. "If the child's sickness is the result of natural law, just as the carburettor is broken for lack of a screw, then why is Divine Providence responsible for the American ambassadress's offer of the missing part, or, in this case, the missing medicine?"

"Because a child isn't a carburettor, that's all," said Don Camillo calmly. "A carburettor can't have a child's faith in God. And this child gave proof of his faith in a spectacular way. The human machine, its disturbances and remedies are material and natural affairs. Faith in God is something quite different, which you, Comrade Carburettor, seem unable to understand. Instead of seeing Divine Providence, you see only the United States ambassadress and the Atlantic Pact. A man without hearing can't hope to understand music, and one without faith in God can't fathom the workings of Divine Providence."

"Well then, this Divine Providence is something for the privileged rather than the needy. If a hundred persons are starving and only seven of them have faith, then God is unjust to send a tin of Spam only to these seven."

"No, Comrade Mayor, God sends the Spam to the whole lot of them, but only seven possess a tin-opener, with which the rest will have nothing to do."

Peppone had once more lost his self-possession and was sweating under the collar.

"Father, let's drop the parable and look at reality. In our country only seven people out of a hundred and seven eat meat, because they believe in Divine Providence and have the tin-openers with which to get at it. Whereas in Russia, where nobody believes in Divine Providence, there are tin-openers for all."

"But no tins of Spam," said Don Camillo.

The bystanders laughed at Don Camillo's thrust and Peppone was beside himself with fury.

"You're clever at playing with words, Father, and you reduce every argument to a word game. But we have concrete facts for our premises. This whole thing is a political trick, an American propaganda stunt built round an innocent child. None of your big words have proved the contrary."

"I know," said Don Camillo, with a shrug of his shoulders. "I'll never be able to prove a thing to you, not even that two and two make four, because you've been taught that they make five.

253

I can tell you this, though. If political propaganda saved a child's life, then I say Hurrah for political propaganda. If I had a child and his life depended on some Russian medicine, I can assure you that I . . ."

"Not I," Peppone interrupted. "I have children, but if their lives depended on medicine flown in by the United States ambassadress, I'd let them die!"

Don Camillo only opened his eyes wide in horror.

At three o'clock in the morning Peppone was still unable to sleep. He got up and dressed, then with his shoes in his hand went to peer into his young son's room. He switched on the light and scrutinized the child's face. After some time he put out the light and tiptoed away. A few minutes later, with his coat collar raised all the way to his eyes, he walked through the icy streets to the church square. Under the rectory windows he stooped to look for a stone, but the hardened snow had stuck them all to the ground. He scratched at the frozen ground and with every passing minute his anxiety grew. Finally he loosened a stone and threw it at the shutters of the second window from the left of the second floor. The sound that it made when it struck the shutters was somehow reassuring. The shutters were thrown open and a rough voice called down:

"What do you want?"

"Come downstairs."

Don Camillo draped the bedspread over his shoulders and came to open the door.

"What can you want at this hour? What's the matter?"

"Nothing's the matter," said Peppone glumly.

"Good. When I first saw you I was afraid."

"Afraid of what? I'm not a burglar."

"I'm always afraid when someone rouses me at night. People don't come to see a priest at an hour like this just in order to tell him a funny story."

Peppone stood with lowered head for a minute and then mumbled:

"When a fellow holds a public discussion, he often says more than he means."

"I know," said Don Camillo. "There's no use taking such things too seriously."

"But other people take them seriously."

"Nonsense! They know what kind of reasoning to expect from a carburettor."

Peppone clenched his fists.

"Father, you're the one that's talking stupidly."

"You may be right. But then a carburettor has no right to wake up a priest at three o'clock in the morning."

Peppone stood his ground until the priest asked him:

"Is there something you want, Comrade Peppone? Do you need a tin-opener?"

"I have a tin-opener," said Peppone gloomily.

"Good! See that you don't lose it. And may God shed a little more light upon you next time you talk in public!"

Peppone went away, and before Don Camillo got back into bed he knelt down before the crucifix in his room.

"Lord," he said, "he hasn't become a carburettor, or anything else soulless and purely mechanical. He's just the same poor fellow that he was before. May Divine Providence be praised!"

And then he, too, was at last able to go to sleep.

15

THE CLOSED GATE

THE highway unrolls its asphalt ribbon along the bank, matching the peaceful flow of the river. But the tributary roads which run into it, although they come from an area as flat as a billiard-table, are tortuous and winding. A city driver, bitten by the mania for speed, would find them unutterably irritating, but they exactly suit a man who works his own land and is jealous of its boundaries.

The Quarta road, doubtless a former cow-path, is such a one. Just a few hundred yards beyond the village it leaves the north-bound highway and winds its way for five miles or so before rejoining it, only one mile farther on. The last section of it runs parallel to both highway and river, then, just half a mile away from the junction, it makes a right-angle turn and climbs straight up the bank. The farm known as the *Cantone* is there at the turn, with the road bounding it on two sides and the farm buildings right at the corner.

The curve is a dangerously blind one, and because the Quarta road runs by a number of properties and is the only line of communication between the village and the outlying community of Torricella, it is heavily travelled. The farmhouse is at the side of the road just before the right-angle turn to the east, and the barns, which are joined to it, just after. Between them lies the bare, rectangular barnyard, open towards the south and towards

256

the river. The main entrance to the farm was originally at the south-east corner of the house.

All these topographical details serve only to explain something very simple: if some luckless fellow were to come carelessly out of the barnyard and another, equally luckless, were to drive at top speed towards the curve, it was obvious that they might run straight into each other. Something of the sort did happen, and as a result the gate was closed and creeper allowed to grow over it.

Marco Stocci had inherited the farm from his father, after many years of working at his side. Now he continued to work, with his wife and one hired man to help him. He was forty years old, but he had married late and Gisa, the eldest of his three children, was only just over twelve years old. With this family to bring up and a large amount of land to till, it is not surprising that Marco was a difficult and sometimes intractable man. He had an exceedingly quick temper and if his children annoyed him, he struck out at them with a violence which might have caused pain even to a grown person. The two little boys, eight and ten years old, took all this in a sporting spirit and were careful only to stay out of his reach. But twelve-year-old Gisa had a more sentimental nature and was mortally afraid of her father. Being a delicate and sensitive child she suffered most when he struck her in the presence of strangers, and in this he seemed to take particular joy. The last time that Marco mistreated his daughter was when the barnyard was full of men who had come for the threshing.

The threshing was a meagre affair that year; after an unusually severe winter, the wheat yielded very little grain. Marco Stocci was boiling over with resentment. Every now and then he plunged his hand into the sack hanging under the threshing-machine, pulled out a fistful of grain and then put it back, cursing. There was another major worry on his mind: his best cow was mortally ill and the vet showed no signs of coming. His two sons, aware of the oppressive atmosphere, had taken to the bush, but Gisa had been given the job of carrying water to the men on the machine and could not get away. The vet arrived around noon, when the men had just come in from the fields and were sitting down to lunch, amid considerable confusion. He went to look at the ailing cow, wrote out a prescription and said to Stocci:

"The pharmacy's closed at this hour. At three o'clock, when it reopens, send someone there to pick up this medicine. I'll be back at four to give the injection."

While the men lingered over their lunch in the cool hall, Stocci went into the parlour. He remembered that the pharmacist had sent him a bill the month before and it seemed like a good time to pay it. The bill was in a yellow envelope; it came to 4,500 liras, which meant that 10,000 liras would easily cover the present prescription as well as those that had gone before. He put the prescription into a pink envelope, lying on his desk, together with a 10,000-lira note. Then he thought it would be simpler to have everything together, and put it all in the pharmacist's yellow envelope.

It was a hot day, and the men were anxious to finish the threshing early and go on to another job. Stocci had barely enough time to eat a few mouthfuls of lunch and gulp down half a bottle of wine before they were ready to return to work. At half-past two, when the machine was just about to swallow up the last bale of wheat, Stocci remembered the vet and the sick cow and called to his daughter:

"Take the yellow envelope from the parlour table and run to the pharmacy. Hand him the envelope and then wait for what he gives you. Hurry!"

Gisa took the envelope and started off walking alongside her bicycle, as her parents had always told her she should do until she was on the open road. She went through the gate and contined to walk until she was round the dangerous curve. Then she mounted the bicycle and rode to the village by the shortest road, which was that along the bank of the river. When she came back the threshing was over, and while some of the men were making the machine ready to go, the others were cooling off with glasses of wine. Stocci was in the loft, over the sealed door between the house and the barn, and when he saw Gisa arrive with a small parcel attached to the handlebars of her bicycle, he called down from the window:

"Have you got everything?"

"Yes, father."

"How much change did he give you?"

"What change?" she stammered.

"Change from the 10,000 liras that were in the envelope!"

"There were two sheets of paper in the envelope, and nothing more," she said, shaking her head.

Money is a sore subject where a peasant is concerned, because it is so very hard for him to come by. It's safer to cut off his ear than to touch his money. And so Stocci let out a loud cry.

"Nothing more! I put the money in with my own hand! And now you've gone and lost it, you little good-for-nothing! If you don't find it, I'll kill you!"

Blind anger made the veins stand out on his forehead and muddled his brain. Not content with shouting, he started to climb down the wooden ladder up which he was later to carry sacks of wheat. And Gisa, instead of waiting for him, fled in terror. She jumped on to the bicycle and pedalled furiously in the direction of the gate. Her father ran after her, but she had a head start, and had already reached the road. The road was covered with gravel, and as she turned to the right, she lost control and went off to the extreme left, at the edge of the ditch. Just then a truck roared down the road at full speed, and as it cleared the curve Gisa was directly in its way. She was killed on the spot, in plain sight of her father.

This was why Stocci closed the gate to his farm. He fastened it with a heavy chain and lock, and put the key in his pocket so that no one could ever go through the gate again. The portion of the highway which ran parallel to the country road, some hundred and fifty feet away, was connected with it at another place, where there was no blind corner. The creeper, which formerly had covered only the gate-posts, now ran over all the iron grating. After a month had gone by, Stocci recovered a measure of calm. He was not very different from what he had been before, but he no longer shouted, and he let his wife look after the little boys.

One of the gate-posts was up against the corner of the house, while the other marked the beginning of the hedge which separated the barnyard from the road. Beside the latter post grew a tall poplar tree, and in the summer Stocci sat in its shade looking out through the over-grown bars of the closed gate at the dusty, white road, with the sun beating upon it.

It was an August afternoon, and the air was particularly heavy. Almost everyone was asleep in the river valley, and silence and solitude reigned. Stocci sat under the tree, staring at the gate. Suddenly someone rode up the road on a bicycle and stopped directly in front of it. The leaves had grown so thick that Stocci could not make out who it was. He got up and went nearer. It was Gisa, staring at him out of her deep blue eyes. Stocci searched his best pocket for the key. The lock was so rusty that the key was hard to turn, and it was no easy job to tear away the vine, but there was a feverish strength in Stocci's hands and soon he had the gate open.

"Come in," he said to his daughter, but she only shook her head, remounted the bicycle and rode off towards the fatal curve.

For a minute Stocci could not move. But when she was out of sight he ran back to his own bicycle, which was leaning against the wall of the house. He leaped on to the saddle and pedalled out through the open gate, just as fast as Gisa had pedalled to her death before him. He skidded on the gravel and veered to the left just in time for the luckless driver coming round the curve to find him in his way and run him down.

It was two o'clock in the afternoon, and old Antonietta, whose insomnia made her the only person left awake in the heat, swore that she saw Stocci and Gisa riding their bicycles along the road in front of her house. They rode side by side, in true cyclists' fashion, and every now and then they looked at each other and smiled.

Sheer imagination, of course. But in the secret compartment of Stocci's wallet they found a pink envelope containing the 10,000-lira note which Gisa had never lost because her father, in the confusion, had never put it in with the bill and the prescription. This part of the story is absolutely true, and Stocci's widow gave the 10,000-lira note to Don Camillo.

"Say some Masses," she told him.

"For whose soul?" he asked her.

"For both of them, Father."

So spake Stocci's widow, and she closed the gate again, this time with the aid of a blow-lamp. After which the creeper resumed its temporarily interrupted process of growing.

16

LULLABY

PEPPONE sat in front of the fireplace, while his wife and children set the supper-table, at the same time watching the pot and frying-pan on the stove. Just then Smilzo burst into the house with a large rolled-up paper in one hand.

"Here's the corrected proof, Chief," he said. "If it's O.K., we're ready to print it."

"Stand away," ordered Peppone. "I want to get the general effect."

Smilzo stepped several steps back, unrolling the paper. At this distance the poster was most effective. It stated very clearly that a Very Important Party Person would come to the village at three o'clock Saturday afternoon and explain to the citizenry "the true story of the Hungarian counter-revolution".

"All right," said Peppone. "The posters have got to be up by tomorrow morning."

After Smilzo had gone away, Peppone's wife said:

"Haven't you killed those poor devils enough by now?"

"What nonsense are you saying?" asked Peppone, wheeling brusquely around.

"It's no nonsense. If you were an honest man, you'd get out in a hurry."

Peppone was in no mood for an argument and so he turned back to the fire, with one parting shot over his shoulder.

"I'm an honest man. But a soldier can't abandon his post just because the general has changed his tactics. Ours is a just struggle, because we're fighting for the good of the working-class."

"You don't do much good to the working-class by killing it off," said his wife severely. "They weren't capitalists, they were peasants and workers, and students, peasants' and workers' sons."

"That's all propaganda," jeered Peppone; "just the usual line."

"Propaganda isn't what goes over with me," said his wife. "I listen to my conscience, and I'm getting out of the Women's League, I can tell you."

Peppone wasn't prepared for such a drastic decision, and for a few minutes he was left speechless.

"Keep your mind on the supper," he said in a surly voice. "I don't feel like joking."

"It's no joke," she retorted, and taking a card out of the top bureau drawer she tore it into tiny pieces and threw them on the table. "There is my membership," she said, "and tomorrow morning I'll go and tell Gisella to take my name off the list."

Peppone jumped to his feet in a towering rage and shook a fist in his wife's face.

"You'll do no such thing," he shouted. "You'll stay right here. I wear the trousers in this house."

Peppone's wife wasn't a woman to be easily buffaloed. Taking advantage of the fact that she was on the other side of the table from Peppone, she seized the pot and frying-pan off the stove and threw their contents down the sink.

"If you wear the trousers, then eat the supper."

Such a bit of rebellion would have indisposed the most peaceful of men, and Peppone was anything but peaceful. Because of his bulk and masculine dignity he couldn't very well jump over the table, but he did move with astonishing swiftness to lay hands on his wife. He had counted without her bodyguards, however, and his impetus was checked by four little children crawling around his legs and shattering his eardrums with their cries. A second later his wife had disappeared up the stairs and his pursuit was blocked by the attic door.

"Open up, or I'll break through!" he roared, hammering at it with his fists.

When he received no answer, he threw the full weight of his

shoulder against the door and erupted into the attic, which, to his discomfiture, was empty. His wife had climbed through the skylight on to the roof, and there, in spite of the darkness, Peppone finally detected her, hanging on to a chimney. His rage was transformed into worry and he drew back, with cold sweat breaking out on his forehead. Meanwhile the children too had reached the attic, weeping and calling for their mother.

"Shut up and get out of here!" said Peppone irritatedly.

Fearfully they retreated towards the door, until the oldest suddenly broke away from the rest, scuttled up the ladder standing under the skylight and joined his mother on the roof. With this Peppone turned tail and fled.

When Peppone came home, after midnight, he found things just as he had left them: the table still set and the scraps of the membership card scattered all over it. The big double bed in the bedroom was empty and so were the beds of the children. The rebels, all five of them, had taken refuge in the room which had formerly belonged to his wife's parents. Peppone made a feeble attempt to force the door but soon realized that it was barricaded. Back in the empty, disorderly kitchen, where the fire in the stove was dead and cold, he attempted to stay his appetite with bread and cheese, but they only made his stomach turn over. Before going out again he knocked once more at the rebels' door.

"Tomorrow noon, if I don't find lunch, I'll smash everything in sight."

"Smash what you please," his wife answered calmly. "Either you let me go and see Gisella, or else tomorrow you'll find the house empty."

Peppone started to kick at the door, but the children's weeping and wailing caused him to desist.

"I said noon, mind you!" he shouted. "That's the deadline for putting everything in order. I'll go and see Gisella myself. If you resign, we'll have to publish an announcement to the effect that you've been kicked out for deviationism. I've got to settle things in such a way that I won't be a laughing-stock."

"Go ahead," said his wife, "but just don't try to put over anything on me like what they pulled in Budapest!"

Peppone roared for an answer.

263

Gisella, the fiery head of the Women's League, had, with Don Camillo's accidental assistance, been tinged in red of the deepest hue by the most ferocious of her former adversaries, now her husband. She had turned into a professional politician, which meant that her husband, after working hours, had to do the housekeeping, to cook his meals if he wanted to eat, to make his bed if he wanted to sleep and to sweep up, if he didn't want the place to be a pigsty. Ever since Gisella had become a big wheel of the Party, the poor fellow had lost all his revolutionary spirit. He confined himself to being a good proletarian husband and let politics strictly alone. Indeed, to talk politics in his presence was like referring to rope in the house of a man who has died on the gallows.

At ten o'clock in the morning Peppone went to the People's Palace to hold a private meeting with Gisella upon the subject of his wife's rebellion. But Gisella was at home, ill. In view of the fact that the big rally was to take place at three that afternoon and Gisella was in charge of the women's participation, she must have been very ill indeed or else nothing in the world would have kept her away from the job. And so Peppone went to the forsaken shack where she and her husband lived and found her in bed, looking anything but well.

"What's the matter, Comrade?" he asked her.

Gisella only shook her head sadly, for she had not strength enough to speak.

"Arthritis," said her husband, who had stayed at home to look after her. "The poor girl's bones are broken."

To tell the truth, if Gisella had a bad case of broken bones, arthritis wasn't the reason. It had all happened the previous evening, after supper, a sketchy sort of supper prepared by Gisella's husband while she worked for the second consecutive day on the speech she was scheduled to deliver at the rally. When the comrade from the city had finished telling the true story of the Hungarian counter-revolution, Gisella was to voice the village women's acclaim of the peaceful settlement effected by the glorious Soviet army. Naturally, so important a speech couldn't be improvised from one moment to the next, and by the time Gisella had said everything she had to say, her crude handwriting covered some twenty long pages. At the end of the meagre meal, Gisella's husband sat down by the fire while she put the finishing touches. When it was all done she had an urge to rehearse it.

"Even if you don't care a fig for politics," she said to her husband, "you can tell me whether or not my speech makes sense. Just listen. . . ."

The poor fellow threw out his arms helplessly, and Gisella launched into her oration. When she got to the end she asked him:

"Well, what do you say?"

He tapped his pipe on one of the bricks of the fireplace, then put it back in his mouth and jerking his chair round said brusquely:

"Eat it."

"What do you mean?" she asked in amazement.

"I said to eat it," he repeated, pointing to the pad on which the speech was written. Gisella stood with arms akimbo and looked at him with disgust, as if she were about to put him in his place. But before she could open her mouth she received a stunning blow across the face. The blow was painful, but Gisella was even more pained by the fact that the browbeaten little man should have found the nerve to administer it. The worm had turned at last.

"Eat it," he said again, following up the first blow with a second.

Gisella didn't understand for some time, but at last it got into her head that if she wanted the blows to let up she would have to eat all twenty pages of her speech and her card of membership in the Women's League as well. That evening Gisella couldn't get up the stairs by herself. Alone, she had received enough blows to fell the entire women's group of the local party. Her rebellious spouse carried her upstairs, as if she had been a sack of potatoes. And that is just about what she was.

Now Peppone told Gisella not to worry. "While you're recuperating I'll put a substitute in your place. We'll wait for you to get well."

"She's not going to get well," said her husband darkly. "It's a chronic disturbance, isn't it, Gisella?"

Gisella nodded assent.

"It's not really a substitute that I'm putting in," said Peppone.

"No one can take your place. The best thing is to disband the group and build it up again on a new foundation."

"I agree," said the husband.

"Take good care of yourself, Comrade," said Peppone moving towards the door. "The Party needs you."

"I'll take care of her, don't worry," said the husband. "I need her too."

When Peppone came home at noon, he found everything in good order. He sat down cheerfully at the table, with a whale of an appetite, as his wife knew very well. But she stood skittishly near the sink, holding the bowl of spaghetti in her hand and ready to repeat the gesture of the day before.

"Well?" she queried at last.

"Everything's all right. Gisella is ill and I've had to disband the group."

He exhibited a copy of the announcement, and in return was served his portion of hot food.

The rally was scheduled for three o'clock in the afternoon, and by two the square and the road leading to the highway were patrolled by a detachment of police sent from the city. It wasn't clear what had drawn out so large and aggressive a crowd. The windows of all the houses were shut and the storekeepers had closed their stores, making the village seem quite dead. At a quarter to three Smilzo arrived breathlessly at the house of Peppone.

"Everything's ready, Chief. The comrades have gathered in the auditorium, and outside all is quiet. The enemy doesn't dare let himself be seen."

At that very moment, however, the enemy let himself be heard, for from the church tower the death-knell sounded. Deeply and gloomily it tolled against a background of perfect silence. Peppone listened for a few minutes and then said:

"Go back to your place. I'm going to do something about this."

"Be careful, Chief," said Smilzo; "it's a critical moment."

"In moments like this we must show that we are not afraid."

He put on his coat, pulled his hat down over his eyes and hurried off towards the church.

Up in the bell-tower, Don Camillo was pulling intently at the rope when Peppone's head appeared at the trap-door, followed by his body.

"Father," he said, "there's got to be an end to this provocation."

"There's an end to everything," said Don Camillo. "In human affairs, nothing is eternal."

"I can't answer for what may happen."

"Never mind, Comrade Mayor; I'll answer for it."

Peppone looked cautiously out of the window. From this height he had a clear view of the empty square, the police car and the forces of law and order. It was a grey day, and even without the tolling bell there would have been something infinitely lugubrious and funereal about it. Punctually at three o'clock, the Party speaker's car, with its police escort, drew up in front of the cinema.

"Comrade, aren't you going to the rally?" asked Don Camillo, between one sound of the bell and another.

"I want to see for myself exactly how long you'll go on with this music," said Peppone, sitting down on the floor.

"For a very long time," said Don Camillo. "This is no ordinary death; it's the death of a whole people."

Peppone sat haunched up in one corner with his hat over his eyes. He was dead tired and soon this gloomy lullaby sent him off to sleep. So it was that he never heard the true story of the Hungarian counter-revolution.

17

TOGO THE BULL

It was one of those things that usually come out in the tabloid papers. If it didn't, the reason was that certain ramifications of the affair induced the village people to pretend to have seen and heard nothing.

It was the afternoon of December 31, and everywhere people were preparing to celebrate the arrival of the New Year. Those who weren't at home were out going from shop to shop or else just loitering in the square. Children had been dashing madly about all day long, whiling away the hours before the climactic noise-making, with the explosion of an occasional firework.

In the Rotti farmyard there was a big band of boys, letting off crackers in this way, in spite of their elders' admonitions. But when it was time to lead the animals out of the stable to water, old man Rotti came into the yard and said that if he heard as much as a squeak, he'd give the whole lot of them a beating. The boys quieted down, and the animals enjoyed their drink. But just when Togo reached the trough, an unfortunate cracker rose up from behind the fence, whistled across the yard and landed on his nose.

Togo was a Carnation-type bull, a Sherman tank of such massive proportions that the very sight of him was intimidating. With a single leap he broke away from the cowherd, smashed the bars of the gate and rushed out on to the road. The Rotti farm was hardly outside the village; fifty yards away the road became a village street, leading in a few hundred feet to the square. And by the time the Rottis had recovered from their surprise and started to pursue him, this was where Togo had arrived, or rather erupted. It was a confused scene, and one of only a few minutes' duration. Togo started to vent his wrath on a group of hysterical women, who squeezed themselves into the narrow space between a wall and two big trucks, while the sergeant of the Carabinieri appeared from nowhere and stood in the way with a pistol in his hand.

The sergeant's shot grazed the bull's side and only intensified his anger. It looked as if both the sergeant and the little group of shrieking women were in danger of being trampled down. Only a volley of machine-gun bullets into Togo's brain could have stopped him in his mad course. And, just in the nick of time, there was just such a volley. No one knew where it came from, but it hit the target, and the bull collapsed at the sergeant's feet. He put his pistol back in the holster, took off his cap and wiped the cold sweat from his forehead, looking down all the while at the great carcass of the bull.

People all around him were making a racket, and the women were shrieking just as loudly as if the bull were still charging upon them, but in the sergeant's ears there rang only the rattle of the machine-gun. The gun was silent now, but he felt sure that he had only to turn round and look up in order to pick out the window from which it had been fired. This was the real reason for his sweating. He knew that he ought to turn and look, but he didn't have the courage to do so.

The sergeant's paralysis was broken by a heavy hand on his shoulder.

"Good for you, Sergeant!" said Don Camillo. "These people owe you their lives."

"He's a very brave fellow," wheezed an old crone who was standing near by, "but if it hadn't been for . . ."

She meant to say "for the fellow who fired the machine-gun", but she never finished the sentence because someone stepped on her foot so hard that she almost fainted away, and a moment later the gathering crowd absorbed her.

"Good for you, Sergeant!" everyone was shouting.

Don Camillo went back to the rectory and waited for the

sergeant to turn up. After an hour he did free himself and turn up, as expected.

"Father," he said, "you're the only person to whom I can say what's on my mind. Will you listen to me?"

"That's why I'm here," said Don Camillo, seating him in front of the fire.

"Father, did you see exactly what happened?" the sergeant asked him after a few seconds had gone by.

"Yes, I was just coming out of the tobacconist's, where I had gone to buy some stamps, and I saw the whole thing. I saw you throw yourself in front of the bull and shoot him down."

The sergeant smiled and shook his head.

"Did you see me shoot *at* him with a pistol and *bring him down* with a machine-gun?"

Don Camillo threw out his arms.

"Sergeant, I'm not an arms expert. I know you had a firearm of some sort in your hand, but I couldn't swear to what it was."

"Do you mean that you can't tell the difference between a pistol-shot and the crackle of a machine-gun?"

"It's not taught in the seminary, Sergeant."

"But it's taught at the public schools, I can tell you. And so I can't help knowing that the animal at which I shot my pistol was milled by a volley from a machine-gun."

"Sergeant, if you say so, I can't contradict you. I repeat, that's not my speciality. The main thing is that the bull was killed before it could gore the life out of you and those poor women who were huddling behind you. I don't see any point in a discussion of ballistics."

"Yes, the machine-gun volley did save the lives of quite a few people. The only trouble is that it had to come from a machine-gun."

Don Camillo shrugged his shoulders.

"I'm no expert, as I've said twice before," he insisted. "But I may say that what you call a 'machine-gun volley' might just as easily have come from a shotgun. I don't see how your higher-ups could find anything wrong with that."

"If it were just a matter of explaining to the higher-ups, that's a plausible story," said the sergeant. "But how am I to justify it to myself? You see, Father, a Carabiniere is never alone; there is always another Carabiniere on watch inside him."

The Carabiniere touched his breast, and Don Camillo smiled.

"If you were dead, would he be dead too?"

"Exactly. But I'm not dead, and the Carabiniere inside me says: 'Someone in the village has a machine-gun in perfect working order. This is against the law, so you must proceed against him.'"

Don Camillo lit and puffed at the butt of his cigar.

"There's no use talking in riddles," he said. "Say what you have on your mind. If you suspect me, I am at your disposal. You and your double can proceed against me."

"Father, let's drop the joking. I know who shot the machine-gun, and so do you, because you saw it."

"You've come to the wrong place," said Don Camillo harshly, looking him straight in the eyes. "I'm the last person in the world to give out such information. And, if you like, you can summon me for failing to co-operate with the law. I haven't another Carabiniere inside me, but I have my conscience, and there is a lot that the both of you could learn from that."

"There's one thing it couldn't teach us! A private citizen, who is the local leader of a movement in favour of revolution and mob rule, has no right to own a machine-gun!"

"I don't care about revolutions and their local leaders," said Don Camillo. "I only want to tell you that I'm neither a spy nor an informer."

"You've misunderstood me," said the sergeant, shaking his head. "I only came to ask you how an honest man can report and turn in someone who has just saved a number of lives, including his own. And how can an honest man *not* report and turn in the owner of a weapon which is a menace to the community?"

Don Camillo was somewhat pacified.

"Sergeant," he said, "as you've just put it, the weapon is the menace, not its owner. There's been entirely too much melodrama for strictly political reasons, over machine-guns. They're certainly lethal arms, but not everyone that has one in his possession is a criminal. The owner of a hammer or a kitchen knife may be just as much of a threat to society. When a man has been through the war, his machine-gun may be a sentimental reminder of an honourable past, of days of faith, hope and self-sacrifice. . . ."

"I see," the sergeant interrupted. "Just a well-oiled

little souvenir that can fell the biggest bull for miles around!"

"And save the lives of several citizens, including a sergeant of the Carabinieri!"

"Father," said the sergeant, rising from his chair, "I can look, successfully or unsuccessfully, for the machine-gun's owner. But I simply *must* find the gun."

"You'll find it," said Don Camillo, rising in his turn to bid his guest good-bye. "I'll bring it to you myself."

Once the sergeant had gone, Don Camillo hurried over to the house of Peppone.

"You did a good job, killing the bull," he told him. "Now hand over that machine-gun."

"Are you trying to make me laugh?" asked Peppone.

"Peppone, the sergeant knows that you fired the gun. Even if you saved his life, it's his duty to report you for the possession of a concealed weapon. . . ."

"The sergeant must be mad. He can't know anything of the kind. I don't own a machine-gun, and I never, even in my wildest dreams, killed a bull."

"Peppone, stop joking. You shot the bull; I saw you with my own eyes."

"Then go and tell the sergeant. Why come to me?"

"I'm not a spy, I'm a minister of God, and God doesn't need me to tell *Him* anything."

"You're a minister of the Vatican and the U.S.A.," Peppone retorted; "that's why you want to make trouble for honest men."

Don Camillo had resolved not to let himself be drawn into an argument, and so did not answer, but merely sought to convince Peppone of the gravity of the sergeant's dilemma. But Peppone jeered at all his supplications.

"I don't know what you're talking about," he said. "All these machine-guns, bulls and sergeants have nothing to do with me. You'd better knock at some other door. Better luck next time! You might try the parish priest. See if he doesn't come up with a machine-gun!"

Don Camillo was disconsolate as he left Peppone's house. From the door he fired his parting shot:

"I shan't mind if you're called up by the police. It's no more than you deserve. But I *am* sorry for the sergeant because he'd never choose to repay you in this fashion for saving his life and the daily bread of his children."

"Don't worry about me," sneered Peppone. "If I'd had this machine-gun you're talking about, I'd have shot the sergeant, not the bull!"

When he got back to the rectory Don Camillo paced restlessly up and down the hall. At last he came to a decision and went precipitately upstairs. The dusty attic was pitch-black, but he needed no light to find what he was looking for. Immediately he located the brick which had only to be pushed at one end to open out at the other. He removed this from the wall and stuck his arm into the opening until his fingers caught hold of a nail with a wire wrapped around it. He unhooked the wire and pulled until a long, narrow box came out of the wall. Then he took out the contents of the box and went to his second-floor bedroom in order to see if it was in good condition. After that he put on his coat and left the house, making his way first through the hedge and then across the open fields. When he came to the area of underbrush near the Canal he waited for midnight to arrive. As the bells rang and fireworks and guns began to pop, he contributed a salvo of his own. Then he made straight for the headquarters of the Carabinieri. The sergeant was still there and Don Camillo said at once:

"Here's what you called a machine-gun. Don't ask me where it came from or who gave it to me."

"I'm not asking anything," answered the sergeant. "I'm simply thanking you for your co-operation, and wishing you a Happy New Year."

"Happy New Year to you, and to the other Carabiniere inside you!" muttered Don Camillo, wrapping his coat about him and hurrying away.

Ten minutes later the sergeant's doorbell rang again, and when he went to open the door a heavy object which had been leaning up against it fell on to the floor. Attached to it by a wire was a piece of cardboard, on which someone had pasted letters cut out from newspaper headlines. These bore the message: "A machine-gun guilty of having saved the life of a police *sargint*."

"By their spelling, ye shall know them," the sergeant said, laughing to himself.

Then, having laid the object beside the one brought in a few minutes before by Don Camillo, he threw out his arms and exclaimed (contrary, perhaps, to the feelings of Togo, the bull):

"Thanks, all too many thanks, to Saint Anthony Abbot, patron saint of the lost-and-found!"

18

A POACHER'S PENANCE

DON CAMILLO had planned an epoch-making celebration of the New Year, based on the simple slogan: "A Chicken in Every Poor Man's Pot". He started a fortnight in advance, to take a collection, visiting every landowner and tenant-farmer in his parish and receiving their unanimous approval. Unfortunately, in many barnyards he was told that there had been a round of diseases; in some all the poultry had been sold and those that were left after a penurious autumn were noticeably scrawny. In short, Don Camillo found himself on December 30th with only half a dozen chickens, the fattest among them looking like Smilzo in disguise. Six chickens, when he needed at least thirty! In his distress he went to the crucified Christ on the altar.

"Lord," he said, "is it possible for people to be so niggardly? What's one chicken, to a man that has a hundred?"

"It's one chicken, after all," Christ answered.

Don Camillo threw out his arms in protest.

"Lord," he went on indignantly, "how can people fail to make a small sacrifice which would yield them so much joy?"

"Don Camillo, too many people regard any sacrifice as a great one and are entirely wrapped up in seeking their own happiness. To them happiness may mean *not* giving something they don't need"

"Lord," said Don Camillo impatiently, between clenched

teeth, "if You know these people so well, why don't You treat them the way they deserve? Why don't You send a frost to freeze the wheat in their fields?"

"Bread belongs to everyone, not merely to the man that sowed the wheat. The land does not bear its fruits only for the benefit of those that own it. It is blasphemy, Don Camillo, to ask the Lord to freeze the wheat in the ground. Don't we all say: 'Give us this day our daily bread'?"

"Forgive me," said Don Camillo, bowing his head. "I only meant that certain selfish people aren't fit to own land."

"If they had sown stones instead of wheat, then they wouldn't be entitled to any reward. But if they raise what it is proper for the land to bear, then they are entitled to own and run it their own way."

Don Camillo lost patience altogether.

"Lord," he said, "You're on the side of the landowners!"

"No," said Christ with a smile: "My interest is in the land itself. . . . Once upon a time there was an island, inhabited by very poor people. There were two doctors on the island, one generous, the other grasping. The first doctor asked very small fees, but unfortunately he was less skilled in his art than the other. And all the sick flocked to the more competent man. Was this fair?"

Don Camillo shrugged his shoulders.

"It was only normal that they should go to a doctor who could cure them. But I can't accept the fact that a good man should be in need, while a bad one should be making money. That isn't just."

"It isn't just, Don Camillo, but it's human. It's human that sick people should pay heavy fees to the abler of the two. On the other hand, it's just that God should punish him for abusing his God-given talents."

"Lord," insisted Don Camillo, "I . . ."

"If you lived on the island in question, would you ask God to destroy the competent doctor and preserve the inept one?"

"No," said Don Camillo, "I'd ask Him to teach the competent man to be generous and the generous man to improve his skill."

"Well, isn't a farmer a kind of doctor responsible for the health and prosperity of the land?"

276

"Lord," Don Camillo explained, "I understand now, and beg God to forgive my foolish words. But I can't help worrying about the fact that I need thirty chickens and have no more than six in hand."

"Eight," Christ corrected him.

"Yes, eight," said Don Camillo, who had forgotten the fact that there were two capons in his own yard.

It's no easy job to find twenty-two chickens from one day to the next. Don Camillo knew this perfectly well, because he had searched a fortnight for half a dozen. But he had no intention of falling down on his slogan, "A Chicken in Every Poor Man's Pot".

He was eating out his soul for an answer, when suddenly another question rose before him.

"Yes, a chicken's just a chicken. But what is a pheasant?"

To be logical, a pheasant is a pheasant. But is it necessary to be so precise? Couldn't a pheasant be called a "flying chicken"? He concluded that the celebration would be the same with the slogan of A Pheasant in Every Poor Man's Frying-pan. There were only two drawbacks to this variant. First, the question of finding twenty-two pheasants, and second, the lack of time for them to season. Don Camillo walked for miles up and down the rectory hall, debating these problems. Finally he resolved them by a further modification of the original slogan. Now it was A Pheasant in Every Poor Man's Shopping Bag. All the essentials were there.

Don Camillo's dog, Thunder, agreed that the main thing was to find twenty-two pheasants to replace the missing chickens. He found it quite natural that his master should don a pair of trousers, a corduroy jacket and a cyclist's cap. It wasn't the first time that Don Camillo had gone hunting in places where a cassock would have been in the way. What was unnatural was that Don Camillo should go out of the house without his shot-gun over his shoulder. The dog felt sure that it was a lapse of memory, and just as the priest was about to step through the garden he barked at him to return to the house. When they were back in the dining-room, Thunder looked up at the gun and cartridge-belt and game-bag that were hanging on the wall.

"Come on, Thunder!" ordered Don Camillo.

"Take your gun, and then I'll come," Thunder answered, without moving. He said all this by barking, but it was perfectly understandable to Don Camillo.

"Stop that noise and come along," the priest answered. "The shotgun's staying there. We can't possibly take such a noisy weapon."

Then, when Thunder remained obstinately still, Don Camillo dug into the left leg of his trousers and came up with a single-barrelled gun. Thunder looked at it in a puzzled fashion and compared it with the gun hanging on the wall.

"That isn't a shotgun," he said at last. "The shotgun's up there."

Don Camillo knew that Thunder's pedigree lent him a certain dignity and entitled him to be treated with respect.

"This is a shotgun, too," he explained. "A small, old-fashioned model, with the charger on the barrel. It's not very powerful, of course, but if you shoot at a distance of two or three yards at a silly pheasant it will bring him down."

He gave a demonstration of how to load it and then, opening the window over the garden he aimed at a tin can which someone had mounted on the end of a pole. The gun gave a faint click, and the can hit the dust. Thunder ran downstairs to follow up the prey. Soon he called back:

"Let's go hunting for tin cans, then, if you insist!"

The pheasants perched lethargically on the lowest branches of the trees. For three years the Finetti family had lived abroad, and in all that time no one had fired a shot on their preserve. The pheasants were so fat and self-confident that it was hardly necessary to shoot them; they could have just as easily been swept up in the crown of a hat. Nevertheless, Don Camillo chose to use his gun. Every time the gun clicked a pheasant fell to the ground. Although he had to waste considerable time searching for the bodies, Don Camillo bagged twenty-one pheasants without the least trouble. But the twenty-second was appointed by fate to give him trouble.

Thunder was showing signs of restlessness, and this signified the presence of something other than pheasants and rabbits. But Don Camillo was so intent on bagging the twenty-second "flying chicken" that he told the dog to be quiet and let him get on with the job. Thunder unwillingly obeyed until, just as Don Camillo was shooting his intended victim, he really barked an alarm. It was too late, because the game warden was already near. Don Camillo threw his gun into the bushes, and picking up the bag that contained the twenty-one pheasants, he ran off on the double. Evening was starting to fall and a thick fog mercifully interposed itself between Don Camillo and his pursuer. Thunder masterfully led the strategic withdrawal, and having found a hole in the high wire fence around the preserve he stood by it until Don Camillo had passed through.

Don Camillo was of elephantine proportions and the bagful of pheasants was quite bulky, but he dived into the fence with all the ardour of a goalkeeper in a soccer game. The warden arrived only in time to see Don Camillo's hindquarters disappearing through the fence. He shot at them, without much hope of hitting the mark. A few minutes later Don Camillo emerged on to the road. He couldn't cut across the fields because just opposite the fence there was the eight-feet wide canal, swollen with water. The road was the only way he could go, and here the warden would surely have found him, because it ran parallel to the fence for half a mile in either direction.

"Home, Thunder!" he shouted to the dog, who set out immediately in the right direction, while he himself continued to run. "He's not going to identify me, even if I have to throw myself into the canal," he muttered to himself.

At the curve of the Wayside Shrine, Don Camillo saw a big truck coming down the road. He stood on the ridge along the Canal and waved his cap. Then, without waiting for the truck to stop, he jumped on to the running-board. The driver wore a concerned expression as he jammed on the brakes. Within a second Don Camillo had opened the door and installed himself in the cab.

"Keep going, man, for the love of God!" he shouted.

The driver depressed the clutch, and the truck regained speed as if someone had kicked it in the rear. After half a mile or so, the driver mumbled:

"I took you for a gunman. Why, in heaven's name, are you in such a hurry?"

"I've got to make the six-twenty-two train."

"Oh, you are a wild-fowl fancier, are you?"

"No, I sell detergents for washing black souls."

"I was a fool," said the driver. "I should never have picked you up, and then the game warden would have seen your typically Vatican-agent face. Well, I must admit that you've done things in a big way. Are you expecting a lot of people to dinner?"

"Yes, thirty. I had two chickens and people gave me six more. After that, I had to find twenty-two birds of some other kind, in order that there should be one for every neighbour of ours that couldn't afford it. I had just taken aim at the twenty-second when the game warden saw me. That's the whole story. Do you need any more data to report to your Party?"

"All I need is some idea as to what is your moral code."

"That of a good Christian and an honest citizen."

"Then, Mister Priest, let's take a look at the past," said Peppone, slowing the truck down. "Last month, when I suggested that we make common cause to procure firewood for the unemployed, you wouldn't hear of it; in fact you fought me all along the line. Why was that?"

"Because I couldn't encourage people to break the law," said Don Camillo, lighting the butt of his cigar.

"What law?"

"The law for the protection of private property. The poor have a right to firewood, there I agree. But one can't say to them: 'Let's go and take it from the rich landowners!' 'Thou shalt not steal' is the law of both God and man."

" 'Thou shalt not steal,' is that it?" shouted Peppone. "If workers can't touch the property of the rich, what right have the rich to rob the workers of a decent wage and thus make it impossible for them to go on living?"

"It's no use your haranguing me as if I were at a political rally," expostulated Don Camillo. "I can't help anyone to break the law."

"Very well," said Peppone. "Then let's look at the chapter you've just written. The poor have a right to a good New Year's Day dinner, but the rich won't give it to them. So what does the priest do? He breaks the law of God and man by stealing pheasants from a private hunting preserve. Do priests have a moral code all their own, or have they a right to violate the so-called public law with impunity?"

"Comrade, I claim no such right. I took off my priestly garb and disguised myself in order to break the law without attracting attention to my person. But last month I couldn't parade through the streets, arm in arm with our comrade mayor, shouting: 'The law is unjust! Down with the law! We're taking the law into our own hands! . . .' If I am a soldier parading before a general, I have to salute him; if I don't want to do it, then I must get out of the parade. The one thing I can't do is parade in front of him with my hands in my pockets, shouting: 'I'm not saluting any such no-good general as you! . . .' Yes, I did steal the pheasants. But I didn't call out: 'Come on, Comrades; the pheasants are ours!' "

Peppone shook his head and pounded with one fist on the steering-wheel.

"You preach against stealing, and then you steal!" he objected. "Your preaching is one thing, and your practice another."

"According to your standards, Peppone, I preach what's wrong and practise what's right. But I still maintain that the opposite is true. If I tell people the right thing, then I am doing them good. And if then I go and do something wrong, quite off my own bat, I'm wronging only myself. Of course, I must answer for my wrongdoing and be punished for it. I may elude human justice, but God's justice will catch up with me, sooner or later."

"That's a convenient way to look at it," sneered Peppone. "You allow yourself to get away with practically anything in this world, by saying that you'll pay for it in the next. I say that you ought to pay up on the spot!"

"Don't worry; I'll pay soon enough, because my conscience will prick me. As a good Christian and an honest citizen, I'm aware of having violated the law of both God and man."

"Hmmm . . ." said Peppone. "I tell you where that Christian and civic conscience of yours is—it's at the . . . base of your spine!"

"Very well, Peppone," said Don Camillo, with a sigh. "Granted that my conscience is located where you say, does that have any effect on what I have just told you?"

"What are you driving at now, Father?" asked Peppone disgustedly.

"Nothing so very deep. I'd just like to know, Comrade, whether you've ever had a bullet in the base of your spine?"

Don Camillo's voice seemed to come from very far away,

and when Peppone switched on the light on the dashboard he saw that the priest was deathly pale.

"Father! . . ." he gasped.

"Put out that light, and don't worry," said Don Camillo. "It's just a little prick of my conscience, and I'll get over it. Take me to the old doctor at Torricella; he'll take the lead out of my pants without asking any questions."

Peppone drove as if he were jet propelled over the bumpy road and put Don Camillo down at the doctor's door. While he was waiting for him to come out he wiped the blood off the seat. Then he hid the bag of pheasants below it and went for a stroll in the course of which he had ample time for meditation. An hour later Don Camillo emerged from the doctor's house.

"How goes it?" asked Peppone.

"Well, my conscience is at rest, in a manner of speaking, but for spiny or spinal reasons I must admit that I'm better off in a standing than in a sitting position. If you don't object, I'll stand in the rear of the truck, and mind you don't go too fast!"

Fortunately the rear of the truck had a canvas cover, so that Don Camillo did not suffer too much from the wind. The fog was thicker than ever and so he was able to slip into the rectory unnoticed, followed by Peppone, carrying the bag of birds, which he deposited in the cellar. When Peppone came upstairs he found Don Camillo back in his priestly uniform. The black cassock made his face look all the whiter.

"Father," he muttered, "if there's anything I can do for you, don't hesitate to call on me."

"I'm quite all right," said Don Camillo, "but I'm worried about Thunder. See if you can find him."

There came a whimper from under the table, which was Thunder's way of answering "Present!" to the mention of his name. Peppone bent over to look at him more closely.

"It seems as if his . . . conscience were bothering him too," said Peppone. "Shall I take him to the same discreet doctor?"

"No," said Don Camillo. "This is a strictly family affair. Carry him up to my bedroom and I'll operate on him myself."

Thunder allowed Peppone to carry him up to the second floor. When Peppone came down he stood at the door, with one finger pointing to heaven, and looked severely at Don Camillo.

"The sins of the priests are visited upon the innocent dogs," he observed sententiously.

"Not fair!" retorted Don Camillo. "The priest in question is half-dead!" He was still standing on his two feet and still looking very pale.

When Peppone had gone he barred the front door and went down to the cellar to look at the twenty-one "flying chickens". There turned out to be twenty-two of them, because while he was waiting for Don Camillo to come out of the doctor's Peppone had bought a magnificent capon. Before Don Camillo went to throw himself (face down) on his bed, he went to kneel before the crucified Christ on the altar.

"Lord," he said, "I can't thank You for having protected me, because I was doing a dishonest deed and one that deserved to be punished. Perhaps the game warden's shotgun ought to have dispatched me to the next world."

"Even the worst of priests is worth more than twenty-two pheasants," answered Christ severely.

"Twenty-one, to be exact," whispered Don Camillo, "I'm not responsible for the twenty-second."

"You meant to shoot him down, however."

"Lord, my heart is very sore, because I know that I have done wrong."

"You're lying, Don Camillo. Your heart is full of joy, because you're thinking of the happiness coming to thirty needy families tomorrow."

Don Camillo rose, stepped back and sat heavily down in the first pew. Perspiration trickled down his increasingly pale face.

"Rise!" said the crucified Christ. "*Ego te absolvo*. Your sins are forgiven."

19

AN EXCHANGE OF COURTESIES

"THE only way to have a genuine exchange of courtesies with the Catholic workers is to belabour them with a stick. But directives are directives, and so we'll simply tickle them with a feather."

These were Peppone's words to his lieutenants, and he accompanied them with the observation that talk is all very well, but that to get anything concrete accomplished by workers—Catholic or non-Catholic—you must begin by subtracting something from their wallets.

"When the priest is in the pulpit, he's unbeatable," Peppone went on. "If he has nothing better to say, he can always fall back on dogma, the Ten Commandments, Heaven, Hell and all the rest. But when he stands behind the counter of the Co-operative Store, then his authority is not the same. There's where we must attack him."

For a long time the "People's Co-operative" had been a thorn in Don Camillo's side, a thorn whose sting even the "White Co-operative" of his own creation could not remove, because the Reds dealt not only in food and other articles but they had also a bar, a tobacco shelf, a television set and petrol pump. Altogether it was big business and functioned very smoothly; he knew that he would never be able to transform his frail enterprise into one equally powerful. He ate his heart out continuously, and every time he was told something new about the Red Co-operative he felt as if he had taken a beating.

As soon as the plan for "an exchange of courtesies" was put

into action, Don Camillo's beating was worse than ever. For one day the Reds lowered the price of bacon, another the price of cheese, the next oil and so on. Soon Camillo could not compete with these crazy reductions and so he simply tried to stop up as many holes as he could and stay afloat. He was hardened by now to adversity and when he felt especially low in his mind and sought the succour of the Christ on the main altar, he simply threw out his arms disconsolately and said:

"Lord, You see how things are. I don't ask You to take an interest in my paltry shop, but I do beg You to help me keep my temper."

God did help him and he achieved considerable self-control, but when he heard about the new department in their Co-operative store his temper boiled up within him. He was not satisfied with other people's description and went to see for himself. The window which had formerly served to show groceries was now given over to the new merchandise, and a big sign explained that in order to meet its customers' every want the Co-operative had undertaken to sell materials and patterns for making baptismal, First Communion and wedding outfits, not to mention handsomely decorated candles. "Compare prices," said the sign, "and see who is exploiting the religious feelings of good Catholic workers." This sign was set up in the middle of the display, at the feet of a big statue of Saint Joseph the Worker, while another sign, nearby, explained that the "People's Co-operative" also furnished printed invitations to any of the above functions, with a wide variety of conventional texts.

As if by chance, Smilzo appeared at the Co-operative door and whispered into Don Camillo's ear:

"Father, you'd better get some of those candles. We give a fifteen-percent discount to active clergy. That means we lose money, but what does it matter? We want to help the Church."

There was a small crowd in front of the window, and Don Camillo could not afford to lose his temper. All he could do was seize the peak of Smilzo's cap between the thumb and forefinger of his left hand and pull it down all the way to the chin. But Smilzo managed to have the last word.

"Nothing doing, Father!" he exclaimed from under his cap. "The Dark Ages are over!"

285

The next morning Don Camillo found three handsomely decorated votive candles burning in the Lady Chapel. The day after there were six, and it was quite obvious that the Reds had put them there, simply to annoy him. In order to be certain he hid in a confessional, and sure enough, that very afternoon an elderly man came into the church, crossed himself and made resolutely for Saint Anthony's chapel. From underneath his coat he extracted one of the famous candles, which he proceeded to light and then to fit into a holder. It was just at this moment that Don Camillo appeared at his side. To the priest's amazement, the fellow was not a Red but one of his own faithful, Matteo Frossi by name.

"Matteo," exclaimed Don Camillo; "I'd never have expected *you* to play a filthy trick like that!"

"Is it a filthy trick to light a candle to Saint Anthony?" asked the astonished old man.

"It's a filthy trick to light one of *those* candles, and you know it!"

"Father, if I can give thanks to Saint Anthony and save thirty liras at the same time, why should you object? The wax of this candle and the wax of yours come from the same place!"

After Frossi had gone away, Don Camillo gave vent to his feelings before the crucified Christ on the main altar.

"The human race is growing cheaper and cheaper, Lord," he told Him. "Judas sold You for thirty pieces of silver, but this fellow sells You for thirty miserable liras!"

"Who are you talking about, Don Camillo?"

"This fellow, Frossi, who just lit a candle to Saint Anthony."

"Don Camillo, didn't you promise never to drag me into the affairs of your paltry shop? Have you lost your memory?"

"No, Lord; I've lost my temper." And Don Camillo humbly bowed his head.

Eventually, although it cost him a considerable effort, Don Camillo regained his composure. In the pulpit and out of it he said what he thought he should about the ridiculous tactics with which certain people tried to deceive the faithful. He explained that Satan employs the most devious means to win men's souls, and that, like the Greeks, he is most to be feared when he brings gifts. For every apparent gift, Satan extracts a hundred-fold return; he exploits our sloth and our avarice together.

Certainly Don Camillo himself didn't play Satan's game. Rather than buy it at the "People's Co-operative", he ate a whole meal one day without salt, and one rainy night he rode eight miles on his bicycle in order to purchase a cigar at Torricella. This was the least of what he was willing to do for the sake of boycotting Peppone. He was called upon to make the supreme sacrifice the day when he went to collect donations for the Orphan Asylum. As usual, he borrowed a truck from Filotti and with the aid of a husky boy picked up produce from all the neighbouring farms. When the truck was filled with wheat, maize, potatoes, apples and wood he drove happily back to the village. The motor had worked like a dream, the farmers had given cheerfully and it was a mild, sunny day. He turned down the main street of the village, which went by the "People's Co-operative" and then, two hundred yards farther on, to the square in front of the church. Just thirty yards from the "People's Co-operative" the engine began to sputter. It seemed as if Satan himself must have had a hand in the matter, for it came to a stop in front of the petrol pump. Don Camillo got out, opened the hood and then went round to take the cap off the tank.

"We're out of fuel," he told his helper.

"Well, we're pretty lucky," said the boy gaily. "There's the pump, right beside us."

A roar from Don Camillo compelled him to silence. But the enemy was already in the know. The enemy was standing at the door of the Co-operative, enjoying the autumn sun. And he had not only keen hearing but also knew a lot about engines.

"Good evening, Father," he said amiably.

"Good evening, Mr. Mayor," Don Camillo answered between clenched teeth, and turned to talk to the boy.

A minute later the entire group of Peppone's lieutenants and a large number of his followers poured out of the door and stood round their leader.

"What's up, Chief?" asked Smilzo.

"He's out of fuel," answered Peppone.

"Too bad it didn't happen out in the country," said Smilzo. "Here, for just over a hundred liras, he can get enough to take him home."

287

"You mean to say he'd have the nerve to buy no more than a quart?" muttered Bigio.

"He's just as likely to ask for a pint," Smilzo answered, with a mocking laugh. "You don't know how tough and stingy these priests can be."

They talked among themselves, turning their backs to Don Camillo, but in such loud voices that they could be heard all the way to the edge of the village. It was only natural that Don Camillo's temper should rise to boiling-point, but he held it in and continued to confer, from the place where he was standing, with the boy in the seat of the truck. At this point Peppone entered his henchmen's discussion.

"A pint, did you say? He can't use a single drop of it. This is the devil's own petrol, and if he were to take so much as a teaspoonful the Standard Oil Company would excommunicate him."

"Then what's he going to do, Chief?" Smilzo asked.

"That's easy," said Peppone to the small crowd which had gathered about him. "Priests' cars have two fuelling systems: one of them runs on petrol and the other on prayers. He'll fill the tank with Our Fathers, press the starter and the Holy Ghost will ignite the motor."

They all laughed. At this Don Camillo couldn't resist looking them in the face and saying what was on his mind. Swelling up his chest and shaking his fist in the direction of Peppone, he said:

"You can leave the Holy Ghost out of it. I'll manage alone."

"That's what you think," Smilzo retorted. "But a Don Camillo won't do; it will take a Don Caterpillar!"

Don Camillo lost control of himself altogether.

"Hold the wheel!" he shouted to the boy, leaping to the rear of the truck and pushing on it.

Something creaked: either Don Camillo's bones, or the rear of the truck, perhaps both of them together. Don Camillo was no longer a man, he was a living jack. Peppone's gang was breathless, for one of two things was bound to happen: either the truck would move or Don Camillo would break into small pieces. With God's help the truck moved slowly ahead. Peppone's gang paraded after it, in horror and fascination. After fifty yards Don Camillo had to catch his breath. He stood up straight and turned around:

"If four of you big oafs are capable of doing what I did alone, let them step forward," he said.

Naturally no four of them moved; only the massive Peppone solemnly answered the challenge. He signalled to Don Camillo to get out of the way and applied his shoulder to the rear of the truck. Once more there was a creaking sound; once more nothing broke and the truck moved slowly ahead. Ten, twenty, thirty, forty, fifty yards, but Peppone did not stop even when he had reached a hundred. As the truck rolled down the street the Reds exulted; they broke into loud shouts and soon the street was filled with people. Peppone was like a powerful traction-belt; he went on to a hundred and ten, a hundred and twenty yards, and finally all the way to the church square, where the crowd thunderously applauded him. Don Camillo did not bat an eyelash; he waited until Peppone had stopped panting and the applause had subsided. Then he raised his arms to ask for silence.

"Good enough," he observed. "I was looking for some sucker to push the truck all the way home for nothing."

"I'm not so much of a sucker as you may think," shouted Peppone.

His henchmen caught the idea. Smilzo edged the boy out of the seat and took the wheel; the others hurled themselves at the front of the car and pushed it all the way back to the petrol pump. There they stopped, and when Don Camillo re-joined them Peppone had his say.

"He who laughs last laughs best. The rectory is still two hundred yards away. Go to it, Father!"

Don Camillo kept cool and lit the butt of his cigar.

"Will you have some petrol, Father?" asked Smilzo, going over to the pump.

"Thanks, I've got some," said Don Camillo, climbing on to the seat, opening the emergency valve and pressing the starter. Under its own power the truck went triumphantly back to the church square. Peppone's gang looked on with their mouths hanging wide open, until their leader threw his cap on the ground and began to protest:

"That's the second time he's fooled me with his emergency valve!"

But Smilzo had something more to say:

"Chief, you did a hundred and fifty yards to his fifty. You lost one to three, and saved your honour."

Thus they sought to find what consolation they could in writing an end to the story. But people still talk about it and bid fair to go on talking.

20

A SPEECH TO GO DOWN IN HISTORY

"For that meeting on the twenty-sixth, we've got to think up something special," Peppone said gravely.

Bigio, Brusco and Smilzo all looked puzzled and Peppone hastened to enlighten them.

"We're lucky enough to have our rally scheduled as the last one before the election, which means that no matter what we say no one can contradict it. But we're called upon for some substantial oratory, not just the usual hot air. There's no question of bringing in a speaker from the outside, because this is a local election, and we're on our own. We've got to produce something smashing, something that will go down in history."

His three aides relaxed. If this was all he had on his mind, there was no need to worry.

"Chief, we're riding the crest of the wave," Smilzo answered gaily. "All you have to do is drive the last nail in their coffin!"

Peppone shook his head.

"A concluding speech is no joke. Election eve is not the time for a political harangue. It's got to be something factual: a record of past accomplishments and a pledge of others to come. It's one thing to promise social justice, and another to date the opening of a public laundry. Big ideas are all very well for a national election, but on the local level it's better to stick to the concrete. The question is how to make parish-pump politics sound epoch-making."

Smilzo continued to dissent.

"If a fellow knows what he wants to say, it's simple enough to say it."

"Simple, indeed!" retorted Peppone. "But one point I grant you. It's a question not of just the appropriate thing, but of what you *want* to say. An historical speech can't be improvised; it must be thought out in advance, with every word weighed and every effect calculated. Words aren't enough; you've got to know their meanings. It takes spadework with the dictionary."

"You have a big enough vocabulary, Chief," Smilzo assured him. "Why work so hard over it?"

"A big vocabulary isn't enough, I tell you," shouted Peppone. "I need peace and quiet, for purposes of meditation. That's why I've called you together. Even if the People's Palace goes up in smoke, or Togliatti himself makes a tour of inspection, yes, even come the revolution, I'm not to be disturbed. No one must break the continuity of my speech. Have I made myself clear?"

They understood him perfectly.

"Chief," said Smilzo, "even if we have to guard your house with machine-guns, no one shall come near you. Just leave it to us!"

This is why, at a certain point, Peppone disappeared from circulation.

Just as election day was drawing close and the atmosphere was growing hotter and hotter, when his enemies were showing their claws and a strong hand was needed to put them in their place, Peppone vanished from sight. Had he been taken ill? Purged? Gone underground? Sent on a secret mission? His workshop was silent and the sign hanging on the door carried the simple word "Closed". The windows and doors of his own house were barred and his children were staying at their grandmother's, with not a word to be got out of them. Even his wife was gone.

Don Camillo sent out spies and alerted all the gossipy old women of the village. He himself walked by Peppone's house, but found no clue to the mystery. But in a village so small that everyone knew everything about his neighbour, such a situation could not long endure. News leaked through to the rectory that Peppone's house was not deserted, that his wife had been seen at the window and every night Smilzo delivered a parcel there and then came home empty-handed. Smilzo was tailed and found to be going every day to buy food at Castelletto, food sufficient to fill two hungry mouths. When it was discovered that Smilzo also bought cigars, then it was obvious that although one of the mouths might belong to Peppone's wife, the other indubitably belonged to Peppone. Decoys dogged Smilzo's footsteps, and one evening he let them treat him to too many glasses of sparkling red *lambrusco* wine. They brought up the subject of politics and remarked how strange it was that Peppone should be absent from the scene. One of the decoys said argumentatively:

"There's nothing so strange about it. It's a bad case of yellow liver. He knows the game is up and doesn't dare show his face."

"Just wait till you hear his historical speech, after all the work he's putting into it!" said Smilzo, falling like a ton of bricks for their little game.

Five minutes later Don Camillo was informed, but the news did not disturb him.

"Is that all?" he puffed. "Not worth talking about!"

And indeed he did not bring up the subject again. But that very night an unknown hand wrote on Peppone's door:

"Here lies Comrade Giuseppe Bottazzi,
 Who has sought solitude
 In order to write an historical election-eve oration.
 The question is whether, when it's written,
 He'll know how to read it."

Although Don Camillo had dismissed the matter as unworthy of mention, this epigraph caused all malicious tongues to wag about it. Such tongues are not too numerous in the Po valley, or at least there is no more than one to every inhabitant, and not the six or seven which seem to be the sources of so vast a volume of gossip.

Meanwhile the blissfully ignorant Peppone continued to toil over his epoch-making speech. His faithful and discreet wife moved about the house in bedroom slippers in order not to break its continuity. Peppone had never worked so hard in all his life. He worked as hard as if he were forging a hundred-foot iron fence, complete with an ornate gate. The stakes were high. His enemies were dead set on getting into power, whereas Peppone and his gang sought their third consecutive re-election. What with weighing every word and polishing every sentence,

Peppone expended far more time than he had imagined, and the final touches were added no earlier than the Friday morning before the historical Saturday night. Then, oddly enough, the scribbler's prophecy was fulfilled, and Peppone was unable to read what he had written. Fortunately this possibility had been taken into consideration. Smilzo had been standing by for two days, and now he took over the precious manuscript, jumped on to his motor-cycle and rode madly to the city, where a loyal typist proceeded to tap out two copies, one for Peppone and the other for . . . history.

It was late at night and Don Camillo was about to go to bed when Caroline, a poor old creature that went about collecting wood and stale bread, brought him a cardboard folder.

"I found it on the edge of a ditch down near *La Pioppaccia*," she told him. "It's full of papers and they may be important to someone. Can you say something about it in church and see if there are any claimants?"

After she had gone away Don Camillo examined the papers. Soon he realized, to his amazement, that he had Peppone's historical speech in hand, the original and two copies.

Meanwhile Smilzo was sitting under a poplar on the river bank, with death in his heart. He had lost the folder containing the speech. It had slipped out of his pocket while he was riding home, full speed, from the city. Twice he had retraced a portion of the route, vainly searching, and then he had sat down to nurse his despair.

"If I come back empty-handed, the chief will kill me," he said to himself over and over.

And he was not far from right.

Peppone spent an agonizing night. After waiting and waiting for Smilzo to come, he put in a long-distance telephone call. The typist told him that Smilzo had left four hours before, with the masterpiece under his arm. Then he called his general staff, and they sent out search-parties. At four o'clock in the morning, there was still no news of Smilzo, and Peppone, who had been angrily pacing up and down the hall, suddenly collapsed.

"Traitor!" he exclaimed, and let himself be carried off to bed, where he fell into a leaden sleep, accompanied by a high fever.

Smilzo turned up at Bigio's house at nine o'clock. When Bigio heard that the speech was lost he was speechless with dismay. He stared hard at Smilzo and said:

"You may as well emigrate to Venezuela."

New orders were sent out to the search-parties. They were to stop looking for Smilzo and watch out for a yellow folder which the miserable fellow had lost on the road. A large-scale manoeuvre of this kind could not escape attention. People took note, asked questions, gossiped, put two and two together and came, by afternoon, to this conclusion: the text of Peppone's famous speech was lost and that evening he would find himself in exceedingly hot water. Which meant that a large crowd would gather to see him squirm.

The meeting was to start at nine o'clock, and by half-past eight the square was full. At this last minute Peppone's henchmen collected their courage and went to wake him. They had quite a job to get him even to open his eyes. He was still feverish and his eyelids were leaden. They explained that a huge crowd had gathered in the square and he must make up his mind what to do.

"How about Smilzo?" Peppone asked in a dim far-away voice.

"He's found," said Bigio.

"And the speech?" Peppone panted.

"It's lost," said Bigio, prudently retreating three steps.

But he need not have been so cautious. Peppone was too far gone to be a menace. He simply closed his eyes and sighed.

"Chief, what are we going to do?" asked Bigio anxiously.

"Go to the devil, the lot of you," murmured Peppone, as if in a dream.

"What about the crowd? And the Party?"

"Devil take the crowd and the Party too," said Peppone pacifically.

His henchmen stared at one another. This was the end.

"There's nothing we can do," said Bigio. "We'll have to tell the crowd that the meeting is adjourned because the speaker is ill."

Just then Don Camillo appeared upon the scene. Obviously he did not expect to find Peppone so stricken, and he looked down in bewilderment at the inert form on the bed. He did not say a word or make his presence felt in any way, but in a few moments Peppone opened first one eye and then the other.

"I'm not ready yet for Extreme Unction," he muttered.

"Too bad," said Don Camillo.

"You can go; I don't need you."

"You always need me, Comrade!" said Don Camillo, taking a big yellow folder out of his pocket and throwing it on to the bed. Peppone reached out, opened it and stared at the contents.

"Check it now, Comrade," said Don Camillo, with a laugh. "Everything's there: the original manuscript and two copies. Remember that 'incontrovertible' takes only one *b* and be thankful to your parish priest."

Peppone slowly slipped the papers back into the folder and hoisted himself into a sitting position. Then he clenched his teeth, looked into Don Camillo's eyes and said brusquely:

"I'd rather not thank him."

Peppone's hands were as big as shovels. With a single gesture he ripped the folder and its contents in two, then, as if he were prey to some uncontrollable madness, he tore both pieces into shreds, rolled them up in a ball and threw them out of the window. Next, he leaped out of bed.

It was nine o'clock, and the crowd in the square was beginning to murmur, when suddenly Peppone walked on to the platform. His fever had fallen or rather it was not the same sort of fever. This was clear at once from the way he said: "Fellow-citizens! . . ." The crowd was silent and Peppone spoke. He improvised; a dozen times he said "ain't" and "don't" for "isn't" and "doesn't"; he referred to the "Nemesis of history" and the "Nemesis of geography", but the most awkward phrases quite plainly came from a full heart, so that even his severest critics had to admit that he was a good fellow.

So it was that Smilzo didn't emigrate to Venezuela and Peppone was re-elected mayor, without having to thank Don Camillo, but indebted, none the less, to Divine Providence for preventing him from pronouncing a speech that would have gone down in history as abysmally stupid. And Don Camillo was not too perturbed by the outcome of the election, for he knew that in politics we can often obtain more from our enemies than from our friends.

21

THE WAR OF THE CARNATIONS

THIS is a commonplace sort of love-story, which had an unexpected ending on the main square of the village, to be exact, near one of the low stone columns which divide this square from the smaller one in front of the church. There were a large number of witnesses, because the main square was occupied by the May-Day celebration of Peppone and his gang, wearing red carnations in their buttonholes, and the church square by the white-carnationed followers of Don Camillo.

In some broken-down shacks in the Po River valley there are still to be found cheap prints of an old religious painting which shows Jesus and Saint Joseph, clad in unmistakably red garments, working at a carpenter's bench. This was quite a find, from a political point of view, and it was taken up, at one time, by the old-line socialists. Long after they had abandoned it, the representation of Christ and Saint Joseph as workers and craftsmen was re-introduced as the theme of a May the 1st Catholic Labour Day.

The final episode of our little love-story took place on the first of these new-style holidays, celebrated on adjacent squares by the conflicting Red and White parties. It was a cool Spring morning, but political temperature was boiling over.

Among the most active members of the White team was Gilda Marossi, an exceedingly pretty young girl, whose political ardour was as great as that of two men put together. And among Peppone's most active henchmen was Angiolino Grisotti, nicknamed Gioli, a heavy-handed sort, who if he hadn't been such a violent Red might have passed for a normal, handsome fellow. The story wouldn't be so commonplace if the two had never met. But they did meet, when they were mere school-children and politics was a complete mystery to them. They met several times after that, too, upon various festive occasions, when they had some notion of what politics was about, but cared more for dancing. Then, when they were in politics up to the ears and discovered that they were sworn enemies, they began to avoid such meetings. One day, however, they found themselves face to face on a bus. For a time they tried to outstare each other, but finally Gilda could hold her peace no longer and said brusquely:

"If some people had the least bit of self-respect they wouldn't stare at their betters."

"Just what I was thinking, myself," said Gioli.

Having said all they had to say, they continued to exchange lowering glances all the way to their destination. In spite of their mutual disdain, it was obvious that she was prettier than ever and that in spite of his association with the Reds he was a strikingly handsome fellow. When the bus reached the city, they went their own ways, but a few minutes later Gioli could have kicked himself for his stupidity. He had taken courses in propaganda technique, sponsored by the Party, and now he realized that he had muffed the chance to use an old friendship either to make a convert or to gain insight into the tactics of the enemy. In order to wipe out this error he hatched a new plan.

"A good Communist," he said to himself, "must be a psychologist as well. And what does psychology say? It says that a girl who takes a bus to the city must be going shopping. She won't go into the first shop she sees, no, not she; she'll look into a dozen windows and compare qualities and prices before she buys a single thing. After wasting so much time window-shopping, she'll be dead tired and just manage to catch the last bus home. That's where I come in. . . ."

And so Angiolino Grisotti, nicknamed Gioli, was one of the first to arrive at the last bus, where he put down a parcel on the seat facing him and patiently waited. According to the dictates of psychology, Gilda should have been the last to arrive and have found every seat except the one which he had reserved for her taken. Unfortunately, she arrived shortly after Gioli, and when he saw her coming he turned pale. When Gilda got on the bus, she could have sat anywhere she pleased, but psychological considerations made her set her mind upon the seat occupied by Gioli's parcel.

"Is this place taken?" she asked firmly, tossing her head in the parcel's direction.

He picked up the parcel and she sat down. They sat stiffly, face to face, for several minutes, until Gioli was inspired to take out a packet of cigarettes and offer one to the silent figure across the way.

"*We* don't smoke in public places," said Gilda coldly. "*Your* girls do practically anything, either in public or in private, but *we*'ve been taught better."

"Let's leave politics out of it," said Gioli, putting the cigarettes back in his pocket. "Why not talk about you and me?"

"What do you mean by 'talk'?" queried Gilda aggressively.

"I mean the way we used to talk when we went dancing together."

"Only a godless Communist would have the nerve to throw a woman's past weaknesses in her face," said Gilda stiffly. "Why don't you print on one of your posters that for a while I lent an ear to your foolishness?"

"Why should I?" asked Gioli. "This is a personal matter, not a Party one. Of course, if you can't talk to me for fear of offending the fiancé whom the parish priest has forced upon you, that's a different story."

"I have no fiancé," Gilda retorted. "You're the one that had better step softly if you don't want to arouse the jealousy of Comrade Gisela Cibatti."

Gioli protested, Gilda answered him back, and so they went on for the rest of the journey. Even then the argument wasn't over, and they continued it all the way to Gilda's house. It was dark, and after more discussion Gilda started to say good-bye and go in.

"Too bad," she said on the threshold, "that politics should divide us!"

A silly comment, if ever there was one, because a few minutes before, when she and Comrade Gioli had embraced each other, politics hadn't entered into it at all. Love-stories are all exactly the same, and it's absurd that after so many hundreds of thousands of years the human race should take any interest in them. Be that as it may, two evenings later Gilda looked out of her window and saw Gioli sitting on the parapet of the bridge nearby. She gazed at him for a while, until sheer annoyance impelled her to go down and ask what he was doing. She was ready for anything and prepared to repay it in kind, but when he said quite simply that he had come in the hope of seeing her, she was so taken aback that he was able to kiss her. Instead of taking offence she decided to reap full advantage from the situation.

"Since this jackass is so crazy about me," she said to herself, "I may as well give him some encouragement. I'll get him to the point where he leaves the Party and then drop him like a hot potato!"

For several evenings Gilda proceeded to encourage him. Then, at the psychological moment, she brought up her heavy artillery.

"Gioli, you swear you love me. Are you willing to prove it?"

"I'm ready for anything."

"Then get out of that cursed Party! I can't marry a man who's been excommunicated."

Gioli drew back.

"Gilda, you swear you love me, don't you? Then the burden of the proof is on you. Get out from under those Christian Democrats! I have no intention of marrying a priestess!"

Gilda's tone of voice altered.

"Then you and your filthy Russia can go straight to hell!"

"All right! And while I'm on my merry way, I only hope a fate worse than death overtakes you, and your Vatican and your America!"

Proudly they turned their backs on one another. But the God of lovers had other designs. No sooner had they parted than both their families joined the fray. According to Gioli's relatives and friends, the young man owed it to his own dignity never to look at that pious and pretentious little fraud again. And Gilda's people were equally vociferous in arguing that Gilda ought to give up seeing that dirty Bolshevik for good and all. Both sides hammered away for a whole week, at the end of which time, the mulish Gioli wrote Gilda a special-delivery letter: "If I look for you tomorrow evening on the bridge in front of your house, will you be there?" To which Gilda made answer: "I'll meet you at eight o'clock on the Molinetto bridge, where more people will see us!"

They met, then, at eight o'clock, and practically everybody in the village saw them. And those that didn't see them heard about it from those that did. The opposition became more violent than ever. Both Gilda and Gioli found all their friends and acquaintances, including of course their fellow party-members, against them. But the more all these well-intentioned people sought to separate them, the closer they were drawn together.

The subversive Gioli was fundamentally a good boy, and the virtuous Gilda had a strongly rebellious, perhaps even revolutionary nature. Because they were both very proud, they did not speak of the battles they were waging inside their own camps; they relieved their tension by loving each other more and more every day. But when Gilda's people came out with ugly threats, she lost patience.

Peppone was flabbergasted to receive her visit at such a late hour. He wondered what could be the ulterior motive of this girl who had made a fool of one of his most stalwart followers.

"Can you keep a secret until tomorrow morning?" Gilda asked him.

"If it's an honest secret, I can."

Gilda took out of her pocket-book a card with the party emblem of shield and cross, tore it into pieces and threw it on to the table.

"Give me one of your cards, now," she said, "and keep quiet about it until tomorrow morning. I want to surprise Gioli and also those wretched people who've been trying to get me away from him."

Peppone remained for several minutes with his mouth hanging open, and then objected:

"But you've come here out of sheer spite. It's not true faith that makes you want to join our party."

"What does that matter? Since when have you Communists been such sentimental souls that you wouldn't delight in thumbing your noses at the parish priest?"

Peppone had been eating his heart out over the rival May-

Day celebration, and these last words roused a definite reaction.

"I'll make you a member thirty times over, if it will make the priest suffer!"

With card in hand, Gilda went away. And when Peppone had time to think it over, he concluded that Comrade Gioli had scored a personal and party triumph.

"Love is on the Communist side," he observed sententiously.

The next dawn was that of the First of May and the main square was filled with red, the church square with white carnations. Peppone was overcome by excitement. While on the one hand he hoped to avoid Don Camillo, on the other he would have given almost anything to run into him. Finally they did meet, near the row of low stone columns which separated the two squares.

"Hurrah for Christ the Worker!" exclaimed Peppone, smiling broadly.

"Exactly! He may not have belonged to the union, but He worked as a carpenter, at the side of His father, Joseph."

"I seem to remember hearing that God was his Father," Peppone retorted.

"Just so, Mr. Mayor. His Father is the greatest Worker of all. He created the universe before there was any such thing as raw materials!"

Peppone swallowed hard and then said between clenched teeth:

"And all the rest of you clerics that are taking part in this labour celebration, just what work do you do?"

"I pray for your sin-stained soul," said Don Camillo, "and that's hard work, I can tell you!"

Peppone looked around, and seeing that everything was in good order, he came out with his sensational news:

"There's another soul you can pray for," he said, pointing to a certain segment of the Red throng.

Don Camillo's eyes popped with astonishment. There in a red dress, with a red carnation in her hair, standing close to the red flag, stood Gilda Marossi. What could he say? But before Peppone could enjoy his triumph to the full, a horrible sight met his eye. In the church square, with a white carnation in his buttonhole, practically wrapped in the folds of the Christian-

Democrat banner, stood ex-Comrade Angiolino Grisotti. After a moment, Gilda and Gioli caught sight of each other, too, for both of them had been scanning the rival assembly. After standing thunderstruck with amazement they moved instinctively towards the columns dividing the two squares, by which Don Camillo and Peppone still lingered. They exchanged curious glances and then Gilda said:

"I wanted to surprise you!"

"Same here!" said Gioli.

Some of the bystanders burst into laughter. Gilda and Gioli looked into each other's eyes and reached a speechless understanding. As if by preconceived accord they stripped themselves of their carnations, and laid them on one of the low stone columns; then arm in arm they walked away from the centre of the village and out of political life for ever and ever. Don Camillo and Peppone stared raptly at the two carnations.

"Well! . . ." muttered Peppone, shrugging his shoulders.

"Well! . . ." echoed Don Camillo, characteristically throwing out his arms.

And these were the most eloquent speeches that either of them made during this May-Day celebration.